WHITE EMERALDS

DON KAFRISSEN

International Digital Book Publishing Industries
Florida, USA

WHITE EMERALDS

A book from IDBPI published by arrangement
with the author
All rights reserved
Copyright (c) 2015 by Don Kafrissen

For information address:
International Digital Book Publishing Industries
Brooksville, Florida, USA, 34601

Visit our website at
www.idbpi.wordpress.com

ISBN – 978-1-57550-057-7

IDBPI and the digital book logo are trademarks belonging to
International Digital Book Publishing Industries

PRINTED IN THE UNITED STATES OF AMERICA
10 9 8 7 6 5 4 34 2 1

This book is dedicated to my late, great friend

Tom Navickas

Although he isn't the Tom Novak of the books, he was my inspiration for the character; and quite a character he was.
I will miss him always.

I would also like to thank my wonderful wife, Diane, for putting up with me and helping with suggestions when I'd written myself into corners.

Thanks to my editor Marlene Becker; and my cover artist, compiler, formatting artist, and friend Johanna Bolton.

And to all my friends in the Brooksville Writers' Group. You all know who you are!

PROLOGUE

Antonio Jesus Locarno was sure he was going mad.

All night he'd tossed and turned in his blanket. The bleating of the sheep was incessant. They were usually quiet at night, with only an occasional bleat marring the cool darkness. He'd walked round and around the small flock looking for predators but saw nothing. He didn't know why they were so restless. Finally he'd herded them into a small pocket in the rough hills and dragged some brush into the entrance to block them, but all night they milled, sometimes almost trampling the lambs.

"*Madre Dios*, what was happening?" Antonio murmured to himself. The night was warm, but not unpleasantly so. The air smelled funny, like rotten eggs, and the moon swirled with rapidly tumbling clouds. He crammed the worn sombrero on his head and leaned back against a rock. The sheep moved closer to his little fire, unafraid, seeking him for comfort. His dog, Pepe, crouched close by his side, paws over his muzzle. He, too, fidgeted, rocking, pumping his small paws.

It was the mid-eighteen hundreds in the hills above the small village of Hidalgo in what is today Northeastern Guatemala known as Tikal. Antonio lived in a small but neat hut on a hillside sprinkled with mahogany tree groves with his wife and two small boys. The fold of hills thrust out of the jungle, changes in vegetation and wildlife apparent, even though the hills weren't much higher than the tops of the tallest trees below. Antonio herds a small flock of fine Merino sheep, no more than fifty at a time, and that was in the spring when the lambs came. Though he was considered a poor man, he managed to feed his family well. They always had mutton or the long silky Merino wool for sale at the marketplace in town so they could buy the few staples they could not grow or raise themselves. His wife, Felicia, tended their garden, raising the beans, tomatoes and chilies that grew so well on the open hill. The area was volcanic and there were several active volcanoes visible far to the south.

There was a warm stream that flowed in a grove of trees about a mile from the house and he and Felicia used to go there often when she first came to live with him. She was a lovely, longhaired mestizo girl from a village far south of Hidalgo. He'd seen her one Sunday in church, helping the priest with his robes. He thought she might be his niece or a relative. He learned that she was an orphan whose parents had been killed by banditos while coming home from market one day. The priest had found the little girl hidden beneath her mother's body as he passed by on his rounds the next day. He took her in and raised her as his own. She had been fifteen when Antonio first saw her and he had fallen deeply and completely in love. The next time the priest had come again on his rounds was some six months later.

Antonio had smiled at her and she had shyly smiled back. At the time, he was lean and hard from living in the hills with the sheep. His parents, too, were dead, though from some mysterious disease that took first his beloved mother, then a short time later, his father. Antonio had been sick for almost a month but had slowly recovered with the assistance of a nearby family of Colombian Indians who had been resettled near Hidalgo a century or more before by the Spanish. After he recovered, he lived alone, herding his sheep. His family was gone and he didn't believe that another woman would ever come into his life.

But the human heart is a strong muscle, and all things must pass. The hole in his heart was still there but the driving, passion of his Castilian and Indian ancestors burned within him. When he saw Felicia, he knew he must be with her. He approached the priest and, though terrified of the church, stated his case simply and eloquently. He was a strong man and not without a means to provide for his wife. She appealed to him and he could tell she was attracted to him also. The priest, though disappointed at losing his fine assistant was also aware of her glowing beauty and firm figure. The father wasn't a saint and although some of his brethren took women to their bed, he considered it a sin. He knew she was ripe for marriage and after inquiring as to Antonio's character with the local town fathers, he finally, although reluctantly, gave his blessing. The simple wedding was performed that Sunday after mass and the shy Felicia gathered her small bundle of belongings, kissed the priest good-bye, and rode off on a donkey led by Antonio.

She knew he lived in the hills, but that was all. Felicia still grieved for her barely remembered parents and had promised the priest that she would raise all children in the church and would visit him whenever he came to town. The priest was not an old man and she hoped he would be there to baptize her babies in the years to come.

After several hours travel, they came out of the jungle onto a plateau, and Antonio lifted her gently from the donkey's back. She was drowsy, yet excited by this change in her life. Felicia knew that what was coming from her husband was supposed so be painful but she had assisted the priest in delivering babies since she was a little girl. Some of the ladies had told her of the pain of first intercourse and some had even described the ecstasy they found in sex.

They rested for a long hour, Antonio ever solicitous to her needs. He had a jug of water he kept wrapped in wet rags and some smoked meat and even two fresh mangos from the market.

He described the little hut he'd built and told her how they would enlarge it and how some day he would have the biggest flock in all of the highlands. She listened as he wove his dream around her. She knew the practical side of life would be her responsibility, the garden and raising the babies that were sure to come. Felicia was a practical girl, solid, sturdy, and safe. She would make a good wife and someday her sons and daughters would walk proudly into the towns and cities of the entire world the priest had spoken of. She could even read some and would teach her children, perhaps even teach Antonio.

She looked at him from under lowered lashes. He sat with his back against a tree. His skin was dark and there were two faint lines from his nose to the corners of his mouth. His jet-black hair was straight and pulled back, tied with a string of leather. Her gaze paused at his strong, ropy arms and hard, though slim hands, almost like a woman's. Though of average height, he was hardly more than 5'6" tall, he towered over her by several inches. His warm brown eyes were tilted downward at the outer corners, like a puppy dog, she thought. Felicia sighed, with those eyes, he will melt the hearts of any woman and many men will think he is easy and will try to take advantage of him. She must discover if he was strong or weak.

That he had dared to approach the priest at all must mean that he has a strong streak inside of him, she thought, all the time trying to fathom this man that was now her husband and soon her lover. They packed up the donkey and soon were walking side by side, she holding his free arm, the donkey resignedly plodding along behind them.

In late afternoon they came to his hut. It was simply made with a log rear wall and woven and plaited sidewalls and roof. He'd always meant to plaster the sidewalls but hadn't had time somehow. He was glad now because he would have to enlarge it for Felicia and the coming children. The thought pleased him and he smiled under his sparse mustache, which only grew at the corners of his mouth, a trait that would be inherited by generations to come.

Felicia appraised the clearing, noting the neat hut, the tiny garden, the sheep pen behind the house and the small lean-to across the clearing. It was acceptable, not big and beautiful like the houses she'd seen in the larger towns, but acceptable just the same. She asked for some water to wash and he smiled.

"Wait," he said. "Put your things inside and come with me. I will put Pedro with the sheep for a rest." He turned and led the donkey off. She pushed open the door to the hut and a low growl greeted her. A yellow mixed breed dog crouched beneath a narrow bed, fangs bared, low growls coming from him. She carefully set her bundle down and held out her hand. The dog crawled out, belly to the floor and sniffed at the proffered hand. In a moment she was scratching the dog behind the ears and murmuring endearments to him. The dog looked mournfully at her and licked her face, long red tongue lolling out.

Antonio came in and smiled at the scene. "That's Pepe," he said. When the dog saw him, he bounded over and jumped up, putting his paws against Antonio's stomach. He fondly patted his head.

"Come," he said taking her by the hand. Her long skirt swept the packed dirt floor as she followed. He led her up and over the top of the hill behind the house and down through a large grove of trees with brightly colored flowers growing around them. Their bright blooms seemed to follow them as they walked. In a moment they came to a small clearing. A tiny stream trickled over stones and fed a pool not more than ten feet around. The brilliant sunlight was filtered and muted by the overhanging branches, the moss and dead leaves forming a natural bed at the end of the path.

Antonio led her to the water's edge. "Here, feel this."

She thrust her hand in the shallow pool and pulled it back in astonishment. It was warm, almost hot. Carefully she fingered the water again. It was quite pleasant.

Antonio was already shedding his clothes -- first the woven rope and leather sandals, then the thin cotton shirt, and finally the trousers. He stood nude before her.

She blushed furiously. She had never seen a man without any clothes. Nor had a man ever seen her without clothes. But she was curious. How different he was from her. His long penis hung down from under his flat belly. She turned her eyes and slowly began shedding her clothes, too. First her light, knitted shawl, then her cotton blouse with the carefully embroidered flowers on it. With great reluctance she untied the sash holding her dark skirt around her waist. It dropped soundlessly to the forest floor. She only had a pair of thin cotton drawers remaining and she was very embarrassed. She felt rather than heard him behind her. His hands caught her thick, ebony hair and carefully removed the two ivory combs that had been her marriage present from the priest. It fell and tumbled over her shoulders, dropping almost to her waist.

Antonio's hands were now gently caressing her shoulders. He gently turned her toward him. She didn't know where to look. Facing him, she found she couldn't meet his eyes. Looking down, all she could see was that man thing, now beginning to rise toward her. He lifted her chin until she looked in his eyes, which were as black as the darkest night. She hiccupped and smiled.

"My little flower, I am now your husband. You are my wife. We are both without parents. It is up to us to bring forth children, to make a family so that we will have young ones to care for us when we are old, to delight us when we are young, no?" She nodded.

He went on, this little speech carefully rehearsed for many days, "Felicia, I love you more than life itself. You must know that I will never hurt you. However, the first time for a woman, I am told, is sometimes painful. I will be as gentle as I can and I will wait until you heal. I do not know what you have been told about the love between a man and a woman, but I am told it can be beautiful, yes?" Again she nodded, he eyes large and luminous. "Let us make it beautiful. First, let us wash. Come."

And he knelt and carefully untied the tiny bow and slipped her drawers over her smooth brown hips until they, too, lay on the soft ground. Then he leaned forward and kissed the softness of her smoothly rounded belly and then the silky hair just below. She shuddered, not knowing she had these feelings in her. Until now, she had yearnings and urges but they were ill defined and without form.

Antonio got to his feet and took her small hand in his and led her to the pool. He stepped in and turned and pulled her to him, holding her against his hard body. Her high round breasts flattened against his chest and now she could feel his man thing poking against her belly. He sank into the water kissing her face, her neck and then her breasts, gently tugging and pulling at the hard nipples. She held him by the head while he did this, just letting the feelings course though her, the feelings coming from the ends of her toes and building a fire in her stomach. She wanted him to touch her between her legs, to feel his lips lower but was too shy to ask. She carefully took one of his hands and placed it between her thighs. He drew back and smiled at her and kissed the tip of her nose, all the time massaging and rubbing her sex.

She felt a giant bubble swelling and growing inside her. At first she was scared but it felt so good, so wonderful that she just waited. Antonio gently lifted her to her feet and sat her on the edge of the bank, legs spread and his hand still rubbing and gently squeezing until she was very moist. She lay back and looked at the small patches of sky between the trees and wondered if this was the heaven the priest was always talking about.

Antonio's face blocked out the sun. "I think you are ready, little one. I will be gentle."

And she felt a firm, yet insistent pushing between her legs. She struggled to her elbows and watched wide eyed as his now large, purple-headed penis was slowly pushed inside her. She couldn't believe that it would really fit. It seemed as long as her forearm and just as big around, another trait that would be inherited by the future generations of Locarno men.

She felt a moment of resistance and furrowed her brow in pain. Antonio stopped but she reached for his hips. "*Andalay, me hombre*, do not stop now." She thrust her hips at the same time he thrust forward and the resistance was gone and he was buried deep inside her. She wrapped her arms around his neck and thrust in time with Antonio's furious plunging. The bubble exploded inside her at the same time he gave one long thrust and clutched her, squeezing the breath out of her small chest, face buried in her neck at her shoulder, her hair twined around his head.

They fell back exhausted; Antonio sprawled on top of her now sweat-covered little body. All will be well, she thought with satisfaction.

She finally got her breathing under control. "Will it be like that every time?" She asked.

"No," he replied, equally out of breath. She was disappointed. "Sometimes it will be better!" And he laughed. Pushing himself up on his arms, he looked at her, hair disarrayed, sprawled on the leaf mold, legs hanging in the water. Then she laughed, a high, lilting laugh, matching him. They laughed at the absurd joke until they were gasping for breath.

This time she led him into the water and washed him with her hands, again and again coming back to his softened manhood, fascinated that it could be hard one minute, soft the next. It looked so forlorn that she leaned down and kissed the end. It tasted a little salty. She kissed it again and it started to rise. She kept kissing it until it was long and hard again. She marveled. I did that, she thought. Just by kissing it.

Felicia smiled shyly at him, "Can we do it again?"

"As often as you like, my little love." And they did. Again and again until it was nearly dark. The small pool became their favorite place and many afternoons they would steal off to bathe and make love. Even after the children came, they would still set them down on the soft carpet of leaf mold after they had bathed them, and then make love nearby. Pepe would quietly sit and watch the tumbling babies, careful to keep them away from the pool until they were older.

As the flock and his family had both grown larger, they came less often to the grove. And tonight, he scarcely thought of it as the rotten egg odor penetrated his nose. He blew out, trying to exhale the odor. Beside him, Pepe whined and growled. The sheep grew more restless, sometimes stepping into the small fire. He finally arose and kicked dirt over the smoldering twigs.

With a rumble that he felt through the soles of his feet, the earth trembled. "*Madre, Dios,*" he mumbled and crossed himself. The sheep were frantic now and it was everything he and Pepe could do to keep them from scattering in all directions. The mother of all things was crumbling. The earth rumbled again, this time louder.

Far below, the earth was adjusting, plates of thick rock rubbing together, each side searching for a fault, a weakness in the crust that would allow one or the other to rest. It was like two strong men searching for an advantage over the other. Finally, one found the other's weakness and pushed hard. The earth split with a loud crack like thunder.

The sheep bleated and ran, some falling. Antonio was knocked off his feet. He reached behind him and felt the bark of a tree. He clung to it fiercely, fingers digging into the rutted bark. The earth buckled again and cracked, a fissure appearing from between two rocks nearby and racing past him like a cut in a piece of meat. The tree tilted and leaned toward the fissure. Antonio scrambled up into the sparse branches and clung for all he was worth. The rumbling continued, louder and louder as the two strong men felt each other's muscles and tested their strength. The tree was whipped like a reed in the wind. Still Antonio clung. He no longer cared about the sheep or Pepe. He said a short prayer for Felicia and the boys.

Suddenly the tree was flung backwards, white-hot rock thrust up before his eyes, searing and curling the leaves before him. He cried out, trying to keep the tree between him and the thrusting rock. The heat was intense and the hairs on the backs of his hands curled, smoked, and disappeared as the skin reddened. With another loud crack, the earth split wider, the tree falling forward and across the fissure, barely resting on both sides. A branch struck Antonio on the back of the head and with a swirl of bright lights, the darkness closed in.

The sun was burning the back of his head as Antonio slowly awoke. His head hurt and his whole body was sore as if he'd taken a severe beating by that bully Francisco. He managed to pry his eyes open. Where was he? He was looking down into a large crack in the earth through blackened branches. Foul smelling smoke swirled out of the crack, looked around and was swept away by the morning breeze. The strong men had settled their differences and all was peaceful now. An eerie silence hung over the scene. No birds sung. No small animals made noises.

Antonio managed to raise himself on the branches and look around. Though he'd used the little cleft in the hill many times, now he barely recognized it. New rocks had thrust up, and trees lay on the ground where they'd been toppled. The entire valley tilted like a table with two broken legs. He managed to carefully crawl backwards down the tree and slide off to the ground where he sat, head in hands. He turned and leaned his back against the trunk, looking into the fissure. The breeze blew the smoke away for a minute and he clearly saw something flash brightly. Antonio squinted and craned his neck lower. Under a small outcropping of dusty, pale, broken rock was a streak of some shiny green rock. Looking about, he spotted a small fallen tree, no more than four or five inches in diameter. He shakily staggered to his feet, half-leaning on the fallen tree behind him. After stripping some of the smaller branches from the sapling, he thrust it across the fissure and into the side of the crack under the green streak.

Firmly planting it into the small crack, he felt secure enough to shakily slide down until he was balancing on the branch, palms against the wall before him. He slid down into the fissure carefully until his eyes were level with the brightness. The green glass rock stretched for eight or nine feet before disappearing under the larger overhang. Reaching for a loose stone, he pounded against some small nubs of the glass until several broke off into his hand. They were almost perfect hexagons. Antonio had never seen such stones! He had seen something similar in the church, when the visiting priest came bringing the beautiful cross decorated with green colored rocks. But they weren't nearly as brilliant as these, he thought. Somehow, subconsciously, perhaps through racial memory, he instinctively knew that these rocks were valuable. The fat streak twinkled and glittered before disappearing beneath the rock.

After climbing out, he marked the spot with a piece of cloth torn from his shirt, and then went looking for the path home. After a mile, he came upon several of his sheep grazing in a thicket of thorn bush and green grass. Pepe was perched on a nearby rock and barked a greeting before rushing up to him to get his ears scratched. He sank to his knees and hugged the scruffy dog, all the while speaking to him and telling him of his find. He took the nuggets out of his pocket and the dog looked at them, then back at him as if to say, *"So?"*

His hill was little changed, and he hurried up to the small house, calling out for Felicia and his sons. They came tumbling out of the narrow doorway. Felicia threw her arms around him, squeezing him tightly, the two boys clinging to his legs.

"Antonio, Antonio, I was so frightened for you. The house shook and moved so much!"

"I am fine, little flower, although we may have lost some of the sheep. Pepe is bringing those that remain in with him." He held her close, caressing her shiny black hair, breathing in the scent of her.

Later, after the children were asleep, he showed her the two shining green rocks. *"Esmeraldas,"* she breathed, crossing herself. They gleamed in the light from the battered oil lamp.

"Esmeraldas?" He asked. "What are *esmeraldas?"*

"These," she said thrusting them beneath his nose. "You must never show them to the priest. He will take them from us. I have seen it happen."

"But I took them from the earth. They are pretty, no?"

"Yes, Antonio, they are pretty. But you must never show them to anyone else and you must allow me to deal with these pretty rocks. Are there more where these came from?" She grasped his wrist tightly. He was a little frightened by Felicia's intensity, but the pattern was now being set for generations to come: the men would do the mining and cleaning of the emeralds, and the women would arrange for the family's wealth to accumulate -- handling the finances and investments. It was not that the men were stupid, but the Locarno men just seemed to marry sharp, avaricious, fiercely family-oriented women.

And so it went for six generations. The boys helped the fathers raise fine Merino sheep when they were small, and as they reached maturity, they helped in the mine. Always the men worked and always the women went away to school, some studying business, some languages, and some medicine. Once in a while, the boys went away, too, but they seemed to always gravitate back to the family business.

Felicia arranged to have the Colombian Indian family take those first emeralds back to Bogotá for cutting and polishing, selling them off to the church or on the open market -- never too many to make waves and never in Guatemala. The Colombian family became inextricably entwined with the

Locarnos, occasionally one of the offspring marrying into one family or the other. Antonio Locarno became the *padrone* in the village, eventually building a fine though small medical clinic, a school and finally a fine house for the growing family.

Antonio went back to the fissure and eventually filled it in up to the level of the vein of emeralds, roofing it over and planting trees, tying the branches together to grow like a natural bower. The vein wasn't large but it was long and he only had to work it two or three days at a time to gain more than enough money for them to live comfortably. The town's people watched Antonio's flocks grow, and just assumed it was the source of the family's wealth.

In the hills nearby lived a tribe of Mayans who had escaped the slavery of the Spanish and the diseases that had slain so many of their brethren. Felicia occasionally saw them and one day rode Pedro into their small village. She assured the chief she meant no harm and that they were welcome to visit the town and clinic for trading any time. Although the town people were wary at first, they soon grew used to the dark, partly naked people with the strangely cut hair and body ornaments. Felicia and Antonio occasionally visited, especially when the boys were small. The Mayans came to the house to trade for tobacco and salt. At one meeting they indicated they knew of the emerald mine but had no interest in it. They would watch over it for Antonio.

And so a strange relationship was forged between the Locarnos, the Mayans, and the people in the small town of Hidalgo tucked way back in a fold in the hills, surrounded by jungle in the highlands of Guatemala. For more than a century the Locarno men removed the emeralds from the earth, the women handled the finances, the Mayans guarded the mine, and the townsfolk gained schools, hospitals, shops, and employment.

Until the drugs came.

CHAPTER 1

The sun was hot and beat down on the open plaza like the heat from a pizza oven. Dave Manley sat in what little shade there was in front of the dirty cafe and sipped his rapidly warming beer. Dave was a tall, well-muscled guy in his early sixties. His dark red hair was worn long and was just starting to gray at the temples. Sitting beside him, Tom Novak appeared to be dozing, his white cowboy hat pulled down over his face, chair tilted back against the peeling whitewashed wall. Around their feet a small, naked, brown boy chased a mangy mutt puppy trying to get a piece of rope back. Near the center of the square stood a low fountain, stilled now and judging by the green slime in the pool, it had been that way for quite some time.

Across from them several women were lined up at an outdoor faucet filling an assortment of plastic and metal cans and jugs. Their chatter was muted, their movements painfully slow. Even the water that spilled from the faucet came slowly, like oil or some equally viscous fluid.

At the far end of the plaza, a fat policeman with an aging AK-47 rifle slung over his sweat-stained short leaned against an equally aging jeep talking to two peasants and a priest in a long dusty cassock. The policeman shrugged and gestured with the stub of a cigarette in the direction of the small café.

In a few moments the priest and one of the peasants sauntered across the plaza and approached their table.

"Senor Novak?" the priest asked politely. He stood with his gnarled, work-hardened hands clasped in front of him like a schoolgirl. Dave glanced up as the shadow of the two men fell across him. Tom stayed asleep. The priest was no youngster, but he wasn't old either. He wore a ragged, plaited straw hat pulled forward over salt and pepper hair, which peeked out in random intervals. His deeply seamed and rutted face was dark with shocking black eyebrows, which crept and crawled along a heavy brow ridge. There was lots of Indian blood in this guy, Dave decided.

He and Tom had come down to this flea bitten town on Mexico's Yucatan peninsula, right up against the border with Guatemala, two days ago to pick up a helicopter and fly it back to the States.

Tom had made the deal and there was $2,000 for each of them plus expenses for this milk run. Dave had let Tom handle all of the details. He didn't even know what model it was. On the plane down Tom had muttered something about how it was a Hughes or Bell or Martin-Marietta or something. They were supposed to meet a man in this town who would lead them to it. Dave didn't care. Tom was reliable, a friend and would make good on the money. He always seemed to have money, though where he got it, Dave didn't know and wasn't sure he wanted to know.

The priest waited, looking down.

Tom finally heaved himself upright and thumbed back the cowboy hat. He regarded the priest through his pale blue eyes framed by a darkly tanned face. Then he spoke rapidly in Spanish to the priest who listened and nodded. He motioned to Tom to follow and turned.

Tom leaned over to Dave, smiled easily and said in a low voice, "Me and the *padre* here are going to see some guys for a little bit. He said the chopper isn't too far. Get our stuff, and then come back and sit right here, ready to leave. I'll come and get you or one of these *campesinos* will. Okay, Buddy-boy?"

Dave nodded. He wanted to argue but it was just too hot. He'd been waiting two hot days for something to happen and nothing had.

After Tom left carrying a small duffel bag, Dave ordered another beer. When he finished, he went up to their room in the adobe hotel, paid the

bill and returned with their one large carry bag. He
flopped back into the chair and ordered another ice-
cold beer. He wondered how many hours he'd have
to wait now. The shadows were lengthening across
the plaza and the sun was losing some of its mind
numbing brilliance. A few wispy clouds tried to
gang up on the sun, but it just baked them like
muffins and they headed west.

Suddenly Dave was brought back from his
torpor by a roar, which quickly developed, into an
earth splitting, teeth rattling, all encompassing
hideous howl. It came from nowhere and
everywhere at once. Dave looked wildly about. A
fierce wind was now blowing through the plaza.
The ladies at the fountain scurried into an alley. A
fat Indian woman ran into the bar after scooping up
the kid and the dog.

Papers and chairs and sunshades were blown
around as if by a tornado. Dave kept a hand over his
eyes to keep the flying grit out. He was backed up
against the wall now, the bag at his feet pressing
hard against his legs. The sun went out and the
plaza was in dark shadows. He peeked through his
fingers and saw a black, sharklike helicopter
hovering just to the left of the fountain. Inside a
hand was raised and was waving at him. There was
urgency in that wave. Dave put his head down and,
scooping up the duffel, ran toward the howling
chopper.

He recognized it as one of the newer models of
the Cobra Gunship, actually a Super Cobra, a model
usually assigned to the Marines due to its armor,
awesome firepower and twin jet engines. This one

was painted matte black and had no markings, and that usually meant DEA or Customs or a military "Black Operations Unit" or BOU. He squinted and, yep, there was Tom in the rear pilot's seat jockeying the controls, the aircraft rocking side to side, now tipping forward, now back. He recognized the wide grin and the white cowboy hat.

Jesus, Dave thought, *Tom must be in hog heaven flying this thing!*

Dave ran in front of the pilot's bubble and lifted his arms in an exaggerated shrug. Tom gestured toward the left side. As Dave got beside the hovering beast, he was just able to hoist himself up on the skid. The duffel tugged against his shoulder. He looked for a latch or access hatch but before he found one he felt the big chopper lift. He hung on, the duffel still slung over his shoulder. As soon as Tom saw that he was on the skid, he lifted the machine up and out of the plaza. Just in the nick of time, too. Charging down the street leading into the plaza from the south was an old rusty red Toyota Land Cruiser with a machine gun mounted on the back. A couple of black clad figures clung to it precariously as it skidded and tried to follow the rapidly ascending black bird. The bullets fell behind them harmlessly as Tom rapidly lifted them over the roof of the café and headed north, out toward the placid blue of the Gulf of Mexico.

Dave stood on the skid and clung to the short hard point wing for support. Just above his head, only inches from his ears, an engine intake duct and it was deafening. He squatted to get out of the roar and noticed that the wing actually held two blunt ended missiles. He knew the Cobra usually held some rocket launchers in round pods under the stubby wings, too, and had a nose mounted, multi-barreled 20mm rapid-fire chain gun. What an awesome, deadly machine. He'd occasionally flown an older version in Vietnam, but these newer twin-engine machines were a completely reworked model.

His eyes were streaming and his hands hurt. He tried to crane his neck around to see what Tom was up to but the wind pressure kept him pressed against the cockpit side, and hard against the stubby wing. Peering down, he saw the blue water rushing up at them. *Oh, shit, we're going to crash,* he thought. *Maybe, if I can jump off at the last minute, into the water, I'll be thrown clear.*

The chopper gently settled lower, and then Dave saw white sand flickering by. Tom headed the ship into the wind and lightly flared the blades. Suddenly they were down on a deserted stretch of beach. The blades slowed and stopped. Dave had trouble prying his hands off the grips. He realized that he had been holding his breath and let it out with a whoosh.

Tom popped the side-opening canopy and hauled himself up and over the side, feet feeling for molded-in steps in the side of the skin. He came around and helped Dave to the ground, taking the dark blue nylon duffel and dropping it on the sand beside him. Grinning like a little kid, Tom slapped Dave on the back and said, "Well, what do you think of our new toy?"

Dave was dumbfounded. For once in his life he was totally at a loss for words. Tom squatted and rummaged in the duffel, finally coming up with a small brown bottle. He unscrewed the cap and took a long swig. Then he handed it to Dave. "Here, you look like you could use this." As Dave tentatively sipped, Tom let out a loud burp and patted his flat stomach.

"Do I dare ask what this is all about?" Dave growled. "You know, I might have been killed. I could have fallen off!"

"Nah, you had a good grip. There just wasn't enough time to set it down and get you all tucked in. Let's get out of here. We're only about thirty miles from town." Tom turned and started back toward the cockpit.

Dave reached out and gripped his arm, feeling the hard muscles go rigid. Tom was wearing a khaki short-sleeve shirt, military style khaki shorts, cowboy boots, and his white Hoss Cartwright Stetson.

"Hold it, Pally. Give me at least a thumbnail sketch. What's going on? Is this the chopper we were sent to pick up?"

Dave was fuming and when Tom turned, he could see that Dave was in no mood for an argument. Though Tom was a stocky 5'10" and well muscled, Dave had three inches and twenty pounds on him. And he knew that Dave was one mean son-of-a-bitch in a fight.

"Okay, okay. See, here's what happened. The DEA guys went into Guatemala on a drug bust with a couple of Hueys and this Cobra for backup. Well, they shot up the neighborhood pretty good and then landed to mop up, and torch the lab and hanger. Only there was about a hundred of the suckers waiting for them, hidden in the bush. Caught our guys in a crossfire. The pilot didn't even know what hit him." He gestured toward the starred holes in the helicopter's Lexan canopy. "Well, the Hueys we don't give a shit about. You can buy them anywhere. But this Cobra is not exactly available through the classifieds."

Tom fidgeted, scratching his butt before he continued. "A guy I know at DEA called me and said they found the chopper, but couldn't pull a raid with their guys 'cause it was in Belize now. He asked me if I could go get it. I said yeah, and asked you if you wanted to go. That's it." He grinned again.

"That's it? That's it?! This thing is worth maybe $50 million, and we're getting a lousy $2,000 each? No way, Jose." Dave was still steamed.

Tom fidgeted, swinging his boot toe back and forth in the sand, eyes lowered. He said nothing.

Suddenly Dave understood. "How much are we, with the emphasis on "*we*" getting? For real, this time, asshole!" His voice was low and menacing, ice in it. He glared at Tom, cords standing out on his neck, hands involuntarily flexing open and closed.

"Fifty grand," Tom mumbled.

"Fifty grand? And you were going to give me a measly $2,000! Arrgggghhh!" Dave turned and stalked off. He spun on his heel and came back until his nose was only inches from Tom's. "Half, Pally. I get half or so help me I'll drop you where you stand." He cocked a big fist under Tom's chin. Tom's eyes flickered down. The scarred fist looked as big as his head.

"Oaky, okay! Take it easy, will you? Jesus, no patriotism in you, is there!"

"Fuck you."

Tom shrugged, went around to the right side of the ship and carefully climbed up on the short wing. He reached up and with a flick of his wrist slid a blade out of his back pocket. After unscrewing the access door, he checked the fuel level, sticking his hand in to see if he could feel fuel. He could, but just barely. Without a change in expression, he announced, "Good. Full tank."

Dave climbed up and dropped the bag in the forward gunner's seat. It was lower than the pilot's seat and had great visibility. He managed to jam the bag in beside the small seat allowing him room for his long legs. He took in the target sighting eyecups. That much hadn't changed. The gun control that stuck up on the side of the seat was a stick with a handgrip and a button. He climbed in and slithered down until he was comfortable. Hanging on a hook next to the seat was a helmet with a cable attached to it. It was the Heads Up Control for the chain gun. Whichever way he looked, the guns would follow. Looking over his shoulder, he saw a flash of Tom's finely tooled cowboy boot just disappearing over the side. A couple of seconds later he felt a tap on his head and Tom was gesturing him to put on the helmet. He was just slipping it on when the huge, almost 50' rotors started turning, casting alternating shadows over him. With a thunderous roar, the twin G.E. jet engines screamed to life as Tom poured the fuel to them.

"Can you hear me, Buddy-boy?" Tom called, once again his cheerful self.

"Five by five," Dave replied. "Where's the radio control?"

"How the fuck should I know? I never flew one of these until an hour ago." He laughed loudly.

Dave shook his head in quiet desperation. He finally found the digitized radio controls by his right hand and turned the volume down. "Where are we headed, Tom?"

The chopper got light on the skids and after spinning it 360 degrees, Tom easily hopped it forward and up, up, up over the blue sea. After a few minutes, Tom replied, "Well, we've got to get it to an Army Helicopter base outside Houston. At least that's to get paid. Hang on a minute, will you? I've got some figuring to do."

Dave lazily dreamed about the times he and Tom had flown together in Vietnam. Usually Dave was the pilot and Tom, a year younger, had flown second seat. They made an impressive team, Tom being the more daring of the two. He'd finally been picked to fly brass around and, though they seldom saw each other during those waning days of the war, they remained friends.

"We're, uh, just a little shy on fuel, looks like," Tom reported casually.

"Jesus," Dave muttered. "How shy is a little shy?"

"Well, this bird does about 150 knots and gulps down about 100 gallons an hour. It holds about 3500 pounds of fuel. Let's see, there's about 6.8 pounds to the gallon..."

"Yeah, yeah, about 500 miles. So how far do we have to go?" Dave was rapidly figuring in his mind.

"We-elllll," Tom drew it out. "There's an oil platform out in the Gulf we can stop at but it's about 550 miles from us." There was no comment from the front seat. "Maybe we'll pick up a tailwind?" he suggested.

Dave drew a deep breath. "All right, all right, let's not panic. So we have to either find a closer spot or some fuel. Take it up high and feather it back a bit. I'll see if we can lighten this bird." Dave unzipped the duffel and pulled out his good hat and a cell phone. The rest of the stuff would have to go. Most of it was Tom's anyway, and Dave relished the idea of tossing his stuff over the side. Serve the bastard right. The canopy tilted to the side. Dave wedged the duffel through the opening and over it went. He slammed it closed and sighed.

"Well, we're about thirty pounds lighter now. How about getting rid of some of the armament?"

Before Tom could answer, a speck flew at them out of the sun. Dave could tell it was a helicopter, but it was flying too fast for him to get a good look at it. As Tom yanked the stick to the side and pulled away, a chatter of bullets pinged at their armored hull. The skid on the left side fell away.

"Shit," Tom quietly cursed. "Where the fuck did that come from?"

"He's behind you and above. Better get a move on, Pally. Looks like a 500. Fast little sucker," Dave added this last almost as an afterthought.

Though the top speed for the Cobra was over 200 MPH, the Hughes 500, though slower, was more agile.

Tom dropped the huge twin-engine chopper in a nose down dive that took them almost straight down, the smaller and more nimble ship following. Once again, gunfire raked the cockpit, pinging and zinging. The radio antennas disappeared in flashes of glitter, bullets skidding off the armored skin.

"He's right behind you!" Dave yelled into the mike.

"Not for long, "Tom yelled back. With an awe-inspiring howl, he pulled back on the cyclic, giving it maximum throttle. The nose came up fast and kept coming up until they were upside down in a loop. Tom kept it pulled back and came level again, closing the loop.

"Where is he?" he yelled.

"Still right behind us," Dave called, swiveling in his seat. "The bastard followed us. He's good. We're in deep shit."

"Hang on, Buddy-boy." Tom hauled on the stick again and once again they were nose up. This time at the top of the loop, Tom flipped the big bird over and twisted it around 180 degrees, a screaming, shuddering awkward maneuver. They were at the top of the loop and facing back the way they'd come. In any other chopper, the rotor would have been torn away at the mast from the drastic maneuvers. The other chopper rose in front of them still upside down. Dave held down the firing button on the stick and let the multiple-barreled gun rip. The much more lightly armored 500 shivered and shook from the repeated impact of the heavy slugs. The chain gun fired 3000 banana sized bullets a minute, a speed so fast it was like trying to fly through a wall of steel. The 500 couldn't, and didn't.

It exploded in a fiery ball of burning fuel, pieces hurtling toward the sea. Tom turned toward the north again and they resumed their flight.

"Who the hell was that?" Dave demanded.

"Dunno, " Tom replied thoughtfully. "Sure hope it wasn't one of ours."

"Now what are we going to do? We used up a bunch of fuel back there. That platform is about out of reach now." Dave sat back exhausted.

"Get on the radio. Try calling the Coasties. Maybe they can help."

"Negative. Antennas are gone. So's our left skid, by the way." Dave was feeling gloomy. This was supposed to be a milk run, a fast $2000. Now he'd trade his $25,000 share for a flat, hard spot.

"You'll think of something." Tom said. Dave always did.

Dave's gaze wandered around the crowded cockpit and settled on his cellular phone. He shrugged. What did he have to lose? He picked it up and clicked it on. The readout said "Roam." He cursed. What the hell was the roaming code for the middle of the Gulf of Mexico? He tried the few he knew. Suddenly the phone came alive. The readout now said "Receive."

He looked at it stupidly. His mind was blank. Then his fingers reached out and touched someone. He dialed 911. The phone was answered on the second ring.

"911 Operator. What's your emergency?"

"Uh, can you connect me with the Coast Guard?" Dave didn't know what to say.

"What is the nature of your emergency, sir?"

"We're in a recovered military helicopter out over the Gulf at the following co-ordinates." He read them off the small Global Positioning System panel before him. "We're low on fuel and won't make landfall."

"Just a moment, sir." He heard muted voices, then a strong male voice came on. It had a military tone to it.

"This is Sergeant Kowalski of the Brownsville P.D. If you're in a military chopper, why are you calling on a cellular phone? Is this some kind of a joke?"

"No, Sarge. We lost our antennas. Look, it's a long story and I really don't have time right now to get into it. Patch me through to the Coast Guard, please, and when we get to shore, I'll explain it all to you."

There was silence for a minute, then the Sergeant said, "Okay, but if this turns out to be a joke, I'll fry your ass. I have your number here."

"Thanks, Sarge." Dave waited, the roar of the engines behind him. He knew Tom was listening to his part of the conversation.

In a moment, the Coast Guard was on the phone. Dave explained their situation to the young woman at the Coast Guard Station outside Corpus Christi, putting a note of urgency in his voice. She quickly turned him over to an officer, a Commander by the name of Michaelson.

In rapid order, Dave explained their situation again and asked if they had a cutter with a flight deck nearby.

"Negative," Michaelson replied. "However, we have one without a flight deck about 80 miles north of you. Can you make it that far?"

Dave relayed the information to Tom and waited. Tom checked the fuel gauge and did some rapid mental calculations, then tapped Dave on the head and acknowledged.

"Yes sir, it's on flight path. Could you patch me through to them?" Dave asked.

"I could, but there's no need. They all carry cellular phones these days. Here's their captain's number. Give me about ten minutes and I'll brief him. Good luck." And he was gone. Dave had written the number on a scrap of chart tucked into a corner.

In a few minutes, Dave called the number and surprisingly heard, "This is Captain Roxanne Stevens. How may I be of assistance?"

"Captain Roxanne Stevens?" Dave asked cautiously.

"Yes, this is Captain Stevens. Who are you, sir?"

"This is Dave Manley and I'm with Tom Novak. We have a recovered stolen AH-1W Super Cobra Helicopter, black painted, no markings. Our left skid has been shot away along with our antennas. We don't have enough fuel to make it to land. Can we get some fuel?"

"Mr. Manley, I've been instructed to render you what assistance I can, but we have no av-gas aboard. If you want to ditch close by, we can put an inflatable out and haul you in." She paused as if thinking of alternatives.

Dave relayed the information to Tom.

Tom was smacking him on the head and yelling no into the mike as soon as he heard the word "ditch."

Dave waved his hand aside.

"Dave, we don't get paid if we don't deliver this bird intact, or at least repairable," Tom insisted.

"Shit," Dave muttered again.

"What was that, Mr. Manley?"

"Nothing. Look Captain Roxanne, this bird is worth a whole lot of money to the US Government. We'll give it our best shot. If you have two five gallon jugs of diesel, we can fly her on that. That ought to..." Tom was hitting him on the head again. "Just a minute, Captain."

Tom was holding up three fingers and smiling. "And a hand pump, too," he said.

"Gee, guess who's going to have to pump that stuff," Dave muttered darkly at Tom. *Let's see,* Dave figured, *15 gallons of fuel at almost seven pounds per gallon...* He groaned. A hundred and five pounds. Plus maybe another ten for the pump.

"Uh, Captain, could you lend us about 15 gallons of diesel and a small hand pump?"

"Roger that, Mr. Manley. That still won't get you to land. However, there's a Unocal oil platform about 50 miles north of here. 15 gallons may give you enough to get there and they have a heli-pad." The line was silent for a moment. Dave could hear talk going on in the background. "You realize it will be getting dark soon and if you can't land, how will we get the fuel to you?"

Dave thought for a minute. "Do you have one of those line throwing guns aboard, Captain?"

"Yes sir. I understand. We'll tie the fuel jugs to the end of the line and then what?"

"Well, you turn into the wind and we'll fly alongside. When we match speed, just shoot the line over the one skid we have left and I'll snag it and pull it in." It sounded real simple on paper. "Captain, our rotor diameter is over 50 feet so we won't be able to get all that close. That and the rotor wash will make it a little difficult. How far can that gun of yours shoot?"

"Don't worry Mr. Manley, we'll put a higher charge into it. You just get it alongside and we'll get it to you. My boys are real good. We do lots of rescue work."

"Okay, Captain Roxy, we'll be alongside in about ten minutes. My phone number is 480-9876 if you need me again. This is Dave Manley, we're out." He flipped the phone closed and stuffed it into a crack in the seat.

"Tom, you ready?"

"Ready, willing, and able, Buddy-boy. I wonder what Captain Roxanne looks like?" Tom speculated.

"Just keep your mind on the mission," Dave admonished.

In a few moments, they saw the lights of the Coast Guard Cutter just where they said they'd be. It was twilight, just enough light left for one pass. Tom eased back on the throttles and dropped the nearly invisible chopper down to wave top level. He skimmed alongside the cutter, matching speed. Dave eased the canopy back and stepped out and back onto the skid, holding on with one hand above his head as he did so.

A searchlight blossomed and Dave was caught in its beam, wind whipping his hair in his eyes. He saw a small figure standing on the port rail, feet braced and what looked like a short-barreled shotgun at its shoulder. The figure had three yellow plastic Jerry jugs at his feet. Dave couldn't see the thin line but supposed it was firmly tied on to the handles. Tom was nearly matching speed now and a figure waved from the bridge.

Just as Dave waved his free hand, the figure at the rail fired. Dave felt rather than heard the heavy warhead whiz past his head to bury itself in the instruments to the left of his seat. The crash was loud, explosively loud. Tom reacted and the chopper rose sharply. The fine nylon rope tightened across Dave's chest as fifteen gallons of fuel and ten pounds of pump leapt free of the slowly rolling deck below. He was pinned to the side of the fuselage with the rope cutting into his chest. He couldn't breathe and pounded frantically on the side of the chopper with his free hand. Tom looked down and grinned. He eased back on the throttles and tilted the chopper to the left until Dave could get free. He quickly scrambled back into the cockpit and squatted on the small seat breathing hard.

"My God, what's next?" he muttered to himself.

As soon as his arms stopped trembling, Dave began the necessary chore of hauling in the gas cans and pump. It was heavy going and, without gloves, his hands were soon streaked with blood. After what seemed like hours, Dave finally had the jugs resting on the skids.

Tom kicked the engine back into drive and once more they headed north.

Dave struggled to get all three jugs and the pump into the crowded gunner's seat. Then he unwound the thirty feet or so of fuel tubing, and strung it back through Tom's command seat and over his shoulder. Next he scrambled over his own seat and slithered into Tom's lap. It was a tight squeeze getting over the gunner's headrest but finally Dave managed it.

"What the hell are you doing?" Tom asked peevishly, trying to peer around Dave's legs.

"I'm trying to find a way to put the fuel tubing into the tank without going outside and pulling the cap." Dave wormed his heavy Swiss Army knife out of his pocket and unscrewed an inspection cover behind Tom's head. He kneeled on the seat between Tom's thighs. The access cover gave way to the pipe that led from the fuel filler tubing to the fuel bladder. Reaching in as far as he could, Dave finally felt the rubbery bladder. The knife made a neat hole and Dave managed to get about a foot of tubing into the slit. It was a tight fit and ought not to come out. "There, that ought to do it. Here let me get out of your way." Dave turned and before he slipped over the back of his seat, managed to break wind loudly. He turned and grinned. Tom was grabbing for the oxygen mask.

Dave settled down and tried to get comfortable while pumping. Up and down, up and down. It was exhausting and there was barely enough room in the tiny cockpit. After thirty or forty strokes he had to switch arms. The handle was getting slippery from his bloody palms, too. By the time he'd pumped the second container empty, he was very tired. He signaled Tom that he was going to open the canopy. Tom held onto his cowboy hat and Dave deep sixed the two empties.

"You know, Tom, you could offer to do some of this pumping."

"Sorry, I'm driving," Tom replied. "Hey, look at this. Look what I found. It's a Heads Up Display." Tom slipped the hat off and put the structure over his head, one eye covered by the display eyepiece. "Wow, cool. I found the switch for an infrared searchlight, too. I could see anything … if there was anything to see."

"Yeah, bully for you. Just get us to that platform. I'll try to raise them." Dave fished around for the cellular phone again and dialed the Coast Guard cutter.

"Hey, Captain Roxy," Dave called as soon as the Captain was on the line. "If I ever get my hands on that son-of-a-bitch who almost shot me, I'll kill him!"

"Relax, Mr. Manley, you got your fuel, didn't you?" There was amusement in her voice. "What else can I do for you?"

"We need to get ahold of the oil platform and notify them that we're coming in for fuel. And that we've got a skid gone. It's our port skid and it's about eighteen inches high. See if you can get them to rig something up for us, please. I'll have to pay them with a credit card." Dave felt around in his pocket making sure he still had his wallet.

"Roger that, Mr. Manley. They have a ring of lights around the platform. I'll ask them to have a ground crew to assist you. Anything else?"

He was about to say no when Tom rapped him on the head again. He knew what Tom wanted and just handed the phone over his head to him. He swore. If Tom hit him on the head one more time, he was going to climb over the seat and toss him over the side.

In a few minutes Tom tossed the phone into his lap and said into the mike, "Well, I've got a date next week. I'll have to steal a chopper and get back here." Dave could hear him chuckling to himself.

When Dave finally finished pumping the last five gallons of diesel into the tank, he tossed the pump and jug over the side. His hands were throbbing and starting to swell now from a combination of the diesel fuel spilled on them and cuts from the nylon line.

They were flying now at maximum altitude, almost 14,000 feet. Tom, in a daring move had decided to dump the armament, having Dave fire the two remaining TOW anti-tank missiles at an oil slick and a few minutes later a slew of 70mm rockets, so fast that Dave couldn't even keep count. He enjoyed himself by pointing the twin gun barrels down and unloading about three minutes worth of ammo from the chain guns. Tom had the infrared searchlight on and Dave pulled the heads-up gunner's reticule down over his right eye. He aimed for wave tops and damned if he didn't hit every one. They were several hundred pounds lighter now and, though the fuel gauge didn't seem to be moving any slower, Dave felt more confident that they would make the platform.

Tom was humming softly to himself when Dave called, "Tom, I think I've got the platform on radar. Crank on your infra-red again and see if you can get a visual."

"From 14,000 feet? You've got to be joking. What's your range?"

"Well, it's the only thing on the screen and it just crossed the max line. That's probably 25 miles or so. I can't find an indication. I see that our fuel is about on empty."

"Yeah, I was noticing, too. Think this bird will fly on one engine?" Tom was sounding a little worried now. "If it will, I think we can coax it in."

"Only one way to find out. Cut the starboard engine. That's the side we took the most hits on and might be a little weaker." Dave gulped and waited.

"Weaker? It's a sixteen hundred horsepower engine! Weaker." He snorted and cut back on the "weaker" engine. The chopper maintained its height, though its speed dipped. "Looks okay," Tom said. "I'm not going to shut it down altogether, though. We might need a burst of power at the last minute." He clicked on the external searchlight and wiggled the little control around until it was pointing down and forward. In a few seconds, far below them and a little to their west, a circle of lights came on, flickered off, came on, and stayed on.

"Looks like they see us, Buddy-boy. Grab your cock and hold your socks!" The chopper seemed to fall out of the sky in a nose down attitude. Dave dumbly watched the altimeter spin downward, downward. When Tom came in, he flared with a wrench about 100 feet above the circle of lights. A figure with waving light sticks indicated their direction. Tom carefully eased the big bird downward until they were only a few feet above the deck. A pile of sandbags had been placed to one side of the circle. Tom gently feathered the blades and just as he was about to set it down, the port engine gave a loud bang and the chopper dropped the remaining feet, settling awkwardly on top of the sandbags. The blades stopped turning and Tom switched everything off.

"Lucky bastard," Dave muttered unbuckling his harness and flipping back the canopy.

"Lucky, my ass. I planned it that way all along." Tom was hauling himself over the side as three men ran over to them. Two of them had tie-down straps over their shoulders. The third man wore a beat up leather jacket and a faded ball cap, which read 26 MEU and had a Marine Corps emblem on it.

"Welcome aboard, gentlemen. I'm Colonel Sykes. I've been waiting for you. Let's grab some coffee."

They introduced themselves and hurried below while the other two men busily pushed and pried the chopper over a foot or so and threw the straps over it.

Dave hurried after the other two men, but took time to look around. In the dark of night there was little to see, but the enormity of the platform was unmistakable. Lights flickered and glowed from a hundred windows and levels. He heard the waves lapping gently against the gigantic pilings. In the moonlight he could see another helicopter hanging in slings from a huge crane. Even in the reflected glare of the searchlights it barely returned an image. It was flat black like the Cobra but all angles and planes. He could see the shrouded tail rotor and the drooping five blade main rotor.

Just before he entered the lighted hatch where Tom and the colonel had headed, he looked back at

their bird. Already there were men working on the
skid, and he saw the flash of a welding torch.

CHAPTER 2

They were waiting in the passage for him along with a third man in military fatigues. Colonel Sykes glanced at Dave's hands and called for the soldier to take him to sick bay and get him patched up.

"The Army appreciates all that you men have been through," he said in his official, stilted voice. The colonel was of medium height, had a salt-and-pepper crew cut, a straight nose that had once been broken and a thin, lipless mouth. He wore a set of fatigues with no unit insignia. If it weren't for the black eagles on the collars, no one would be aware of his rank, though it would have been hard not to pick him out of a crowd as a military man. His back was straight and he had a habit of rubbing his thumbs against his pant legs as if searching for the seam. Tom in his cowboy hat and boots seemed incongruous slouched next to him.

"Let's us go get a drink, Colonel. Davey-boy can catch up to us later. That okay with you, Pally?" Tom slapped Dave on the back, smiling.

The Colonel turned to the enlisted man, "Corporal, bring Mr. Manley back up to the mess hall when you're through." With that he turned and led Tom down the corridor.

The enlisted man led Dave a short way after them, then turned down a corridor set at right angles. Soon Dave was lost in the maze of passages and stairways. He was bothered by the enlisted man's familiarity with the passages.

"Excuse me, Corporal," Dave said, noting the rank on the man's collar. "Does the military come here often? You seem awfully familiar with the layout."

Reluctantly the corporal said, "I've been here before, sir."

"What's that mean? You've been here before. Isn't this an oil platform? Let's see if I remember correctly, it's owned by Unocal, isn't it?"

"Yes sir," was all he said continuing along the sparsely lit corridor. It was like going through the passages on a ship with occasional watertight doors with levers around the outside for sealing each compartment in the event of water intrusion.

They soon entered a brightly lit compartment, which Dave guessed was down near the water. The slapping of the waves was a little louder. A man wearing a white coat was seated at a small desk reading a colorful magazine.

"Brushing up on your gynecology, Doc?" Dave asked. The doctor hurriedly crammed the magazine in a desk drawer, jumping to his feet.

"Ah, good evening, gentlemen. I believe you are the fellow off the helicopter that just landed?" The doctor came forward, hand outstretched. "I'm Doctor Morrison. The Colonel asked me to take a look at your hands." He absently lowered his hand.

"Yeah, Doc. It's nothing that some cleaning and a couple of Band-Aids won't cure." Dave held out his hands, palms up. The meat was lacerated in a dozen places, though the blood had just about stopped flowing when the diesel fuel splashed over them. The doctor grimaced and shuddered.

"Come over to the sink here and let's get them washed out." He led Dave to a large, deep sink where he proceeded to gently swab the flayed palms with a soothing soap and warm water. Next he carefully looked at them with a large illuminated magnifier. "Well, I don't see any bone or tendon damage. Can you wiggle all of your fingers?" Dave did so and the doctor nodded. "I'll just put on some antibiotic cream and dress them. Sorry, son, but there'll be no beating your meat for a week or two." He broke out into a loud cackle as he set his supplies on the exam table.

Dave looked sideways at the corporal standing beside him. The corporal shrugged.

"Been a while since you were ashore, Doc?" Dave asked innocently.

"About a month," replied the Doc, bent over the pink, rutted hands. He gently smeared the white cream over them and worked it into the cuts, then placed two large gauze pads on top, finally taping them with multiple wraps of adhesive tape. "There, do that every couple of days, don't get them wet if you can help it. And put the cream on every time you change bandages." He tossed Dave a long white tube, which Dave awkwardly stuffed in a jacket pocket.

"Thanks, Doc. Send the bill to the Army or Marines or whoever these guys are with." But the doctor was already back at his desk, feet up, reading his magazine.

The corporal escorted Dave to the mess hall, and in a few minutes they were both seated with Colonel Sykes and Tom, steaming mugs of coffee before them.

The debriefing took over an hour with Tom doing most of the talking. The Colonel was most interested in the Hughes 500 they'd shot down, asking them to describe it over and over. He wanted to know where it had come from, the maneuvers it made, how many shots they'd put in it, and identifying marks. Finally Tom got tired and went to get a tray of food. Dave followed and got close to Tom.

"What the hell is going on? We got their stupid chopper back didn't we? How should we know who was in the 500?" Dave awkwardly put two large cheeseburgers and a pile of mashed potatoes on his tray. Tom did the same and added more coffee to both of their cups.

"Listen, just play along. Tell him what he wants to know. He's the guy who's got our fifty grand. Did you see his chopper hanging in the slings under that crane outside?" Dave nodded. It was a weird shape, all flat surfaces.

"Yeah, what the hell was that? It looks foreign." Dave racked his brain trying to put a name to it.

"I think it was one of those new Comanches. Mean lookin' mother, wasn't it? I'd sure like to drive that guy." Tom was incorrigible. "Maybe the Colonel will let me fly that one and you could fly the Cobra?"

"Not with my hands taped like this," Dave replied, holding up one white-swathed paw.

They approached the table and sat down again with Colonel Sykes and Corporal McNeil.

"The welders are taking care of the skid and one of the radio jockeys said he could rig up an antenna for you," the Colonel said, sipping his umpteenth cup of coffee. "You'll be ready to go as soon as its light."

The corporal spoke up, "As soon as you gentlemen are finished, I'll show you where you can sack out for a couple of hours."

"Where are you going to be?" Asked Dave, mouth full.

"We're heading back tonight," Sykes replied. "The delivery location is marked on a chart I'll leave in the cockpit. We'll meet you there. And Novak, don't lose it, okay?"

"Colonel, you just have our dough waiting. We'll get your bird there in one piece," Tom replied, a wide grin splitting his face.

A half-hour later, Dave and Tom were in a small but comfortable room, laying back on the narrow beds. Tom was already snoring, but Dave couldn't get to sleep. Something about the delivery was bothering him. Why hadn't the Colonel sent a BOU squad to get the chopper? Why hire a couple of civilians? And why was he so concerned about the other chopper – the one that attacked them? What was so important about that bird? It was probably stolen or maybe even purchased by the druggies sometime in the past. After all, Hughes 500's were a dime a dozen. So it had a couple of guns on it, so what?

They were questions that had no answers, and stewing over them, Dave fitfully dropped in and out of sleep until Tom roused him just as dawn was creeping up the harsh, angular towers and turrets of the platform.

Blinking sleep out of his eyes, Dave peered out the small window set into the bulkhead. From his vantage point, he could just see the edge of the landing pad. Next to it, the yellow painted crane no longer held the other helicopter. They hadn't even heard it take off.

In an effort to wake up, Dave stuck his face under the cold faucet, trying not to get his hands wet. He let it run for a minute over the back of his neck, finally standing and shaking his head vigorously. Tom tossed him a towel and he quickly dried himself. He felt like a shower but both he and Tom were anxious to get the job over with. When they went to the mess hall, no one was around except a pasty-faced cook who shrugged when asked about the military pair who had been there the night before.

Dave found a window that looked out on the landing pad. "Looks like we're alone again." He signaled to Tom to come look, but he had his face buried in a tray of pancakes and bacon. Across on various catwalks, men were working, moving unconcerned over the choppy sea far below.

Fifteen minutes later, he and Tom were airborne once again, the rotors beating him into drowsiness. After flying for a while, Tom roused him. "We're coming up on land, Sleeping Beauty. Get the chart out and guide us in. I'll rouse Customs."

Dave located the course on the chart left by the Colonel and busied himself with an approach to Houston. It was fairly straightforward. In his earphones he could hear Tom clearing them with U.S. Customs. Obviously Colonel Sykes had smoothed their way because they didn't even need to deviate from the course they were flying. Tom dropped down a few hundred feet so as not to interfere with civilian aviation in the Houston area. Off on the eastern horizon, Dave could barely make out the sprawl of the city. Tom was swinging wide to the west and dropping still further toward the undulating ground.

"What are you doing?" Dave asked, keying on the internal mike in his mask.

"I just want to see if these guys are awake," Tom replied, a grin in his voice.

"Shit, you'll probably get us shot down. We're supposed to come in from the south and set down next to that hanger," Dave held up the chart and indicated the X mark.

Tom dropped the ship lower until they were flying NOE (nap-of-the-earth) at over 150 knots. They were coming into the target area from the northwest. Directly ahead of them was a low range of hills. Tom slowed down and crept up behind the hill, skids only a few feet off the ground, dust being blown around them. He slipped sideways until they could look around the side, the crest hiding the rotor.

"Well, well, there it is," Tom chortled. "Let's give 'em a surprise."

Dave knew better than to argue. Tom again slipped around the hill and the big ship leaped forward, slightly nose down. Tom wanted a good view. He was just approaching 100 knots when he jerked up then down, barely clearing a high chainlink fence with concertina wire on top. He continued to hop over objects and bumps in the terrain until they were hurtling at the hanger at high speed. As they approached, men started running away from the hanger, fearing an impending crash. There were two other helicopters on the pad outside the hanger. A large circle was painted on the ground beside the western most chopper. It was the angular bird they'd seen on the platform. At the last minute, Tom pulled back on the cyclic and up on the

collective, climbing, climbing, up and up. The ship
rapidly gained altitude, the rotor blades screaming.
The nose with Dave in it was pointed up towards
the sun. Suddenly she rolled to the right side. Tom
jammed the cyclic forward and the collective down,
wildly over correcting. The ship tipped, fell, lost
altitude. Dave felt rather than saw the ground rush
up at him and he prepared for a crash. Good-bye
Chris, I love you. Good-bye Vinny and Joan. And
Rusty and Mom and Dad and...

With a howl, Tom flared again and the heavy
ship came to a shuddering halt just feet above the
white circle. He set it down gently and began
throwing switches above his head and on the panel
before him. Dave gulped and tried to calm his
racing heart.

Tom hoisted the canopy up and swung his
cowboy boots out of the cockpit, toes feeling for the
indents. He jumped the last few feet and strolled
around to Dave's side and twisted the handle.

Dave was leaning back in his seat, drenched
with sweat. "Are we there yet?"

"Yup," Tom smiled and looked over his
shoulder. "And here's our welcoming committee."

A half dozen camouflage clad soldiers were
double timing towards them, M-16 rifles at port
arms. They stopped short of the two men, rifles
pointing at them menacingly. Tom and Dave were
unmistakably civilians. Tom stood, hands on hips,
white cowboy hat tilted at a rakish angle over one
eye. Sweat stained khaki shorts rode up inside his
thighs and white sweat socks could just be seen
peeping out of the tops of his shiny boots. Dave had

a silky flamingo encrusted shirt on over cut-off jeans and Nike running shoes.

The squad leader said something into a hand-held radio and then motioned his men to stand easy. In a couple of minutes a Humvee sped across the tarmac at them, skidding to a halt just inches from Dave's shoes. Colonel Sykes slowly removed his mirrored sunglasses. Glaring at Tom, he swung his long legs out and stood, nearly stepping on Dave who stumbled backwards.

"Novak, you hot rodder, you dumb fuck! We almost shot you down. You know there were six missiles aimed at you when you got within three miles of this base?"

Tom still had the cowboy hat tilted down over his nose. Slowly he pushed it back with his thumb. Squinting up at the Colonel, he smiled. "Sykes, you couldn't shoot me down if you were sitting next to me. Now why don't you give us our dough and we'll get out of your hair." He held out his hand, palm up.

The Colonel reached into the Humvee, brought out an envelope and withdrew some papers. He laid them on the hood and handed Tom a pen. "Just sign where I've marked and you'll be out of here and out of my life," he said, jabbing a stiff forefinger at the top sheet.

Tom scribbled on the paper and tossed the pen down. "You know, Colonel, when your boys get their peckers caught in a vise, you call in a well trained civilian to do your dirty work. Well, that's why we do it for money."

The Colonel tossed him a white envelope with a rubber band around it. Tom hefted it and tossed it over his shoulder to Dave. "Count it, Buddy-boy."

Dave quickly thumbed through the hundred-dollar bills, counting quickly. "I make it about $30,000, Tom."

"What the fuck's going on, Sykes? The deal was for 50 grand."

"Well, with the damage to the ship and having to get you fuel and a night on the platform, I figure all that was worth $20,000. You don't like it? Sue me." Colonel Sykes was almost nose-to-nose with Tom, the cords tight in his neck

Just as quickly, Tom smiled again at the Colonel. "Sykes, you have definitely picked the wrong guy to fuck with. The way I figure it, you now owe me another $50,000."

Dave didn't like the way this was going so he stepped between them, his Hawaiian shirt contrasting sharply with the khaki of the Colonel's clothing and Tom's shorts and T-shirt. "Now, now, boys, let's just all keep our cool. Colonel, may I suggest a compromise? If you will just pay us what you owe, I'm sure we can forget this unpleasantness. Tom is just talking, and if the deal was for $50,000, I don't think you'll have any trouble persuading your superiors to honor their commitment. So why don't you just drive on back to your office, open your little safe and get our $20,000. We'll wait, won't we, Tom?" Dave was talking fast now, trying to diffuse the tension.

Tom raised his eyebrows. He was itching to nail Colonel Sykes on his thin, aristocratic nose.

Dave's hand rested lightly on his chest, holding him at bay. The Colonel's men slowly formed a ring around them, weapons still at port arms. The Colonel stepped back in disgust.

"You fuckin' civilians make me want to puke. You're asked to do something patriotic for your country and all you can think of is the almighty dollar. Well, no sir. No way. No fuckin' way." He turned to the squad leader. "Corporal, escort these men to the #2 gate. Tell the guards to shoot them if they ever try to get on this base again."

He turned in disgust and climbed back into his Humvee. He nodded sharply to the driver and the vehicle sped away, tires squealing in protest.

Tom kept smiling at Dave and the Corporal. "Well, Davey-boy, looks like we just got screwed again by Uncle Sam. Getting to be an everyday feeling." He turned to the Corporal. "I don't suppose you'd let us take our chopper back and fly out of here, would you, son?"

The Corporal grimly shook his head and motioned for them to precede him to a nearby 4x4 truck. Tom easily hoisted himself into the rear and gave Dave a hand up. Several soldiers scrambled up and sat beside and across from them, gunstocks on the floor between their feet, barrels pointed upward. The Corporal climbed up beside the driver and slammed the door. The truck lumbered off the tarmac and down a dusty road, finally coming to a stop before a high chain link fence. A Marine guard in fatigues stood under an awning strung from poles and surrounded by a waist high sandbag barricade.

This obviously wasn't the main gate but some back hole in the fence. Dave and Tom looked at each other.

"What the hell is this?" Dave asked. A narrow, rough road ran away into the scrub covered low hills and out of sight.

"I don't suppose you could tell us which way to the nearest town?"

The Corporal gestured with his gun barrel. "About a mile down there, take a right. Can't miss it." The guard opened the gate and stepped aside.

Tom pulled his hat down tight over his head and strode through the gate muttering, "Thirty-thousand fucking dollars in my pocket and can't even get a fucking ride to town..." Suddenly he whirled and pointed to the Corporal, "You tell that goddamn Sykes, I'm not through with him yet!"

A few weeks later, Tom and Dave were hunched over their drinks at Chesney's. This was their bar and watering hole, and Dave's home on Florida's West Coast in the tiny town of Sunset Pointe. Tom toyed with his Sam Adams longneck while Dave idly stirred his iced tea with a thick forefinger.

"I still can't figure it out. If Sykes has used you a few times in the past, why was he being so stingy this time? You know he'll call on you again someday." Dave glanced up at Tom, his eyebrows raised.

"Maybe he's under the ax, too. You know, cutbacks and all?" Chris ventured. Chris was a pretty little blonde, Dave's wife of nearly 10 years. She'd inherited the old bar/restaurant and marina from J. Chesney Campbell, a prominent Clearwater lawyer and friend of Chris and Dave's. Dave had been living on his boat; a solidly built sloop rigged 40' sailboat at the small marina when he'd married Chris. After she moved in with him, she and the old lawyer had become closer than father and daughter. She had baked him special pastries when Charlie Potts let her into the kitchen, and had generally assumed supervision of the local hangout. It was a terrible blow to her when the old man died, and she'd been surprised when he'd deeded her the old bar. In deference to Chesney, she'd hung a large photo of the old man over the bar draped in black. The tradition had started soon after that the last round was dedicated to him. Near closing time, one of the patrons or Chris or Dave would stand and raise a glass to the portrait. "To you, Ches!" was the usual toast. After the drink was downed, more often than not the drinking and conversation would simply continue until Chris threw everybody out.

Gathered around one of the scarred wooden yard sale tables with Dave, Tom, Chris, were Rusty and Anna who lived aboard a restored World War II vintage PT boat, and Vinny and Joan who also lived at the marina on an immaculate thirty-eight trawler. Rusty was a big old fellow with a great shock of pure white hair, a prodigious beer belly and a smooth, seamless face with a ready smile. His wife,

Anna, was a florid woman with a tight cap of bright
red curls, arms and shoulders to rival her husband's
and a small cigar, which stuck out of the corner of
her mouth. Vinny, a small, wiry Italian ex-plumber
and trivia buff, sat to her left. His wife, Joan, sat
back with her feet curled under her on a director's
chair, her cut off T-shirt barely concealing her small
hard breasts. Her short hair poked out from under
the Yankee's baseball cap she had pulled down over
her forehead.

The discussion had degenerated from "what are
we going to do with Dave's share of the money" to
"I wonder why he did what he did?"

"Well, all's I know is that someday I'm going
to get that prick," Tom growled. "Oops, please
pardon my French, ladies."

Joan gave him a grin of understanding.

"Who's hungry?" yelled Charlie Potts, the ex-
Army cook, from the pass through behind the bar.
His fat face nearly filled the square opening, loose
lips hanging open. "Steaks all around?"

Tom nodded, Vinny and Joan shrugged an
affirmative, Rusty raised an assenting finger and
Dave agreed. Chris left to give Charlie a hand. Tom
watched her walk away, her round bottom twitching
in her tight cutoff jeans.

Dave grinned and muttered, "Eat your heart
out." Tom grinned sheepishly, having been caught
in the act -- again.

Just then the door opened and a woman stepped
through. She was dressed in a simple cotton dress
that was obviously expensive. Her open toed
sandals showed dark red nails and the short dress

displayed her magnificent legs. The great mass of black hair tumbled over her shoulders and was held with a simple clip. She glided over to the group at the table and asked a fateful question. "Which of you is Senor Thomas Novak?"

CHAPTER 3

At another table, thousands of miles away and a month earlier, another family sat deep in conversation. This was a more formal grouping. At the head of the table sat Enrico Ernesto Locarno, the present head of the Guatemalan sheep ranchers and clandestine emerald mining family. He was fifty-eight years old. Enrico oversaw more than 50,000 hectares of fine grazing land, had many thousands of fine Merino sheep, and sometimes dispatched his boyhood friend Gregorio Mauro to Colombia with as many as seven or eight fine quality emeralds to be sold quietly and discretely. The money was dispatched to an old banking house in London where it was even more discretely invested under a number of family member's names with the interest being deposited into a Swiss bank under a number only. Occasionally some of this money was transferred to the British-Canadian Bank of the Caribbean in Nassau, Bahamas, and Enrico would take one of his infrequent vacations. Few people knew why he liked the Bahamas so much, but gossip had it that he was a gambler. When discussion in the local cantinas came around to the family's fortunes, it was always assumed that their holdings would have been more extensive but for the *Padrone's* habit. Few people realized that their village was unique in that they possessed one of the few hospitals in a small town, that their doctor, one of the *Padrone's* nephews, was a brilliant surgeon trained in the city of Nuevo York in *Los Estades Unidos* and in London in the country of England.

They also rarely discussed why they had been almost entirely free from political strife in a country seemingly at war almost since its inception. That they sat in a fine, deep valley surrounded by thickly wooded hills helped, but that wasn't the entire answer. Through the many years, the Locarno family had made official "presents" to government appointees, occasionally to highly placed military men, and even more rarely to rebels who had inadvertently strayed into their valley. Once, Enrico's grandfather, Nicholas, had gone to the Mayan Chief and asked for some help in discouraging a particularly persistent band of thieves composed of all around bad hombres. He was a bit flustered one late evening when the chief unceremoniously dumped a burlap bag containing the grinning head of the bandit leader on his doorstep. Fortunately, the children had been asleep.

At the table, sitting to Enrico's left was his Aunt Roberta, his father Armando's sister. She wore a black dress with a finely woven black lace shawl over her head. Though Aunt Roberta was seventy-seven years old, she conveyed great dignity, which belied her earlier years. Pregnant and married at fifteen to an Italian adventurer, she soon found herself alone after the baby had been stillborn. It seems that Mario, her husband, upon being informed that she couldn't bear anymore children, had simply packed one night and left. Many years later, she'd gone looking for him and had been trapped in Italy by the war. Alone in a foreign country, surrounded by foreigners, she had nevertheless managed to find the resistance fighters, allied herself to them and had come through the war, though physically unscathed, a much matured and quiet woman. By the time she'd found her way back to Guatemala in the early 1950's, she had seen most of Europe and had helped her brother Enrico to set up his little investment scheme. Though Enrico was one of the more worldly men to be born into the Locarno clan, he was known to have never made an important decision without consulting with Aunt Roberta.

Sitting on Aunt Roberta's left hand was her grandniece and Enrico's daughter Alexandria. Alexandria was coming onto 30 years old and Enrico was afraid she'd soon be too old to find a husband. She was an elegant, dark-haired beauty, educated first at the Americano college of Boston

University and then at the London School of Economics. She had recently enrolled in a prominent, though little known academy in Amsterdam where she planned on studying Geology with particular emphasis on gems and their formation. It seems that the Locarno's little mine, which had brought them so much wealth, was, if not exactly giving out, was certainly not producing the deep green, gem quality stones that were its trademark. In fact, on the table before them sat a pure white emerald, as it is known in the trade, of approximately thirty carats, rough cut.

Across the table from Aunt Roberta sat Enrico's friend and their emerald broker Gregorio Mauro, with his son Sergio. Gregorio spoke in the strangely accented Colombian Spanish inherited from his ancestors. "*Padrone*, my son tells me that these white emeralds are worthless. The men who buy the stones don't want them. Have we no more green stones?"

Enrico glanced at the remaining member of the group. He was Bernardo, Enrico's son and pride. He was one year older than Alexandria, a fine looking lad with the family's silky black hair, broad shoulders, and finely formed hands. His well-shaped nose was aquiline and his lips slightly thin above a strong jaw. In the local village he was known as a ladies' man and many a father would have shot him, or at least threatened to shoot him had they been able to catch him. It was Bernardo's job to mine the emeralds, as had been his father's job and his father's before him.

"Poppa, I can see no more of the green pipe. However, the white goes on for quite a ways. I have dug along its length for approximately fifty meters and, if anything, it grows larger. Perhaps we can find an industrial use for the white esmeraldas?" He neither knew of a use nor cared. That was for the others to deduce. His job was to mine the pipe and give the *esmeraldas* to his father. After that, he didn't care. If there was money to spend and local girls to dally with, he was happy.

"Perhaps we can create a need, a desire?" Sergio suggested.

"Perhaps," Enrico agreed. "We will all think on it. However, I think our problem with the Colombian drug people is a greater one. Forgive me, my old friend, I mean no disrespect." He glanced at Gregorio. He knew Gregorio was of Colombian ancestry and did not want to show disfavor to his race or nationality. He was usually quite sensitive to these things but their current problems had him confused.

"No offense taken, my friend. I must agree that the problem is pressing. May I summarize the problem for those present who do not have all the information?"

He looked from one face to another. Roberta Victoriana Locarno nodded once firmly. Bernardo nodded with interest. Here was something exciting, something more interesting than grubbing in the dark earth. The Patron gave one slow nod. Alexandria said nothing, just sat looking from one male face to another. She saw that they were troubled.

Gregorio spoke, "Several months ago some men came to our village. They were inquiring about some land -- land suitable for an air landing field. Someplace, shall we say, private, secluded. As you know, they have made arrangements to purchase land in the Piedra valley. Observations made by our Mayan friends indicate that these men are bringing in cocaine, *narcoticos*. The *Padrone* and I have concluded that these men are not seeking to sell these *narcoticos* to our people but for trans-shipment to *Los Estates Unidos*." He stopped and cleared his throat, stroked his fine, thick mustache.

He continued. "In normal times, this would not affect us but there have been reports that they have been sending men to some of the outlying farms and taking the people to work for them." He paused for effect. "Yes, my friends, taking them at the point of a gun and forcing them into their valley. And as you know, that valley lies only one over from ours. The Mayans also report that they are clearing land for a much larger settlement." He paused again and let that sink in.

Aunt Roberta raised an eyebrow, her lips imperceptibly tightening. The *Padrone* leaned forward on his forearms. "If we allow this to continue, they will soon be coming over the hills and taking our people!"

"Poppa," Bernardo spoke for the first time. "I have heard that they have approached some of the Mayans for help in finding workers for them." He looked around the table. "They wouldn't help them, would they?"

"I don't think so, Bernardo." He looked bewildered.

Finally Aunt Roberta spoke. "You fools. Don't you read the newspapers? Don't you watch the television? Do you not know what kind of men these Colombians are?" She looked at the *Padrone* and finally at her niece. "If they captured Alexandria, you, Enrico, would give them anything they want. Would you expect any less from the Mayans?" No one spoke, all forced to agree with the old woman.

"Si, *Tia* Roberta, but what can we do? Can we make peace with them? Can we negotiate with them to stay away?"

"Pah," the old woman spat. "They are worse than the Nazis. You fight them, you kill them. That is what you do, Enrico."

"But Roberta, we are not soldiers. Beyond our few shotguns and hunting rifles, we have no weapons. Besides, they have more than fifty men at their camp now, all of them armed." Gregorio shrugged helplessly. "We need an army."

"Exactly, Gregorio, you are brilliant!" Enrico clapped him on the shoulder. "Now where are we to get an army?" Once again he looked around the table. "Alexandria?" She shrugged. "Gregorio? Bernardo? Sergio?" They all looked down. "Yes, the last thing we want is the government army in our valley." He thought for a moment. "Can we hire an army somewhere?"

Roberta snorted. He looked at her and asked, "You have something to add to this little discussion, *Tia* Roberta?"

"Last week when Padre Lazaro was here for a visit, he spoke of a raid recently by two *Americanos* who came and stole an *Americano* helicopter back from these same Colombians. Maybe they have an army?" She spoke quietly yet firmly.

Now it was Enrico's turn to snort. "Two men, what can they do?"

Now Alexandria spoke. "Maybe they have friends in the *Norte Americano* army. Don't they fight against the drug people?" Again they looked around at each other. No one knew but they were grasping at straws. "We have no one else to turn to. One of us must go and ask them."

"But these *Americanos*, according to the television, they do nothing unless they get paid. We must offer them some money, some incentive to make them want to assist us." Enrico was silent for a moment lost in thought.

Roberta spoke again, "*Esmeraldas.*"

"What did you say, Tia Roberta?" Enrico asked.

"*Esmeraldas.* Those stupid *Norte Americanos* will think they are worth a fortune. They cost us nothing. Offer them some of the *esmeraldas blanca* and they will come with winged feet. But let Alexandria go to them. They love women and the combination of a beautiful woman, tears -- you must remember to cry, my pretty one -- and the white emeralds will assure us of their cooperation. We have nothing to lose." She crossed her thin arms across her bosom and sat back.

Alexandria blushed and lowered her eyes. Sergio shyly searched for her glance.

The *Padrone* considered this. "Does anyone have any other ideas?" There were none. "Meanwhile, Gregorio, you must ask the Mayans to place themselves in the paths of the *Narcoticos*. We may need some of our people on the inside," a term he'd learned from watching the *Americano* television show Miami Vice. He was proud of himself and stroked his narrow mustache with the back of a forefinger. They were doing something, something positive.

"But Poppa, how do I find these men? I don't even know their names. And America is a very large country."

"Don't worry, *mi flora*, I took the liberty of writing down the one man's name the *Padre* knew. Here," *Tia* Roberta reached into an inner pocket and withdrew a scrap of paper which she handed over to Alexandria. On it were two words, 'Tom Novak.'

The men arose from the table, each nursing his own thoughts. *Tia* Roberta took Alexandria into her sitting room, quietly speaking to her, giving her instructions based on her experiences in the resistance in Italy. She knew ways to trace men, to obtain information and how to use it. In her more than four decades at the ranch, she had quietly and without seeming to, given her knowledge and strength to the family and especially to her nephew Enrico.

At 58, Enrico is a tall, sparse man, impeccably dressed, usually in a pair of black trousers, a white silk shirt open at the throat and finely tooled calf high boots. His wife of six years, Julia Martini, an ash blonde he'd met in college in Texas many years before was gone. The remote valley, the tiny village proved too remote, too quiet, too sedate for the vivacious Julia Martini. One night, like her *Tia* Roberta's husband Mario, she was gone, leaving her two small children alone in their beds.

Enrico took it all with quiet grace. His sister Dorotea and her husband, the jovial Ricardo, had taken on the task of raising the children, mixing them with their own Lazaro, Dominguez, and Claudio. Alexandria grew up with the boys, riding, shooting, and scrambling up the steep hills with them. Though he'd had many opportunities, Enrico never remarried, preferring instead to await the return of his beloved Julia.

CHAPTER 4

Tom looked up at the comely young woman. She stood by his chair in a simple yet obviously expensive cotton dress, her perfume wafted to him, swirled around, mixed with another, stronger scent. It was her scent, the one that made her special, unique. It was a delicate muskiness, the smell of the outdoors, of sun warmed skin, of clean, a scent not altogether familiar, a scent somehow foreign, not of America. Tom decided he liked it. Looking up at her after a long, deadpanned minute, he said, "I'm Tom, who wants to know?"

She looked confused for a moment. A tiny frown crossed her face like a flickering shadow, then was gone. She smiled a warm smile, her generous red lips crinkling with pleasure. She

looked down at him liking what she saw. Then she
lightly rested a slim hand on his shoulder and bent
so her lips were only millimeters from his ear. "I
want to know. And I'd like to speak with you in
private."

Tom raised his eyebrows at Dave who was
looking at him questioningly. They were all looking
at the young woman who still had her hand resting
on Tom's shoulder. He shrugged and slowly
climbed to his feet, topping her by barely two
inches. Tom's five foot ten and 220 pounds sure
wasn't overpowering against this woman. He was
broad in the shoulders with a great barrel chest and
thickly corded arms. His sleek auburn hair, shot
through with gray, was carefully brushed back over
small ears with a casual wave over his forehead.
Today, he was wearing faded jeans tucked into a
pair of scuffed Wellington boots and a Harley-
Davidson T-shirt -- a wild looking eagle screened
on the front. He stood before her and gestured
elegantly at a booth in the corner. Alexandria
preceded him. As Dave watched, Tom put a hand
behind his back and theatrically crossed his fingers.

In a few moments they were seated inside
Chesney's, leaning across the table almost head to
head. The woman was speaking intently, making
strong jabbing gestures and occasionally pounding
on the table soundlessly, her tiny fist clenched tight.
Through it all, Tom just listened, finally shaking his
head from side to side. She grew more demanding,
poking him in the chest, fire in her eyes. Finally
Tom brushed her hand away and stood up, took a

last look and came back then sat down next to Dave again.

Dave glanced at Tom, then back at the woman hunched over in the booth.

"Aw, shit, Tom, what did you say to her? She's crying. Look at her," Vinny moaned almost to himself. He made as if to get up but Dave reached out to him, as did his wife, Joan.

"Sit still, Vince. I'll handle this." Dave pushed back his chair with a creak and resignedly strolled over to the silently weeping woman. He slid into the booth and touched her on the hand.

"Excuse me, Ma'am, but I want to apologize for my friend Tom. He sometimes says the wrong things. Maybe I can help." He sat back expectantly, hands clasped on the table before him.

She pulled a tiny wisp of a handkerchief out of a small handbag on the table and dabbed at her eyes. Dave idly noted that she was either wearing waterproof mascara or her deep, dark shaded eyes were that way naturally. He fervently hoped the latter.

With a final sniffle, she looked up at him. "That pig friend of yours I have been searching for two weeks and he won't help me. He won't even listen to me."

She seemed about ready to unleash another torrent of tears so Dave hastily said, "Wait, wait. Maybe I can help."

It seems that in some men there is a nasty disease often observed but until recently never named. This debilitating disease is called Damsel in Distress Syndrome. It has been known to deprive strong men of their will, money, and sometimes marriages. Men have died attempting to placate this Syndrome and even taken hoards of friends with them in the mistaken assumption that there was 'Something they could do to help.' Dave had long suffered from advanced stages of this terrible tragedy and it was only with the able and diligent assistance of his wife, Chris, that he was able to fight off the more expensive stages.

Tom, on the other hand, failed to become infected. He was able to say no clearly and succinctly, feeling no qualms or remorse. He did, however, tend to accompany Dave on the occasional outing when Dave was infected, often to his dismay and disbelief that he was actually doing something that stupid, but by then it was usually too late to back out. This is not to say that Tom wasn't a kind and uncaring human being! It was just that Tom had his priorities. The first was money. The second was the well being of his hide. Next came his friends. He sometimes confused the second and third, but rarely the first.

As Tom glared at the two in the booth, Dave tenderly patting the lady's hand, he had the uncomfortable sensation that he was being inexorably sucked into a whirlpool that he really wanted no part of, a black hole that would cause him to be made to do things he really didn't want to.

He began to shout, "Chris!" Louder now, "Chris, come out here!" The others at the table started at his shouts.

Rusty reached across and gently cuffed Tom up beside his head. "Get it together, man, you're starting to lose your marbles. What did she say, anyway?"

Just then, Chris Manley came rushing across the floor, vigorously wiping her hands on a stained white apron. "Whatever is the matter, Tom? I could hear you yelling over that awful country music Charley plays in the kitchen."

Tom just pointed to Dave and the young woman. She groaned and muttered, "D-I-D?"

Tom nodded slowly, wishing he were somewhere else. He felt his world slowly sinking into a quagmire.

Chris stalked over to the booth, her every fiber bent on undoing what had just been done, knowing that her attempt was probably doomed to failure. She slid into the booth next to Dave and wrapped an arm around his neck, kissing him possessively on the cheek. Then she smiled broadly at the woman opposite. "How do you do? I'm Christine Manley, David's wife, and you are...?"

The woman appraised her coolly. After all, it is only what she herself would do with a man such as this. "How do you do, Mrs. Manley? I am Alexandria Locarno. Please sheath your claws. I came here to see that pig, Thomas Novak." She gave a contemptuous shake of her head in Tom's direction. "Your husband was just comforting me after Mr. Novak refused to even hear me out. Now I am not sure what to do." She slumped back in the booth.

Chris appraised this woman, tall, taller than Chris, with a good figure, if you liked that heavier, voluptuous Latin look. Good hair and from what she could see, good teeth. Therefore, not poor. Spoke excellent English with just a hint of an accent, probably went to school in the U.S. Chris looked at her hands. Well cared for but she'd done hard work in her time. Several small scars were visible on the right forefinger and the nails, though well manicured, were natural and slightly uneven. Chris lifted her gaze to the woman's high forehead and the tracery of fine lines at the corners of her eyes that the makeup couldn't hide. Not a spring chicken, but not old either. Chris estimated her age at 30 or so, maybe a year older than she was.

"So what's the problem? Why are you here to see Tom?" Chris inquired.

With a sigh Alexandria retold her story of the Colombians, the small village, the Padre who gave her Aunt Roberta the name of the *Americano* who had stolen the helicopter back from the Colombians. She explained her family's decision to send her in search of the elusive Mr. Novak.

Dave interrupted, "I was with Tom on that trip. I helped him fly it back. Boy, the Army sure screwed us on that one," he said ruefully.

Alexandria looked at him in astonishment, "Then you know the Army people of the United States? You can get them to help us?" She eagerly leaned forward. Chris noted the front of her dress displaying a great expanse of creamy tan cleavage at about the same time Dave noticed. She squeezed his thigh hard under the table.

He smiled through the pain. "I'm afraid that when we parted company with the military people, they weren't too happy with us -- or us with them," he added.

She slumped again in the booth. Chris asked, "Why don't you join us for something to eat and we can discuss it. Maybe one of the others will have an idea."

"Thank you, Mrs. Manley. You are too kind."

"Please, call me Chris. May I call you Alexandria?" Her New York manners came to the fore even in an informal setting like this. *Good breeding always tells,* Dave thought.

"Thank you, Chris," this last hesitatingly. "Please call me Alex. It is what my family calls me and my friends at college when I was in Boston."

Dave followed along and drew up chairs for the two women, being careful to keep Alexandria away from Tom. Tom hunched over his steak ignoring his surroundings and most pointedly their new companion.

Dave made the introductions. Alex coolly extended her hand to each person as the introductions were made. The men rose to their feet. The women reserved judgment. Dave encapsulated her story and threw it open for discussion.

"Where's Guatemala?" asked Vinny. "Ain't that somewhere down in South America or someplace?"

"Ah, you dumb guinea," said Joan. "It's just below Mexico in Central America. Isn't that right, Alex?"

Alex smiled and nodded. Charlie Potts came out of the kitchen holding two plates. "I brung the lady a little something to nosh on." He leered at her, thrusting the plate before her. On it were three small lamb chops, little bows of white satin tied around the shank ends, julienned carrots artfully arrayed in a spray and several small boiled new potatoes. Wedging his plump torso between Alex and Vinny, he pulled a chair up and plopped down his own plate. He gave Alex a huge, fleshy, openmouthed grin, winking at Chris. "I unnerstand you got a problem. Well, lemme tell ya, we're here to help ya out." His glance challenged them to say differently. Tom squirmed uncomfortably in his chair.

"All right, all right," Charlie said. "Let's have some of the details. How many of these Colombians did you say there are?"

"Two weeks ago there were about fifty of them. There may be more by now," Alex said in a small voice.

"Okay, okay! So that's about ten apiece. That's no problem. What else?" Charlie surveyed the men at the table. He knew that Dave and Tom could each handle at least ten each. Rusty was about seventy-five so you probably could only count on him for five or so. And Vinny? Well Vinny was maybe sixty-five or sixty-six, but was a tough, wiry little guy so he could probably handle about five, too. Let's see, that left twenty. Charlie didn't think he could handle that many by himself. "We'll probably need a coupla more guys," he admitted glumly.

"Yeah, no shit Sherlock," Dave retorted.

"What's in it for us?" Tom asked quietly.

"I beg your pardon, Mr. Novak?" Alex asked frostily, an eyebrow arched.

"I said, 'What's in it for us, Miss Locarno?'" Tom leaned his meaty forearms on the table and looked directly into her eyes. "You expect us to gather up an army, and transport them and our pathetic little group down to your country. We're supposed to smuggle all our gear as well as all these people in so we can take on a Colombian drug cartel with God knows what kind of resources?" He raised an eyebrow. "I ask again: what's in it for us?" He waited, never taking his eyes off her.

She shifted under his gaze and wormed her hand into her small purse. She slowly placed her hand on the table and opened her fingers. There in her palm lay a gem, pure white, almost clear, 30 carats at the least. The sun glinted off its many facets.

Everyone stopped eating and you could hear the quiet whooshing of the overhead fan blades. Vinny broke the silence. "Holy Shit, what a rock!"

It was about the size of his thumb, cut rough but clear enough to look like it needed little more work.

Tom took it from her hand and held it to the light. It sparkled and gave off almost its own heat. There are few things in the world that stir men's loins than gems, the larger the better. Piles of money look great, gold bars are impressive in their heft and dull gleam, but it is gems that turn the innards to water.

"Is it real?" asked Anna.

"Is it a diamond?" asked Tom, "Or a cubic zircon?"

She hesitated, "It is neither. It is a white emerald."

"There's no such thing," Tom stated flatly. "Emeralds are green." He'd had a couple of friends in the jewelry business once and picked up quite a bit of information.

"Well then Mr. Novak, what you are holding in your hand is something that does not exist although that my family dug it out of the ground. And, there it is." She indicated the gem.

"So what's this got to do with us?" asked Dave.

"If you will help my family, we will give you one-hundred carats of these white emeralds. They are probably worth about $5000 per carat. That is one-half million U.S. dollars." She pushed the stone toward Dave with a long forefinger.

Dave hefted it and said thoughtfully, "We'll need to do some checking and talk to some people. We need to find out about these white emeralds." He turned to Tom. "Tomorrow we'll go up to that synagogue in Clearwater and see the Rabbi. Maybe he knows someone who knows the gem market. Seems to me that lots of Jews are into gems."

"Rusty, you and Vinny nose around and see what you can find out about what the gun market is like these days. I'll need to know what kind of expense money we might need." He thought for a minute. "See if you can get a line on couple of AK's, M-16's, shotguns, grenades, light stuff like that. Not much ammo, though. The Colombians are probably using AK's and there's no sense carrying lots of ammo when we can steal it. Anna, you and Joan get together with Emil and see what we can get off the Internet about emeralds and explosives. I think we may need them. Charlie, you can do what you do best." Dave put his hand on Charlie Potts' meaty shoulder. "We'll need some sandwiches for tomorrow, and a jug of iced tea wouldn't be too bad." He grinned at Charlie's crestfallen face.

He stood and steered Charlie toward the kitchen, arm still around his shoulders. "Listen, Buddy, I've got a feeling about this. I'm going to need somebody here I can trust. Somebody to keep an eye on things and look out for the women and Ringo – that is, if we take this job. And sometime before we leave, I'll slip you a piece to keep in the kitchen, okay?"

"Sure, Dave, but don't gimme no gun of yours. I've got my old .45 I keep under the service shelf in there. An' don't worry about them women. I'd sure hate to get inna fight with any one o' them, never mind all three." Charlie looked at Dave speculatively, "You've made up your mind then?"

Dave shrugged. "I don't know. A half a million bucks is a lot of dough. I'll sure sleep better knowing you're ready, Charlie, if I need you." Dave slapped him once and turned back to the table. Chris was showing Alex the stairs behind the end of the bar, which led to the loft overhead. They had a spare bedroom that they sometimes used when they didn't feel like sleeping on the boat. The adjoining bath was rather minimalist but would suffice for a few days until they could get her back aboard a plane to Guatemala.

Tom still slouched in his seat, fondling the gem, turning it this way and that, the glints flickering across his face like a mirrored ball in a dance hall. He heard Dave approach. Without looking up he said, "A million bucks, Buddy-boy, a million bucks."

"A half million, slugger, and if we need the rest of the guys, the split is equal. But if I know you, you'll find a way to make off with some more bread out of this gig. If we take the job."

Tom raised an eyebrow. "Think we could pull it off and get out of this with our skins whole?"

Dave was mildly startled. This was Tom's fastest turn around he'd ever seen. "I'll be damned if I know. The part that really bothers me is the Colombians. We've got to get some real bad dudes to go after them. It can't be us, you know. Those greasers get a look at us and we'll never be safe, ever. Plus, they've got to think that they will never be safe in that part of Guatemala. Damn, we need an army." He mused some more, taking a swig of Tom's beer. Ringo Star, the bald old man with the floppy ears who lived with Charlie Potts in the Airstream Trailer up the road came over to the table and slowly began clearing the remains of the meal.

Tom spoke in a loud voice, "How're you doing, Ringo?"

Ringo nodded his head once, the small knitted cap bobbing, his long overcoat nearly touching the floor. He hefted the plastic tub and smiled toothlessly at them. "Fine, Tom," he replied shyly, then shuffled off toward the kitchen. Both Ringo and Charlie Potts came with the place when Chris had inherited it. It never entered either her mind or Dave's to dismiss either of them.

"Okay, guys. What do you think?" Dave looked at each of them for a long moment. "Do we take this gig on or not?"

Tom grinned, "I'm in, of course."

"Of course," repeated Dave. "Vince? Rusty?"

"Boy I don't know, Dave. If we do, it sure ain't going to be easy, you know?" Rusty shook his shaggy head. Anna patted him on the forearm.

"Yeah," chimed in Vinny. "If we get caught, we're totally screwed."

"Look, guys, we'll try to keep you two just in a support role. Frankly, if we don't find an army lying around doing nothing somewhere, we're going to have to pass on this." Dave slumped in his chair rubbing his stubbly beard.

"Aw come on, buddy boy. For half a million, we owe the lady to at least go down and have a look." Tom's eyes were still shining thinking about the rock, which Rusty was now holding up to the light.

"Christ, we can't 'just go down and have a look. We'll need weapons, transport, intel... You know the drill." Dave shook his head, rubbing his hand through his sandy hair. "Besides, what are we going to do? Go down, meet the family, look over the situation, and then tell them we can't handle it?"

"Sure, why not?"

"Naw, Tom. Dave's right. We either do it or not." Rusty agreed. "Let's work on this some more. We ought to be able to come up with a plan."

"Besides," Joan piped in, "if Dave and Tom are going to do all the work, you two Bozos ought to be able to support them."

The conversation continued back and forth for another hour as Tom and Dave hammered out the basics of a plan. When all were agreed, they finally broke for the evening and went to their own boats.

Tom arranged to pick Dave up early the next morning. He left, humming quietly to himself. Dave stood in the doorway listening to the clacking of the diesel engine in Tom's new Dodge truck as it disappeared down the road. Rusty's bulk cut off the light as he moved up next to Dave. He stood quietly for a few moments, lighting his pipe, the sweet smelling smoke filling the warm night air.

"What are you going to do, *Amigo*?" Rusty's voice was a deep rumble.

"I don't know, Rus. This isn't going to be easy -- if we decide to help her. 'Course, if we were smart, we'd walk from this one, you know. There's no way we're going to beat the Colombians, for her family or for us." He mused for a long minute. "We're going to have to get an army of our own, not let the Colombians ever see our faces, while we kick their butts out of Guatemala. At the same time, we can't let them know that all this is being done for the Locarno's. And then we have to collect the gems, sell them, and finally split the dough. And one last thing…"

Rusty looked inquiringly at Dave, pipe stuck into a corner of his mouth, "What's that?"

Dave jammed his hands deeply into his jean pockets and looked up at the stars. "We've all got to come out of this alive."

"That may prove to be the hardest part, *Kimo Sabe*."

CHAPTER 5

Tom was just finishing his breakfast when Dave and Chris pushed through the back door of Chesney's. The day promised to be a warm one -- clouds scudded past the low lying spoil islets just west of the Intercoastal Waterway 100 yards beyond the docks. The boats bobbed gently in their slips, riding on the wake of a large Hatteras fisherman that passed on its way north. Out on the dock, Rusty was filling the water tanks on his converted PT boat while Vinny just made a nuisance of himself. Their wives were sitting on the after deck of Vinny and Joan's trawler enjoying the first of many cups of coffee.

Dave looked around for Alex. She was sprawled in an old leather chair in the reading corner idly thumbing through a fashion magazine. Her long dark hair was pulled back into a loose ponytail. She was wearing cut off jeans and a tank top, acres of *cafe au lait* skin showing everywhere.

Tom studiously avoided her and slurped from his outsized mug. He greeted Chris with a smile and waved Dave to a chair opposite. Dave dropped in and rested his forearms on the table edge.

"Well, big guy, have you figured out our next step?" Tom asked.

Dave pondered the question a minute, thoughtfully rubbing his jaw. "Waalll," he drawled, "I s'pose we'd better find out if the stone's worth anything. Then we can figure out the rest." He sat back, obviously exhausted. "Oh, and don't call me big guy."

Tom looked at him Poker-faced. "That's it? That's your plan?" He shook his head disgustedly. "Did you stay up all night figuring that out?"

"Relax, that's what we do today. We'll figure out the rest as we go along. We've got to figure out where to get an army -- one on our side anyway. We can't fight these guys alone."

"You really figure we'll have to fight them? Shit, I was hoping we could go in, finesse them a little, and they'd just go away." Tom shrugged and sipped his coffee.

Dave looked at him incredulously. "That's *your* plan? Finesse them? Jesus, these are Colombian drug dealers, not some dime bag pushers." Chris put a plate of pancakes and sausages down in front of Dave, and another beside him. She gestured for Alex to join them.

"So what are you boys up to today?" she inquired. "Alex and I thought we'd do some shopping, have lunch at Harringtons, and maybe stop at the beach for a swim." Alex smiled in assent.

Tom looked uncomfortable and squirmed in his seat. Dave chuckled and said, "We're off to see a Rabbi about a rock. Alex?" He held out his hand. She reached into her purse and reluctantly placed the shining stone in his palm. He hefted it and slipped it into his pants pocket.

"Let's go, flyboy. We'll take my wheels. Yours might be a little too intimidating for the good Rabbi. That synagogue is just off Belcher road, isn't it?"

Tom didn't say anything.

Dave leaned over and kissed Chris on the nose. "Later, hon."

Tom leaned over to do the same but she deftly put a sausage in his mouth, smiling and patting his cheek. "Nice try, junior, but you're out of your league."

Alex smiled sweetly at him and resumed her breakfast. Tom and Dave walked out and got into Dave's old Mercury Station Wagon. The hand polished wooden exterior panels gleamed in the morning sun, the last few drops of morning mist drying rapidly.

While the engine was warming up, Dave turned to Tom. "So what's up with you and Alex? I never saw you like this. She's a good looker, nice figure, and a certain amount of intelligence. Of course, that might count against her, in your case."

Tom shrugged and crossed his arms over his chest, saying nothing. Finally he snorted and said, "Maybe I like her and maybe I don't. I'll have to reserve judgment. But I'll tell you this, that's one tough broad. Don't let those tears fool you."

Chris watched as her husband and Tom drove off to find the rabbi, then turned to Alex, "So, Alex," Chris asked, a forkful of pancakes halfway to her mouth, "are you still mad at Tom?"

Reluctantly Alex gave a small shrug, "I still think he is a pig for not listening to me and then agreeing when he knew there was money involved." She smiled down at her plate. "He is cute, though, in a loud American way."

Chris chuckled. Alex sure had Tom pegged. "Just a caution, *Amigo*. Tom is not, shall we say, for the long haul. He's…" Chris was at a loss for words. Most people were when it came to describing Tom.

"Please, Christine, you don't have to explain. I've met many men like Tom. Loners, wanderers, the Yankee Gypsies, my *Tia* Roberta calls them." She paused for a mouthful, then continued, "However, they are fun to play with – and very useful at times." She continued eating.

Chris watched her and thought she must be nuts. Playing with Tom was like playing with a poisonous snake. It might give you a real sense of power – if you could pull it off -- but in the end, dangerous as hell. Oh, well, she was a big girl; she could learn the hard way.

Dave drove on in silence. Soon he was in Clearwater, weaving through the traffic, the old wooden-bodied car garnering an occasional thumbs up from a passerby. These he acknowledged with just an upraising of a forefinger from the steering wheel. He was still deep in thought when he swung into the parking lot of the Beth Israel Jewish Community Center. It was housed in a modern building, all brick and glass with the expected thermometer on the lawn.

"Let me do the talking," Dave insisted as the pulled open the tall, frosted glass door. Tom just shrugged.

The receptionist was a mousy little woman, gray and wrinkled, hair pulled back into a tightly wrapped bun. But her eyes were a bright, shrewd blue as she scanned the two jeans and T-shirt clad men standing awkwardly before her desk.

"May I help you?" She asked in a surprisingly strong voice.

"Yes, we'd like to speak to the Rabbi for a few minutes, please." Dave felt as if he were standing before his first grade teacher, Miss Nolan.

"What about?"

"Umm, it's a personal matter." Dave replied shortly.

"Do you two boys want to get married? The Jewish faith doesn't condone that sort of thing, I'll have you know." She cocked an eyebrow at them.

"Oh, Christ," Tom muttered and turned away steaming.

Dave grinned, "No, Ma'am, it's nothing like that. We just want to see if the Rabbi could help us locate a member of the congregation who is or was a gem merchant."

"What for?" Now she was interested.

Dave looked down at her nameplate. "Look, Mrs. Leven, our Mom died and left us some jewelry and we want to get it appraised and we don't know anybody locally. We thought the Rabbi might be able to sort of steer us in the right direction." He gave her his most winning smile.

"Well, the Rabbi can't be disturbed right now, but I can give you a name, or rather a couple of names." She flipped through a rolodex on the corner of the desk by her elbow and extracted a card. Quickly she wrote down a name and address and handed it to Dave. "These two brothers will be able to give you any information you need. They live out by the golf course off Sherwood Street."

Dave glanced at the slip of paper. Sid and Jerome Tischler, it read. "Thank you, Mrs. Leven." And he and Tom quickly exited the building.

"Jesus, what a battle-ax," Tom exclaimed. "Do you believe that old broad? She wanted to know if you and I wanted to get married! Can you believe it? Do you think I look gay?" Tom wrenched the mirror on the passenger door around so he could get a look at himself. "Hell, No!" He hummed a few bars of Macho Man as he entered the car.

They drove out toward the golf course, admiring the houses along the way. As they got closer, the houses got progressively larger and more ornate. Dave turned onto Sherwood Street and glanced down for the number. Tom looked and pointed at a large cedar and glass place set back off the street behind a long circular drive. As Dave took the car out of gear, he thought how at home the Woody looked in this driveway. In front of him were parked two Lincoln Town Cars, one steel gray and the other dark blue, both current models.

Tom whistled. "I guess the gem business was pretty good to these guys." Dave nodded and they approached the doors. There was no doorbell but as Dave raised his hand to knock, the door opened. Before them stood a short, gaunt gentleman, slightly bowed, a thick shock of pure white hair was pushed back and held in place in a short ponytail with a rubber band. His large, hawk like nose preceded him and he glared at them though close-set, slightly bulbous eyes. He was wearing a tiny Speedo bathing suit and had an ornate silk robe thrown over his shoulders.

"Whadda ya want?" He sneered at them.

"The Rabbi at Beth Israel gave me your name." Dave began.

"Bullshit!" The man exclaimed. "Mrs. Leven called. You got our name from her. You never even saw the Rabbi, that *gonif*," he muttered. "He's always looking for money -- for the school, for trips, for the poor. Jesus, Moses, and Abraham, does he think we're made of money? Well, you boys come on in. Me and Morty are out by the pool. We got food and drinks out there." He turned and shuffled out toward a pair of large sliding doors giving onto the pool and garden area.

Tom whistled again. They were passing through a grand entrance hall, tiled in marble with plants all around. To one side sat a grouping of white wicker chairs and sofas, several newspapers strewn on them, the typeface in what Dave took for Hebrew. The ceiling rose two stories and was crisscrossed with massive wooden beams. Soft sunlight filtered down, sunbeams dancing in the shafts of yellow light. Tom raised his eyebrows at Dave and pantomimed a whistle. Dave motioned him for silence.

Ahead of them, the slight figure of Sid Tischler shoved open the door to the pool area. Around them, a profusion of plants rioted, everything from Royal palms towering overhead to birds of paradise, bougainvilleas with their brilliant pink blooms. Impatiens with waxy white, pink and red flowers hugged the ground and peeped out from under soft shield ferns. There were many other plants and flowers that Dave couldn't identify. *Boy*, he thought, *Chris would love this place!*

They followed Sid between the plants on a narrow graveled path, finally emerging beside a waterfall that splashed noisily into the beautiful natural pool. In the pool was a huge bear of a man sitting in a plastic beach chair suspended on bright red floats. Two young ladies who were obviously as naked as the day they were born were noisily propelling the chair through the water. They were giggling while the big man in the chair roared boisterously, having a great time while attempting to keep his drink from falling out of its holder in the armrest.

Tom gawked at the sight. The girl on the big man's right was bleach blond with white lipstick and high firm breasts. The one on the left was a brunette, had long hair, which floated behind her and larger breasts which also seemed to float. She kicked with both her feet together, giving her the appearance of a mermaid. She had large, sensuous lips and was one of the loveliest girls Tom had ever laid eyes on. As they came near the waterfall, Sid cupped his hands over his mouth and yelled, "Morty, stop screwing around for a minute. These guys want to talk to us." He indicated the gaping Tom and Dave.

Morty reached a huge, hairy paw around the blonde and squeezed her right breast. The chair angled for a platform just under the water against the near pool edge. As the chair drew near, Morty hopped nimbly out and propelled himself up onto the apron.

"Thanks, girls, go play. Sid and I will be back in a few minutes." They waved and dived, their lovely rear ends breaking the surface momentarily.

"Hello, boys, I'm Morty Tischler and this is my kid brother Sid, whom you've already met. Follow me, will you? We've got something to eat on the table over here." He parted some ferns and there was a little clearing decked over in redwood. In the center were a round, glass-topped table and a half dozen plastic chairs. The table was heaped with bowls of fruit, baskets of bagels and Danish pastries, assorted jams and preserves. With an expansive wave, he said, "Help yourselves. It's just for me and Sid this weekend. Oh, yes, and of course the girls." He reached for a thick, peach colored towel that was lying atop a stack on a nearby bench. Morty vigorously toweled his thinning, salt and pepper crewcut. He had a neatly trimmed grayer mustache and a huge barrel chest. His entire body was covered with hair. Dropping the towel, he turned to them. He must have been six foot two or three, Dave estimated and weighed at least 250 pounds.

He stood before them and smote himself a resounding blow on the chest, "Seventy-six years old. Not bad shape, hey?" He smiled, showing even teeth. "Of course, my kid brother would say it's the young tootsies, but I say it's a cigar a day." He fished a huge panatela out of a rosewood humidor that lay buried beneath the plates, trays, baskets, and bowls of food. He bit the end off and spit it into the bushes. With ceremony, Sid brought out a gold Dunhill lighter and held it for Morty. Morty carefully and slowly twirled the cigar above the flame and finally sucked it into life. The aromatic smoke wafted through the air and Tom's nostrils widened and inhaled the pleasant aroma. He'd given up smoking several years ago but always loved the smell of a good cigar.

Sid and Morty pulled up chairs and Sid asked, "Well, what did you want to see us about?" They were all business now. Dave guessed that they'd been a formidable negotiating team before they retired.

Dave held out his hand, "I'm Dave Manley and this here's Tom Novak. We've got a stone we'd like your opinion on." Dave withdrew his handkerchief and unfolded it, revealing the white gem.

"Ah, shit, diamonds are Sid's field. I'm strictly a colored stone man, mostly emeralds and rubies." Morty shoved the stone toward his little brother and made to rise.

Dave reached out his hand and held Morty's arm. "Just a minute. Mr. Tischler, let's see what Mr. Sid has to say about it." Sid had taken one look and disappeared in the direction of the house. He returned several minutes later with a pair of eye loupes and a small electronic probe. He tossed one of the loupes to Morty and touched the stone with the probe. It emitted a muted shriek.

"Not a diamond, Mort," he muttered. "Let's see," he held the rock up and squinted at it, "about thirty-two, maybe thirty three carats, it's only rough cut, so finishing would pare that down to twenty or twenty five. Still not bad." He handed it over to Morty who engulfed it in his paw.

A moment later he screwed to loupe into his right eye socket and grunted. "Emerald, I'd say." He grunted a few more times, turning it over and over. "Oops, looks like a small occlusion down in that right hand corner." He handed it back to Sid.

"Yep, I see it. But I probably wouldn't have if you hadn't pointed it out to me." He squinted at it. "A nice rock though. Where'd you guys get it?" He asked this last in an offhanded manner. Dave caught the glance that passed between the two brothers.

"Ah, I really can't say at this time, Mr. Sid, but is it worth anything? I thought emeralds were always green."

"Yeah, yeah," replied Morty. "Mostly. As they get lighter, they're worth less. But this beauty, trim that little occlusion off, give it a nice long marquis cut and nobody would be able to tell it from a high dollar diamond. But I got a better idea. So far, kid," he turned to Dave, "I've never seen a white emerald this clear. Usually they're lousy with occlusions and flaws. Let us cut it and polish it up. Finished, it'll bring maybe $75 grand. We've got a guy in New York you can take it to." He still squinted at it through the loupe. "Have you got any more?"

Dave glanced at Tom who was busy stuffing a third Danish into his mouth. He shrugged. Dave said, "We can probably get another hundred or two hundred carats." Now he shrugged, "Beyond that, I don't know."

Morty let out a roar and clasped his hands across his belly. "A couple of hundred carats, Sid!" He gasped, laughing so hard the tears rolled out of his eyes. Sid, too, was laughing, small squeaks filling the air while he pounded the table. Tom and Dave looked at each other, perplexed. Were these guys nuts?

In a few minutes they'd settled into a more or less normal attitude. Morty leaned across the table rubbing his hands together. He looked at each of them from under bushy eyebrows. "You boys don't know much about the gem business, do you?"

They shook their heads no.

For the next fifteen minutes, both Morty and Sid described the politics and workings of the giant VanHerff diamond conglomerate, how over the years a succession of directors had each strengthened the company's grip on the wholesale trade to the extent that anyone who was a serious merchant had to buy what they were offered at annual "showings." At these showings, a select group was given the opportunity to purchase a selection of rough-cut diamonds. Each *brifke*, a small five-sided folded envelope contained from two to ten, sometimes more, diamonds. The price was fixed, there was no negotiating. The quality and quantity was also fixed. Sometimes the dealer got a fair deal, sometimes he didn't. One refusal and he was never summoned for the opportunity again. VanHerff controlled the entire wholesale trade. Lately the Soviets had tried to break into the lucrative market. However, VanHerff, through its Security Forces had let dealers know that anyone who trafficked with the Soviets, now the Russians, would be forever blacklisted and perhaps worse. After all, VanHerff was THE diamond supplier and had been for almost 100 years. They'd never missed a sale and although their tactics might be a bit high handed, they were always a sure thing. Who knew with the Russians? The Russians had finally caved in and agreed to market all their precious diamonds through VanHerff. Except for the occasional maverick shipment, VanHerff had an iron grip on the market.

The present head of VanHerff Security was a man known as Michael "Mad Man" Boettcher. His father had been a Security man and his father before him. Boettcher was a third generation Boer from South Africa and was fanatically loyal to the Company. He and his men roamed the world, monitoring the wholesale diamond business. They had informants everywhere, from the huge diamond capitols of New York, Antwerp, Brussels, and Johannesburg. Lately Tel Aviv was gaining in popularity as a finishing and distribution center.

Finally Morty wound up, "You see, *boychik*, there's no way you guys are going to dump a couple of hundred carats of stones like these on the market without him getting wind of it. You threaten the diamond market. Suppose the public decides they like white emeralds more than diamonds? After all, they are rarer, no?" Boom! He slapped his hand on the table, making plates jump, "We want white emeralds, not diamonds. The public is very fickle. If Mrs. Astor tells her friend Mrs. Fitzwilliam who tells her friend Mrs. Harriman that she has just got to have a white emerald necklace, then that's a big bunch of diamond sales down the toilet."

Sid snorted, "And that prick, Boettcher, will have your *kishkas* on a spit if he finds out that it's you who are dealing."

"Big deal, we can take care of ourselves," Tom leaned forward, eyes flashing.

"Hah," snorted Morty. "These guys have an army. Yeah, an army with guns and helicopters and all. I heard they can call up troops from the South African Army. After all, it's in the best interests of the country to keep the diamond business for South Africa. What the hell else do they have down there - - some chromium or some shit like that?"

"Tell us about this army they have. How much discretion does this guy Boettcher have in using its forces?" Tom was interested now.

"Well, let me tell you about an incident that we heard happened a couple of years ago in Yemen." Morty pulled off a handful of grapes and stuffed them in his mouth. The cigar had long ago gone out and rested on the edge of the table.

"We heard that a small mine had been found on the southern shore near the town of Al Mukah. The stones were not large but of a particularly fine quality. When the Yemeni government refused to deal the stones through VanHerff, Boettcher and his men flew in one night and blew the place up."

"Yep, blew it off the face of the earth," Sid chimed in. "Of course, nobody could prove who did it, but we all knew. Those are some bad boys. Thanks God we're retired now and that *gonif* can't do a thing to us, but we'd sure like to stick it up his *tukkis* just once." He slumped in his chair, a beatific smile on his face.

"So, boys, why don't you leave the stone with us? We'll cut it and polish it and give you a name of a landsman of ours you can take it to up in the big apple who will buy it and give you cash. For that, all we want is ten percent. That's only about seven-five, maybe eight grand. Payable after you sell it." Morty smiled benignly at Dave.

"How do you know you can trust us for your share?" asked Dave.

Morty smiled again, "Mr. David Manly, our search shows that you are an honest man, you drive a 1947 Mercury Station Wagon, own a 1985 Endeavour 40 foot sailboat and live with your wife Christine Bennett Manley at the end of Fisher's Road in Sunset Pointe at a joint called Chesney's. We used to know old Ches, and if he left that gin mill of his to your wife, that must mean you're okay. We don't know who this *putz* is," he indicated Tom, "and frankly we don't care. Besides, you'll still need somebody to move the rest of the stones, and you sure can't do that yourself." He sat back and waited, Sid helping him light his cigar again.

"How'd you find out all that information, if you don't mind my asking?"

Sid smiled, "The Jewish Mafia." He laughed at their perplexity. "Gloria Leven gave us your license plate number. I called a cop friend of mine and he ran the plate. Given more time, I would have found out more. *Nu*, just because we're old, doesn't mean we're stupid." He winked broadly and patted Dave's hand in a fatherly way. Just then Dave heard giggles behind him.

"Ooohhh, who are your cute friends, Morty?" The two girls stepped into view. They were both wearing thong bikini bottoms, their breasts free. The blond slipped her arm over Morty's shoulder, her hair hanging over his eye. He pushed it aside and smiled up at her.

"Jacqueline, this is Mr. Manley and…" he raised a hand indicating Tom.

"Tom Novak," Tom leaped to his feet hand outstretched, a huge grin on his face.

"Relax, *boychik*." Morty waved him back to his seat. "So, you got the information you wanted?

Dave nodded. Tom nodded, not taking his eyes off the blonde's breast, which, was only inches from Morty's face. Kiss it, he urged, kiss it, kiss it, kiss it. He was almost drooling.

"Tom, let's go," he heard Dave call him from a far off place. A large hand hauled him to his feet.

"Yeah. Yeah, right. Well thanks for everything, Mort. Sid." He hadn't even seen the stone disappear into Morty or Sid's pocket.

"I'll call you when our little project is completed, boys! Have a nice day!" The last Tom saw was Morty's hand caressing the blonde's rear-end, a small smile on his face. She didn't look like she was unhappy either.

CHAPTER 6

Dave drove in silence. Beside him, Tom babbled on and on about the two half-nude girls, which, if Dave had let himself think about it, was a nice bonus for visiting with the brothers Tischler. Round and around his thoughts went. The VanHerff people had an army. We need an army. How to get the VanHerff people to Guatemala and fight with the Colombian druggies. Several problems to solve. One, how to get them there. Two, how to get them to fight. Three, would their army be a match for the firepower of the Colombians? And four, how to keep the Locarno's and their people out of it, or at least out of sight.

Finally Dave turned off the main north-south highway and headed toward the water. They drove past the small store-post-office and through the old housing development. After passing through a beautiful old stand of trees, they reached an ugly trailer park squatting on both sides of the potholed road like a somnolent virus. Old pine trees festooned with cancerous growths of Spanish moss spotted throughout the park. Dave liked it. If it weren't for the trailer park and its grandfathered-in zoning, Chesney's would have been gone long ago. Chesney's and their neighbors existed as an anachronism in the late 20th century. The trailer park tenants tended to be elderly on minuscule pensions from Akron or Dayton or Pittsburgh. An occasional group of bikers or other rowdies came and went. Sometimes Tom and he joined with the permanent residents to "suggest" that it wouldn't be healthy for someone to stay on. Of course, the rule was that if someone weren't annoying the others, they would not be bothered, no matter who they were or what they did.

Charlie Potts often told him of a time in the mid seventies when the first black family moved in. Some of the tenants were all for moving them along, but he and Ringo stood up for them, even became friendly with them. Occasionally Jeddah Huxley visited with Chris and Dave and told of the terrible times his parents experienced in Detroit in the twenties and thirties. Dave liked old Jed because he'd worked with Zora Argus-Duntov, one of the early pioneers with Ford and Chevrolet.

Over the years the trailer park had become a hodgepodge of races and nationalities. Some

Saturday nights, Chesney's resembled more the bar scene from Star Wars than a neighborhood-drinking emporium. People now tended to move into the trailer park as a temporary halt between jobs, divorces or between convenience store stickups. The old timers were getting really old and they tended to have more funeral parties than bowling nights. One of Charlie Potts old army buddies, Patsy Clarke, was sort of the unofficial mayor, handling the leasing and rent collections for the absentee landlord, a Mr. Griffin, from Cincinnati. Nobody had ever met the man. The hiring had been all done by phone and mail. As long as the three hundred or so checks showed up each month made out to Mr. Griffin, Patsy was free to do as he wished.

Dave gave a cursory wave to Ringo who was just pulling out onto the road on his three-wheeled bike heading for Chesney's to help Charlie Potts with the lunch crowd and the cleanup after. Charlie Potts and Ringo shared an old Airstream trailer that had been parked under a huge old cypress tree so long ago that the doorway was only a couple of inches from the ground. Ringo Star was a gaunt old semi retarded fellow who had been the sweeper at Chesney's as long as anyone could remember. He always rode his three-wheeler with the basket on the back, wore a moth-eaten khaki watch cap and a long overcoat, summer and winter. He spoke little and always had a toothless grin for everyone. His gaze, while not exactly vacant, was inward looking and as he swept, he hummed a tuneless few bars. Dave had listened a time or two but couldn't recognize it. He was always careful to give short, specific instructions to Ringo and the reply was always the same, "Thank you, Dave." Sometimes Dave felt like he was listening to HAL, the computer from 2001, A Space Odyssey. However, Ringo was always there, always did what he was asked and never had a bad day.

Dave pulled the old Woody into the yard and parked under the overhang from his workshop, a steel-framed building that sat to the right of and about twenty yards from the big barn main building. Out behind Chesney's, the assorted sailboats, trawlers and houseboats gently bobbed at their docks. At the end on the T-pier, Rusty and Anna's restored PT boat barely moved in the swells from passing fishing boats. Rusty and Vinny had scoured the country trying to keep its ancient Packard engines running, but it brought diminishing returns. For a boat built cheaply in the early forties, Rusty was lucky to still have her. Then the year before, he and Vinny and assorted friends and neighbors had worked all summer helping Rusty re-power the aging but immaculate boat with twin diesels which had come out of a sunken 75' Custom built Rybovitch cruiser. The disgusted owner had given them the salvage job, but when saw what the unforgiving gulf had done to his lovely yacht, he'd taken the insurance money and reluctantly walked away. The twin Caterpillar diesel engines were more than enough power for the 90' PT boat, and now she flew like the wind.

Rusty'd drifted after the war. Eventually he married Anna Rose Baldwin, a former USO singer-dancer he'd met on liberty in Hollywood just before shipping out in a PT Boat squadron based in the Pacific. After the war he'd come back to Hollywood looking for her, but she was gone. It was the merest co-incidence that he'd run into her again in a small town in Oklahoma where he was working as an oilfield roustabout. She was singing in a local nightclub for just a day or two, and he'd waited for her after the show. That was the end of Rusty's carousing. A year later they were married, and Rusty started his own drilling business. Fortunately he'd been lucky enough to retire before the West Texas boom collapsed. He and Anna were vacationing in New Orleans when Rusty saw a flyer about a government auction. He'd gone just as a lark, and there was his old PT boat for sale. Without telling Anna, he bid and bought it. After a lot of fixing up and some memorable trips on the refurbished vessel, he and Anna had ended up on Florida's West Coast. They made their base in the backwater town of Sunset Pointe and at the T-dock at Chesney's. Since then he and Dave had become fast friends. Anna occasionally belted out some of the old songs out on Saturday nights at Chesney's.

With its new engines, the beautiful old boat often ripped through the waters of the gulf at forty or more knots. Below, the boat was a home to Rusty and Anna, often joined by one or more of their grandchildren. The retired Chief Warrant Officer was a favorite at the hospitals around Christmas time, playing Santa, and he and Anna made sure that the poorer people in the trailer park were not forgotten.

That evening, Dave called a war council. Vinny and Joan, Anna and Rusty, Chris and Alex, and he and Tom all sat at a round oak table. Chris had wanted their resident computer and technical whiz, Emile, to sit in but he was at a meeting with his fellow programmers in Tampa.

After outlining their conversation with the Tischler brothers, Dave threw open the discussion for ideas.

Vinny asked, "How many guys did you say these Colombians got at their base?" This was directed at Alex.

"The last count was about fifty. I do not know what it is since I left two weeks ago."

"Wow, fifty guys! How the hell are we going to get rid of them? Cripes, you're nuts if you think we can just go down an' scare 'em off." Vinny nervously lit a cigarette and blew the smoke out behind him. Chris scowled, but let it go.

"I know, I know," answered Dave. "If we can just get the VanHerff guys down there, maybe we can pit them against each other."

"Yeah, sure, Dave, but how are we going to do that?" Rusty shook his shaggy head, his faded cap pushed so far back on his head that Dave thought it would fall off any minute. It never did.

"Hey, it's the only army we've got. You figure it out. Meanwhile, Tom and I will go to New York, meet with this friend of the Tischlers' and sell the rock Alex brought and feel out the market."

"Honey, don't forget you and I have that boat delivery to New Orleans next week." Chris reminded him.

Damnation, he'd completely forgotten. "I guess you'll have to handle New York, Tom."

Before Tom could do more than nod, Alex jumped in, "Not without me, you will not." She looked at both Tom and Dave defiantly. "It is still my family's stone and where it goes, I go."

"Bullshit," Tom replied hotly. "Then take it up yourself." He sat back, arms folded across his chest, glaring hotly at her.

"Hold it, you two. If we're going to be in this together, we've got to get along," Chris reminded them. "So Thomas, if you're in, you're in all the way. If not, leave now."

Tom looked pleadingly at Dave, but Dave refused to meet his eye. Finally he visibly gave in, expelling a great breath and then extending his hand to Alex. "Okay, Miss Alex, I'm in. But the price is two-hundred carats, not one-hundred."

She looked him shrewdly in the eye and offered, "One -hundred, fifty, Mr. Novak, IF you deliver, IF you get the Colombian drug people completely out of my country."

"Nope, *Chiquita*, its two-hundred or I don't go." Tom stood over her, pointing a thick forefinger at her face. "And, whether or not you know it, you need me."

She looked pleadingly at Dave and Chris who nodded.

"Yes, we need Tom," admitted Dave. "In fact, we could use about a dozen Tom's. Sorry, Alex, no Tom, no us."

She looked at the assembled figures. They all nodded. "Alright," she agreed, "I will see to it that at the end, you will have two-hundred carats of white emeralds delivered to you. The stones will be rough-cuts and you may do with them what you wish. But I want a solemn promise from each of you." Her eyes flashed as she leaned forward looking each person in the eye. "No more bargaining, no more negotiating. Once we have agreed, we will work toward our common goal, yes?"

She pointed to each of them and one by one, they either nodded or spoke yes aloud. "Good," she sat back satisfied. "And, you, my new friend, " she smiled sweetly at Tom, "and I are going to New York City as soon as these brothers are finished cutting and polishing the stone, yes?"

"Yes," Tom agreed, though still with a remnant note of reluctance.

"So if we are all in this to help this young woman's family and people, we all have a hell of a lot of work to do in the next couple of weeks," Dave announced.

Vinny and Rusty reported that they'd attended a gun show at the Tampa Fairgrounds the past weekend. They were able to make deals for two Winchester pump shotguns, three M-16's converted for civilian use. At the same time, Rusty was busy three aisles over, bargaining for kits to convert the

M-16's back to military full auto. They had even located a source for flash-bang grenades and smoke bombs. Since both men possessed concealed weapons permits, they were able to actually purchase several semi-automatic pistols. The makes didn't matter as long as they were all 9mm.

The discussion went on until well past midnight with various other tasks assigned.

CHAPTER 7

The Tischler brothers had the emerald cut and polished by early the next week. When Sid handed it to him, it was in a soft leather pouch with a drawstring.

"That's for good luck," Morty promised. "That pouch once held the Hope diamond."

Dave opened the pouch and spilled the stone onto his palm. It glittered, gleamed, sparkled in the sun. If it wasn't a diamond, it sure looked like one. It was cut in a long oval shape with many facets. Dave was by no means a gem expert but the quality of the workmanship was unmistakable. The gem was almost as big as his thumb. He and Tom were both impressed.

The reverence in Morty's voice was unmistakable. With final instructions on the location of their friend in New York's busy diamond district, Tom and Dave bid the brothers good-bye, this time the topless girls were not in evidence, much to Tom's dismay. That evening, Tom dropped Dave and Chris off at the municipal marina where their delivery boat waited. It was an elderly, yet graceful Bermuda 40 sloop, and Dave knew the trip would be enjoyable.

The next day Tom and Alex flew to New York by commercial jet. Tom had looked desperately for a private or corporate jet to ferry north but in vain. Alex laughed at his discomfort, all the while swallowing her own queasiness. She dozed most of the time while Tom twitched at every bump. The trip was unusually rough occasioned by a storm off the East Coast that was slowly making its way onshore. The pilot flew almost directly over the coast, turning inland over the Carolinas, but the big jet was buffeted by the thermals rising off the mountains. Once Alex came awake to find her hand gripped firmly in Tom's. He smiled an apology and reluctantly released her hand. She patted him with some affection. He wasn't so tough, after all.

The taxi took them swiftly downtown to the smallish hotel where he'd made reservations. The desk manager came out from behind the counter to greet them. He was a man of medium height and build, balding but immaculately dressed in a dark pinstriped business suit. A snowy handkerchief peeped out of his breast pocket. Beneath his aristocratically thin nose rode a thin, carefully trimmed mustache. He had slicked back thinning salt and pepper hair and appeared to be about fifty, but a well-kept fifty. To their left was a double door leading to a dining room and to their right, twin elevator doors. The lobby was spotless, done in lustrous woods and brass, looking for all the world like a British gentlemen's club rather than a very private hotel in the center of Manhattan.

"Ah, Mr. Novak, so good to have you with us again. *Guten tag, freulein.*" He addressed Alex and kissed her hand with a short, stiff bow. As he shook Tom's hand, he raised one eyebrow.

"Yes, Willi, *freulein* it is." Tom grinned. "You have a package for me?"

"Ya, ya, of course." He went behind the counter and reached into a cabinet quickly emerging with a brown paper wrapped box the size of a shoebox and addressed to Tom Novak, c/o The Chesterfield Hotel. He handed it over and Tom thanked him courteously, finally introducing Alex Locarno, a friend from Central America.

Willi pivoted on one heel and signaled to a bellhop standing in one corner, unnoticed. The bellhop silently took two keys from the manager. Hoisting Tom and Alex's bags he strode toward the elevators. They bid Willi good-bye and followed. The elevator stopped at the third floor and the bellhop opened a door two rooms to the right of the elevator and entered. Alex followed and noted the exquisite decor. The furniture was French provincial and a small painting she took for a Degas hung on the wall next to the bed. With an arched brow, she noted the large bed and looked about for another.

She was about to protest when Tom handed a folded bill to the bellhop who smiled his thanks and exited with Alex's bag. He paused at the door and gestured her to follow.

"Relax, sweetheart," Tom cautioned, "you have the adjoining room. And by the way, the door," he indicated a thick dark wood panel, "locks from both sides." As she left, she heard him chuckling softly to himself.

A few minutes later he knocked at the adjoining door. "Alex?"

She started. *Oh, no*, she thought, *not already!*

"What do you want?" she asked through the panel.

"Open the door, for Chrissakes. I just want to talk to you." His voice, though muffled, was still irritating to her.

She opened the door a crack and shrewdly looked at him.

"Look, it's too late to do our business with the rock," Tom said. " I'm going to make some phone calls, and grab a shower and a nap. Would you like to have dinner later?"

She shrugged her acceptance. He slouched on the opposite side of the door, one arm leaning on the frame. She took him in, the well-muscled arms, narrow waist, and barrel chest. He wore a pair of gray flannel slacks with an off-white golf shirt and well-worn boat shoes. Tom's one grudging acceptance of modern civility was the navy cashmere blazer he'd worn to the big city. It was now thrown over the back of a Louis XIV chair. His fine brown hair was pushed back but a lock had escaped and hung just above his right eye. Her hand moved almost involuntarily to brush it back. She stopped herself, hoping he didn't notice the movement.

"What time?" she asked.

He glanced at the stainless steel Rolex and shrugged, "About eight okay with you?"

She nodded again in what she hoped was a casual affirmation, smiled and closed the door.

That night they ate in the hotel's small dining room. Tom had the grilled pork chops while Alex opted for the chef's special, salmon almandine. The dinner was excellent, the wine chilled and subtle, the cheesecake for desert light and delicate. Afterward, they took a stroll along a busy street, stopping for a cappuccino. Tom asked for and received a shortened life history of her and the Locarno family, and he told several humorous stories from his youth in New Jersey. Soon they found themselves back at the hotel entrance, her arm through his, a finely embroidered shawl over her shoulders.

"Tom, I had a lovely evening," she said at the door to her suite. "I'd almost forgotten why we're here. Thank you so much." She smiled a heavy lidded and sensuous smile.

"Let me ask you one question, Alex. What will happen to you after this is all over? Assuming that we're successful, of course."

"Of course," she agreed.

"Are you going to be satisfied stuck in some jerkwater town in the middle of Guatemala doing God-knows-what?"

She smiled at his suggestion, not at all offended. "Maybe after you have seen my little 'jerkwater town,' as you call it, maybe you will change your mind."

"Well, it's possible, but not likely. There's just too much world to see. I like flying, I like traveling. Why would I want to stay in one place?"

"I see," she uttered softly, eyes cast down. She turned to go and he caught her arm.

"Maybe someday," he said, softening the words, "maybe someday." He saw her to her door and she lightly brushed his cheek with her lips.

"Thank you once again for a lovely evening, Thomas." She pronounced it with the Spanish accent on the second syllable.

"*De nada*," he replied. "It was nothing."

He lay awake a long time, imagining her disrobing for bed, imagining her curling up next to him. Could he imagine being married to her, raising children? He fell asleep with images of little Toms running around an imaginary yard.

They were up early the next morning and, after a light breakfast, headed for 42nd Street and Fifth Avenue, the heart of the diamond district. Even at this early hour, the streets were jammed. Many in the crowd wore the traditional garb of the Hassidic Jews, high crowned black beaver hats, long sidelocks, beards and prayer shawls under dark suit coats.

Alex was amazed. Tom explained what little he knew of the Hassids, an ultra religious Jewish sect. They were probably Russian or Eastern European, and many of them had drifted into the money lending and gem brokering when all other doors had been closed to them. She stood in the middle of the sidewalk and stared when a Hassidic family came by, the mother walking respectfully behind with a four or five year old daughter. A pair of sons walked beside their father, a tall, ascetic man with protruding eyes. Both sons wore round framed glasses sitting low on their noses in imitation of their father. He carried a black covered prayer book in one hand, his lips moving as he read although they could hear little in the noisy crowd.

Tom and Alex threaded their way down a side street and came to a doorway in a narrow building. A bronze plaque set into the grimy brick read "Goldfarb and Son." Below it was a push-button.

Tom pushed the button in a pre-arranged signal. A moment later, the latch was withdrawn and a short, plump woman opened the door. She signaled them to follow her upstairs. At the top of the stairs was a brassbound glass door, very ornate. Tom could see that the glass was over an inch thick. A voice came from a speaker to their right and set into the wall.

"Good morning, Mr. Novak and Miss Locarno. Mrs. B. will show you in. Please deposit your gun in the box to your left, Mr. Novak. I assure you it will remain there until you depart."

Tom was startled and after a long moment reached into his waistband and removed a slender 9mm Beretta automatic pistol and placed it in the box.

"And the one in your ankle holster, please."

Shit, he thought. He reluctantly removed the small stainless steel AMG back-up gun from the soft leather holster beneath his right sock and it, too, clattered into the box.

"Thank you," the voice murmured. An audible clunk was heard and Mrs. B pushed open the heavy door. She turned and smiled.

"Through the door straight ahead, please. Mr. Goldfarb will see you now." She disappeared down a side corridor.

"Where did you get the guns, Thomas?" Alex asked, eyes flashing.

"The package at the hotel. I sent them to myself before we left. You think I'm going to carry around a rock like this without protection?" He pushed open the office door. Mr. Goldfarb sat behind a huge desk. Behind him on the wall was a map of the world with pushpins in many colors all over it. On his desk sat a laptop computer and an eye loupe. That was all. Mr. Goldfarb himself was an average looking man. In any other context he might have been mistaken for a small town banker or insurance salesman. He sported a fringe of hair from ear to ear, most of it dark, thick glasses which tended to distort his eyes and wore a brown tweed jacket over a tan V-neck sweater over a yellow shirt and oddly patterned tie. The most Tom could say was that he was average. He wore neither jewelry nor a watch that Tom could see, nor was there a phone in evidence.

When he spoke, it was with a slight accent, which Tom couldn't place. "Good morning, Mr. Novak, Miss Locarno."

"Good morning, Mr. Goldfarb." Tom replied. Thanks for seeing us at such short notice."

"Not at all. I spoke with Sidney Tischler last week, and he suggested that you might be stopping by with something interesting." This last was drawn out as if Goldfarb had been searching for the proper word or was rapidly translating a word in his head.

Alex started to say something and Tom nudged her under the table. He said, "Yes, Mr. Goldfarb, we have a stone that we'd like to sell. It was part of an inheritance and Sidney suggested that you might be interested in it. It is quite unusual." Alex scowled at him but kept quiet.

Tom reached into his jacket pocket, withdrew the soft suede pouch, and handed it to Goldfarb. Goldfarb then drew out a square of black velvet from a drawer and spilled the contents of the pouch onto it. The jewel tumbled out and lay face up, sparkling as it jiggled. Goldfarb then produced a pair of tweezers with blunt tips and oriented the stone at six and twelve o'clock to him. He sat staring at it for a long moment, mentally classifying, grading, and weighing it. About twenty-two or twenty-three carats, long oval cushion cut, quite deep from the crown, high quality. He then delicately, almost effeminately put the loupe in his left eye, pushing his glasses up onto his forehead.

He studied it carefully, turning it slowly this way and that. It was flawless. From another desk drawer, he withdrew an electronic probe and placed the tip against the stone. It gave a quiet series of clicks. This seemed to startle the gentleman who then placed the tip against it again. Once again the clicks sounded. He frowned, deep furrows wrinkled across his forehead. From another drawer he removed what looked like a small telescope. He gazed at the brilliant stone and gave a short, dry laugh.

"George, would you come in here, please?" he said to no one in particular. Tom looked at Alex and shrugged. She shrugged in reply.

In a second a discreet knock sounded and a second man came in, a thinner, much younger version of Mr. Goldfarb. "My son, George." He introduced them.

"I want you to look at this, George, because you may never see another. Please." He handed the loupe over to young George. George then picked up the stone and held it up to the light, face screwed up in concentration.

"What is it, Papa? A CZ?" He asked, referring to a Cubic Zircon, a cheap imitation of a diamond.

"No, George," he explained patiently. Look at the crystalline structure, especially in the lower quadrant. What does it remind you of?"

George answered promptly, "A beryl, Papa. An emerald. But there is no color and no occlusions." He sounded baffled, but the father saved him.

"Look at it carefully. It's a flawless piece of goshenite. Sometimes known as a white emerald. An extremely rare gem. This is only the second one

I have seen in thirty years," he mused. "The one I saw over twenty years ago had several small flaws, yet it was still beautiful." He leaned back in his chair and pulled his glasses down onto his nose once again. "They sometimes place them in a closed setting with colored foil behind the stone." He stared shrewdly at the couple before him. He'd never seen them before and they were as unlikely a pair as he'd ever seen in his years in the gem business.

The man sat easily in the chair, his dark suit well fitted, but older, seldom worn. The young lady was beautiful, lustrous dark hair caught up in a single braid that hung over one shoulder, a simple strand of pearls at her throat offset by her light olive skin. His professionalism overcame him and he estimated the pearls as being nearly perfectly matched at about eight millimeters. Not bad. Eighteen hundred, maybe two thousand at wholesale. The way they sat and darted looks at each other, he did not think they were married. She sat perched on the edge of her seat, eyes fixed on the gem. It was obvious that she had more at stake in it than he did. She would make a deal. He would be more difficult.

George finally placed the gem back on the velvet mat. "Thank you, Papa. Thank you also, Mr. Novak, Ms. Locarno." He bobbed his head and left through the door from which he'd entered.

"I'm so sorry, my friends. May I offer you some coffee? Or tea?"

"No thank you," they chorused. Tom laughed. "We just had breakfast."

"I want you to know the reason I called George in was to show you that I am an honest man."

"Can we get down to business, Mr. Goldfarb?" How much will you give us for the stone?" Alex asked bluntly.

Goldfarb idly spun the stone on his desk. "Eighty-five thousand." The number hung in the air between them, and when no one responded he asked, "Can you get more?"

Before Alex could answer, Tom put his hand on her arm. "Possibly, Mr. Goldfarb. And if we do, can come to you first?"

This seemed to satisfy Goldfarb who pursed his lips and made a steeple of his hands. If he offered what the stone was probably worth, it would set a precedent that would drive future purchases. If he offered too little, the Tischlers would probably advise these folks to go elsewhere with other gems. He sighed. This really was a no-win situation for him. He knew he could easily sell the stone in a simple pendant setting to any of a dozen New York society matrons. Just a whisper that it was a white emerald would set hearts fluttering.

"Thank you, Mr. Novak. I think I can offer you $100,000 for the stone."

Tom countered, "I think $150,000 would be a more appropriate figure, Mr. Goldfarb. After all, you'll be the only one in the city to have one."

"One hundred and twenty, and I want exclusive brokerage rights on any future stones."

Alex gasped. This was more than she'd been expecting. Tom continued, "One-hundred and thirty and you will have first refusal rights."

"Done." Goldfarb was pleased. He would probably clear $50,000 on the sale. He thumbed a button under his desktop. Mrs. B. had been listening and came in with a check for $130,000 as they were shaking hands. "My bank is just down the street. I'll call ahead and authorize the funds. Thank you Mr. Novak, Ms. Locarno." He ushered them to the door.

He sighed as they left. Of course he'd have to call and inform the VanHerff people. They insisted that any colorless stones of magnitude be brought to their attention at once. He knew that they were beginning to loosen their grip just a little with the new finds in Australia, however, best not to tempt fate just yet. The Australians were poorly organized and the South Africans have had a century to get their act together. Look what they'd done to the Russians when they'd tried to flood the market with their high quality blues just a few years ago. A pity, he supposed, that they exerted such control. However, in reality they did.

"Mrs. B. Would you please get the VanHerff security people on the phone for me?"

Tom and Alex had no trouble cashing the check. The bank manager showed them into a small office where he counted out the money. It was all in used one hundred-dollar bills. He only asked once if they would like to open an account. He knew it was fruitless but his responsibility was to at least ask. They seemed like a nice couple. The young lady instructed him to have fifty thousand sent to a bank in Mexico City. She wrote the account number in a small notebook and tore the page off. There was no name.

Alex smiled sweetly at him as Tom went back to his counting. He removed the paper bands with the bank's name and counted the hundreds into piles of $10,000, then put a rubber band around each pile and placed the bundles in her large purse.

In a few moments, they were out on the crowded street looking for a cab. The cab took only fifteen minutes to get them back to their hotel. As they entered, the manager called them to the desk.

"Mr. Novak, a moment, *bitte*."

"Yes, Willi?"

"A gentleman called a few minutes ago. He said he would like to meet you for a drink. He said his name was Boettcher." Willi was sweating slightly. "He spoke excellent German, but I do not think he was from Germany. My guess would be a Boer. You know, South African?" Willi drew himself up to his full height. He ran a hand over his slicked hair. "No trouble, please, Mr. Novak, *hein*?" He handed Tom a small slip of paper.

Tom put his hand on the older man's arm, "Don't worry, Willi. If there is any trouble, it won't come from us. Besides we're leaving in the morning. Thank you."

While this exchange was going on, Alex strolled to the door and casually glanced out. If they were being followed, she couldn't tell. There were no men in trench coats loitering across the street, nor men with newspapers in doorways that she could see.

Tom signaled to her and they rode the elevator silently to their rooms. She was about to enter when Tom took her elbow and steered her into his room.

"What's going on?" she asked when the door was closed.

"I don't know, but, boy, that was fast. I didn't know that Boettcher was in the city. I figured he was headquartered in South Africa or someplace nearer to home."

"You think that nice Mr. Goldfarb called him?"

"Of course. But that's not his fault. He has to play by their rules. They're his lifeblood, not us. But, Jesus, we're going to have to be very careful. And move fast." Tom was busy pulling a soft, beat up duffel bag out of his suitcase. "Here, put the money in here." He threw the old blue bag beside her on the bed. "Put a few essentials in there, too. We may have to move fast and light. I'm going to call this guy. We're going to have to get him really pissed to mobilize his troops."

Tom settled himself back on the bed, pulling a couple of pillows behind him.

He dialed the number and waited.

"Hello, Mr. Novak. This is Michael Boettcher." Tom heard the accent behind the voice and knew what Willi meant. German, but not exactly German. "I'd like to meet with you and discuss distributing some stones for you."

"What are you talking about, Mr. Boettcher?"

"Come, come, Mr. Novak. I've seen the lovely goshenite you sold today. Let us not play games with each other." He let an edge slip into his voice. He knew he was speaking with an American, yet he couldn't help thinking of him as a stupid Pollack or Czech, a member of a sub-species. He smoothed his voice out. "Mr. Novak, all I wish is for us to talk, to prepare the groundwork, so to speak, for a profitable business arrangement."

"Profitable for whom, Mr. Boettcher?

"Why for both of us, Mr. Novak. We would be prepared to purchase all the stones you have for a very good price. You do have more, don't you?"

"Yes, I do, but I have other buyers who may be interested in some of them. Would that be a problem?" Tom was enjoying himself. Alex sat still beside him, one warm thigh pressed against his calf, her brow furrowed in concentration.

"Ah, I'm afraid that my principals would require me to make an arrangement for them to acquire all of the stones. We may also be interested in acquiring your mine as well. Couldn't we speak about this in person?" Boettcher was uncomfortable discussing this over the phone. He liked to look a man in the eye, physically overpower him with his mere presence. He knew he cut an imposing figure being over two meters tall and large overall, his blond, almost white hair cut to a military brush cut, a several times broken nose below icy blue eyes. His thin, almost lipless mouth seemed in keeping with his Prussian ancestors. He kept wiping his brow and the back of his neck with a large linen handkerchief, yet a thin film of dried salt always seemed to reappear. He couldn't figure it out and so far had resisted the desire to go to a doctor. Right now he was pacing in his office high atop a modern steel and glass building off 100th Avenue.

"I don't think so, Mr. Boettcher. I'm flying out early in the morning and I have several meetings, which will take the rest of the day. However, thanks for the offer and if we're ever interested in selling, I'll be sure to give you a call. I've got your number." And he hung up.

Boettcher cursed and threw the portable phone at the wall. He looked down at his desk at the digital indicator. Novak had been calling from his room at the Chesterfield hotel, the caller I.D. told him. Well, tonight they'd have their little talk whether that eastern European peasant wanted to or not.

Alex placed a hand on his thigh. "Was that wise?" She shivered. "He'll come looking for us, won't he?"

Tom grinned a cold grin. "That's the idea. And when he doesn't get to talk to us, he'll follow. All the way to Guatemala, we hope." Tom hopped off the bed and threw the small gun in the bag with the money and Alex's small packet. From his big bag he removed a small leather pouch. In it were several tools and a hand drill with bits and two hypodermics. Alex watched curiously as he unscrewed the light bulb from the lamp on the table next to the door. Next, Tom brought the bulb to the bed and began carefully drilling a hole in the globe. In a couple of seconds, a tiny whoosh could barely be heard as the drill penetrated the vacuum. Tom pulled a screw top baby food jar out of his luggage and carefully filled one syringe. He squirted it into the light bulb, then gently eased it back into its socket.

"Just a tip," he said with a leer. "Don't flip on the light until I tell you!"

"Why are you doing this? Do you really think they'll come here?"

"Who knows? Better safe than sorry. Look, get some sleep. We'll probably have a long night. If nothing happens, we'll be out of here tomorrow and be home safely."

Alex arose and headed for the door.

"Wait, better use the connecting door," Tom gestured.

"But the door is locked from the other side." She was perplexed.

"Nah, I picked it last night. Never know."

"You mean you could have come into my room at any time?" She stood with her hands on her hips.

"Well, yeah. But I didn't."

She tapped her foot on the floor. "Too bad," she said and pulled the door shut behind her.

CHAPTER 8

Tom sat cross-legged on his bed, a hotel water glass half filled with bourbon on the night table by his side. He had the heavy automatic pistol in pieces on a newspaper and was carefully lubricating each piece as he reassembled it. He hummed softly to himself, taking an occasional swig from the glass. He heard a soft snick of a knob being turned and the nearly noiseless opening of the connecting door. Without turning his head, he saw the shadow of his next-door neighbor creep toward him along the wall.

Alex moved to Tom's side. She wore only a slip. "Aren't you going to offer me a drink?"

He smelled the warm muskiness of her, no makeup, and no perfume, just her. If he turned his

face, his nose would be on a level with her hip. He
slipped the slide in place, cocked it and sent it
home. He swung his arm smoothly in an arc and
pressed the barrel to her gently rounded belly. She
froze for a minute then stood on her toes and pushed
the top of the barrel down until it was pressed
against her mound. Tom looked up and saw the
beginnings of a smile just touch the corners of her
mouth.

"Is that a substitute for the real thing?" She
reached a hand out and lightly ran it over his head.
Slowly, slowly she caressed his slightly damp hair.
It was mesmerizing. Her hips were now
imperceptibly moving against the gun, the oil
staining the satiny fabric. With a viciousness he
didn't know she possessed, she grabbed a handful
of hair and twisted it in her hand, forcing his head
back.

Her other hand stiffened awkwardly in a karate
chop position poised just inches from his throat.
"Poor little man. I could kill you right now. And
you with an unloaded gun."

She felt his gun hand move. She looked down.
Her slip was now up over the barrel and the warm
steel pressed against her mound once again, this
time without the benefit of the scant covering. She
shuddered, licking her suddenly dry lips. She still
held the smiling face back. She knew it must hurt
but he gave no sign. Suddenly she bent forward and
covered his lips with hers, grinding her lips and
teeth and tongue against his. Tom dropped the gun
and wound his fingers in her hair wrapping it
around his own head, kissing her lips, her eyes, her

nose and the hollow of her throat. She moaned and pushed away from him. She was panting now.

"Not here, my room." And she was gone. Tom quickly loaded the clip, wiping each shell with an oily rag before inserting, a trick he'd learned in Vietnam from an unnamed, unmarked soldier whom he was later told was NSC. Now he'd met men from all intelligence branches, ONI (Naval Intelligence), G-2 (Army), CIA, even FBI. Most of them he considered bozos with a few exceptions but the few NSC operators made even his ice-cold blood run cold. Dave had nicknamed him "Carbide" because he was so hard. He reached down with his clean hand. Yep, he sure was carbide tonight.

He brought the gun with him into her room. Only a shrouded bedside light was turned on. Alex laid on the bed totally nude, legs together, hands by her side. Tom could only stand and stare. The shadows outlined her hills and hollows. Her hair was now unbraided and spread in a semi-circle on the white pillow. She lay with her eyes closed, as still as death. Her beauty awed Tom. Hers was not the fashion model beauty, not the cool, hairlessness of the Nordic princess that was all the fashion. She was dark and olive skinned, her hair was jet black and thick, her breasts were heavy with deep, almost purple nipples that stood up at the moment. Her waist was taut with muscle, a rounded belly over a dark thatch of hair. No, this was a woman, a woman born of Mediterranean and Castilian, and Indian blood. The blood of conquerors and warriors. And she waited for Tom. Slowly, quietly, almost afraid to make a sound, he slipped out of his T-shirt, letting it drop. His trousers fell next around his feet. He took one small step toward the bed. His briefs fell next and then he too was nude.

His hands slipped up from her knees to her thighs and she shuddered, opened her eyes and smiled at him. Her arms came up and opened in invitation. He sank to his knees beside the bed, laying his head on her breast, breathing shallowly, afraid she would throw him off. She held him and stroked his shoulders, his neck. Tom turned his head slightly and took a taunt nipple into his mouth, letting his tongue circle the hard jut of flesh.

Behind him, he thought he heard a noise. Suddenly a loud bang could be heard through the half closed connecting door and a man screamed in pain. The light bomb, Tom thought, leaping to his feet. He fleetingly glanced at her, only a split second given to regret. Alex also leaped to her feet as Tom threw himself to the floor by the door. He crawled rapidly forward and glanced around the doorframe. The room was shrouded in acrid smoke, a figure was on its knees hands over his eyes. For an instant, Tom felt regret. My God, suppose it was Willi. But then he saw the gun by the figure's right knee. A second figure loomed behind the first, a gun in his hand. Quickly Tom noted details: tall, taller than me, white or blond hair, leather jacket, white scarf. The gun was a revolver, long barrel, thick at the end. A silencer, he thought. Before he could get off a shot, the figure strode forward, roughly pushing the kneeling figure aside. That may have saved him. As he stepped, his booted foot nudged a thin monofilament line only an inch off the rug. The line jerked and the pin from a nautical smoke flare pulled free. The room rapidly filled with smoke shrouding everything with a thick, dense white cloud. Tom quickly snapped off a shot and groped around beside the door until he snagged the small duffel bag full of money and his other pistol, and he scurried backwards. Fleetingly he thought, "I hope Alex doesn't shoot me in the ass." Just as he was clear of the door, it slammed heavily and the latch was thrown. Alex stood above him breathing heavily, eyes wide with fear.

Why wasn't she dressed? Then he realized that it had been only seconds since he had heard the first noise.

"Quick, grab some clothes. We've got to get out of here." Tom leaped to his feet and ran for the corridor door, pausing just long enough to grab his pants and T-shirt. Alex was next to him, a bundle of clothing under her arm. Tom cracked the door and peered out. The corridor was empty, smoke billowed out but no one was in sight. A feeble whimper could still be heard. Tom supposed it was the kneeler.

He glanced at Alex and nodded. They slipped into the carpeted hall. Just as they rounded the corner, a voice called, "Hey!"

Alex grabbed Tom's hand and ran as fast as she could, turning another corner. A man stepped out in front of her, a pistol leveled at her waist. For a split second he glanced at her naked breasts. It was all the time Tom needed. He brought his gun hand up and squeezed off a shot, barely missing her rounded hip. The gunman spun, clutching at his leg. He slammed against the near wall and fell heavily. He scrabbled for his gun.

Damn, thought Tom, *down but not out*. He raised his gun for another shot but another voice called out, "Down here. They got Jules," and a bullet whizzed by his head.

Alex kicked out the window in the wall overlooking the alley. Firmly she pulled on Tom's arm as she stepped out onto the foot wide ledge. Tom quickly followed, edging along, his bare buttocks scraping against the rough brick. A head poked out the window and Tom snapped off another shot, pinging the brick beside the face. A yowl rang out and the face disappeared. *Cripes*, Tom thought, *could it get any worse?* A fine rain started to fall.

"Jesus, we're sitting ducks out here." Tom frantically looked around. Ahead of him a thick drainpipe blocked their way. Alex was wild eyed with terror, swinging her head from side to side. Below, Tom saw a dumpster, lids thrown back. It was outside the kitchen and a man was upturning a garbage can into it. It was two stories below them. He pointed. Alex looked down and shrank back against the wall, trying to press herself into the mortar between the bricks. She shook her head frantically. Tom estimated the distance at no more than forty feet. He slid his hand up her arm and pulled her to him. He kissed her quickly and then pushed her sharply out into space. Her legs made a frantic effort trying to climb the air, and then her natural athletic ability took over. She curled into a

ball and landed on her back, narrowly missing the
side. She was stunned. Stunned at finding herself
still alive. And stunned at seeing a large, naked
figure hurling at her from an incredible height. She
quickly pushed with her feet until she was pressed
into the corner of the filthy garbage bin. Tom
landed with a thud beside her. A great whoosh of air
escaped his lungs. He looked up and gave a short
bark of laughter.

"Boy, lady, you sure know how to show a guy
a good time!" She looked at him in a daze. "Let's
get the fuck out of here."

Tom scrambled to his feet shaking a slime of
vegetable scrap off his leg. After peering over the
edge, he hauled Alex to her feet and pushed her
over the edge. She hit on her shoulder and rolled
shakily to her feet. Tom jumped down lightly beside
her just as a short oriental man shouldering a large
garbage can stepped out the door. They must have
been quite a sight, Tom decided, both nude, covered
with garbage, a small duffel bag clutched in one
hand and, miraculously, his gun in the other. He
scooped up both his and her clothes with the gun
hand and thrust them at Alex.

"*Konichi-wa!*" Tom greeted the oriental, not
knowing if the man was Japanese or not. The short
man bowed, the cloth tied around his head dripping
a pinkish dye down the side of his face.

At the far end of the alley, a voice yelled out,
"Stop!" Tom grabbed Alex's hand and they ran
away from the voice. The dark swallowed them up

and soon all sounds of pursuit faded. They stopped and leaned against a rough wall breathing hard.

Only the normal sounds of the city echoed. Tom quickly slipped into his jeans, first trying to scrape off some gooey green slim off his leg. The jeans and T-shirt were damp and smelled awful. Tom gingerly pulled the collar over his head. Beside him, Alex slid her pants over her hips, wiggling rapidly from side to side.

"Yuck," she wrinkled her nose. "I think the shirt landed in some spaghetti." She shook it and scraped it against the wall, some unidentifiable red lumps sticking there. Before pulling her shirt together, she flashed Tom one last look and gave him an impish grin. "Aren't we a sight? Where are we going to stay now?"

Tom frowned for a minute and thought. Finally he shrugged, "Well, we smell like shit, we look like shit, got no shoes. All the money in this bag won't get us into a fancy hotel." He dangled the small bag by one finger. "Ah, come on, we'll find something." He took her hand and led her down an alley and out onto a street in a run-down section of the city. They'd gone farther than he realized.

Up ahead the mournful sounds of a small, out-of-tune band came from a brightly lit doorway. As they got closer, Tom made out the faded letters on the hand-painted sign. Third Evangelical Baptist Mission. *Perfect*, he thought. *Nobody will look for us here.* "Besides, it's probably the only place that would let us in," he said out loud.

Alex looked at him strangely. "No, not there, Thomas."

"Yeah, there." He spoke quietly, but forcefully. "If we try to get into a hotel, the desk clerk would remember us, if they let us in at all. Where the hell are we going to get a shower and clean clothes this time of night?"

She had no answer for that. They stopped in the doorway, yellow light spilling out over their bare feet. Inside an old black man with white hair stood slowly stirring a large pot. There were only two or three derelicts hunched over chipped mugs of coffee. They hardly looked up as Tom and Alex stepped inside. As they did, a small man wearing a priests' collar hurried over to them. He had on lime green windowpane slacks and sandals. The black priest's shirt contrasted sharply, as did the Boston Blackie pencil thin mustache. His voice was high and his eyes were bright but he motioned them forward.

"Come in, come in, my children." As he got closer, he wrinkled his nose. "God, but you two smell awful. Have you been dumpster diving?"

Tom smiled and answered, "Yes, Padre, we could really use a shower and a rack for the night. That coffee smells good, too."

"Yes, yes, definitely a shower. If you'll go through that door," he indicated a narrow door behind the kitchen area, "there are towels and soap on the shelf outside the shower. And, one at a time in the shower. House rules, you know." He fussed over them, drawing cups of thick, black coffee for them. "I'll go through our lost and found and see if I can find some clean clothes for you." He sized Tom up and said, "Five, ten; five eleven. About 180 or so?" He turned to Alex and smiled a pinched sort of grin, his eyes never leaving her breasts. "Uh, five-eight, about 125?"

She nodded and clutched Tom's arm with her free hand and crept closer.

"Go on, children, clean up. Cleanliness and Godliness and all that sort of thing." He shooed them through the door. The short corridor was in sore need of a paint job, long curls of some indescribable color paint peeling from the plaster walls. A single dim bulb lit the corridor. Alex found the recessed shelves and handed Tom a threadbare towel.

"I'll go first. You stand guard. I don't trust that little sneak."

"No kidding." Tom leaned against the wall, towel over his shoulder. He heard the shower running and the sighs of contentment coming from the closed door. In a moment, the water stopped. Tom wished he were inside doing the soaping, front as well as back. He'd about made up his mind to go in when the small priest came down the corridor with an assortment of clothes over his arm.

"Here you are, my son." He handed Tom a worn pair of corduroy trousers that looked like it was standard wear in Bulgaria or some Eastern Bloc country. The flannel shirt marked him as a logger from Oregon or Washington and finally the shoes were patent leather, white. Altogether, a fitting ensemble for a night out on the town in Moscow or Miami Beach.

The priest edged by Tom and started to open the door. Tom slammed his big hand against it, closing it firmly. "I'll take those, if you don't mind, Padre. My, uh, old lady, she don't much like strange men, even holy Joe's like yourself. You understand." Tom relieved the priest of a flowered skirt and a man's dress shirt, white with blue stripes and a pair of mules with white straps. He waited a minute until the priest scurried back out the door, then knocked once and opened the door a crack and handed the clothes to Alex. She stood pink and clean, one hand over her pubis and the other across her breasts, sort of like the Botticelli print of Venus. Only this Venus was a full-blown fleshy woman with all the curves in the right places.

Tom wiggled his eyebrows at her as she snatched the clothes and slammed the door. A few seconds later she threw open the door. Her hair was wrapped up in the towel like a turban. "The shower is all yours, Thomas."

Tom eyed her carefully. "Well, you certainly smell a hell of a lot better than you did a few minutes ago."

"Yes, that is true, and right now I smell much better than you. You smell like a pig that my Uncle Rojas once had." She thought for a minute, a finger against her cheek, one hip thrust out. "In fact, I think his name was Thomas, too."

Before Tom could spank her, she scampered out of the way, laughing. "Hey, keep an eye on the bag while I'm showering. If that little rat faced preacher sticks his nose in here, shoot it off." Now

it was Tom's turn in the dingy shower. It was only a
tin enclosure painted what was once white, now an
off color that gradually ran to beige with darker
blotches near the floor. The curtain had a dark
brown crust that swept the rusty floor, but the water
was hot and the bar of soap felt good. Tom
scrubbed his hair twice with the strong soap, letting
the warmth of the water seep into his taunt muscles.
He was of a mind to pull the beautiful Alex into the
little room with him and finish what they'd started
earlier. He sighed. Time and place. Time and place.
There would be other opportunities. First they
needed a night's sleep away from prying eyes, then
to get out of New York.

Well, Boettcher had taken the bait, a little faster
than he'd have liked but they'd escaped and were
safe for the moment. He'd phone Dave in the
morning. He was sure Dave would have the rest of
the plan in place by the time he and Alex returned.
On second thought, things were starting to hop. It
might be best if he got her back to her people to get
things started on that end. Oh, well, what happened
happened. Tom was, after all, a bit of a fatalist and a
linear thinker. Dave and Chris were the empirical
thinkers and planners.

After drying off, Tom dressed in the ugly
clothes provided by the weasely padre and slipped
out the door. Alex was gone.

Tom frantically looked both ways in the short
corridor then went hurrying toward the door they'd
come through. Storming through, he saw with relief
that Alex was seated having a cup of coffee, one
foot slipped through the handles of the small duffel

bag. The padre was sitting across from her, leaning forward on his elbows, speaking rapidly. Alex looked up from her conversation and rolled her eyes at Tom. Tom slipped in beside the little man and put an arm across his shoulders.

"You know, padre, me and the little, uh, lady here could sure use some shut eye. If you could show us where we could bunk down, we'd really appreciate it." Tom grinned and squeezed the little man's shoulder affectionately.

"Yeah, yeah, sure, friends. If you go up them stairs, the men's dorm is on the right and the woman's dorm is on the left. Sorry, we ain't got no couples quarters, if you know what I mean." Now it was his turn to smile. "Oh," he said as they rose, "try'n keep the noise down and not wake any of the other tenants."

"Sure thing, padre." Tom and Alex parted at their doors, Tom taking the bag. "I'll see you in the morning, baby, and after breakfast we'll get some new clothes. I think we can afford it."

"I know, and I feel guilty taking food and a bed from these kind people."

"Aw, don't worry too much. They get a good hunk of change from the state for this fleabag. We'll leave a big tip for the padre and his good works, okay?"

Alex nodded and Tom kissed her on the tip of her nose. She smiled shyly and squeezed his arm. They went into their respective rooms.

Tom entered and stood just to the side of the doorway. Old training dies hard. Never stand directly in a doorway. He waited until his eyes adjusted to the gloom. In a few minutes he could make out the sleeping forms of about twenty men on a double row of narrow metal beds. It reminded him of a military barracks. God knows, he'd slept in a few of those in his time. The room was fairly quiet with a low buzz of snoring and an occasional rheumy cough punctuating the dark. Tom slid swiftly and silently to one side and took an empty bed near a window. He fell asleep with the duffel bag beneath his head, a satisfied smile on his face.

CHAPTER 9

A cold, blue light threw harsh shadows across the desk and man seated behind it. His right fingers beat impatiently on the bare wood.

"What do you mean, you can't find them?" His voice was calm but with a thin, brittle veneer. The two men seated across from him fidgeted nervously in their seats.

"*Herr Captain*...." The first man began.

The man behind the desk held up a hand, palm outward, "Dieter, you are in America now, you will speak only American English. How many times do I have to tell you?" He was seething. Were they only sending him fools, and incompetent ones at that, now? "How could a naked man and woman alone in the night slip through your hands?" *Idiots*, he silently fumed.

"Mr. Boettcher, you were with us. You saw them jump from the ledge. It was… unexpected." He sat silently.

The second man, an older one said, "Sir, they can't have gone far. I have men checking the hotels in a ten-block area. I have not heard reports on the police radio of any stolen cars in the area, and the taxi frequencies are being monitored. No one matching his or her description has been picked up recently. In the morning we will check car rental agencies, the airport, bus station, and all other methods of egress from the city through our contacts. However, I must warn you that it will be nearly impossible for us to stop a determined man and woman from departing this city if they wish to do so unnoticed." He too lapsed into silence.

The man behind the desk drummed his fingers once more. He was stocky, over six feet with a thick neck and small features. His hair was cut short in a military brush cut, which was nearly white and had been so since early childhood. His hands were thick fingered with the nails bitten off to the quick. Several scars wound their way across the backs of his hands and the corner of his mouth sagged a bit on one side, the result of a fight many years ago.

He was just a youngster then and assigned to an elite police unit that patrolled the Soweto slum outside Johannesburg. There had been a shooting two days before and a young black man had been killed by a rival tribesman. At the funeral, the rival tribesmen attacked the procession. The police waded in, bashing heads indiscriminately. Boettcher had become separated from his comrades in the melee. He soon found himself backed against a rickety fence in a small alley between two shacks. He was clubbing a young woman who was trying to get away from him when a huge shadow loomed over him. It was an angry Zulu man, gone to weight from living in the city, but big and solid, nonetheless. Before he could draw his revolver, the young black had lifted him over his head and hurled him through the fence. He'd landed on his face against a pig-feeding trough set partially in the ground and been stunned. Blood trickled down the side of his face. The giant had crashed through the fence after him. As he reached for his weighted baton, the man's booted foot had come down on his hand, grinding it and tearing the flesh. The man laughed and said, "Not such a big man now, eh police fellow?"

Before Boettcher could reply, he was kicked in the face and his other hand was ground into the dirt. The giant was about to finish him when a whistle blew. A voice called "Michael, where the devil are ye?" The foot lashed out once more and Boettcher lapsed mercifully into unconsciousness.

He came to in a hospital bandaged and sore. The next day, his friend Karl came to visit. "Ah, Michael, it's good to see you alive. That wog was looking to do away with ye." He smirked and pulled a chair up.

"And what did you do to him, Karl?" Michael struggled to sit upright, pulling a pillow behind him.

Karl rose to assist him but one glare from Boettcher and he sat back down, crossing his legs.

Karl shrugged and lit a cigarette. "Do? I shot him but I must have only winged him a wee bit. He got away." He added almost as an afterthought, "Sorry, laddie."

Michael glared at him in disgust. "Did you get a look at his boots? I think he must work in the mines. He was big and strong enough to. I'm going to find the black bastard and kill him." He seethed, reliving the scene of his humiliation.

A week later he was back at work. It took him almost a month to find the big black man, and a week of following him to locate his family. The man was something of a tribal leader in his neighborhood, if you could call the collection of shacks in the shantytown a neighborhood. He had a wife and two young daughters. Michael sat in his car smoking and watched through tinted windows as the man got off the ramshackle bus, and the two little girls ran up to him. A moment later, the young woman he'd been beating walked up and wove her arm through his. The family, Boettcher thought.

Since the black family lived not far from the edge of the camp, Michael was able to slip in unnoticed several nights later. He was dressed in black and carried only a knife, a lead filled sap and a roll of duct tape. Quietly he slipped inside the shack. It was surprisingly clean and swept. The man had obviously built the table and two low benches, but the workmanship was quite good. Against a wall, a rack of shelves held clothes, kitchen utensils and a row of books. Michael looked at the books.

They were in both English and German.
Philosophy, he noted, and economics. Steady
snoring came from an adjoining room and he
peeked in. The giant and his wife were asleep
wrapped in each other's arms. The two young girls
lay in small cots just inside the doorway. Quietly he
reached in and clasped the nearest one over her
mouth in a crushing grip. She kicked but Boettcher
lifted her clear of the bed and pulled her around the
corner. Her eyes were huge in her head as she
looked at him. He grinned at her and gave her head
a quick jerk. The snap was audible and she sagged
in his arms. Boettcher quietly placed her small body
against the wall.

Once again he reached into the next room and
slowly gathered up the smaller figure. The little girl
squirmed and pressed her head against his chest,
finally settling back to sleep. Boettcher pressed her
small face into his stomach, holding his hand on the
back of her head. She struggled briefly trying to
turn her face away from the smothering flesh. When
her feet stopped kicking he placed her on the floor
next to her sister. Two down, he thought. He wanted
the man last. He wanted the black bastard to watch
him.

Once again he slipped into the room. The man
and woman had rolled apart at last. That was good.
He pulled the heavy, leather-covered sap from his
rear pocket and brought it down in a crushing blow
on the black man's head. The man jerked once and
was silent. As his wife slowly came awake,
Boettcher ripped a long strip of tape off the roll and

wrapped it over her mouth before she could scream. He quickly pulled several more strips off and wrapped her hands together tightly. In a second, he was astride her and had her ankles taped. She was immobile. Next he did the same to the giant, dragging his body across the room to the table where he strapped the man down to the tabletop, using almost the whole roll of tape. Back into the bedroom, he jerked the wife to her feet, tearing her thin shift to pieces and throwing the pieces across the room. She was small but ripe, had high breasts and a jutting rear. Her color was dark, almost purple. He grabbed her hair and pulled her back against him. She smelled of soap and sleep. He reached between her legs. Not wet so they probably hadn't had sex that night. Good. He didn't want to be second behind the giant. Boettcher dragged a bench over just under the giant's face and placed her face down, her gleaming buttocks rising high. When he had her placed just the way he wanted, he looked at the giant. His face was no more than a foot from his.

Boettcher glanced around and saw a squat bucket of water. He reached and threw it in the black man's face. The man blinked and shook his head, throwing drops around the room. Slowly his eyes came into focus. He was looking at his wife's rear end. When he raised his eyes he was looking into the grinning face of Michael Boettcher. "Hello," he sneered, "Remember me?"

Boettcher laughed in the man's face. "Can't talk? Cat got your tongue?" The black giant squirmed and tried to pull free but Boettcher had done his work well. Slowly he unzipped his trousers and pulled out his member, stroking it up and down slowly while rubbing the woman's sex. Despite herself, she grew moist. Tears dripped from her eyes. She tried to speak through the tape, to assure her husband she loved only him. But she could barely move her head and her wriggling only served to inflame Boettcher more.

"You watching now? You watching me do your wife, Kaffir?" He slowly pushed into her and pulled back till the cap of his penis was just visible. The black giant twisted and thrashed, banging his head against the table in frustration. "Come on, now. Keep watching. You ready?" He was pumping faster now, on the verge of climaxing. The black man's eyes were wide. Suddenly Boettcher pulled his knife and just as the spasms came, reached around and slit the woman's throat. She jerked upward, arching her back and pushing back against him. "Oh, yes, that's good, that's very good." Her blood spurted, one great gout, then silently spilled out onto the floor in slower spurts, then drips. Boettcher sighed and hung his head as she slipped and fell on her side. Great beads of sweat stood out on the giant's face, his shoulders rippled but the layers of tape held fast.

Boettcher shoved the wife's body aside and casually sat on the bench, his face close to the giant's. "Well, now, my wog friend. I've managed to kill your wife," he nudged the still body with his foot, "your children," he gestured with the blood smeared knife at the corner where the two stiffening bodies lay. "Now I guess it's your turn." He rose and walked behind the black man. The shoulders slumped, the man stopped his wriggling, resigned, quiet. Boettcher placed the tip of the knife at the base of the man's thick neck and swiftly hit it with his palm. The thin blade slid between the vertebrae, severing the spinal cord. The man was dead before Boettcher withdrew the knife. He carefully wiped it on the man's pants and placed it back into its sheath strapped to his left arm.

He went back to work the next day and one-month later was diagnosed with a minor kidney malfunction. The doctor told him it might have come from a bout of unprotected sex or the blood transfusion he'd had in the hospital. Boettcher was warned not to drink alcohol. He went out that evening and got blindingly drunk. Several years later, he noticed a light, salty dusting of his skin but thought nothing of it. He continued to drink, though the quality of the alcoholic beverages increased as he rose in stature in the police force.

One day a pair of men in well-tailored dress suits visited him. They offered him a position with the VanHerff Mining Company in their security division. The money was good and there was great chance of advancement and travel. Two weeks later he handed in his resignation to the provincial police captain and cleaned out his locker. Since signing on with the diamond merchants, he'd performed a variety of tasks including intercepting a shipment of Russian diamonds destined for Antwerp, had tortured and killed the courier and had shipped his head back to Leningrad to his employers. He had

led a commando team into Yemen and blown up a
small mine which was supplying gems to a French
jewelry chain, had recovered any number of raw
gems for various dealers and had returned them,
less his commission, of course. Finally, he was head
of Security, worldwide for VanHerff. He was
nominally headquartered in New York but roamed
the globe, plotting with thieves, hiring informants,
supplying the muscle for various company
operations. His title as head of Security also gave
him access to the huge pit mines in Kimberly, South
Africa where his Lieutenant, Raoul LaPierre, a
former Legionnaire presided over internal security.

Boettcher drummed his fingers on the desk.
"We must find them. It is imperative. If they have
access to weight and it hits the market, then we'd
better start looking for new jobs." He thought for a
minute. "Dieter, you and Axel go pay a visit to the
hotel manager. Find out where that man came from.
I don't like wild cards."

"Ya, Mr. Boettcher," Dieter was almost out the
door, Axel closely following in his wake.

CHAPTER 10

The next morning, Tom and Alex rose early and slipped out before breakfast. Tom left a $100 bill in the donation plate. Hey, in New York, you sure couldn't get a decent bed and breakfast for a C note!

They stopped in the first clothing store they found open and bought new clothes. Next they caught an early cab for the airport. The day was overcast, but the fine rain had stopped. The city almost looked good, the wet streets still reflecting the cab's headlights and the neon signs not yet turned off. Tom tipped the cabby a ten-spot, and they dashed into the Kennedy terminal. At Tom's insistence, Alex bought a first class ticket to Miami, then to Cozumel before catching a short hop to Guatemala City.

"I want you out of here, and I want your people to know we're coming." Tom was holding her by the upper arms and looking deeply into her dark eyes, eyes you could drown in, 100% eyes. They were in the departure lounge and Alex was protesting. "Look, everything that's going to happen now will happen down south. Don't worry about us getting there. By this time next week, we should all be together again." He impulsively pulled her to him and gave her a deep kiss just as the final passengers were being loaded.

"Don't fail me, Thomas, or I shall hunt you down like the coyote you are. *Via con dios, me amore.*" And with a turn, she was gone. Tom waited in the passenger lounge until they threw him out. His flight took him back to Tampa and he never saw the pimply-faced young redcap who glanced nervously at the sketch in his hand and repeatedly looked at Tom as he strode toward his gate. The youth noted the flight number and destination before hurrying to a phone kiosk.

"This is Richie. The guy in the drawing? He's on flight 237 to Tampa. You got it?" He waited for confirmation. "When'm I gonna get my money?" he whined. "Yeah, yeah, sure." And he hung up.

The flight was uneventful and landed in mid afternoon after wheeling around over the barrier islands of the Gulf. Tom was able to identify John's Pass, Indian Rocks Beach and Clearwater Beach. He couldn't quite see as far as Travis Key and the small inlet with Chesney's nestled in its arms. He also failed to see the girl in the blue Avis uniform

who was loitering at the end of the tramway
bringing him into the main terminal from concourse
F. She followed him to the cabstand and heard him
say, "Chesney's in Sunset Pointe," to the driver.
Then she, too, made a call.

Tom arrived at the old bar/restaurant about an
hour later, paid the cabby and strolled in through the
front, pushing open the double screen doors and
letting them slam behind him. Rusty looked up from
the big screen where he sat with Vinny watching a
basketball game, and grunted at Tom, a beer nestled
in his big paw.

"Hey, Tom, how they hanging," Rusty
commented. "Nice threads," he added. "They new?"

"Hey, Rusty. Vinny. Where's Dave?" Tom
dropped his small bag and looked around, squinting
to see out the back door to Chris and Dave's
sailboat.

"Not back yet. They had that Hinkley Bermuda
ketch to deliver to New Orleans, remember? Dave
called and said they'd be back tonight or tomorrow.
Grab a chair," he gestured at an old but serviceable
recliner.

Tom slumped into the chair. "Who's playing?"

"Bulls and Magic. Jordan's dancin' rings
around Hardaway."

Tom let all the tension go out of him and
relaxed. He hadn't realized what a strain he'd been
under these last few days. He pried one eye open
and aimed it in Vinny's direction. "You get your
end taken care of okay?"

Vinny jumped up and squatted next to Tom's
recliner. He pulled out a small notebook and rapidly

flipped through it. "Tommy, you know you can depend on us," he said indignantly. "Me and Rusty and the wives went to the big gun show in Sarasota at the Convention Center the other day and picked up four M-16's, sportsterized, of course, but Rusty called the guy from Tampa who sold us four fully auto conversion kits. Then Joanie bought them two pump shotguns and we all bought ammo, a little here and a little there." He was fairly hopping around now. "We got six extra clips for each M-16 and about 10 boxes of double ought for the shotguns." He checked the notebook again. "We all used cash and we changed it at three banks before we went to the show. Chris gave it to us before she left. And, oh, yeah, we got some smoke and flashers. We called J.B. and he made us up a box of dragon's breath shells for the shotguns." He flipped a page and consulted a note and smirked. "Rusty and me used Dave's shop and made up a silencer for one of the pistols." He snapped the book closed and leaned his head back and thought a minute before speaking again.

"All told, we got about 5,000 rounds of ammo. Oh, yeah, Anna and Joanie picked up a dozen camo suits and a couple of black suits. We've got six sets of those radios that go on your belt with the earphone-microphones and half dozen walkie-talkies that Emile fixed up to all be on the same channel. Not a regular one, though. We got them at Radio Shack." He thought for a moment. "We met a guy at the show who wanted to sell us a heavy machine gun, a .50 cal. But I didn't have a good feeling about the guy." He gestured behind him, "Neither did Rusty. He might have been ATF." Vinny frowned. "Oh, yeah, I picked up a couple of night scopes, too." He thought for a minute. "I think that's it."

Rusty cleared his throat and spoke from the nearby recliner. "We put a couple of extra fuel bladders in the PT and built a couple of flip-up-and-lock-in-place racks that look like extra railings. They'll hold a couple of tons like Dave asked. What're they for?"

Tom ignored Rusty's question and said nothing for a while, mentally going over his checklist. Except for rations, web gear that they all had, there was really nothing else they needed. He hoped. "You have charts of the Western Caribbean, Rusty?"

"'Course," answered Rusty, taking a long swallow of his beer, spilling a little as he watched Jordan take a long pass from Barkley and Alley Oop it in. "Damn, that man can fly!" He exclaimed.

"Say, Tommy, did you manage to sell that jewel that Alex whats-er-name let you have?" Vinny was almost beside himself with anticipation. "Was it really what she said it was? A white emerald?"

"Yeah," Tom replied. "It's called goshenite and is real rare. The guy the Tischler brothers sent us to gave us a lot of dough for it. I sent Alex back to Guatemala to get her people ready for us. I told her we'd be there in a week or so." Tom rubbed his eyes with his thumbs, the basketball game droning in the background. All was normal around him. He and Vinny and Rusty sat in the worn but serviceable recliners, the late afternoon sun shone through the large windows overlooking the bay, sparkles winking at him like the facets of the gem they'd sold in the Big Apple. He'd done everything he was supposed to do, Alex was safe and Dave would be back this evening. After that, it was his show. He didn't know what Dave had planned for all of them but he was confident that he was working on a long-range plan for ridding the Locarnos of the Colombians.

In a few minutes Tom was fast asleep and didn't even wake up until the Friday evening dinner crowd raised the noise to a level even he couldn't sleep through. A rough hand shook him, and Charlie Potts was grinning his slack lipped grin at him. Ringo stood just behind him, also grinning.

"Tom, wake up. I've got a table set for you and Rusty. Anna's eating with Vinny and Joanie."

"Okay." Tom shook the cobwebs from his eyes, pinching the bridge of his nose for a long minute. "Thanks, Charlie, I'm going to grab a quick shower upstairs. I'll only be a minute." He hauled himself to his feet and took the stairs two at a time. Chris kept a small set of rooms upstairs in a loft over the bar. He entered and suddenly Alex was all around him. Her scent filled the air. She had walked here, sat here, slept here. He stood for what seemed like eternity, every sense open and receptive. Finally, struggling to regain his center, he stepped into the bathroom and turned on the shower. He reached for a fresh towel from a stack on a shelf in the open closet but stopped. On the towel bar beside the shower stall was a slightly mussed towel. He slipped it free and held it to his face. Yes, she was still here.

The hot shower soaked into his skin and into his bones. Tom leaned forward against crossed arms and rested his head against the far wall, the hot water beating down hard on his broad back. He reached down and kneaded his calves, working the knots and aches out. He stretched down and placed his palms flat on the floor, water dripping into his eyes. Below him, the floor thumped loudly three times.

Charlie Potts lowered the broom handle and tossed it back into its accustomed place beside the stove.

Tom smiled and felt fortunate to have such friends. In a moment, he was toweled dry and had slipped into a pair of Dave's khaki shorts, bleached almost white from repeated washings. He rummaged through the dresser until he found a pile of T-shirts and selected a dark gray one from Westwinds Cycle, a local custom Harley-Davidson shop. A pair of clogs completed the outfit and he was out the door and down the stairs.

Charlie Potts was just putting a large plate of nachos in front of Rusty as he slipped into his seat. "Good thing you got here when you did. I can eat a whole plateful of Potts' nachos by myself, you know."

"No kidding," replied Tom scooping up a large chip loaded with beans, thin strips of beef, sour cream, vegetables and salsa. Tom looked around

and nodded at the few faces he recognized. He tried
to memorize everyone, every candle flicker, and
every streak of dying sunlight. They were going up
against the toughest enemy they'd ever faced, and
they'd faced a few.

Rusty was swigging on a longneck of Ybor
Gold, a local brew, the bottle looking like a toy in
his huge mitt.

"Rusty, tell me about your boat," Tom asked
the big fellow. He knew that boaters never tired of
talking about their boats, any more than he never
tired of talking airplanes and helicopters.

"What do you want to know?"

"How'd you get it? What have you done to her?
You know, the facts, man, nothing but the facts."

Rusty burped and shoved himself back from the
table. "Well, I found her at a surplus sale in Miami
about 12 years ago. You know I was with Bulkeley
in the Pacific when the war broke out. We were the
guys what got MacArthur out of Corregidor back in
'41. Well, anyways, I saw this old plywood job
come up for bid and me and Anna put in a bid for a
grand, you know, just for the hell of it." He paused
and took a long pull at his beer. Magically, a full
one appeared at his elbow. Without looking, he
said, "Thanks, Ringo," over his shoulder.

"Let's see, where was I? Oh, yeah, so a month
goes by and we get a letter from the Government
Accounting Office telling us to come and pick up
our boat and assorted spares and that we had ten
days to move it out. Well, we went down and there
she was. She'd float, but that was about all. The

engines was seized up and it was kinda mildewy
down below but it was just like I remembered." He
shook his shaggy head and smiled a dreamy smile.

"We took her into a yard up by Lauderdale and
had her hauled. Me and Anna put our trailer, we had
a trailer then, right next to her and spent the next
year working on her." Rusty looked off into space,
not hearing the slowly building noise in the bar.
Tom hauled over a vacant chair and put his feet up.

"Yeah, so what did you do?"

"Well, we had to replace a lot of the plywood.
This was one of the Higgins class boats built up in
Jersey by Electric Boat. She was 78' and after we
replaced about 25 sheets of plywood, lengthened
her to 90', we fibre glassed the whole bottom. You
know, they were only supposed to last for a year or
so. The damn Packard engines were the biggest
problem. We got some spares but trying to keep
three engines going was just too much and finding
spares got to be a nightmare. We tried pulling one
and using it for parts and just running two but she
wouldn't get up and move, you know?"

Tom nodded encouragingly. Rusty went on.

"Well, after we moved here, Dave convinced
me to pull the old Packards and put in a couple of
Cat diesels. It runs farther, faster and doesn't use as
much fuel. The old Packards used to get about five-
hundred miles on a tank full."

"So what's she do now, about six or seven-
hundred?" asked Tom.

Rusty burped again and sat toying with a left
over French fry. "Nope, with the new fuel tanks,
she'll go about eighteen-hundred miles without

refueling. And that's running about three-quarters throttle. About thirty, thirty-five knots. Not bad for a fifty year old boat, eh, Tommy?"

"No kidding, Rusty!" Tom's enthusiasm was almost as great as the old sailor's.

Rusty continued, "With the two extra fuel bladders, we can carry an extra five-hundred gallons. "Course, it slows us down some, but sure extends the range. You know the originals carried a 40 mm and a 20 mm ak-ak gun besides the two torpedo tubes." He leaned across the table and whispered conspiratorially to Tom. "You know the two machine gun dummies I've got on the mounts?" Rusty was referring to the wooden replicas he'd carved and painted that the Coast Guard occasionally inspected.

Tom leaned forward, too, their heads almost touching. "What about them?"

Rusty was into his fourth or fifth beer now and his words were, if anything, more precise. "Well, the forward one is real, the wood cover is the dummy!" He gave a huge wink, his snowy eyebrow threatening to leave his face. "Me and Vinny found it a couple of years ago at a fucking yard sale. The barrels were plugged with lead but we managed to melt it out without damaging it. Dave helped us get some shell casings and belts. Then we made a mold and a loader. We've got about a thousand rounds buried in the bilge." He winked again. "You never know."

Tom sat back astounded. This World War II warrior was a constant surprise to him. *Well*, he thought, *we've got a Navy, the diamond guys were supplying an Army, and all's we need is an Air Force.* And he knew just where to get one.

Just then Vinny came in the door. "Hey, everybody, look who's back!" With a flourish he bowed out of the doorway, and Dave and Chris came in behind him.

"Hey, Dave, where you been, Bro?" a black motorcyclist called from a corner booth beneath a huge set of shark's jaws.

"Out in Texas, Homes. How you doin'?" Dave smiled and waved. He had a large duffel bag over his shoulder and as he set it down next to the bar, he called, "Hi, everybody. Mikos, I've got that part made up for your compressor." He gestured to a slim, dark, curly haired man with a thin mustache. Mikos waved and shouted over the din.

"I'll get it tomorrow, Davey. *Efaristo.*" Thank you in Greek.

"*Pa-ra-ka-lo,*" Dave answered -- you're welcome.

Chris walked over to Tom and Rusty, and slumped into a vacant chair. First she leaned over and kissed the old fellow on the cheek, and then Tom gave her a dazzling smile and patted her rump. "You look beat, Nick." Tom chuckled at his lame joke. "How was the trip?"

"Oh, the sailing was all right, though we had to motor about half way. But the asshole owner didn't want to pay us all the money we'd agreed upon. Dave finally took the boat out into the bay and threatened to pull the hoses off the thru-hulls if he didn't pay up. Then he wanted to give us a check but I put my foot down. Cash or down she goes. I gave him half an hour to come up with the dough. He made it by five minutes." She was tired and babbling and knew it but didn't care. "The good news is that David called Skip, Chip, Flip -- damn, I can never remember his name -- and he had a corporate jet coming back from Houston so we got a free ride back." She slumped back in the chair as Dave pulled up a seat and handed her a tall glass of iced-tea. "Oh, thank you, baby. That looks so good." She impishly smiled at him and patted his hand.

"So where is the bodacious Ms. Locarno, Tom? Did you kill her in New York?" Dave asked offhandedly, swigging from his own iced tea.

Tom gave him a rundown on the previous days' activities and finished by pulling a roll of cash from his jacket pocket. "Here's our seed money for this little venture. Alex has her share with her, and she and the family will be waiting for us. I've worked out the frequencies and locations with her." Tom sipped his beer. He tentatively said, "You know, she's not that bad at all."

"Ooohhh, Tommy's got a girlfriend," Chris ribbed him. Both Rusty and Dave grinned. "I'm going back into the kitchen and see if Charlie Potts needs some help. You boys work out whatever details you need to and I'm going to bed as soon as I can get away."

"Okay, babe. Later." Dave quickly kissed her and sat back down. The night was humid and the packed humanity only increased the heat. He gestured to Joanie who was tending bar to turn up the ceiling fans. She gave him a thumbs up, and the multi-colored fans increased their stirring of hot air.

"Okay, Tom, you're fairly certain that the VanHerff people will follow us to Guatemala?"

"Guatemala? Shit, they're probably outside right now!" He glanced over his shoulder anxiously. "Dave, those are some bad dudes. We sure as hell better convince them that the Colombians are emerald miners. Meanwhile, I think we'd better be off and running in the morning. I don't think we're going to have as much time as we had hoped. This guy's going to fly soon."

"Okay, relax. We'll leave in the morning. Rusty, you and Vinny'd better do the same. We'll meet you at the pre-arranged spot. We've got all the gear? Everybody got a personal weapon besides the long guns?" Nods all around. "Good, get some sleep and leave at dawn." He paused. "Just in case, do the women have weapons?"

Rusty nodded. "Anna's got that little Ladysmith I got her and a shotgun. Joanie has a Mini-14 that she keeps under the bunk. Charlie's got his .45 in the kitchen and also another one under the bar. Chris?" He raised his eyebrows.

"Yeah, yeah, don't worry about Chris." Time was short. He was tired and getting testy. "Tom, why don't you sleep here tonight and we'll get an early start."

"Early start for where?"

"Well, how do you think we're getting to Guatemala? Walking? I figure our pal Col. Sykes owes us a little something. So we'll just borrow that Comanche we saw."

Tom's eyes lit up. He and Dave were on the same wavelength. He stood and clapped Dave on his broad back. "Pally, you're a wonder. But you know they'll follow and try to get it back."

"Good," Dave smiled a wicked grin. "Now we'll have two armies fighting the damn druggies. We ought to be able to get lost in the shuffle."

After Chris asked Charlie to close up for the night, she and Dave strolled out onto the rear deck. The moon hung low on the horizon lighting up the small offshore spoil islands with a surrealistic silvery glow. The pathway led from the end of the dock out into the gulf like a silver road. They stood a moment with their arms around each other.

"How many more nights will we have like this, babe?" Dave asked, giving Chris a gentle squeeze.

"Lots, I hope," she answered leaning into him. "Why? Are you scared?"

Dave thought for a minute. "Yeah, I guess so. I hope so. It'll keep me on my toes. But we've never come up against a group like this before. If we can pull this one off, I swear I'll stick to deliveries from now on. Jesus, babe, I just hope none of this comes back to haunt us."

"I know. But if it hadn't been for your D.I.D. syndrome, you wouldn't be concerned about this."

"Aw, I know," Dave smiled. "But how can we say no? She needed help."

"David, they all need help. But why is it you and Tom always fall for their sob stories?" Before he could answer, she said, "Aw, hell, I liked Alex, too. And, yes, she and her family do need help, but you better be careful." She grabbed him by the ears with her small hands and pulled his face down until they were nose to nose. Very seriously she said, "You better come back to me in one piece."

He started to open his mouth to reassure her, but she placed a finger against his lips and went on. "And I'm holding you responsible for Tom and Rusty and Vinny. You do what you have to do and come back. Now let's go below and make love."

Dave slid the hatch back and helped Chris down the companionway ladder. The sailboat floated gently in her slip, the small wavelets slapping against the hull. At the base of the ladder, Dave took Chris in his arms and kissed her deeply. She kissed him back with a pent up fervor, arms wrapped tightly around his neck. Chris stumbled back and fell on the starboard settee pulling Dave down on top of her. Never once taking her mouth from his, she tore at him, shredding the old T-shirt. Dave was mildly surprised and pleased.

Chris loved Dave's chest. He had broad flat pectoral muscles and just enough hair to make kissing him interesting. His flat stomach was covered with a tapering arrow of hair, which seemed to point south. She covered his chest with kisses, gently pulling at his nipples. Chris squirmed out from under him. She quickly stepped out of her shorts and rolled her panties down until they were just a line across her pelvis. Reaching behind her, she unsnapped her bra and let it hang. She knew Dave liked to remove the rest himself.

She was warm. No, hot. She grinned seductively and straddled him, a knee on each side grinding her pelvis into him, kissing him all the while. Her hot breath left a trail of kisses down his chest and belly. She held firmly to his love handles and he lifted his hips and slipped out of his cut off shorts, letting them drop to the deck. Dave slipped his hands under her T-shirt and felt the weight of her breasts, kneading them, lifting one, then the other. He pulled a nipple into his mouth through the thin fabric, pulling the bra aside. She moaned and pulled his head hard against her. Dave pulled her T-shirt over her thrown back head and tossed both it and the bra across the narrow space onto the opposite settee. He slipped her panties off, an inch at a time.

And then he was in her, deeply. She groaned and squeezed her legs against his hips, rocking back and forth, side to side, making circular motions. Dave lifted his hips to meet her, his strong hands holding tightly to her waist as if she were a bronc and he was a helpless cowboy just trying to stay on for the mandatory eight seconds. She pulled his face into her cleavage, holding him there tightly while Dave moved his hands to her hips, cupping, lifting, and pulling.

Chris moaned deep inside, an animal like growl. She was moving faster now, almost vibrating. Dave held on for all he was worth, loath to break contact. He knew the signs, she was approaching her climax. He was just meat now, a hard jut of flesh that she was using for her own gratification. He felt the heat beginning to build inside him. When his climax came, it was fast and hard, and almost violent. He squeezed her buttocks hard against him and clamped his teeth down on her shoulder.

But Chris was beyond caring now. She pulled him deep inside her and ground her pelvic bone against his, hard, fierce, and unrelenting. The cries came out of her, "Unh, unh, unh!" The last long and drawn out, against his ear like the last gasp of a steam engine. Her damp hair hung down over his face, his chest soaked where they'd rubbed together. They panted in unison, trying to regain their breath, Dave twisting his head from side to side, slower and slower until he was spent. He was glad that Chris was rarely multiple orgasmic. Though she was small, he was sure she'd kill him if this went on much longer.

She was collapsed on top of him now, dragging in great breaths, her weight almost dead, her skin glowing with that sexual afterglow women get. He rubbed his hands over her back and buttocks smoothing, wiping, soothing. She liked this after play, the touching and rubbing. She stroked his hair back, the way she liked it, smooth and slick. With a last gasp, Chris felt him slip out and she rolled off him with a sigh. They sat next to each other, feet up on the table. Dave slipped into the head and ran the water until it was hot. He wet two washcloths and brought her one. They sat, the warm cloths between their legs. In a few minutes, they went to bed in the big aft cabin.

When Chris woke in the morning, Dave was gone.

CHAPTER 11

In the early morning stillness, Rusty eased the throttles forward. The twin Caterpillar diesel engines grumbled, the wake churning brown water in the shallows. Vinny stood on the stern and waved to Ruth and Anna, a big grin splitting his face. As the big boat rounded a point of land, the tiny marina was lost from view. Vinny sighed and began coiling up the thick dock lines and stored them in deck boxes on either side. He soon joined Rusty at the helm and handed him a thick white ceramic mug of black coffee. Rusty thanked him and swung the wheel to port, pointing the dark green craft toward the open waters of the Gulf of Mexico. As they got out farther and into deeper water, Rusty eased the throttles forward. At 20 knots the big boat started to lift onto a plane and at 30 knots just barely skimmed the tops of the light waves. Rusty kept pushing the throttles forward until the craft just touched 40 knots, almost 50 miles an hour. The turbo-charged Cat diesels were roaring like top fuel dragsters and the boat fairly flew. Vinny had to turn his U.S. Navy ball cap backwards or he'd lose it. The coffee cup was stable in his hand, the deck under his feet solid. On either side of the helm were the twin 20mm guns in their surrounding metal cages. He had an urge to climb into one and pop off a few rounds.

"Wow, this is really something, Rus!" Vinny had to scream over the engine and wind noise to make himself heard. Rusty frowned and shook his head.

He punched a button and put the steering on autopilot while he fished around under the instrument panel in a small horizontal locker and came up with a lightweight earphone and microphone. He gestured for Vinny to put one on while he donned his and pointed to a plug on the dash in front of Vinny's seat. Vinny plugged in and suddenly he could hear his big friend breathing. He repeated his earlier statement.

"Shhhh, Vin, I can hear you fine. Emile helped me rig these up with noise filters and all. You just have to talk in a normal voice." His own voice was crystal clear and deep, just a touch of a rasp in it.

"This is fine. I've never been out with you when you've really opened it up. Is this as fast as it will go?"

Rusty glanced at the instruments and shrugged, "Maybe another 3 or 4 knots. We might be able to pick up 5 or 6 but we'd have to change the props. I don't think we need to go any faster. We'll be at the rendezvous point tomorrow about this time. Why don't you go below and make us some breakfast, then you can spell me at the helm.

Vinny saluted and said, "Aye, aye, skipper!" and slid below.

"Thanks, little buddy," Rusty mumbled to himself.

Tom and Dave had departed from Tampa International on an early morning flight to Houston. There, they picked up an Avis mini-van, tossed their gear in back and headed for the Army base to the north. An hour's drive with Dave at the wheel brought them to the long line of chain link fencing. Two rows of barbed wire crowned the twelve-foot high fence, and warning signs were posted every thirty-feet notifying them that this was a government preserve and no trespassing was allowed.

They sat quietly in the van, their eyes taking everything in. To their left was the main entrance. A small guard house controlled an electric gate that slid open every once in a while to admit a car or allow a truck to leave. Overhead, Dave could see an occasional black helicopter flitting about.

Tom spoke, "Look over to the right where the road goes." He pointed with his chin, "That row of trees looks like officer's quarters. The barracks are in back. Behind them should be the flight line before the hangers."

"Okay, you get things ready. I'll do a quick recon and then we'll hit 'em at about nine, just after dark. I'd rather have a week or two to get to know the guards' routines, but we haven't got that much time." He grinned at Tom. "These guys are amateurs. We'll be gone before they know it." Dave slithered into the back where he changed into a pair of tight cycling shorts and a multi-colored jersey. He slipped into a pair of hard sole cycle shoes and slid the door back. Tom helped him pull the folding mountain bike out of its shipping box and assemble it. Dave buckled himself into a black helmet and finally pulled on a pair of narrow mirrored sunglasses.

"Give me a couple of hours and I'll meet you at that bar over there. While you're there, see what you can pick-up." He hopped onto the bike and was away, easily slipping into the rhythm of a long ride. The narrow road completely circled the base with an occasional side road peeling off and either going back toward town or out into the scrub-covered hills.

Dave rode easily, the exercise feeling good. He noted every building, tried to figure out what it was, and memorized its location. Toward the northwest corner was the smaller hanger they'd flown into. The Comanche was parked on the tarmac outside.

He could barely make it out, but when the road was clear, he pulled a small yet powerful pair of binoculars out of his rear shirt pocket. Yep, it was the Comanche, the latest military attack chopper just now undergoing tests before full acceptance. It squatted like an ungainly bug, low and mean, its five bladed rotor drooping. He slowed and came to a stop. A light breeze swirled dust around his feet. A pilot was alighting from the chopper. Dave carefully zoomed in and focused. *Well, well! What do you know!* It was their old friend Colonel Sykes. Dave watched him toss his helmet to a waiting aide, then climb into a Humvee and speed away. But what he saw next was even more gratifying. A fuel truck pulled up next to the black helicopter and began filling its fuel tanks.

"Yo, Mama! Thank you Col. Sykes!" Dave whispered to himself.

Dave reversed his direction and tried to keep Sykes' vehicle in view. He saw the elaborate eagle, a Colonel's symbol painted on the back. It disappeared into the trees and Dave didn't want to take a chance pulling the binoculars out so close to the front gate. He rode on the other way, circling the base in the opposite direction, noting features, hiding places, access roads, dips in the fence, adjacent properties and other helpful landmarks. He noted a spot at the base of the fence where an early spring rainstorm had eroded a small gully and hadn't been filled in. About a quarter mile away stood the entry road to an abandoned farm where ramshackle buildings seemed to lean against each other. Once more around and he saw a small tree leaning against the fence, touching the barbed wire. It was green and healthy, so the fence wasn't electric.

Satisfied, he returned to the van that was parked on a dusty side street near the Easy Rider Bar. In the back, Dave hurriedly changed back into jeans and a T-shirt, and slipped his feet into a pair of Nikes.

Inside the bar, Tom had a small crowd of fresh-faced pilots around him, and was making aerial motions with his hands, simulating combat maneuvers. The eager pilots asked lots of questions about the war and some even were retelling anecdotes from their own experiences during Desert Storm.

Dave ordered a Sam Adams longneck from the bar tender. "How long's he been going on like that?"

The bartender, a short, pony-tailed Mexican with a Zapatta mustache shrugged, "About an hour. Has he done all that stuff he been saying?"

"Yep. And more he won't talk about." Dave took a long swig of his beer and turned, leaning back with his elbows on the bar. He watched Tom, his too loud voice reverberating in the small bar. Tom had on his old leather flight jacket with a pair of tarnished wings pinned to the left breast. His gold-framed aviator sunglasses hung on one side from an ear. He kept smoothing his hair back with a slim hand, all the while waving the other. At a lull between stories, he spotted Dave at the bar and gave him a barely perceptible wink and a nod.

"Barkeep, another round for my friends, here."
He casually tossed a hundred-dollar bill on the
table. "Boys, I've got to run. I'll see you all later.
Remember, roll off that throttle nice and easy now,
ya hear?" And with that he stood, jammed his ball
cap on his head and strode past Dave and out the
door. There was an excited murmur around the table
as the younger pilots gossiped about the "old man."

Dave took his time finishing his beer, left a five
on the damp bar, and casually left. Tom was leaning
against the side of the van, hands deep in his
pockets when he turned the corner.

"Excuse me, General MacArthur, but we are
supposed to sneak back into town. The operative
word was "sneak," remember?" Dave gave him a
disgusted look.

"Aw, shit, Dave. I was keeping a low profile
but one of those boys remembered me from when
we brought in the Cobra. He was real suspicious at
first, but I told him I was regular Army and was
spearheading an inspection team that would
probably be replacing Sykes. They all wanted to
kiss my ass after that. Bright boys." He climbed into
the driver's side of the mini-van while Dave
relaxed.

"Where we going?" Dave asked, his head
thrown back with his seat in the fully reclined
position.

"Back to Houston. I need a few things before
we go in. Did you find a good entry point?"

"Yeah. Piece of cake. But we'll probably need
a diversion."

Tom nodded thoughtfully. "That's what I was thinking, too. That's why we're going back to the city."

"What do we need?" Dave asked sleepily.

"Well, I thought a bucket, some sterno, a couple of small propane bottles, a half dozen shotgun shells. And, oh, yeah, some gel caps."

"Let's just not kill anybody, okay? Those guys looked like nice kids." He was silent for a minute, squirming to get into a more comfortable position. "So what did you find out that was useful?"

"Well, the Comanche is guarded at all times. That's why the diversion. It's also kept fueled at all times, in case Sykes wants to take a ride. A bunch of rent-a-cops in Jeep Cherokees patrol the perimeter. The Jeeps are air conditioned so they can't hear diddly-squat outside. And it's supposed to be hot tonight." He thought for a minute. "Oh, yeah, Sykes doesn't let anybody fly it but him and some Lieutenant Hooper. Or Cooper. And the flyboys don't like Sykes. That's about it."

Tom hunched over the wheel as they approached Houston's outskirts. In a few minutes he left the highway and pulled into a small strip mall with a pharmacy, a small hardware store, a pawnshop, a deli, and an office supply store.

Dave stayed in the car while Tom shopped. When he came back, he handed Dave a paper shopping bag full of supplies. Then went into the deli. In a few minutes he returned with another bag, this one with the heavy, sweet aroma of corned beef. Dave inhaled deeply and smiled. Tom must be

planning something extremely odious for him to
spring for food without being asked.

"Have we got everything?" Dave asked, now
awake and salivating.

"Yup, I've got what I need. Let's go back out
to that park along the river we passed. Well eat and
grab some Z's before tonight.

"Sounds good to me."

The rumble of the PT boat's engines hadn't
diminished, but after a couple of hours, a person can
get used to anything. The day had passed
uneventfully except when a low flying Coast Guard
SH-60 Sea Hawk helicopter had passed overhead.
Rusty had beaten the pilot to the radio and had
identified himself as PT-108 registered out of St.
Petersburg, Florida, on a fishing trip with friends.
Fortunately the pilot knew him, being out of the
Coast Guard Station on Sand Key, just south of
Clearwater Beach. They chatted for a few minutes,
and then the chopper swung back to the mainland.

They saw no one, passed no one, and met no
one. It was as if they were in an overturned bowl,
just the blue sky and the bluer water. They were
lucky; the water was still with only a three or four
knot breeze blowing. Behind the windscreen, it was
calm. Rusty had on a tape of Duke Ellington, and he
and Vinny grinned at each other occasionally. Once
in a while they could see Cuba, way off on the
southern horizon, but Rusty had plotted a course to

stay away. He thought they could pretty well outrun anything the Cubans had, but best not to test that theory. They'd head south soon, through the Yucatan Channel, keeping in international waters as much as possible. It was almost 16 hundred hours and they'd been running at just about forty knots for ten hours. Five-hundred miles.

Rusty smiled to himself. When he'd been with the PT's in the big one, WWII, prowling along the coast of New Guinea, their range had been barely five-hundred miles. Well, the Cats and expanded fuel capacity had changed all that. He'd seen later models come out in the fifty's, all aluminum, and with much more powerful Packard aircraft engines, but they still topped out at forty or forty-one knots. And he'd bet they couldn't keep it up like this, hour after hour. He patted her instrument panel fondly, checking the gauges as he always did. Once Vinny got over his fear of the speed, he'd roamed the deck, sitting in all the gunner's chairs, swinging the guns around onto imaginary targets. He even kneeled down and looked into the back of the fake torpedoes, spinning the little propellers like a kid. Rusty jiggled the wheel a little and Vinny had to grab a lifeline for balance. He glared at the big man then smiled.

On the instrument panel was mounted a new GPS satellite receiver and a radarscope, supplanting the older style scopes that were fitted late in the war. Nothing on the horizon. Cuba was obscured from view. Nothing on the scope out to ten miles. He reached out and clicked a knob on the Raytheon

R11XX receiver, stepping the range out to twenty-four miles, then thirty-two miles. Nothing. At the edge of the thirty-two-mile range, a fuzzy series of blips stood out, just barely visible. Rusty reached under the counter and pulled out a pair of reading glasses. He checked the range and compared it to the GPS latitude and longitude figures. It had to be Cabo Catoche, the northernmost tip of Mexico's Yucatan Peninsula. He throttled back slightly and Vinny came running at the change in pitch of the motors.

"What's up, Big guy?"

"Nothing, we're just a little ahead of schedule." The light was slowly fading and the sun was beginning to streak the western sky. "I'll tell you what, I'm going to bring us back to about thirty knots. Why don't you go make us a great spaghetti dinner? When it's ready, I'll slow us down, and we can eat out on deck here. Okay?"

"Yeah, sure, Rusty. That's a good idea. I'll make us some garlic bread, too, with those rolls you got. Don't worry about me, I can find everything." Vinny's head disappeared below, still talking. Rusty sat back in his chair and kicked his feet up on the console. He pulled out an old pipe and took his time filling it and tamping it into just the right mixture. At home, Anna didn't let him smoke aboard and didn't like his pipe at all. But out here, he was his own boss, lord and master of his realm, captain and admiral and all the privileges that go with it. He let out a loud, satisfying burp and folded his hands across his lap.

Dave whispered to Tom, "There it is. See that old barn? We'll stash the van there. We can come back for it later or send somebody after it. I rented it for three weeks." It was just full dark and they were crawling down the road, which ran along the fence. Just up ahead, Dave pointed out the hole in the fence. "You ought to be able to get your fat ass under there. Do your stuff and meet me at the chopper. Okay?"

Tom nodded, squinting into the dark. He checked his watch and he and Dave coordinated. "I'll need about ten minutes to get from the barn to here, about twenty to get to where I'm going, a few minutes to set it up, and probably another fifteen to get to the chopper. That's about fifty. Hold until you see me coming, but not more than ten minutes -- if you can hold out that long."

Tom drove slowly past the gate and up the dark road. About two miles from the gate, he slowed, looked both ways and Dave quietly stepped from the van and vanished into the dark. He was wearing black jeans with the rivets blacked out, a navy cotton pullover shirt, a thin black watch cap was in his pocket and a small daypack was over one shoulder. He carried no identification and had no labels in his clothes. If something terrible went wrong, they'd have no idea who he was.

After dropping Dave off in the moonless night, Tom continued around the base road and looked for

the abandoned farmhouse. As he came abreast of
the turnoff, he quickly doused his lights and,
avoiding the brake lights, made the turn. The dusty
road was about one-hundred yards long and turned
into a parking area between the old house and the
barn, hiding him from the road. Taking no chances,
Tom eased to a stop using the emergency brake.
After ascertaining that there was room in the barn
for the van, he again eased it forward until it was
totally hidden from view. Satisfied, he broke a
sapling branch off and, walking backwards with his
larger pack on his back, swept the area before him
of tire marks and footprints. He and Dave were both
wearing latex gloves and earlier in the day had
wiped the van completely of anything they might
have touched. Tom had also burned all the papers
tying them to the van.

When Tom reached the lonely highway, he
tossed the stick in the ditch and began jogging
toward the fence gap. Only once did he have to
flatten himself in the ditch when a car passed. In a
few minutes he was at the hole in the fence, pushed
his pack through and followed it. No more than a
half-mile from the clump of trees where the
officer's housing was situated, he stood still for a
long minute, letting the night sounds come to him,
searching for an odd or out of place noise. The
crickets chirped, the cicadas sang their song, and
that was all.

By now his eyes were accustomed to the dim
light, pupils fully dilated. He slipped the pack straps
over his shoulders and dropped to the ground,
humping across the empty, open ground. In eight

minutes, by his watch, he came to the trees. The trees bordered a narrow road between a double row of brick, government style houses with small neat lawns and an occasional vehicle parked in the driveway or out front. He crept behind the houses on the north side, frequently glancing between them to see if he recognized Col. Sykes' Hummer. At the last house, he saw it, parked on the street in front. There were no lights on downstairs and only one light on in a small back window. Tom slipped the pack from his shoulders and propped it up against the wall behind a bush. The hedge was waist high and gave about one-foot clearance between it and the brick wall of the house. If anyone walked by, he would see Tom unless he already knew he was there.

Tom poured gasoline from a one-gallon can into the metal bucket he removed from the pack. On top of that he pushed a circle of cardboard, fitting it tightly to the edge of the bucket. Then he ran down to the street in a low crouch, and placed the bucket under the Hummer's fuel tank. He ran back to the pack and pulled out a round wire rack, a can of sterno, and a pair of Coleman propane cylinders. Taking a lighter from his pants pocket, he lit the sterno. It burned with a quiet, nearly invisible blue flame.

Tom cackled to himself. Screw them out of twenty- grand, eh? He'd show Sykes. Next Tom took the sterno and the propane cylinders down and carefully put them into the bucket, one cylinder on top of the sterno and the other beside it. He knew he had about ten minutes before it went off.

Swiftly Tom gathered his remaining supplies and started running for the last of the trees. Before him was a line of low maintenance buildings, then a flight line with Cobras parked on it.

Time to be very careful now.

He sat with his back against a building and pulled out three glass containers the size of small pickle jars. Pulling out his trusty gasoline can, he poured just three or four drops into each jar. From his breast pocket, he removed a small bottle of a colorless liquid. Carefully, moving his lips while he counted, he put three drops into each jar and quickly capped them, tossing the small bottle into the last one. He turned the jars so the gasoline was distributed evenly over the whole inside of the jar. The rest of the gasoline he emptied on the ground and tossed the empty can into a dumpster outside one of the buildings. He placed one jar by each door where he saw a light. He placed them so that when the door was swung open, it would knock the bottle off the cement step. That should be enough to make them break.

Tee-Hee! The bottles were now the equivalent of about a half stick of dynamite each. That ought to keep the curious inside!

As he slid carefully around the end of the last building and prepared to make a run for the smaller hanger in the distance, two things happened. He heard a helicopter just winding up in preparation to lighting off. Just before the pilot dumped the fuel to it, a tremendous explosion rocked the night behind him.

Although he knew he must move, and fast, Tom turned his head in time to see a geyser of flame light up the night, and poised on top of the flame was the Humvee in a slight nose down position. The flame looked like the Hummer was equipped with a rocket engine and was attempting a low earth orbit. With a crash, the Hummer embedded itself into the roof of the last house on the block, still shooting flames. When the sterno had heated the propane bottles to the explosion point, they had burst through the bottom of the Hummer's fuel tank. The blast had put out the fire in the sterno can, but by that time, the gasoline in the bucket had ignited and, coupled with the twenty-five or so gallons in the Hummer's tank, had caused the vehicle to go orbital.

Tom grinned in the dark. Take that, asshole.

He lurched to his feet and made a beeline for the now churning helicopter that was dancing on its wheels, barely touching the ground. Behind him he heard a smaller explosion, then another. No one came behind him. In a crouching run he ducked under the blades and pulled open the gunner's door. Dave gave him a thumbs up, and Tom slipped into his helmet, buckled his harness, and flipped down the heads up display. The layout was similar to the Cobra's and he didn't have any trouble locating switches, knobs, and touch screens.

As soon as Dave saw he was secured, he jumped the agile bird up and around the back of the building. He kept low and barely cleared the fence, dropping momentarily to go under a power line.

They were on their way. The fly-low radar kept Dave appraised of ground undulations and obstacles in their path. They were now speeding along at over 180 miles per hour and climbing. The heads up displays kept him in constant touch with engine speed and temperature, fuel consumption, rotor speed, direction, and even latitude and longitude. The amber numbers flickered rapidly on the lexan windscreen as they sped along. In a few moments they cleared the coast, and Dave eased them down until they were just above the water. He knew the radar absorbing skin and angles of the Comanche would make it almost impossible to see them.

Their speed was now over two hundred miles per hour, and radar indicated a few ships to either side, but none directly in their path. In front of him, Tom fiddled with the radio frequency, occasionally getting a blurb of talk. He was looking for the military frequency that would indicate pursuit. He exhausted all their old frequencies and started slowly moving through the channels. In a few minutes he got a squawk from a definite military voice.

"Military helicopter, number alpha, Nancy, tango, four, niner, niner, do you copy, over?" Tom grinned and turned to look at Dave. He thumbed a button to change to the cockpit frequency.

"Uh, Father," Tom addressed Dave, do you think he means us?"

"I don't know, Thomas. Why don't you stick your head outside and see what our designation is?"

"No need, Father, I have a piece of paper taped to the instrument panel with those very call letters. I think we should reply, don't you? They must be very worried about this magnificent machine." Tom chuckled, "Would you allow me the honors?"

"Why, of course, Thomas. Please notify him of our expected destination."

"Thank you, Father." Tom prepared a little speech in his head and thumbed his external radio button. "This is alpha, Nancy, tango, four, niner, niner, military helicopter in flight. What can I do for you guys?"

Col. Sykes' enraged voice filled the speakers and Tom had to lower the volume. "Who is this? You son of a bitch, I'll have you shot down unless you return that chopper immediately!"

"Now, now, Sykes, temper, temper. We're just taking this bird for a little joy ride down Guatemala way. We ought to be back in a week or so. Don't get your military issue panties in a knot."

The amber glow in the cockpit lit up smiles on both Dave's and Tom's faces.

Sykes sputtered, "You know me? How the hell do you know me?" He was silent a moment, then it came to him, "Novak? Novak? You rat bastard civilian puke, I ought to call the Air Force and have them shoot your ass down. I…"

Tom cut him off, "Sykes, you now owe me another fifty grand. You want your chopper, come and get it. And don't bullshit me about shooting me down. If the Air Farce ever found out you let a civilian borrow one of your toys, you'll be the

laughing stock of the Airedales. We'll be
vacationing in the big G. You want us? Come and
get us. This is alpha, Nancy, tango, four, niner,
niner over and out."

Tom clicked around and found an FM station
broadcasting dance music. He sat back humming to
himself, eyes closed. Dave had taken them up to
five hundred feet and had throttled back to an even
two hundred miles per. At this rate, they'd be at the
rendezvous point in about three hours. He had
carefully checked the weather and tested his
portable GPS against Rusty's. They had agreed to
about one to two seconds difference - insignificant
in a huge ocean with good visibility. Rusty had
installed a differential beacon receiver, which
improved the accuracy from about one-hundred
meters to about ten meters. Dave knew that all
military GPS receivers already had this option built
in.

The GPS receivers used a ring of satellites to
pinpoint their place on the earth below, whether on
land or sea. The receivers gave locations in degrees,
minutes, and seconds, both latitude and longitude.
The helicopter-mounted units even gave altitude, so
when Dave and Rusty worked out a rendezvous
point, they would meet within thirty feet in the dark.

Tom woke from his nap with a start. He'd been
dreaming about standing on a ledge in the rain
naked and being shot, the bullet entering his side.
He was doing a slow motion dive, falling, falling.
Then he woke up. Good thing, too. There wasn't
any dumpster full of garbage in his dream.

He checked his instruments. About ten minutes to their rendezvous. Dave was humming along with the radio. He'd switched to a country and western station, and Tom listened to Johnny Cash sing something about getting married in a fever, hotter'n a pepper sprout. Well, the next week would be hotter'n the halls of hell for them all. But -- and this was the big BUT -- if they could convince the Colombians that the VanHerff people were a rival dope cartel, and convince the VanHerff people that the Colombians were mining white emeralds and intended to flood the market, and convince Sykes' guys that the Colombians had the test chopper and the VanHerff guys were running dope, too, they might pull it all off. *Yeah, right,* Tom thought to himself.

"Oh, Father, we're almost out of fuel. Is there a petrol station out here somewhere?"

"Yes, my son. Yonder lie our colleagues with a floating fuel barge." Dave indicated a steadily flashing light aimed at them. He checked his GPS. "Damn, right on target." Dave thumbed his hand held VHF Radio. "PT, PT, this is Big Bird, over."

"Got ya, Big Bird. Cradle is ready for baby. Bring her on in."

Dave turned the big chopper sideways to the slowly moving PT boat and carefully set the cockpit down on the pre-rigged wooden rails Rusty and Dave had installed the previous week. As soon as they were down, Vinny flipped two pair of straps over the gunner's cockpit and the tail boom and cranked them tight.

Dave and Tom hopped down onto the deck. "So how was the trip, fellas?" Dave asked hugging Rusty. Tom grinned widely and slapped Vinny on the back.

"Oh, boy, Dave, Tommy, the weather has been beautiful. This old boat runs like a dream - after you get used to the noise." He laughed and gripped Tom's hand.

The boat wallowed a bit with the nearly 4,000 extra lbs. of weight on deck, but the moon was full and the night was warm, and the 90 ft. boat could handle it. Dave stripped off his shirt and said, "Let's get to it guys. Vinny, give me a hand with the fuel. Tom, will you give Rusty a hand with the guns and supplies? I want to get this bird off and landed in Locarnoville before sunup. And that's in …" Dave checked his watch, "in about two and a half hours."

They worked quickly, Rusty handing duffel bags and boxes up to Tom's waiting hands. Tom stored the gear in every available nook and cranny of the attack helicopter. Dave climbed up on top of the cockpit and stuffed the fuel hose into the opened filler neck. Below, Vinny called, "Say when, Dave."

He stood with his hand on a switch and when Dave called down, "Let 'er rip!" Vinny hit the button and the newly installed fuel pump whirred into life. Dave felt the hose harden in his hand and the fuel gushed into the chopper's tank. Vinny watched the huge fuel bladder wobble and slowly sink into itself as the fuel transferred gallon by gallon. He knew the aircraft used about sixty-five gallons an hour and held about two-hundred and fifty gallons which gave it a range of about seven-hundred and fifty miles, depending on airspeed and combat maneuvers. The fuel bladder held five-hundred gallons. The balance they would transfer into the boat's tanks, and then roll up the bladder and lash it on deck.

In a few minutes Dave could hear the gurgle of the tank topping off. "That's it, Vin!" he shouted and almost immediately, the flow slackened, then stopped. Vinny poked his head out the hatch.

"Reach behind you, Tommy, and unscrew the fuel filler there by your left foot, will you?"

"I'll get it," said Rusty reaching up and taking the hose from Dave. He handed it to Tom who was unscrewing the deck filler. In a minute they had the hose in and Vinny had started the pump again. Fuel once again filled the hungry boat tanks.

Dave wiped his hands on a small towel then slipped into his T-shirt. Tom was throwing the last small bag under his seat. "Let's get going, Dave. Time's a wasting."

"Okay. Vin, Rusty, you know what to do from here?"

"Yeah, Dave, we're going to take the boat over to Belize City, check in with Customs. They're going to search the boat. Thoroughly. Vinny and me are going to give them some free drinks, grease a few palms, and tell them we're going fishing. Then we'll head south for a place called Punta Gorda. We'll keep the radio on all the time and wait for your call. Meanwhile," he stopped for a minute and removed his captain's hat and scratched his thinning

white hair, "we'll fish." He smiled mischievously at
Dave.

"Good, you guys do that. Meanwhile, nose
around, look for Colombians and top up the tanks.
Be ready to go on a moment's notice. We'll see you
in a few days." He touched them both on the arm
and stood looking at them, his friends. So far from
home, away from family and all because of him.
For him. Well, he'd do his best to keep them safe
and out of trouble. "'Bye guys."

Dave turned and strode across the hardwood
deck and once again climbed into the pilot's seat.
Tom was already settled and had his helmet and
HUD settled on his head. The howl from the first
turbine stage was still at a low growl, the blades
still. In a few seconds, the whine went out of human
hearing range and the second stage started turning
up, the rotor lazily gathering speed like an old man
with a hotfoot.

Dave pulled his harness tight and scanned the
myriad of instruments. The fuel gauges read full,
the temperature gauges were all in the green, and
the oil pressure was up. The rotor tach indicator was
rapidly rising toward 100%. The several computer
displays dominated the cockpit, lighting it with an
eerie glow. Dave waved a hand at Rusty and Vinny.
Vinny slipped below his sight and flipped the
buckles on the hold-down straps. Dave tapped Tom
on the helmet and indicated he had control. With a
last look around, he pulled up on the collective lever
beside his left leg just as Vinny and Rusty
unsnapped the restraining straps. The heavy bird

sprang free of the deck and disappeared into the night.

Rusty looked over at his short friend as the chopper disappeared. "Well, they're in it now, Vin. I guess we better get going. No telling what the satellite images picked up. I'd like to get inside Belize territorial waters in case the Coasties are around. Let's haul butt!" He turned and headed for the helm.

Vinny took the tie down straps to the fantail and secured the folded fuel bladder. It looked like a tarp and that's what they wanted. The engines growled mournfully in the night.

CHAPTER 12

Jonathan Lee Stoner closed his eyes and lifted his voice over the din in the cavernous room. The big, old Martin dreadnought vibrated, the deep bases punching through the smoke and noise and into the conversations at the closest tables. These people knew nothing of the blues, he thought. But Chris was his friend and he was getting paid. Besides, he liked singing the blues and always gave it his best.

Across the room behind the bar, Chris caught his eye, winked and gave him a thumbs up. Jon Lee winked back and improvised a short riff, nimbly flicking the strings. He appraised the house. In a corner booth sat three men in light windbreakers. One was so fair-haired, his hair almost white. He smoked a dark cigarette or a short thin cigar. He was lean, and his eyes were almost closed, squinting, always roving. The second man was heavier, dark, a three-day growth of beard. His clothes were neat so Jon Lee figured the beard was a contrived look. He sipped at a large can of Fosters Lager and tapped his fingers in time with the music. Jon Lee couldn't see the third man well, as his back was to him, but he could tell that the man was big. Not especially tall, but very broad, his neck flowing outward and into the thick shoulders. He noted the tight fit of the jacket across the back and the odd strap outlined under it. A bra strap? Nah, that's no broad.

He took in the rest of the house. The seats at the bar were full with some standees between stools. Chris was tending bar along with Anna. Every once in a while Chris stopped at one place and threw a pair of dice into a low box positioned in front of a white haired fat man. Jon Lee knew the game was known as "Horses" here, but in England where he'd lived and toured, it was Crowders or Shut the Box. You threw the dice and flipped a row of pivoted, wooden numbers down. The last one able to flip the numbers down, won. It was fast, noisy and often invited the players to bet, though he was sure Chris wouldn't allow that. Yeah, right!

The fat man slapped his hand down flat on the bar, the noise a crack like a pistol shot. Jon Lee quickly incorporated it into the song, one he made up as he went along. He saw Chris shake her head disgustedly, draw a draft beer, and slide it down the bar to the fat man. She lost, Jon Lee thought with a grin.

At a table in the center of the room sat two men in Florida Marine Patrol uniforms, the Water Nazis. They were with their wives or girlfriends, Jon Lee couldn't tell which. They touched the ladies a little too often for them to be wives, he thought. Beyond them sat a table full of young women, overweight, over-made-up, and two of them obviously intoxicated. The fatter one, a bleach blonde in a stretched-to-the-limit tube top, was trying to lean her chin on her palm, but it kept slipping off. The other blonde, the one with the dark roots, was glassy eyed and listening to a broad faced Hispanic girl who was speaking incessantly and poking her with a stiffened forefinger. She looked as if she didn't really give a shit one way or the other.

Behind them, against a pillar, sat a dark haired man with a Gilbert Roland mustache and long sideburns. He had a soft, dark cap on his head and a cigarette smoldering in the corner of his mouth. The smoke drifting up, gathering under the brim and leaking out the sides. His chair was leaning back against the pillar. At the table were three companions, hunched forward over their beers, drafts, speaking in low voices and ignoring the music.

Jon Lee had this talent for singing and playing, and evaluating, weighing the crowd at the same time. Even the improvised riffs, the made up songs, came out of one part of his mind, the other part thinking private thoughts.

His gaze came back to the three men in the
corner booth. Nothing new. Jon Lee looked at the
clock. Near midnight. Almost time to wrap it up. He
slipped into his personal refrain, Jimmy's Blues, an
old John Lee Hooker tune, his namesake. Now he
was into the song, wailing, giving it his best, the
powerful lungs ringing, and the deep thunk of the
Martin calling attention to himself. Slowly the room
quieted, people looking up from their conversations,
from their drinks. All eyes were on him now and
Jon Lee wailed his pain, his loneliness, and his
frustrations. The fact that he drove a new Ford
Explorer, lived in a luxury apartment in Belleair
Beach and was educated in England didn't interfere
with his music one bit. He *knew* the blues, or at
least convinced others he did.

Jon Lee finished the tormented song with a
complicated piece of fretwork, which he trailed off
into silence, hunched over the guitar until even the
thrum was quiet. The room was silent, then broke
out into applause, a few scattered "Yeas!" a couple
of whistles and even one "Go Man!" Jon Lee smiled
and stood for a small bow before putting his guitar
back into its hard case. The noise level returned to
its former din.

The clock touched midnight, and Chris reached
up and rang a large brass bell suspended over the
bar. "Last Call," she shouted through cupped hands.
For ten minutes the bar was busy then Chris rang
the bell again three times slowly. The regulars slid
off their stools and raised their drinks to the large
portrait of the deceased former owner, J. Chesney

Campbell. The portrait above the bar was suddenly bathed in light, a black drape across its frame's top.

Chris recited the ritual words and the regulars mouthed them with her, "To Chesney, you old scoundrel. May you look down on all who stop here with affection, love and joy. If not, may you rot in the darkest corner of Hell!"

"Hear, hear," shouted those assembled and sipped their drinks. The new fish asked for an explanation from those nearby. Around the room, the new folk were now regulars and never again would remain sitting during the toast. The crowd slowly drifted toward the door, except the three men who continued to sit in their booth.

Chris started wiping down the bar, tossing empties in the large plastic racks on the floor. Ringo continued sweeping, now between the tables. All night he'd pushed his broom around the periphery of the room, softly humming to himself, suffering occasional jibes with a sad, patient smile, his knit cap pulled low, his long overcoat hanging open. The last remaining patrons were the three men in the corner booth.

Chris walked over. "Let's go guys. It's time to close. Drink up." She reached out to take the empty cans and a large hand gripped her wrist. Suddenly a face thrust close, the sour, beery breath wafting around her. She was afraid, but more angry than afraid. She struggled, trying to pull out of the vise-like grip.

"Would you please tell us the whereabouts of Thomas Novak, Mrs. Manley?" The man with the almost white hair asked casually, as if he were ordering a sandwich. Beside him one of the men moved away as if clearing his hand for anticipated action.

Chris looked him in the eye and leaned her face close. "Let go of my arm right now." The pressure increased and tears of pain came to Chris' eyes. She thought about swatting him with her free hand, thought of smashing a beer can into his white, pocked face, thought of a lot of things but the pain was almost overwhelming.

"His whereabouts, please?" The tone still casual but with more of a bite to it, a hiss like a snake.

"He's in Guatemala, goddammit." She felt as if her arm were in a vise. The white haired man's face was lined and pocked, and in the lines Chris could see a fine white dust, like make-up. The eyes were flat, reptilian, a washed out blue. She wanted to cry out but instead leaned forward and, as if to kiss the man on the cheek, bit down hard on his ear. The pressure on her arm ceased and she was flung backward. Her mouth tasted salty, she noted as she slid backward on the floor

The white haired man exclaimed, "Why, you bitch!" He held his hand to his ear and began reaching under his coat as he swung out of the booth. The big man sitting across from him also started to slide out of the booth. As his feet swung out he suddenly tripped and fell on his face, landing heavily next to Chris, his hands outstretched to break his fall. He was a big, bulky man, his head shaved to a mere bristle but he moved surprisingly quickly for a man his size. Ringo was standing next to him carefully pulling the broom out from between his legs.

"Sorry," he mumbled and continued sweeping, positioning himself between the white haired man and Chris. The white-haired man rose and pulled a gun out from under his short jacket, keeping it close to his side. It was a thin, flat-black automatic and he kept it tucked against his leg. He shoved Ringo to the floor, reached down and hauled Chris to her feet. By this time the thickset, balding man had leapt to his feet and stood in a half crouch, the third man, the bearded one was also in a crouch, his gun out, swiveling left to right looking for a target. The building was quiet, only the harsh breathing breaking the midnight silence.

The white-haired man hissed, "Where are the gems?" pulling Chris close, though not as close as before. He had her by the bicep and was squeezing again, pulling her up on her toes. He placed the barrel of the gun against her right breast and gently stroked up and down. Involuntarily, Chris felt her nipple grow rigid and she felt afraid and ashamed, and tried to pull away again.

"What the hell are you talking about? This is a bar, not a jewelry store." She was playing for time, hoping that someone would notice her and Ringo's predicament. Nothing moved. She'd dimmed the overhead lights so only a glow suffused the huge empty room. David and Tom had warned her that she might be questioned but they conveniently forgot to mention the pain she might have to go through.

The white haired man was speaking again. "Novak came back here. You say he's gone to Guatemala? Is that where the gems are?" He squeezed cruelly and shook her. Chris was expecting to be interrogated but the violence and the rapidity were coming faster than anyone had imagined. She and Dave had gone over what she should say, several times. Tell him but not all at once and make him pull it out of you. Don't fight and once they have what they're after, they'll go away.

Ringo struggled to his feet and swung the broom at the white-haired man, but the one with the beard turned and shot him. Ringo spun and fell, hitting a chair, then fell to the floor and was still, arms outstretched.

Chris screamed, loudly. The white-haired man let go of her arm and grabbed a handful of her hair, pulling her head back. The shot had been loud, deafening those who were standing near. Chris' ears rang. Suddenly another shot rang out and the bearded man grunted, a cherry colored blossom of blood appeared on his shirt above his heart and to the left. He spun around and went down on one knee. Chris could see where the bullet had exited. The back of his jacket was suddenly covered with blood. He was down but not out. His gun was still gripped by almost lifeless fingers, the black metal almost invisible in the gloom. The thickset man snapped off a shot toward the kitchen where Charlie Potts was standing behind the pass-through, a smoking .45 automatic in his thick fist. The bullet whined off a cast iron frypan and whizzed through the wall, making a sort of thock as it went through. Charlie ducked back out of sight, not wanting to chance another shot at an alerted target.

"*Merde*, Boss, we gotta take cover. We're too exposed. Bring the broad." The bearded man grabbed the white-haired man's shoulder and pulled him behind the booth. He dragged Chris by the hair, she fell over backwards and was barely able to catch herself on her outstretched hands. The floor behind her was sticky with blood and she frantically tried to wipe it on her jeans.

"What about Brian, Boss?" The beard peered out at the tableau before him. The body of Ringo Star laid half beneath a table, one leg bent over another, the watch cap askew, a chair overturned and blocking his head. Brian still knelt on the floor, gun in his right hand, blood running down his left arm and dripping in a widening puddle, just beginning to soak into his pant leg. He was in shock from the heavy caliber slug ripping through his upper chest. Though the bullet hadn't penetrated any vital organs, the shock might kill him if they didn't get him help soon. The bearded one knew that it was a large caliber slug that had hit his partner. The entry wound would be minuscule compared to the huge exit wound. As far as he was concerned, Brian was a goner.

"Brian, come here!" Insisted the white haired man.

Brian attempted to rise but only made it a couple of inches before toppling over onto his side. The shock of the heavy .45 slug entering his body had torn up his collarbone, a lot of muscles and tendons. The mushroomed slug had exited, tearing a great cavity of flesh as it did so, ripping through veins and arteries as well. Brian had lost too much blood and was in shock, rapidly slipping into unconsciousness.

"I am afraid Brian is no longer of any use to us. Dieter, you must cover our backs and I will…" Just then another shot rang out, tearing a hole in the upholstery of the booth above Dieter's head. It came from an open window to his right. Dieter could just see the barrel and shot quickly three times. The window shattered and the frame splintered. The one called Dieter pulled the white-haired man lower, behind the wooden booth. As he did so, his grip loosened on Chris' hair.

On the floor, Chris managed to pull free and lashed out with a foot, catching the white-haired man in the shin. He gave a short bark of pain and swung his pistol toward her. She spun, scampering back and under a table, pulling chairs in around her. They were poor protection, she knew, but they were all she had. She moved quickly thrusting furniture out of the way and pulling it behind her. Two shots were fired in her direction. One splintered a chair leg and the other whizzed by her ear. She could hear the crackle of it as it spun past, like an angry bee. She hunched lower, trying to squeeze between the floorboards.

Behind the booth, the white haired man rubbed his shin with his left hand and pointed his gun at her. He was about to squeeze off another round when the top of the booth exploded. The deafening boom made the two men duck even lower. It was a load of double ought buckshot fired from a shotgun. "Shit" Dieter cursed. What had they gotten themselves into?

A voice called out, "Sorry about the booth, Chris!" It was Joanie, crouched on the back porch next to the door, the shotgun almost as big as she was. But Joanie knew how to handle the shotgun, as well as an M-16, a deer rifle, and any manner of handguns. Both Rusty and Vinny made sure their wives knew how to handle weapons. Joanie had grown up on a ranch in Wyoming and her father had bought her a simple single shot .22 when she was ten and put her in charge of the chicken house. She'd bagged her first fox at twelve and a deer at fourteen. She'd helped with the yearly slaughter of the pigs and a beef for the freezer. She was no stranger to blood, but it made her sick to destroy good furniture.

The two men were pinned down behind the booth. Charlie Potts was behind the kitchen pass-through with his .45, Anna was at a side window with a Ruger Mini-14 semi-automatic .223 rifle, and Joanie was at the rear door with the Winchester pump shotgun. Chris was slowly slithering back on her belly. She felt the end of the bar and managed to slip behind it. Farther down, near the cash register was a .357 pistol she kept there for protection. It was a small, aluminum framed Smith & Wesson Air Weight and she was familiar with its feel.

She finally had it in her hand. The heft of it felt comforting. She raised her head until her eyes were level with the top of the bar. "What do you guys want?" she called. No answer. "We have four guns to your two and all exits are covered. You better tell me quick because the cops will be here in a few minutes.

Boettcher gritted his teeth. Damn, they had to get out. "Novak, that's all we want. We want to know where he got the gem." He nudged the man next to him and indicated the front door. Dieter nodded and gathered his energy, preparing for a leap and a run. He knew how difficult it was to hit a running figure, especially with a handgun. They figured that the front door was their best chance since it was closest to a single shooter. Besides, it was dark and they'd only be shadows.

Chris calculated. Dave had told her to tell them but she didn't want to give them too much information. "I told you, Guatemala. I don't know where. Someplace in the north near the Mexican border. I…"

She didn't get a chance to finish. The two men leaped up, firing carefully in the direction of the known shooters and ran for the front door, zigging and zagging from table to post. They both hit the front doors as a volley of shots hit the screens and jamb. Chris had the best shot down the long alley of the bar and back wall. Charlie reached over the pass through and quickly fired off three rounds at the fleeting shadows. Joanie had a direct shot from the rear door but the shadows were indistinct at that distance. What was left of the screen doors was reduced to tatters by the heavy load of buckshot.

Anna managed one shot and she thought she heard an "Ow" but wasn't sure. A few seconds later, they heard a car start and tear up the road.

Chris started to get up but a voice behind her shouted, "Everybody hold your positions until I tell you it's okay" Charlie Potts was moving toward the front door through the kitchen side entrance. "Anna, come around the side until you can see me coming through the front door and cover me. Shoot anything that moves that isn't slim and handsome, like me."

Anna groaned but slipped down the side of the building, staying in the shadows. She poked her head quickly around the side of the building, rifle at her shoulder. Charlie's bulk came through the door, crouching, gun out in front in a two handed grip, whipping from side to side. He made a quick tour around the parking lot and around Dave's workshop. Satisfied, he slipped the safety on and shoved the heavy gun under his belly into his waistline. "Okay, all clear," he shouted as he came back through the remnants of the front door.

"Oh my God, Ringo!" Chris dropped her gun on the bar and ran to where Ringo lay on the floor. "Joanie, Anna, turn on some lights!" she shouted. Chris knelt next to the still form. Ringo lay on his side, a small pool of blood under him. Charlie knelt next to Chris and rolled Ringo over onto his back.

"Ringo, Buddy, are you okay? Where you hit?" Charlie felt along Ringo's arms and legs, up his rib cage and his neck. Nothing. "Check him again," he mumbled. He and Chris carefully inspected the unconscious man until Chris jerked her hand back.

"What 'cha got, Chrissy?"

"He's been shot in the ass." She reached again and said, "Yep, the bullet passed right through his left buttock. For Chrissakes, it's just a nick." She gently slapped Ringo's face. "Come on, sleepy boy, wake up."

Ringo opened one eye. It looked from Chris to Charlie. "My butt hurts. Is it okay to wake up now?" He smiled a toothless grin, a dribble of saliva trickling down his stubbly chin.

"Yeah, Buddy, you're gonna be okay. Yer a hero. You saved our lives!" Charlie helped Ringo to his feet, supporting him under the arm, a hand around his waist.

"I am?" Ringo smiled again and winced as Charlie headed him toward the door.

"Yep, you sure are. Why if it hadn't been for you, we mighta all been killed." Charlie's voice tapered off as he left the building, still telling Ringo what a hero he'd been that night. They all watched until Charlie's taillights disappeared up the road. He was taking Ringo back to the aluminum house trailer they shared. Charlie would take good care of him.

"Well," Joan said, "I guess it's up to us to take out the trash. She toed the remaining body.

"Is he, is he? You know," Chris asked.

"Yeah, dead as a doornail," Anna replied. I checked while you guys were fussing over Ringo." She shook her wiry red curls. She had already slung the rifle over her shoulder and was going through the dead man's pockets. "Aha!" she roughly pulled a roll of bills out of his right front pocket. Anna flipped through the bills. "Must be a grand or more here." She tossed it to Chris. "This ought to take care of the booth and the front doors," she snorted.

Chris smiled and stuffed the roll inside her shirt. "Joanie, would you go into the kitchen and get a couple of Charlie's big garbage bags, please?" She squatted and started slipping the big man's jacket off.

Anna frowned and asked, "What are you doing, Chris?"

"Well, it appears that the cops aren't coming and we'll have a hell of a job explaining a body shot with one of our guns, plus Ringo shot in the ass. Not to mention the whereabouts of the boys, so I figured maybe we'd go fishing tonight."

She shot a glance at Anna who shrugged and said, "We really ought to call the police, you know. Suppose his friends do?"

Joanie came over and joined in the discussion, "Anna, this is the real world. You know what the Sheriff's department is like, especially that big jackass, Reese. They would shut this place down in a minute."

"I suppose, but they did attack us."

"And how are we going to prove it?" Chris asked sharply.

"I don't think his friends will be back looking for him. I think he was an expendable. So we'll expend him." Joanie was already sticking his feet in a garbage bag.

"And we'll burn his clothes and ID and if somebody does find him, they'll have a great deal of trouble identifying him and certainly won't be able to connect him to us." Chris spoke more confidently now.

"Sounds reasonable. Here, let me help you," sighed Anna. She squatted beside Chris and Joan and together they stripped the big man until he was naked on the floor. "Oooh," sighed Anna, looking at the size of the man's genitals. "Look at the size of this guy. Too bad Charlie had to kill him. We could have kept him for a while."

Chris giggled. "Maybe we ought to stretch it out until rigor mortis sets in."

Anna cackled, lifting the limp penis. "As big as he is, maybe we ought to mount it over the bar." The two of them giggled then broke up in gales of laughter, coming down off an adrenaline high.

Joanie came over with another garbage bag under her arm; the shotgun still clutched in her hand. "What are you two hens cackling about?" Chris and Anna had their arms around each other, laughing hysterically. Anna pointed down at the object in question.

"Oh, my," Joan whispered softly.

Chris sputtered, "Anna thinks we ought to mount it over the bar." Again she couldn't stop giggling.

"Are you crazy, we'd lose half our male customers." She appraised the dead naked man. "Let's get him bagged." She began stuffing his clothes into the smaller bag. A little pile of personal belongings lay to one side. "What are we going to do with this stuff?" she indicated the wallet, a pocketknife, a handkerchief a ring of keys and a small gold pinkie ring with a clear stone.

Chris sighed. Dave would want everything destroyed so as to leave no trace. "Bag it with his other stuff. We'll have to burn it all. It's the smart thing to do." She idly flipped through the wallet. No pictures of a wife or family, only a snapshot of the man standing beside a blue Triumph TR-6, three credit cards, two of them international from Swiss banks, an ID card from VanHerff identifying him as Brian Klassen and his position as Security. There was nothing to indicate his address or next of kin.

They slipped the large garbage bag over his feet and managed to work it up and over his hips. While Anna lifted his head and shoulders, Chris and Joanie wormed it up to his neck. That was as far as they could pull it. Old Brian was a big man. Chris tied the loops around his neck. They all stood and admired their work. "Maybe we ought to tie a small bag over his head?" Joanie said sarcastically.

"Why, don't you like him looking at you?" Smirked Anna.

"No, he's giving me the creeps."

Chris reached out and pressed his eyelids down. "There, now it looks like he's sleeping."

"Oh, sure, we always get drunks in here who sleep it off inside big, black garbage bags." Anna cackled again. "Let's get him into the Whaler, and you two youngsters do the deed while I clean up here." The three women tried lifting the corpulent Brian, but his two hundred and fifty-pound frame was just too much for them. Chris finally took one leg under her arm and Joanie the other. With much grunting and cursing, they dragged the inert form out the back door, down the steps, head banging on each step.

"Oops. Sorry old boy," muttered Joanie. They were finally able to roll the body into the back of the 23' Boston Whaler. Anna came toddling down the dock, shuffling, carrying a cement block. "Let's get another one and some coat hangers. No sense having him float around out there."

"Ugh," groaned Chris. "How gross. I don't know if I can do this."

"Yeah, sure you can. This is the asshole who shot Ringo. He'd of shot you if Potts hadn't nailed him. Screw him, he's pond scum." Joanie kicked her boat shoe against the still form. The three women stood on the dock. Anna handed over a half dozen wire coat hangers to Chris.

"Do it and come back. Run out until your depth finder reads over fifty feet and get rid of him. I'll take care of his stuff here." With a farewell hug, she strode up the dock to her odious task.

Chris started the two engines while Joanie threw off the dock lines. In a few minutes, they were out in the Gulf, past Travis Key and headed for deep water. Joanie walked back and untied the plastic bag from the dead Brian. She slid the bag down and with much struggling, pulled it down to his feet. Next Joanie twisted two coat hangers around the now swollen ankles and then around two cement blocks. In a few minutes Chris slowed the boat and slipped the throttles into neutral.

Chris went back and helped Joanie push and shove the naked man into a position bent over the side of the boat. They stood back and studied the plump buttocks. "I can't figure out what men like about this position. I don't find it particularly erotic," pondered Chris.

"Especially one hung like this guy. Can I have one more look?"

Chris and Joanie turned Brian over until he was bent over backwards, his head almost in the water. "Um, nope, still doesn't do anything for me. Guess he's been dead too long. Gimmee a hand." Joanie bent and hefted one of the blocks. Chris lifted the other.

"Ready? One, two, three!" They threw the blocks over the side and the legs followed up and over. For a second the body was poised on the gunwale of the boat, legs spread and then it flipped over and immediately sank beneath the black waves. The last they saw was the body, arms upraised, head thrown back, eyes and mouth open.

"Maybe we should have said something, Chris."

"Yeah, you're right. How about: Fuck you, Brian. May your soul rot in hell forever after. I hope your mother never knows what you became."

"Amen," they chorused. Chris started the engines and headed back toward land.

"You know, at the end, he looked like that underwater statue of Christ down in the Keys," Joanie said wistfully, remembering a diving trip she and Vinny had taken with Dave and Chris the past year. The water near Looe Key had been especially clear and warm. They had begun the trip in Key Largo, provisioning there and then heading into the John Pennekamp State Park, home of the only coral reef in the continental United States. The statue of Christ stood in about thirty feet of water. They anchored nearby and dove around the bronze statue all afternoon. The fish flitted in and out, occasionally feeding from the crumbled crackers they took down with them. That night they'd anchored and motored the dinghy in to Marina del Mar for a delicious dinner of lobster, shrimp, and good wine. She sighed wistfully and looked at Chris out of the corner of her eye. Would they ever have those days again? Would this nightmare ever be over?

When they returned to the dock, Anna and Joan tied up the boat while Chris called the PT boat now in the western Gulf of Mexico. It only took a few minutes to fire up the SSB radio and tell the boys the story of the shootout, that they were all okay, and that she'd given the South Africans the leads as Dave had coached her.

Chapter 13

The charcoal gray Mercedes was stopped by the side of the road. A light misty rain had started to fall. A low hanging tree branch occasionally brushed the roof, sounding like fingernails being lightly scraped over a blackboard surface. The driver of the car was half turned in his seat facing his companion. He rubbed his hand through his fine white hair causing a light dusting of salt crystals to fall to his coat collar. His companion sat staring at the dimly lit dashboard, his large form slightly hunched in the front seat. His position was normally in back, and he felt extremely uncomfortable in his former partner's seat.

"He's dead, Dieter. You saw him hit for yourself. By a .45. You know what that means."

Dieter knew all too well the great stopping power of the nearly half-inch diameter American bullet.

"But we can't leave him there, Herr Boettcher."

"Yes, yes, of course. We must recover his effects and his pistol. Especially, we must recover his identification." Boettcher thought that the Managing Director must never hear of this incident. There must be no concrete evidence linking the Company to these people. He was still baffled as to how an imbecile and a couple of women had defeated them. It had looked so easy. All they wanted was information, but to look at the good side, they had uncovered the information they sought. The man, Novak, was in Guatemala, probably with more of the gems he'd promised the jeweler in New York. Northern Guatemala, probably near the Mexican Border. They'd go in south of Cozumel and pick up his trail there. A man dealing gems leaves a wider trail than he believes, especially an amateur like Novak.

Boettcher nodded at Dieter and started the car. "This time we will go in through the surrounding trees and quietly so as to reconnoiter the enemy. Remember, we seek only to recover Brian's body and effects." Personally, he could care less about Brian. But he wanted that I.D. card. Dieter could only nod glumly.

They drove slowly down the long, dark road through the housing development and then past the trailer park. If Charlie Potts had been on his porch watching, he might have seen the dark car roll slowly and silently past the end of the street and

glide to a halt under a spreading clump of Norfolk
pines that grew up against the fence around
Chesney's. They got out, careful not to slam the
doors and pulled on black silk ski masks. Dark
pigskin gloves covered their hands and dull blue
9mm automatic pistols were in their hands.
Boettcher signaled to Dieter to go to the north and
come upon the building from the sea side, while he
came in from the darkened alleyway between the
main building and the long, narrow outline of
Dave's workshop. Silent as shadows, the two men
crept to the half-opened windows. Illuminated by a
lowered light, Boettcher could see a figure slowly
scrubbing a patch on the floor, frequently ringing
out a mop in a bucket. A pile of sweepings stood
nearby, and a trash can sat next to the scrubwoman.
The handle of a shotgun protruded from the
wastebasket, within easy reach. Boettcher smiled to
himself. He could easily shoot her from his position
by the window, but what did she know? He
suspected that only Mrs. Manley knew of the
whereabouts of Novak and her husband, David,
who were reported to be close friends. Shooting her
would gain nothing, raping her even less. She
looked to be in her 60's or 70's. He grimaced to
himself at the thought. He looked around for
Brian's body. Sliding quietly from window to
window, he saw no trace. Quickly peeking around
the rear corner of the building he saw a darker
shadow within a shadow. It was Dieter. He signaled
him to approach. "Anything?" he hissed.

"*Nien*. I checked the boats and managed to get
a look upstairs using a ladder. Nothing." He was

puzzled. No cars had passed them on the road out to the main highway.

Boettcher held a small infrared night vision scope to one eye and peered around the darkened interior. On a table close to one window he thought he saw a small pile of things, one of which glinted in the dim light. He gestured to Dieter.

"On the table, there. Go around until you are by the window and reach in and gather them up. I will cover you."

Dieter snorted, "Cover me from what?" He thought to himself, "An old woman with a mop?" Nevertheless, he, too, slid cautiously around the building and nimbly stepped from shadow to shadow until he appeared at the proper window. From a sheath strapped to his left ankle, he withdrew a wicked looking dagger, as black as death and as sharp as a viper's tongue. Silently he slit the screen along the bottom and up one side. As he slid an arm in to retrieve the confiscated lootings from their dead partner's pockets, Dieter accidentally knocked over a pile of change. He fumbled quickly for the wallet and other incriminating objects.

In the center of the room, Anna quick withdrew the shotgun from its holder and swung it up. At the same time as she was moving, Boettcher was wiping his brow. He quickly snapped off a shot. The shotgun boomed and Dieter quickly withdrew his arm with a howl, the wallet clutched tightly in his fist. Boettcher's shot barely grazed the back of Anna's right hand and buried itself in the hardwood stock of the shotgun. The power of the shot drove the heavy stock back into Anna's stomach, throwing her onto her back and behind the nearest booth where she lay quietly and out of Boettcher's line of fire, grunting and gasping for breath. Dieter whimpered and ran for the car. Boettcher swung his gun wildly from left to right and was about to enter the bar when he heard the faint whine of an engine. He crouched and waited. The engine was from the dock area. More people coming, he thought. Time to beat a strategic retreat. Once again, he flitted from shadow to shadow, ending at the car. Rapidly, he slipped in, slamming the door and starting the motor. He quickly reversed and then the long, dark car flew up the road to the open highway.

CHAPTER 14

The matte black helicopter came in from the sea in a rush, curving around a small mountain and heading up a long, wide valley. Dave kept them low enough to avoid coastal radar, yet high enough not to alarm early risers. The sky was turning a slightly lighter shade in the east, but the valleys were still dark as pitch. As the chopper headed farther north, the lights from villages grew farther and farther apart until great stretches of jungle flowed beneath them.

"Tom," he whispered. "Get on the horn and see if they're waiting for us."

Tom didn't bother to reply. He rapidly punched in their agreed frequency. All throughout the flight he'd been toying with the CRT displays, the

weapons arming and aiming devices,
communications, and radar gear, until he felt that he
was as familiar with it as he would ever be. It was
new. It was clever, but it was all based on that
previous technology that he was familiar with. So
the screens were larger, and the gauges had gone
from analog to digital. They could now see behind
them and shoot with much more accuracy - if they
had any weapons. There were a few shells in the
chain gun under the chin but they were all that were
left after Tom had shot them off attempting to co-
ordinate the arming and firing sequence. Too bad
Sykes hadn't left the chopper fully armed, like he
had with fuel. Ah, well, can't have everything.

He thumbed the mike button, "Chicken Coop,
this is Big Bird, over." He repeated the call twice
more, letting the atmosphere absorb his call and toss
it around until it found a waiting antenna. Just as he
was about to call again, a faint crackling came to his
earphones. There was a decidedly Chicano accent to
his reply.

"Big Bird, thees ees Chicken Coop. We read
you very clearly. Over."

Tom smiled. He was surely going to get laid
tonight! He consulted the GPS navigation chart and
followed the flickering speck on the large screen.
Then he clicked on the destination reading on one
side and read the estimated time of arrival and
course. "Chicken Coop, our ETA is approximately
thirteen minutes. Turn the lights on in ten, over."
Oh, boy! Oh, boy! He rubbed his hands gleefully.
He happily hummed to himself. He even stroked
himself through his pants a little. "Big fella, you're

going to get your beak wet tonight," he hummed quietly to himself.

"What was that, Tom?" Dave asked. Tom hadn't realized he'd spoken out loud.

"Uh, nothing, Dave. Just thinking out loud."

The night was rapidly fading. Far off in the distance Dave could see the snow-capped peaks of Texupatchalas and Marchianchala, the twin sacred mountains of the ancient Mayans. The terrain was more rugged here, the flattened valleys giving way to higher ridges and narrower gorges. The jungle canopy was now in clumps, like that in Viet Nam's central highlands, a terrain both Tom and Dave were familiar with. Tall ceiba trees reached their tight branches high. Mahogany occasionally vied with a teak giant, still waiting for the woodsman's chainsaw. Dave slowed the chopper and both he and Tom peered ahead trying to see the lights, now about four or five miles ahead by the GPS coordinates. All at once, a circle of lights appeared at about one o'clock. They made for it and came to a hover about three-hundred feet up. The circle of light was flat and clean. No trees were nearby. Tom keyed his mike for intercom, "Well, are we waiting, Father?"

Dave hesitated a minute longer. "I'll ease us around three sixty." Dave pushed a pedal and the big chopper slowly revolved, peering, looking, and attempting to penetrate the shadows. "Well, Thomas, there's another fine fix we've gotten us into. No turning back after we land, you know."

"Ay-yup. Let's shit or get off the pot, buddy boy. Take it down." Tom reached down and released the landing gear. It whirred and then thunked. A green light lit on one of the screens.

"Okay, takin' 'er in. Get a hand gun ready, just in case." Dave cautioned.

"Got one on my lap already. There's one by your right knee, if we need 'em."

Dave suddenly dropped the big bird, pulling back on the collective just scant yards from landing, then lightly setting it down on its wheels. It bounced, before it settled on its shocks. The great five-bladed rotor slowed and finally came to a stop. Both Tom and Dave were flipping switches, shutting down systems and screens. Dave looked up and noted the circle of lights was from a ring of automobiles. Beyond the cars, to the north, was a cluster of buildings. He could make out the vehicles and buildings in the emerging dawn, which was visibly creeping down the row of hills to their right and west.

A figure emerged from the circle of headlights. It was a short, swarthy boy or eighteen or nineteen, with rounded, pleasant features. His hair was jet black and cut around his head like a bowl had been placed on it. He wore jeans and a Hawaiian shirt. The jeans were worn low and every few seconds, he tugged them up, but not too far up. His underwear emerged from the tops of the jeans a good six inches. He wore red, high top Converse all-stars and a Florida Marlins ball cap backwards. He was rapidly going from car to truck to tractor turning the headlights off. As he completed his circle, Tom and

Dave emerged from the now silent chopper, rubbing their backs and trying to get some circulation going in numb butts.

"Dudes! *Hola* and welcome!" He came forward, hand outstretched, and high in a ghetto shake. "Oh, man, are we ever glad you're here. I've got a camo net in the back of the pickup. Give me a hand and we'll cover the chopper. Man, is it ever awesome!" He greeted Tom and Dave by smacking the backs of their hands with his knuckles. As he turned, Tom gave Dave the 'eye', raising his eyebrows. Dave only shrugged.

They followed the boy to the back of a dusty tan Chevy pickup and helped drag an enormous roll of camouflage netting out and spread it on the ground. Then he took two telescoping poles out and fitted them together.

"Come, on, dudes, let's get the net on and get some breakfast. Wow, they're all waiting for you! Alexandria's especially waiting for you, Tom dude!" He leered at Tom and chuckled loudly. While Tom hauled the net from the middle, Dave and the boy lifted the net from either end and walked it over the now drooping rotor. In a moment it was done and the boy walked around silently stabbing stakes in the ground then stepping on them until they hooked the net and then with a final stomp, buried them. Meanwhile, Dave retrieved two of their duffel bags.

He stood outside the camo circle and inspected the work. Fast and efficient. He liked this boy, despite his outlandish dress. "Hold on, what's your name, son?"

The young man turned and came back to Dave, "My name is Dominguez Florio Locarno." He said this with all solemnity, shaking hands with Dave in the proper fashion. Then he smiled a broad grin, "But my friends call me Doby. You can, too."

Tom looked at Dave and smiled. They said at the same time, "Doby Gillis!"

"Who?" The boy inquired.

Dave looked crestfallen. "Never mind."

Puzzled, the boy said, "Throw your gear in the back of the truck and we'll go get some chow. My Aunt Roberta makes a killer breakfast!" The door opened with a squawk and Doby leaped behind the wheel.

Dawn was in full bloom now, the valley enveloped in a deep golden hue, the dew rapidly evaporating. In the distance howler monkeys hurled insults at each other while the bleating of sheep nearby floated across the valley.

The boy was chattering as they bumped along the rutted road. "My pop is out with the sheep and some of the cousins are too, but Pop'll be back later today. I guess you guys'll need a good sleep. Don't worry about the chopper. Nobody'll go near it. Uncle Enrico told the Mayan's to keep an eye on it. Boy, I bet you guys can't wait to see some action, huh? I sure can't." As he ran on and on, Tom looked at Dave out of the corner of his eye and shook his head.

In a few minutes they screeched to a halt outside a modest house of adobe. The roof was tiled with terra-cotta half round tiles. The drive was white crushed stone edged with large pots of flowering shrubs. Three broad stone steps fronted the entranceway. Standing on the steps was a small crowd of people. In the center was a short, heavy woman with dark hair shot through with white. She wore a demure blue cotton dress with a snow-white apron tied about her ample waist. Her face was the color of copper and the creases were deep yet kindly. She had a strong, hawk nose and black, bushy eyebrows. She stepped forward to greet the two men as they alighted from the pickup.

"Tia Roberta, this is Thomas," he indicated Tom who stepped forward and took her hand and brought it to his lips.

"A great pleasure, Senora Locarno," Tom smiled and said in perfect Spanish.

"And this is Senor David Manley." He said the name all as one word and Dave paused to correct him. Before he could, the old lady stepped down a step and looked in his eyes. She stood for a minute staring at him.

"You have beautiful eyes, Senor David Manley. Deep green like our sea so far away. Honest eyes." She paused then said in a quiet voice, "Thank you for coming. May I present my nephew, Enrico, the head of our little family?" She turned and Enrico stepped down, hand outstretched.

"Senor Manley, I am Enrico Ernesto Locarno. I welcome you and Mr. Thomas…" here he hesitated.

"Novak, Senor Locarno. Tom Novak." Tom smiled his biggest grin and clasped the proffered hand in both of his. In a few minutes they had met, shaken or kissed every hand offered. Dave was tired from the long ride but Tom seemed full of energy. He led the way inside, a lady on each arm. But Alex was not in sight, and Tom was almost afraid to inquire after her. He swung his head around constantly trying to look into every room, every shadow.

The large dining room was cool and airy, the breeze coming in through a large pair of sliding glass doors. Outside, the overhanging tiled roof kept the worst of the afternoon sun at bay. The adobe walls were at least two feet thick and the floor was tiled in a dark gray slate that was also cool to the touch. Dave noticed that the majority of the household inhabitants were barefoot and when he inquired whether this was a common practice, he was invited to peel his flight boots off and get comfortable. Young Doby had already taken their duffel bags to their rooms in a remote corner of the sprawling hacienda and now Senor Locarno spoke to them:

"Senors Novak and Manley, many thanks for coming to our poor country to aid us. As you know, you will be amply rewarded for your efforts, but I hope that you will become our friends as well as our employees." This said, he once again shook their hands. "Since my nephew, Dominguez, has taken a liking to you and I'm sure you would like to freshen up after your long flight, he will show you to your rooms." He looked at his Aunt Roberta and raised his eyebrows. She nodded imperceptibly.

"Breakfast will be served in one hour. It will be our

pleasure to entertain you here." With that, he gave a short bow and they were excused.

Doby pulled on their sleeves and led them down a long corridor, leaving the entire family smiling and nodding at them.

"Wow, Tom-dude, they sure liked you, even Tia Roberta and she's the toughest one here. Daveman, you gotta loosen up. They're cool. Most of them don't speak much English but they understand a lot more than they let on." He babbled on as they walked down the shadowy corridor, there were many doors on the right wall. Doby explained that they were various bedrooms, reading rooms and private quarters for senior family members.

"What's on the other side of that wall?" asked Tom, his arm thrown over the shoulders of the youth.

"That's the pool and hot tub. It's in a courtyard in the middle of the house. Only one door, though. The old folks don't use it much, just us kids. They like their privacy and peace and quiet." Dave suspected that anyone who didn't wear his underwear sticking out a foot above this waistband was classified as an "old folk."

Finally they stopped before a close-set pair of doors. Across was another door, this one painted bright red in contrast to the other doors that were all of a natural finish over a deep, grainy wood.

"Senor Tom, this one is yours," he gestured at the first door, pushed it open and lead the way inside, his hand gripping Tom's shirtsleeve. Doby busied himself opening the sliding doors a bit, permitting a gentle breeze to blow back the hand-woven curtains. The curtains were all bright reds, blues and yellows with terra cottas and burnt umbers to offset and mute the brighter colors. On one side was a huge king-sized bed with a beautiful ochre and tan bedspread with four plump pillows at the head. An overstuffed chair of the same dark wood with plump cushions stood at its side. Along one wall was a long table upon which sat a modern Apple computer and printer. Tom noted the phone cord connection and guessed it was for a modem. A double-doored armoire stood next to it and a simple chest of drawers nearby. The slate was carried over into the floor here but with several colorful throw rugs scattered about. At the foot of the bed was a huge ornately carved trunk. To his left was another door inset into the thick wall. Doby pulled it open with a flourish. Tom peeked in. A large bathroom with all the modern conveniences lay behind it. He strode in to check it out and Dave crowded in behind him. To his right was a large tiled shower stall and behind that was a large tub recessed two steps into the floor. Against the left hand wall was a long vanity with two sculpted sinks and a pile of fluffy white towels on one end. Dave could have wept when he saw the toilet. Not only did it have a padded seat but a full magazine rack within reach. These Guatemalans really knew what was important in this world.

"Senor Dave, your room is just beyond. You and Senor Tom will share the banyo, if that is all right?" He looked inquiringly at Dave who was already opening the door to the adjoining room. It was a mirror image of the one he just been in. His bag was on the floor and he shrugged out of his jacket and tossed it on the bed.

"Thanks, Doby. Tom and I'll grab a shower and put on some clean duds and we'll be ready in an hour. Will you come and get us?"

"You bet, Senor Dave. Someone or me! See you in one hour." He smiled a gleaming smile and left them alone.

Dave sauntered into the bathroom and peeled off his shirt. He leaned tiredly against the vanity and peered into the long mirror. He saw a tanned face that had dark hollows under the eyes, sandy hair, graying at the temples, that was in need of a trim, and a beard that needed the same.

"Some digs, Buddy-Boy!" Tom enthused. "I'm going to really enjoy this."

Dave sighed, "Don't get too used to it. Tomorrow we're moving into the bush." He splashed water onto his face, letting it trickle down onto his chest.

"What the hell for?" Tom sputtered. "We just got here! Why can't we hang out a while and enjoy the good life?" He stood in the doorway, his T-shirt pulled over his head but still on his arms. His indignation was apparent and he was belligerent.

"Look, asshole, we're here to fight a fucking war. The last thing we want to do is get these people involved as much as they seem to want. We've got to move away from the house. Period. We've got to scout the Colombians. And we've got to get into a war frame of mind. Look at us," Dave indicated

Tom's not quite solid stomach and his own slightly
protruding love handles.

"Let's just get our rucks and tomorrow find us
a guide so we can look this situation over. Okay?
We can relax when this is finished, if anybody's left
alive," he said darkly.

Tom knew he was right but it seemed such a
shame to leave all this luxury. He grumbled about it
all through his shower and repeated dunks in the hot
pool. He nearly wept when he found the controls
that sent jets of water bubbling into his tired back.
After what seemed like only a few minutes, a
discrete knock on the door was heard. "C'mon in,
Dobe!" Tom called. He was lying back in the tub, a
fine cigar in his mouth, a glass of brandy at his
elbow. Dave was sharing the bottle and sitting on
the vanity between the sinks, back against the
mirror.

Alex strode into the room and laughed at the
two of them. "My, my, look at our army. Enjoying
the good life, are we?" Dave hastened to pull a
towel from the pile and cover himself. He tossed
one to Tom but Tom batted it away.

"Relax, Buddy-boy, she's seen all I've got!" He
grinned at Alex. She smiled back and kicked off her
sandals.

"Oh, yes, Senor Tom and I have been through
some fine times." She stepped down into the pool
and straddled Tom, holding her skirt up around her
smooth thighs. "As much as I'd like to continue
this, Thomas, my father has called for breakfast.
Please get your fat buttocks out of the tub and be
prepared to act gracious to my family." She leaned

down and kissed him on the top of his head. "Say, is that a bald spot I see?" And with that she scampered back out of his reach as Tom came out of the tub in a rush of water.

"What bald spot? I don't have a bald spot!"

Dave casually tossed Alex a towel. She put a shapely leg up on the vanity, her skirt riding up to the top of her thigh. Tom stood next to her, vainly trying to see the top of his head in the mirror.

"Relax. She's just busting your balls. Lemme see."

Tom leaned his head toward Dave who snorted and said, "Nah, there's no bald spot. Maybe it's getting a little thin..."

He winked at Alex who grinned and winked back. "Let's go, my papa doesn't like to be kept waiting. She smacked Tom on his bare bottom and swept out of the room laughing.

"Well, well, flyboy, have we got the colleen befuddled? Maybe she doesn't know about the others. Maybe I'll have to clue her in." This last Dave said over his shoulder as he entered his room.

"Don't even think about it, Davey-boy." Tom yelled from his room. "Besides, there haven't been any since Alex. Who's had time?"

Dave chuckled and slipped into a pair of neatly pressed khaki dress slacks and an orange pleated sport shirt with blue and purple birds of paradise embroidered on the front. He slipped his feet into a pair of Adidas sneakers, then thought better of it and stepped out of them, kicking them in the direction of the bed. Hell, if the family went

barefoot, so would they. Last came his Rolex
Submariner's watch and a quick brush through his
hair. He was ready.

As he came into Tom's room, Tom was just
pulling a pink Izod golf shirt over his head. He
tucked it into a pair of lime green rather long
walking shorts. All this was held together with a
tooled leather Harley-Davidson belt sporting an
enormous silver and gold bullhead belt buckle. Tom
was the picture of sartorial splendor. Only Dave
knew that under the waistband of the shorts, Tom
kept a stainless steel AMG .380 mini-automatic
pistol. Dave elected to go unencumbered this night,
trusting to fate -- and Tom -- to haul his chestnuts
out of the fire should one erupt.

Alex was waiting in the hall as they emerged,
leaning back against the door across from theirs.
"Yours?" asked Tom, inclining his head toward the
room.

She grinned and nodded. Today she had her
thick, black hair up on her head, held in place by a
beautiful clasp of worked silver set with three
smallish emeralds and held by a pair of smooth
wooden pins. The silver looked beautiful on the
field of jet hair, and her neck formed a graceful
curve. Dave knew the Japanese were especially
appreciative of a graceful neck and he thought he
could make a pile of cabbage flying in attentive
Nipponese to view her nape. Personally, he liked
the tender area behind a woman's knee, but then
again, he wasn't Japanese. These idle thoughts
drifted through his mind as he followed the lovers
who played hand tag up the dim corridor.

In a few moments, they reached the great dining room. The family all were gathered again, though each had obviously dressed for the occasion. Faces were scrubbed and in the case of the women, freshly made up. The men and boys had on achingly white linen shirts and various medallions and chains. Mustaches were trimmed and hair was in place. Dave felt like he was on display. A chair had been left on either side of Senor Locarno for Dave and Tom. Next to Dave was the Aunt Roberta, Dave seemed to remember. Next to Tom sat Doby who grinned at Tom and kept patting his arm in a proprietary way. Alex sat somewhere down the table on Dave's side.

The food was a blur. Dish after dish was passed down the table, but Tom and Dave allowed themselves a spoonful of each lest they become overly filled. The wine was chilled and delicious, though Dave restricted himself to two glasses. Everything was delicious and the conversation centered on that year's wool crop and a forthcoming trip to Miami for shopping. It was all so unreal, Dave thought. Here they were about to start a war only one valley over and the chatter was about shopping trips. Dave caught Aunt Roberta staring at him out of the corner of her eye a number of times.

Senor Locarno gently but thoroughly interrogated him and Tom about their respective histories, but the topic of the forthcoming operation wasn't mentioned. Finally, the meal was over. The last course had been served, the last glass of wine drunk, the last mouth wiped.

At last silence reigned. All eyes were on Dave and Tom. Senor Locarno quietly asked, "So Senor Novak, what is your plan?" The quiet could have been cut with a knife.

"A plan?" Tom shrugged. "I don't have one. That's Dave's department." He grinned at Dave and waved in his direction. "I'm just a grunt."

Senor Locarno looked perplexed. "A grunt? I don't understand. That is a noise a pig makes, is it not?" He smoothed his pencil thin mustache.

"In American slang, sir, a grunt is a soldier, a lower grade foot soldier." Dave answered. The slim, immaculate man nodded in understanding.

"Ah, so you are the planner, Senor Manley. *Bueno*. What is your plan?" He raised his eyebrows and nervously tapped his fingers on the tablecloth.

Dave hesitated. Should he tell them what they didn't want to hear or keep them in the dark? He looked around the table at the eager faces and sighed inwardly. They were all looking at him as the great savior. Nothing like a little pressure. Well, 'in for a penny, in for a pound.'

"Senor Locarno, I strongly recommend that you and your family give up this valley and find someplace else to live." He let that sink into the stunned silence. The table erupted into a gabble of indignant voices as his words were translated for those without English. The Aunt to his right smiled a small smile and said nothing but the senior Locarno was heatedly speaking loudly and pointing a slim finger at him. After a moment, Senor Locarno realized that no one could hear a thing and he rapped a spoon against a heavy leaded glass until the din abated.

"Senor Manley, have you come under false pretenses? Have you come to drive us from our homes? Please explain this statement of yours." He sat back, arms crossed across his chest. The others eagerly awaited his reply, leaning forward.

Dave took a deep breath and continued, "I don't think you know what you are getting into. These people are Colombian drug people. They are evil incarnate. They will kill you, and you and you," Dave pointed at one of the younger women and an older man and another woman, "just as soon as look at you. They will burn this place to the ground, rape the women and torture you all for sport. They will seek out all your relations and kill them, too. Do you understand what I am saying?" He glared at them, one at a time. Some wouldn't meet his eyes, some glared back and a few just stared and gulped. He went on, "So unless you are ready to commit yourselves to a fight to the death, move. Get out and go away, because there is a very good chance some of you may be hurt or killed in the next week or so." He looked around at the nervous faces again.

"You have to be worse than they are," he continued. "If you commit to this fight, and we win, some of you will have committed sins worse than anything you can imagine by the time it is over. If we lose, you won't have to worry about your immortal souls." Dave was half standing by this time. He felt a gentle pressure on his arm. Aunt Roberta was gently urging him back to his chair.

She stood, a lacy black shawl over her shoulders. "All that Senor Dave says is true. I myself have been in a war and seen things I would just as soon forget. But this is our home and I for one will not give it up. You younger ones must make your own decisions." With that said, she sat down with dignity, head high.

"Senor Manley, I have listened to you with a great feeling of doom. We have hired you and Senor Novak to fight for us. Must we be drawn into this? Must my family be a part of this misery?" Senor Locarno gripped Dave's wrist and looked beseechingly into his eyes.

"Yes, I'm afraid that you will be drawn into this no matter what happens and I just want you to be ready and aware of the consequences." Dave stood slowly and looked at the rows of faces. He drew a deep breath.

"Senor Locarno," Dave touched the older gentleman on the shoulder, "*Senoras Y Senors*, what we are about to embark upon is a deadly game called war. You have something these men want, your land. You wish them not to have it. All throughout history this has been the case, but if you truly want what is yours, you must fight for it." He looked around. All eyes were on him, while a murmur translated his words for those who didn't speak English. He went on, leaning forward on his hands, "The price of freedom must sometimes be written in blood. Your country's bloody history tells you that. It all comes down to times like this. We do these things," he gestured to Tom and tapped himself on the chest, "because we are paid to or because we come to believe in your cause, but make no mistake, this is your cause, your homes, your land." He emphasized each point with a stiffened forefinger, poking it at the older members of the family.

"We are here to help you, not do your job. We will try to confine this entire operation to the next valley. We will try not to have anyone killed or injured and we will try to make the Colombians go away and not return." He paused again and looked at the rapt faces. "But we cannot do it without your help." With a final pause, he sat down. Tom looked at him with raised eyebrows.

Down the length of the table, voices were raised in discussion. After a moment, Alexandria stood, smoothing her dress. Immediately there was silence. She cleared her throat and spoke, "I have lived my life among you since I was born. I love our little valley where we have lived undisturbed, until now. I have been with Senor Tom and seen him fight. I have been with him and seen him risk his life for mine. I will fight with him. I will do whatever it takes because if I don't, we must go away forever and those Colombians," this last said with disgust in her voice, "will take my home, and this I cannot allow." This last said with a defiant fist pounded on the snowy tablecloth.

"Yeah, right on, Alex!" cried the youngster, Dominguez, fist raised in the air. She smiled fleetingly at him.

The *Padrone* raised his hands for quiet. He stood solemnly and looked at his family, a sad smile

on his face. "All of you, please, I must know now
where you stand. Will those of you who will stay
and do whatever is asked by Senor Dave and Senor
Tom, please indicate by raising your hand. Those of
you who wish to leave may do so and no ill will be
thought of you. But before you decide, I, Enrico
Locarno, the head of this family, tell you that
whoever of you departs, you do so forever." There
were raised eyebrows and murmurs of protest. The
Padrone silenced them with a chop of his hand.
"Yes, my family, if you will not stay and fight for
your land and lives, then go and go for good." Then
he, too, sat down, raising his right hand.

Doby and Tia Roberta next followed the
Padrone. One by one, the hands rose until all were
up. The *Padrone* had a tear in his eye. "*Viva
Locarno!*" he cried and the family members echoed
him until the cry was thunderous. "*Viva, Locarno!
Viva Locarno!*"

Tom was yelling along with them and tossing
back glass after glass of wine. Dave wouldn't want
his head by noon. He wondered who of the family
would be sitting here a month from now.

In a few minutes, after all was quiet, Dave
announced that Tom would begin weapons training
the next day, while he would go with a guide to
scout the Colombian's camp.

"Senor Dave, I'm your man!" piped up Doby,
standing at Dave's side and tugging at his sleeve. "I
know that valley and every rolling stone in it.
Besides, I've been there since the *Cholos* came."

"The *Cholos*?" Dave asked, a puzzled
expression on his face.

"Yeah, the *Cholos*. That's what we call 'em. I was over there about a week ago and stole some boots and a knife." He pulled a well worn folding knife out of his pocket and showed it to Dave and Tom who'd come up to join them.

"What's that?" Tom indicated the knife in Doby's outstretched hand.

"This asshole stole it from the *Cholos*. That's what they call the Colombians." Dave said disgustedly.

Tom threw an arm over the youngster's shoulders, "Kid, do you know what they'd have done if they'd caught you?" Tom winked conspiratorially at Dave. "They probably would have hung you upside down over a fire and roasted you until you talked. You know, made beef jerky out of you."

"Yeah, beef jerky," chimed in Dave.

Doby gulped. "But I wouldn't have talked, Tom, Dave, honest."

"Sure kid, you're tough, but they'd have made you talk. This isn't the movies. I would have talked, Dave here would have talked. These guys are some *loco hombres*, eh? Don't go there again without one of us, okay?"

Doby nodded, wide eyed. "Okay, Tom."

"Tonight, we'll make a recon of the valley and in the morning, you and I will make a map, okay?" Doby nodded again. Tom and Dave left him standing there.

Dave turned back, "Oh, Dobe, sometime today, go out to the chopper and bring back the duffel bags full of stuff, will you?"

Doby smiled, "Sure, Dave. I'll put them in the back garage. You want me to lay the stuff out, too?" He was all eagerness like a new puppy.

"No, leave the stuff alone until we get out there with you. Just bring it in."

He nodded again as Dave and Tom strolled back down the passageway toward their rooms. Tom had seen Alex moving in that direction a few moments before and was eager to get on with his amorous business. Dave just wanted to get some sleep. He was full of food and wine, and was exhausted.

As he entered his room, Tom was splashing on a double handful of a fluorescent green aftershave lotion in the adjoining bathroom.

"Whew, what is that horse-piss?" Dave mockingly asked.

Tom threw him a scornful look. "This, Buddy-boy is Mantastic. It is guaranteed to make me irresistible." He sloshed some more into his hand and, pulling his shirt up, rubbed it onto his chest and belly. "Ah, now I'm ready."

"Jesus, that stuff would knock a buzzard off a shit wagon. You'd better hope your lady is, uh, olifactorily challenged."

Tom grinned and rubbed his hands. "Don't wait up for me, Son. Daddy's got a long day ahead of him." And with that, he slipped out of the door and into the hallway.

Tom knocked softly on Alex's door and was immediately admitted. In fact, her strong, brown arm reached into the darkened passageway and yanked him into the room. The door closed softly behind him and she was on him, squeezing and kissing, running her slim fingers through his hair with an urgency he'd rarely known, except for that one time with the Pan-Am stew, er, flight attendant, just before they got to Hawaii.

Tom responded in kind, his strong arms around her, kneading her shoulders, pulling at the simple clasps holding her hair up. It came loose all at once and tumbled down her back. He slid his hands lower and grasped her buttocks close to him, pulling and squeezing. She ground her hips against him and if she'd been any slimmer it would have hurt. But she was well padded and full of fire. She had one leg up and wrapped around his hip while his hand fiercely rubbed her naked thigh.

"Wait. Stop. Thomas, let me catch my breath." She sagged in his arms, panting, lipstick smeared, hair awry.

"Yeah, sure," Tom gasped, breath rattling in his throat. "I'll wait, I'll stop." He held her under the arms, his back against the sturdy door, trying to calm his breath. They staggered to a low and wide couch a few steps away. Alex collapsed on the couch pulling Tom down on top of her, again kissing him with long, deep kisses.

Tom twined his fingers in her hair, burrowing his face in her neck, kissing her ears and shoulders. She was tearing at his shirt, trying to get it over his head. They broke contact long enough to yank the shirt free and toss it into a corner. Alex had kicked her sandals free and her stockinged legs rubbed his, sending a fire through him. Tom reached behind her for the tiny zipper but his hands were shaking and the position was wrong.

"Up, up," he gasped, twisting and pulling her atop him. Her hair was caught under his arm and she gave a small cry of pain.

He stopped and fell back panting. In a minute, he'd regained his breath. "Take the dress off, please," he begged. "Those things baffle me."

She lay slumped against him, the morning sunlight coming through the large window drawing lines across them both. "Okay, wait a minute." Alex climbed to her feet and stood before him. Slowly, tantalizingly she reached behind her and pulled the zipper down. Tom lay back on the couch, eyes half closed.

Alex slowly slipped the dress forward, baring first one shoulder, then another. It fell to her waist, then to the floor. She was wearing a bright red bra, frilly panties, and a garter belt. Her golden stockings gleamed as if made of neon. She reached her arms behind her and unsnapped the bra, letting the ends dangle while she cupped it over her breasts. She moved her legs in a slow dance, swaying to some music playing inside her head. Tom watched heavy lidded, his breathing slow and deep.

The bra slipped down her arms and noiselessly fell to the carpeted floor. She danced a few more steps, turning slowly, bending, cupping her breasts, holding them as an offering, weighing them, the dark nipples peeking out from between her fingers. She turned her back and began to roll her panties down over the roundness of her buttocks, swaying side to side, sensually, gracefully. They, too, slipped to the floor. She swayed closer then leaned and whispered, "Come into the bedroom in a minute, lover boy." She turned and with an exaggerated swagger, strode to the adjoining room. Quickly shedding the garter belt and stockings, she slipped into the cool sheets. A low nightlight barely illuminated the room. The sunlight peeped through the closed curtains and sent streaks across the wall in the living room. Alex smiled to herself and spread her hair carefully over the peach pillow and waited. And waited.

Five minutes went by, then ten. "Tom," she whispered. "I'm waiting." Still nothing. She slipped out of bed and peeked around the corner of the doorframe. Tom lay with his head on a throw pillow, mouth open, snoring softly, hands clasped on his chest, legs crossed. She slumped against the doorframe. Her man, she thought. The great sleeping bear. Ah, well, she supposed he'd had a busy day. With that, she turned and went back to the bedroom, slipped into a pair of jeans and pulled a Nike T-shirt over her head.

CHAPTER 15

Before the first rays of dawn streaked across the dark sky, Michael Boettcher was on the phone to South Africa. He stood in the near deserted broad concourse at a pay phone in the Tampa International Airport. He had screwed a short cylindrical device onto the mouthpiece and kept his back hunched, concealing his discussion. Across the way, his assistant, Dieter, sat and watched each person who strolled by. His arm was freshly bandaged and covered with a new windbreaker. The air conditioning kept the place cool and he casually watched two students asleep on the floor in a corner, heads propped on a pair of gaudily colored knapsacks. Cheap ones, he noted, not the good brands, like Lowe, Madden, or Karimoor.

"I'm telling you, Karl, the stones must be in Guatemala." Boettcher was speaking forcefully to his superior, Karl Danziger, his contact on the VanHerff Board of Directors. "I know you don't want another Yemen, but we have no choice. We've been met at every turn with violence. There must be much at stake." He waited, agitated, already forming his reply without waiting for the other man to finish. It was inconceivable to him that maybe his violence was the instigation of the reply.

"Ya, Karl, ya. But if they manage to get these Weiss Emeralds onto the market, you know what will happen." It was easier to let the threat of impending doom speak for him. It hung in the air. "Just let me ready the strike force and get them in position. Of course, I will wait for the Board to make the final decision. Ya, Karl, you don't have to keep reminding me about Yemen. The one thing you have failed to mention about Yemen, once again, is that we did stop them, did we not?" He waited while silence hung. Finally, the old man on the other end gave his assent. He would ready his strike force. Boettcher smiled grimly.

He turned to Dieter and gave a short thumbs up, a jabbing in the air. Dieter merely nodded. He was concentrating on the boy and girl asleep on the floor. The girl's skirt had ridden up over one hip as she rolled over. She wore tiny white panties, which he could just make out creased into her pale flesh. He pictured her thrashing about under him, crying and sobbing at his hard thrusts. He sighed. Maybe sometime soon he'd have time to find a woman. He glanced again at Boettcher. Not bloody likely.

Boettcher dialed another international number. A man answered in a bored voice, "Halborg and Ramsey Imports."

"This is Michael. Prepare a team for an export. We will need at least two birds. Make it three. I will relay your course within 24 hours." He hung up without waiting for a reply.

"Where to now, *Mien Capitan?*" Asked Dieter dryly, hauling himself to his feet, casting one more reluctant gaze at the young girl's rear end. He hoisted a bag with all their personal articles and casually tossed it over his shoulder.

"Back to New York." Boettcher spoke in short, clipped sentences. "I need some time to plan, gather information. Then we are going to Guatemala. Come." He led the way to the Delta ticket counter.

On the other side of the world in a small military compound near the end of a short river with no name, a phone rang urgently. A bored woman in khakis dropped her booted feet to the floor and reached for the receiver. Her hair was short, red, and damp. If the phone had rung ten minutes before, she'd have been in the shower and would have missed the call. Her name was Jane Houllihan and she was listed as a clerk/typist on the payroll of the VanHerff International Corporation's office in Springbok, South Africa. Though VanHerff did,

indeed, have an office in Springbok, it transacted no
business, was rarely occupied, and existed for the
sole purpose of providing a telephone with call
forwarding to the military style base.

"Springbok, Union of South Africa." She
answered in English as she was ordered to do,
though the caller spoke hurriedly in Afrikaans. She
listened a moment then smiled and enthusiastically
answered. "Yes, Sir!" She hung up and sat back
savoring the moment. The team was about to go
into action again. It had been almost a year since the
whole team had been called out. Last time it had
been to Morocco and that was to take out a large
transshipment point for Russian diamonds, coming
out of Siberia. Though there had been a leak and
there was a security team waiting for them, the fight
had been fierce and they had shut down the
warehouse. She smiled to herself, remembering.
They'd left the building looking like something out
of Lebanon. She, personally, had been responsible
for shooting the leader, one known only as the
Dancer. Though she'd been wounded, it had only
been a scratch and her team had recovered more
than ten-thousand carats in rough-cut stones.
They'd been rewarded with a two-week all
expenses paid trip to the beaches in Rio de Janeiro.
She'd loved the soft sand, the dancing and the
nudity, for she was a tall, lanky girl who liked to
show off her body.

She stepped out of the small office that also
served as the quarters that she shared with two other
women, and walked to the volleyball court where a

vigorous game was in progress. Her khakis were pressed to razor sharpness and, though she wore no insignia, she carried the rank of captain. The hot sun beat down like a sauna, leaving her hair moist and forming pockets of moisture under her arms and between her breasts.

"Listen up," she called through cupped hands. All activity stopped. The twenty men and women came over to stand under the shade of a thatched roof over a pole structure.

"What is happening, Captain?" asked a young blonde boy from Zimbabwe.

"A and B Teams, prepare equipment. We leave tomorrow. Full gear. Jungle preparations."

"Africa or Sud America?" Her supply sergeant, an older veteran of Angola asked.

"Central America, Sergeant. I will want three helicopters. One troop carrier, one gunship, and one reconnaissance. Do we have room in the freighter for three?"

"Aye, Captain. What about ground transportation?"

She thought for a minute, "I think we will be operating in the jungle. We will dispense with ground vehicles. Let's not take heavy machine guns either. I'm not sure who the target is, but we had better take weapons common to that area. Mostly Cuban and American weapons." She smiled at the older man. "You know what to pack, Angelo. Be prepared for one week maximum after we hit shore." She paused, looking at the eager faces. She knew they didn't see action often, but the teams were always in top shape and ready to respond. The pay was good and there was ample opportunity to share in the pleasures of the world. Sergeant Angelo DeLuca liked young boys so they'd found him a houseboy from the slums of Joburg. Marie, from Marseilles liked her men in teams, so she was bunked with the Broussard brothers, a set of twins from Belgium. They tried to accommodate the desires and wishes of all the team members, for they were handpicked for their skills, ruthlessness and lack of any ties except to the company. All members had been recruited from orphanages at a young age. They worked in offices or counting rooms, or as valets, cooks, yard boys and girls. Some were concubines to more senior men. But the elite, those who were selected, went into the teams.

There were four teams. Two were at the small base near Springbok on the West Coast of South Africa, and two teams were stationed in a similar base near Ubombo in Swaziland on the East Coast. The teams knew of each other's existence, but were kept apart. One never knew when one might have to be used against the other. The director of the teams overall was Michael Boettcher, the Direktor of Security for all of VanHerff, Inc.. His job was to insure that the miners, graders, cutters, other security personnel, rivals, and managers, stole no diamonds. He took over the strike teams to insure that VanHerff would continue to stay in control of the world's diamonds, and that anything threatening its domination would be crushed.

The strike teams had been formed back in the 1920's when VanHerff was attempting to insure its sovereignty. They had slowly built up a network of spies and lackeys everywhere in the world, most of who never knew who their masters were. All diamond merchants who dealt with the company or ever hoped to, were similarly engaged and owed allegiance to the company. Boettcher insured that.

The merchants were the final link in the chain. Each year, selected large merchants were granted a Viewing of rough stones. At that time they were expected to purchase the stones from the company at the company's price. There was no negotiating and no choice. If the merchant exhibited reluctance or haggled, they might not receive an invitation for a Viewing the following year. If all went well, the merchant might be given more valuable gems in the ensuing years. However, the company frequently made up packets or *brifkes* of inferior grade stones and inserted them in the offering as a way of reminding the merchant who his master was. If he protested, he was dropped. There were always dozens waiting to take his place.

Thus went the diamond business. When gems like the white emeralds came along, something that might prove more alluring than diamonds, they must be stopped -- crushed if necessary. If the emeralds had remained green, VanHerff might have ignored them or merely noted their existence, but once they threatened the diamond's dominance, they became Boettcher's province. Though he was nominally under the aegis of the Board of Directors, he'd proven his loyalty so many times that he was given free reign, reporting only to Karl Danziger. At Karl's suggestion, Boettcher had prepared a dossier on each of the other board members, their families and friends. Just as a precaution.

Due to VanHerff's great influence in the South African economy and government, the company was given assistance and aid from the military. It was, therefore, quite easy to assemble strike teams, equip and deploy them with, if not the government's blessing, its determined ignorance. Each base had aircraft, boats, and land fighting vehicles available.

The main form of transport for the teams was by freighter. These freighters had been especially constructed to look like the old rusty tramp freighters that ply the world carrying assorted cargo from port to port on contract. They were registered as independent vessels for hire, and even occasionally served as such for cover. Inside, however, they were a marvel of engineering, with the latest in electronics, communications, and weaponry. So far two of these special freighters had been built and were continuously upgraded. Hydraulic lifts could bring a fully fueled and manned helicopter to the deck in a matter of seconds. Below were comfortable quarters, and pressure hatches for miniature submarines and divers' egress. There were even small shops where specialized weapons, repairs, or last minute modifications could be made. Kept aboard were many sets of identification for each of the crewmembers and for the strike teams.

That evening, the supply sergeant met with the team leader to decide on weaponry for the mission.

Since they were to be operating in dense jungle,
they opted for simple, lightweight weapons. Each
person would carry an SA-80, a British Enfield
Assault Rifle. It fired a 5.56mm shell, which the
Americans had found to be near perfect for jungle
warfare. The bullet was fast and tended to cut
through most foliage rather than be deflected easily.
The SA-80 was short and blocky with the 32 shot
magazine inserted behind the trigger guard. The
design was known as the bullpup. Atop was a four-
power image intensifying scope, third generation.
The newest design used a microprocessor to avoid
the former problems of "whiting out" when
confronted with a sudden burst of light. Though the
gun was heavy, eleven pounds fully loaded, the
weight made it an extremely stable weapon when
used at full auto. And best of all, the guns were sold
in large quantities to Cuba so they were easy to get.

In addition, each member of the team would
carry a personal side arm, generally a Detonics .45
caliber U.S. automatic patterned after the standard
U.S. Army Colt .45. The Detonics was smaller,
lighter and more accurate than its bigger cousin.
The team leaders agreed that heavier weapons were
more hindrance than help. They added two
flash/bang grenades each, a smoke grenade, several
Dutch V-40 hand grenades, and agreed that each
team leader would carry a Mossberg pistol grip riot
control shotgun loaded with special XR-18 Sabot
Rounds. Though the shotguns were only good for
close-in work, they gave the advantage of massive
destruction at close range.

Each team member would wear standard South African Army Issue camo fatigues with a cross-buckled combat vest to which the weaponry, ammo, first aid gear, and all other items would be attached. After a short discussion, it was decided that one team would assign their strongest member to carry a quantity of C-4 plastique explosive and a miniature radio controlled transmitting detonator. If there was a mine to explode, the C-4 would be more than adequate for the job. They decided against shoulder missiles due to the close quarters normally encountered in the jungle and their cumbersome nature. This was to be a fast in-and-out operation. None of the uniforms had any identifying labels or insignia, no personal papers were to be carried, and they were sure that all members of the team were untraceable either through any government agency in Central America or through Interpol. The meeting was short and each team captain made a list of the gear to carry back to his or her members. A team would go in first with B team being held in reserve.

Before dawn two mornings later, the troops quietly glided aboard the rusty freighter at the dock just outside Springbok. They quickly loaded their personal gear and weapons. There were twenty-one in all, Captain Jane Houllihan was in charge of Strike Team A and Julian LeDuc was Team Leader B. Each had ten combatants under them, each team having three women and seven men. Sergeant Angelo DeLuca would stay aboard and act as liaison, supply and communications co-coordinator.

The three helicopters were unloaded from their flatbeds and hoisted aboard with the ship's crane. The reconnaissance bird was a small Aerospatiale II two passenger, a French design that had been discontinued in the mid '70's. However they were still being built in India and had been purchased there ostensibly for aerial survey work. The next was a larger LodeRunner 2000 Troop Carrier, a US designed cargo machine utilizing a modified Jet Ranger power train and a custom airframe, which allowed ten soldiers and their gear inside a cargo compartment aft of the two-person tandem cockpit. It was a slim, shark-like extremely rugged machine that could act as a gunship after discharging its troops. The third was a South African built Rooivalk Gunship, a Red Falcon. This was a pre-production machine, similar to the US built Cobras, though a little heavier and not quite as fast. All three choppers were painted flat black and had no markings at all.

Just as dawn was breaking through the clouds, they were finished loading. Jane Houllihan stood on the bridge with the captain. The day was hot and she was wearing loose khaki shorts and a sleeveless T-shirt. The captain, a short, neat German with a thin cigar clamped between his teeth eyed her breasts from behind mirrored sunglasses. He wore white trousers and a neatly pressed blue and white striped shirt. Upon his nearly baldhead, he had a white captain's hat. The boat's name was the Van der Groot and her homeport was listed as Surinam. Her cargo - machine tools.

Ft. McAndless, Texas:

Col. Sykes paced back and forth, fuming. He yanked the cigarette from his mouth and ground it under his booted heel, then kicked it as hard as he could. In a minute, he lit another, snapping the top on the heavily engraved Zippo lighter repeatedly. "Those bastards. Those motherfuckers! When I get my hands on those two, I'll personally kill them. How dare they? How fucking dare they!"

Sergeant Rossiter stood at loose attention just inside the door. He was almost used to Sykes' towering rages. He'd been off the base the night the Comanche had been stolen and the Colonel's personal Humvee implanted in the roof of his house. The Colonel had wisely made more of the Humvee incident than the disappearance of the prototype helicopter. Only the Colonel and a few select individuals knew that fact. As far as base officials knew, the machine was out on maneuvers and would be back in a few days for more tests.

"Sergeant!" Sykes barked.

"Yes sir, Colonel." Rossiter snapped to rigid attention.

"Get Lt. Graham in here on the double. Then get Sgt. Dodge, Corporals Bettenhousen, Mikkelsen, and Pagano to the hanger. I'll meet you there."

Each of these orders was followed by a Yes sir! Then Sergeant Rossiter left in a hurry. In a few minutes, First Lt. Edward Graham knocked once then let himself into Sykes' office.

"You wanted to see me, Colonel?"

"Yes. At ease, Lieutenant." Graham relaxed, though he remained poised for action at any moment. This was his normal demeanor, ever since returning from Vietnam. He'd been a lowly private then and had slowly risen through the ranks until he'd become an officer. He expected to finish out his time as a first lieutenant. He'd served under Sykes in 'Nam and in Panama, and once Sykes had saved his life, though it was in a bar in Saigon when a grenade had been lobbed through the door.

"Lieutenant, we've known each other a long time. I suppose you've heard about our missing Comanche?"

"Yes sir, it's all over the base." Graham had an uneasy feeling.

"Well, that was a test. We're to locate that chopper and bring it back - quietly. With its stealth capabilities, it will be hard to track, but I, in my infinite wisdom, had a locator beacon installed when we first started tests here. I not only know where it is, I can tell whether it's flying or on the ground." He resumed his pacing. "I have called together a crew of loyal American soldiers to assist in this recovery. I want you to be my second-in-command on this operation. It's all top secret, you understand."

"Yes sir, I understand," answered Lt. Graham. This sounded to him like one of their Black

Operation Unit runs. He also knew the Colonel was full of shit about the theft of the chopper being a "test." Two guys had slipped onto the base and stolen it, pure and simple. Probably the same two guys who had recovered the stolen Cobra, the ones Sykes had screwed out of their money. They wanted their money, that was all. He liked the touch about the Hummer into Sykes' roof. It had a lot of style, and one thing Graham liked was style.

Sykes had his own style, a bit darker, but nevertheless style. Things were always interesting around Sykes. Hell, yes, he'd be the second-in-command. Things were dull these days without a war. He tried to stay in shape, working out at the gym three days a week, but without a definite purpose, it hardly seemed worth it. His weight had ballooned to 235 lbs. on his six foot two inch frame and he felt heavy and loggy. He still kept his hair in a short military crop, though even that lately felt more effort than it was worth. Graham was a Midwestern boy out of the South Dakota prairies and endless days of plowing, seeding, and combining. He loved the military and thanked whatever God he believed in for the opportunity to escape from those endless days of boredom. To pilot a helicopter instead of a New Holland combine was his greatest thrill, and he'd go along with whatever deranged scheme Col. Sykes dreamed up if it meant hours in an attack chopper or even a troop transport. He was checked out on over two-dozen different U.S. and foreign choppers, and leapt at any chance to even sit behind the stick.

They walked out to a waiting Humvee and drove to the hanger. A 4x4 was just pulling up and several men dropped out of the back. These men were Sykes' handpicked crew. He'd pulled them in from units around the world. Sergeant Dodge was a veteran thief and "cumshaw" artist. Cumshaw was a term used in the military to loosely meant: "making better use of government property." It was not exactly theft; *redistribution* might be a more correct definition, at least in Dodge's mind. Anyway, Sergeant Dodge was a senior ranking cumshaw artist. He had a narrow face, close set eyes, a slim, twitchy build, and a long thin nose. He looked like an Irish setter gone to seed. His specialty was supply. His eyes were constantly roaming, looking for that indefinable something that was coming soon, coming to harm or to help him.

Next to him stood Corporal Mikkelsen. His broad, open face had a permanent smile. His blonde hair was cut short and framed clear blue eyes. You couldn't tell just by looking at him that he was a thief and a killer. In another life he might have been a neighborhood priest or a youth leader.

Slouching beside him was Corporal Pagano, a skinny kid from Federal Hill in Providence, Rhode Island. He was a close-in weapons man. Word had it that he was *connected* and that his father had sent him into the army to gain training with a wide assortment of military hardware. Sykes had his doubts as to whether or not that was true. As crazy as this kid was, he was probably sent away just to get rid of him. But he was also a first rate small arms expert, having qualified as expert with handguns, rifles, and machine guns. He could field strip them in the dark, and was a natural mechanic. Sykes considered Pagano one of his star finds. It was a closely guarded secret that Graham was teaching Pagano to fly a chopper, and Pagano had proven such an apt pupil that Graham was of a mind to mention it to Sykes, maybe be able to get the kid into flying school. He hadn't said anything yet, at Pagano's insistence.

Private Bettenhousen was a hard one to figure. Sloppy, overweight, his pocked skin looked as if he'd spent his entire youth scratching his cheeks. He smoked constantly and needed reminding to put it out when around aircraft. He was a pilot in civilian life who'd been busted out of a small commuter airline. He specialized in electronics -- computers and programming. It was he who'd designed, built, and installed the homing device in the now missing Comanche helicopter.

Sykes liked to keep as much information from the military as he used it. His team specialized in Black Operations. They weren't elite. They weren't super trained. They were just expendable. When the Army needed something underhanded and untraceable done, they contacted Colonel Sykes. He always came through. Their former commanders never missed the men he picked. They were never the outstanding members of a unit. They were not military enough, but the Army had them and had to do something with them.

It was rare that Sykes and his men would be given one of the prototype Comanche helicopters, but Sykes was known to have flown helicopters like no other man had in the past, and it was decided to have him wring one out. They gave him two engineers from Bell Aviation and a strict schedule of tests. They knew he'd probably ignore the schedule, but he'd also find its weak spots and make it do things it wasn't designed to do. If it could fly upside down and backwards at 200 knots while firing Tomahawk missiles and its laser guided cannon, Sykes would do it. The engineers would be aghast and dumbfounded, but the Army wanted at least one machine completely wrung out. If putting up with Colonel Warren Emmett Sykes and his BOU was the price, then that was the price. After all, Sykes had been a promising young officer on the rise. He'd been a Cobra Gunship pilot in Nam, eventually commanding a squadron as part of the 1st Air Cavalry. He'd never been convicted or even tried for illegally transporting contraband in country, but his company commander had felt it was in his best interests to have him transferred after his third tour started.

Sykes had been sent to Israel to help train Israeli troops in battle tactics. When Israel had finally sent him back to the U.S. Army, the Israeli Officers knew all about helicopters vs. tanks, and were poorer than church mice, or maybe synagogue mice, thanks to then Captain Sykes' poker playing ability.

After a stint in Florida at McDill Air Force base learning about in-air helo refueling, Lt. Colonel Sykes was ordered to Panama to assist with the extraction of Panama strongman Manuel Noriega.

Though the intelligence was poor and they never did find Noriega, Sykes found that a Cobra really could fly down a street between buildings and land on top of a building such as a bank. As he found, a bank in Panama City was no match for military explosives, and he had the good sense to share his newfound wealth with a certain General Creighton who happened to discover the incident. That Creighton was a little bent himself only served to aid Sykes' career.

Several delicate, yet perfectly executed extractions, assassinations, and operations led to Sykes' posting as a BOU team leader in a sleepy part of Texas. General Creighton convinced his superiors at the Pentagon to assign one of the new Comanche helicopters to Colonel Sykes for testing, and that was that. One of Sykes' discoveries was that the Comanche could fly sideways at over ninety knots, a feat impossible with conventional military helicopters. What use this might be was yet to be discovered, but it was something that only the Comanche could do and this fact was filed away for further tactical study.

Sykes also discovered that its five bladed rotor was strong enough to chop through vines and branches up to four inches in diameter, a fact learned when he'd had to fly cover in the jungle for an assassination team in Mexico. They'd been pinned down by a Mexican army squad on the payroll of a Mexican general who was transshipping cocaine into Texas via Vera Cruz. A two-man assassination team had been landed on the coast and had hiked inland for several days until they reached the general's villa. It took two more days to line up the fatal shot. In the end, they managed and at over 1000 yards at that, but an unlucky break had stymied their escape. The general was feting one of his captains for his birthday and had the captain's personal platoon out for the day.

As the general lay dying, the captain had rushed his men in Jeeps to where he suspected the shot had come from. His lucky guess had pinned the team down for good until dark had overtaken them. The two-man team had night vision gear and quietly slipped through the cordon. The pickup zone was no more than a mile away, so a last minute change was made and the matte black Blackhawk extraction chopper had to put down in a small clearing on the side of a hill poking out of the jungle below. Hearing it, the Mexicans had rushed to the spot hot on the tail of the assassination team. Sykes had sailed the Comanche down through the canopy, raking the mini-gun back and forth just over the heads of the two men now fleeing up the hill as fast as their gear would allow. He'd placed his ship directly in the path between the Mexicans and the Blackhawk, coming down through the trees like a crashing meteor. He'd felt several thunks and clunks but the rotor kept turning and the suppressing fire allowed the hit teams' extraction to be completed successfully. Later inspection showed a series of dents in the leading edge of several rotor blades that were at least four inches in diameter. Sykes remembered thinking at the time: *Gillette thought he had sharp blades, he never walked under a Comanche for a shave!*

Now he was on the trail of those two bastards who'd had the audacity to come onto his base, blown up his Hummer, and stolen his chopper. Well, by goddamn, they were going to get theirs. He'd track them into Hell if he had to and string them up by their balls.

"Men. We've got a mission. Last night two unidentified terrorists entered the base and made off with the Comanche helicopter we've been testing." The men kept silent. This was all old news. "I had planted a homing device in it and our mission is to recover the missing bird." He had a good head of steam up now and was pacing up and down in front of the men. "Lt. Graham will contact the Air Farce and give them the frequency of this homing device. They will locate it by satellite and give us its location. We will load up, take two choppers, and go get it. We'll take a Blackhawk for the commuters and an Apache. I want the black ones, no markings. I want you all in camos, no insignia. Bring small arms and, better, M-16's too. Sergeant Rossiter!"

"Yes, sir," shouted Rossiter, leaping to attention. The other men looked at him incredulously. They knew from experience that when preparing for a mission, rank got left behind, and military protocol was tossed aside. Of course, Sergeant Rossiter was new and hadn't been on a BOU mission yet.

"Relax, Sergeant," Sykes waved a hand negligently at him. "Load up the chin gun on the

Apache with a full complement of 20 mike-mike, and have the gunners put TOW's on the port wing and Hellfires on the starboard. You'll fly gunner for me."

"Yes, sir," once again popped out of Rossiter's mouth, and Pagano snickered.

Before Rossiter could retort, Sykes pointed to Lieutenant Graham. "Graham, you get the ball rolling with the Air Farce yuppies and tell them we'll need an in-air refueling in the next day or two. I'll let them know where and when. Low level, two choppers. Also, get the location of our beacon. Here's the frequency." He handed over a scrap of paper. Graham signaled Private Bettenhousen who took the paper and the two of them trotted over to the 4x4 truck and took off.

"Well, that's it. You men draw your gear from Rossiter, here, and be ready to go by," he pulled back his cuff and squinted at his watch, "sixteen hundred hours." He looked around at his men. "Any questions?"

"Yes, sir," Sergeant Dodge asked. "We going to need anything special? I mean, if I only got a couple of hours, I'll have to get cracking."

Sykes rubbed his hand along his jaw, "I don't know, Dodge. Maybe some night gear? We've got comm gear. I really don't know what we'll be up against. This one is new, we've got no intel. We'll go in light and fast, snatch the chopper, nail the fuckers who swiped it and be gone before they know what hit 'em. Be ready for anything."

"We going to use a ship to get us close, Colonel?" asked Mikkelsen. He hated ships. They were slow and uncomfortable and he got seasick, violently seasick.

"No, the fewer people know about this, the better. We'll use a bird for in-air refueling.

"Suppose the Comanche is, say, in Africa, Colonel?" this from Pagano.

"Nah, shit, Pagano. They'd have to have a ship and maybe a tanker to fuel that thing. No, my bet is that they're close. This'll be a piece of cake. We'll go in, shoot up some bad guys, snatch the bird and be home before you know it."

The men seemed to be satisfied. They knew their roles and it was just another mission to them. Two days later, Lt. Graham was back with the location and they found themselves on the way to the oil platform in the Gulf of Mexico.

CHAPTER 16

Dave woke just as dusk was settling. He came instantly awake, eyes open, body tense, ready to leap up and operate, before he knew where he was or what was happening. He felt electrified and alive. The ability to be asleep one minute and then in a micro-second, fully awake was a trait he'd picked up in 'Nam, a skill that had saved his life on more than one occasion. He listened for a repeat of the sound that had awakened him. Next to his right leg he felt the small Walther PPK pistol he'd placed there when he'd gone to sleep. There were voices, agitated voices. Quietly he slipped out of bed and crept to the window. Silently, he placed an ear to the glass. He didn't recognize the language, though he recognized one of the voices as that of Senor

Locarno. He could barely make out the outlines of a small group of people to his right. Two of them were barely dressed, just in breechclouts and crossed slings of leather over their shoulders. One held a small bow and had a tiny quiver of arrows on his back. The other had a spear as tall as he was, which wasn't tall at all. They both had slightly protruding bellies and hair trimmed in that thatched roof style of primitive people. They spoke to Senor Locarno waving their arms about in exaggerated gestures, stamping their feet and the one waved his spear in a direction over his shoulder.

Dave pulled away from the window and slipped into the bathroom where he flipped on a light. After peeking into Tom's room and determining that he wasn't there, Dave hopped into a hot shower, as hot as he could stand it. He knew it would be the last one for a few days.

Just as Dave was toweling down, Tom quietly slipped into his room. Dave saw the light go on and called, "Thomas, you whore-dog, have you been cavorting all day? Let's go! Time's a wasting." Though he, Tom, and Doby would move their quarters into a tiny clearing in the jungle some two miles from the house that Dave had selected, they'd come back during the night for supplies.

Tom staggered into the bathroom and sloshed cold water on his puffy face. "*Oy vey*. What time is it?"

"Its show time, Pally. We'll grab a bite and you start some weapons training with the family. Doby and I will check out the *Cholos*. Okay?"

"Yeah, yeah," Tom replied, now running water over the back of his neck, soaking his shirt. He peeled it off and tossed it in the corner, slid out of his shorts and tossed them after the shirt. Naked, he slumped down in the sunken tub and ran the water. As Dave was dressing in a clean set of jungle camos, he could hear Tom humming softly tunelessly to himself. Dave knew that he was getting focused.

He called, "I'm going down for some grub. I'll meet you in the kitchen or whatever they call it down here.

Tom muttered some reply and then went back to his splashing and humming.

Dave put the Walther in a shoulder holster under his camo top and slipped on a pair of camo sneakers. He stuffed a make-up kit into one pocket and took his good watch and wedding ring off, carefully placing them in the bureau's top drawer with his wallet and other personal belongings. He'd already removed the labels in the camos. At last, he rolled up a pair of thin rubber gloves and placed them in a pouch pocket of his pants. Picking up a black silk balaclava, he ambled down the corridor toward the kitchen, which, in fact, was called a kitchen, or *cocina* in Spanish.

It was around six, too early for dinner, which these people ate around nine or ten o'clock at night. Doby was sitting at the old pine table eating a small plateful of cookies with a glass of milk. Tia Roberta was sitting across from him while a fat, dark woman rolled tortillas out on a floured board. They were having an animated discussion as Dave cautiously stepped into the room. There was an instant silence.

"Pardon me, I didn't mean to intrude," he hung back near the doorway.

"Senor Dave, please have some cookies. Would you like some milk, too?" Tia Roberta spoke in heavily accented English, picking her words slowly.

Dave nodded his head, looking about the large kitchen. Against one wall there was a large six burner stove with a griddle similar to the one at Chesney's. Next to it was a heavy counter of light colored wood and behind it was a brick oven with a small fuel door under it. In strange contrast, beside it were a stainless steel commercial microwave oven and a four-slice toaster. The sink was a huge double basin made of some sort of stone with two faucets hanging over the edge. The table was set with a hand-woven tablecloth and a rack of cloth napkins in the center. Beside them was a large pepper mill and a square box that Dave imagined held salt or sugar.

Tia Roberta was speaking in rapid Spanish to the heavy woman rolling out the tortillas. She sighed and dusted her hands. Against the far wall was a large double door refrigerator. She removed a wide-mouth bottle, poured Dave a glass of milk and handed him one of the plates of cookies that were sitting on the counter in a row. Dave bit into one. It was soft and had a sweet, crunchy taste.

The others watched him eat. His brows furrowed.

Doby leaned forward, smiling. "Well, wha' 'choo think? Not bad, huh?"

Dave tilted his head and thought for a minute, jaw working slowly. At last he said, "I taste coconut, almond and…." He drew this last out. "Cinnamon?"

Tia Roberta laughed, slapping her palm against the table. The dark woman laughed, too. "*Canela*!" she croaked through her laughter. "*Si, canela.*"

Tia Roberta wiped her eyes with the end of a shawl draped over her shoulders. "You are very good, Senor Dave, but not good enough. There is also nutmeg, what we call *nuez moscada* here. It grows wild nearby. My nieces gather it, and Maria and I dry and grind it." She gestured absently with one hand.

"Nice try, man," said Doby smiling as he dunked another cookie in his milk. It was now dark and the warm light in the kitchen and the family around him made Dave suddenly miss Chris and his friends at Chesney's. His face grew grim.

"Doby, did you get the stuff out of the chopper like I asked?"

"Yep. I put it all on a bench in the garage. Man, you've got some awesome firepower. You know, that's some radio you've got in the chopper. I picked up Miami and a couple of other stations on it. I was wondering what the beep-beep-beep was, though." Doby looked puzzled, playing with a cookie before putting it whole in his mouth.

"Beep-beep-beep?" Dave asked cautiously, a cookie halfway to his mouth.

"Yeah, only the second beep was a little lower than the others. Three beeps, then a pause. Three beeps then a pause. Why, is something wrong?"

The two women were looking at him curiously. Dave smiled a grim smile. Just then Tom strutted into the room looking none the worse for wear, hair neatly combed, a pair of camo pants with an olive drab T-shirt stuffed into the waistband. He plopped down in a chair next to Dave and as he opened his mouth to speak, a door to the outside opened and Senor Locarno stepped into the warm kitchen, hands flexing in agitation. Tom raised an eyebrow questioningly.

Senor Locarno was pacing back and forth after grabbing a cup of thick, black coffee in one hand. "Something wrong?" asked Tom.

The slim man stopped beside Tom's chair and put a slightly trembling hand on his shoulder. "*Si*, Senor Tom." He sighed and pinched the bridge of his nose between a finger and thumb. "This morning the headman of the native Mayan people who reside in the hills came to me. He told me that his son and his sister's son were in the next valley spying on the *narcoticos* yesterday afternoon when they were taken by one of the men." He paused, visibly shaken, steadying himself against the table. "He said that the men burned them with cigarettes until they cried out in pain. When they wouldn't tell them where their village was, they cut the skin from their arms and legs then hung them from trees. The men hit them with sticks until they died. He wants to gather the men in the tribe and seek his revenge. I tried to reason with him but he was deep in his grief." The slim man hung his head. He was clearly agitated and sat wringing his hands.

Dave looked at Tom and motioned him outside with a small movement of his head. They exited the warm kitchen and strolled outside and down a path leading to one of the outbuildings. The hacienda was laid out in a square, the main living quarters facing the front with a large green lawn fanning out before the dun colored portico, bisected by a road, which wound off into the hills. To a casual observer, it would appear that the main building was all there was, comfortable, but not extravagant. The secondary buildings lay behind the main house and slightly lower, as the ground sloped away. They casually walked toward a large garage. Dave assumed that was where Doby had brought their gear. He and Tom said little, each trying to figure out a way to keep the Mayans from committing suicide. They knew the Stone Age weapons would be no match for the automatic weapons of the *Cholos*.

Dave peeked into the garage. There, on a table lay the large green duffel bags Doby had taken out of the helicopter. Tom and Dave each pulled open the tops and began carefully extracting the contents. Dave laid out the M-16 automatic rifles, six in all, and began pulling out metal boxes of ammunition, stacking them beside the machine guns. Tom, meanwhile, pulled out three pump shotguns and boxes of shells. Next to them he piled a half dozen pistols and extra clips. Tom also pulled out several chemical vials and other mysterious gadgets Dave had never seen before.

"What are those?" Dave asked gesturing toward a pile of what looked like small transistor radios.

Tom absently ran his hand through the pile. "The dark ones are two way radios and the gray ones are remote detonators. They can be triggered by the radios as well as these." He handed Dave a couple of keychain size buttons. "Oh, and you'll like this. I got it out of a catalog." He shoved what looked like a smoke detector at Dave and a pocket calculator-sized box. "The smoke detector is actually a video camera and this box is a TV screen." He clicked on a couple of buttons and pulled out a thin wire antenna. "Look."

Dave looked at himself looking down at the round camera and started making faces. Tom laughed.

"What the hell did you bring this stuff for?" asked Dave, amused.

Tom shrugged, "You never know. Maybe we can plant this inside one of their buildings and get some good intel."

"Yeah, sure," snorted Dave. "You probably wanted to plant it in Alex's bedroom so you can watch her strip at night."

"Naw, if I want to watch her strip, I just have to ask her."

They were silent for a few minutes as each carefully checked his gear. Dave broke the silence, "So what are we going to do about the Mayans."

Tom looked at him in dismay. "Do? We do nothing right now. Shit, you going to go in with guns blazing for a couple of kids? No fucking way." He shook his head disgustedly. "You and Doby go in tonight and get us some hard intel, and we'll plan this out properly. You tip them off and they'll come and wipe this whole valley out, you mark my words. We're only a couple of guys, and Doby said there's about fifty of them." He looked disgusted. "We go off half cocked and you can kiss your ass good-bye."

Dave nodded in reluctant agreement. "Maybe if we had some firepower in the chopper, we could really shoot 'em up," sighed Dave.

"Yeah, but we don't, buddy-boy. Don't worry, Sykes will be after us as soon as he figures out where we are, and we'll sic him on the *Cholos*. That'll get rid of some of them. And if the diamond kings are on schedule, they might just get here at the same time. We won't have to do shit except the mopping up." He snorted. "Maybe if we're lucky, they'll all kill each other off and we'll have a few choppers to sell!"

Dave stopped for a minute, "Let's see, Chris said the security guys from VanHerff were at Chesney's," he consulted his watch, "about twelve hours ago. If they move fast -- and with their timing on the Yemeni trip, I think they will -- I'll expect them in four or five days. That doesn't leave us much time."

"No way," responded Tom. "What do you expect them to do, fly over and drop in on us with no way of getting out?" He chuckled, clicked the action back on one of the M-16's and peered down the barrel.

"So that means a ship, if they're bringing choppers with them," Dave pondered.

"And they'll have to if they're operating in the jungle," reasoned Tom

"If they use a ship, that'll give us a week, maybe ten days to get ready." He was making notes on the tabletop. "Sykes won't come alone and I expect neither will the VanHerff laddies. If we can get them here about the same time, maybe we'll only have to direct the action." Dave licked the tip of his pencil, "I figure that if Boettcher gets the go ahead from his bosses, a pretty fast ship doing about twenty-five to thirty knots from Capetown to the Western Caribbean, that's about 8000 miles, give or take, should get here on...," Dave scribbled some more on the table, Tom peering over his shoulder. "Thursday the fourteenth, maybe Friday." He turned to Tom. "We'll have to get Emile to monitor ship movements out of South Africa headed this way for the next few days."

"Suppose their team isn't in South Africa?"

"Where else would it be? They're not exactly beloved by the rest of the world, you know." Dave replied.

"Yeah, I guess," Tom conceded. He was a man of action, not much of a planner. Dave usually took care of that end. "We can call Emile and get the ship schedules."

"Oh, I think Doby detected a homing bug in the chopper."

"Great," Tom enthused. "Let's go get it, and you can give it to the bad guys as a little present."

"Good idea. But we'll shut it down for a while. No sense bringing Sykes in too soon. And before I leave, have Alex get me a few uncut white emeralds. I'll plant them, too, for the diamond kings to find."

They stepped out of the garage and almost walked into Doby and the elder Locarno. "Senor Dave. Senor Tom, my uncle would like to talk to you about the Mayans."

"I'm sorry, Senor Locarno, but you will have to deal with the Mayans right now," Dave replied, looking at the agitated old man. "Just keep them away from the *Cholos* for about a week, and we will take care of everything."

Without waiting for a reply, Dave stepped into an open Toyota Land Cruiser and started it. Tom swung into the other side and yelled something in Spanish to Doby. They left the old man and the boy standing in the dust as they roared away toward the chopper.

Over the noise, Dave hollered, "What did you say to them?"

Tom yelled back, "I told Doby to go back to the house and be ready to go with you in an hour." Dave nodded and swung the truck in a circle next to the covered chopper. They scrambled under the camouflage netting, shining flashlights all around as they pulled inspection covers open and lifted seats.

"What the hell are we looking for?" asked Dave, digging into an instrument package behind a tangle of wires.

"Damned if I know." He thought for a minute. "Look for a stand alone electronics package that looks hand wired. It will probably have one or two wires for power and an antenna, but nothing else connected to the ship and it will be small, maybe like a pack of cigarettes." Tom's voice was muffled as he peered into a belly compartment. They had started in and around the chin gun and were slowly working their way aft, when Tom cried, "Got it." He pulled out a plastic box the size of a small cellular phone with a strip of double sided tape stuck to the outside. The antenna was a wire with a loop on the end. There was a red and black wire twisted together disappearing into the heart of the ship. "This must be it," Tom said, holding it aloft. "There's no numbers or I.D. tags on it and it looks handmade."

Dave came around next to him. "What do you figure the voltage is?"

Tom shrugged, "Dunno. Let me see. Tom dug into a pouch pocket on the side of his pants and came out with a small multi-meter.

Dave shook his head in amazement. Tom unwound the wires and Dave scraped at the insulation on the wires with his Swiss Army knife. Tom put the small flashlight in his mouth and squinted at the digital readout. "Hah," he gurgled. "Twelve volt." He slipped the multi-meter back into his pants pocket. "Reach into the pocket next to the gunners seat on the right, Davey, and get me a couple of 9 volt batteries." Dave did as he was told and handed them to Tom who had wormed a small roll of electrical tape out of a rear pocket. He quickly taped two of the batteries together and, borrowing Dave's knife, snipped the wires and stripped them back an inch or so. He then taped them to the battery terminals. "Well, 18 volts is a little more than we need but it should still work OKAY" He handed the package to Dave who grinned. "That should work fine for a few hours like that. I'll disconnect it for now. See if you can tie it to a 12 volt battery when you get a chance." Tom grinned back.

"Let's get the hell out of here." They wormed their way out of the chopper and stood brushing themselves off. Tom jumped behind the wheel of the Land Cruiser and they sped back to the main house. Doby and Alex were waiting for them. Dave held out the small package, wires dangling.

"What is it?" Alex asked curiously.

"It's a homing device for a high powered receiver. Obviously, the Army likes to keep track of their equipment." Dave smiled.

Alex hugged herself. "So they know where the helicopter is with that?" She shivered. "What will we do now?"

Dave smiled again. "You'll see." He turned to the boy. "Doby, do you think you can show us where our Colombian *Cholo* friends are?" he indicated Tom and himself.

"You bet, Dave-dude!"

"Good. Go get in the Toyota. I'll get our gear." He and Tom walked toward the house. Dave took Tom's arm and leaned close. "We'll set up a perimeter, lines of fire, and that sort of thing. Arm all the family. Get the men carrying all the time. Doby and I will check out the *Cholos* and be in touch. Monitor on three. If there's trouble, we'll come in from the south. Fuel the chopper. We'd better keep it topped up and ready to go." He paused, intent.

"When we need it we'll be in a hurry, right?" Tom asked.

"That's right, buddy." Dave slapped Tom on his broad back. "Let everyone in the family fire off a few rounds from each weapon so they know the feel and the kick. Then keep 'em close. Anyone who doesn't want to come to be part of this, send them down to the capital or someplace else that's safe. We don't need screaming meemies in the way." Dave stopped at the door and faced his friend. "I'd say that we've got maybe a week, maybe ten days before all the players get on stage. We've got to set up everything before then."

"Don't worry, Buddy-boy, I'll do my part. By the way, here's a bunch of the emeralds Alex gave me." He handed Dave a small leather pouch, which Dave stuffed into a pocket.

Dave went into the garage, gathered up several items, and put them in a small rucksack, which he casually tossed over his shoulder. He took one last look around and hurried to the waiting truck. Doby was already in the driver's seat, engine running, face agleam with anticipation.

"Okay, young fella, let's rock and roll!" Dave smiled and waved him forward. The small truck lurched into gear and sped out of the yard in a cloud of dust. In a few minutes they were out of the clearing and into the jungle heading west through a dense thicket of vines and closely woven trees. The road looked as if it had been bored through the bush even though it had been there a long time.

Soon they reached the bottom of the valley and were headed up toward a ridge on a long gradually ascending cut in the hillside. Before they'd gone too far, Doby pulled the truck under some huge mahogany trees and turned the motor off. The only sounds were the clicking and creaking of the cooling engine and an occasional bird call. They sat in silence. Soon the air was filled, once again, with the chattering of monkeys and the screeches of parrots and other wildlife. To the south they heard the deep cough of a large cat.

"I didn't think we ought to go any closer, Dave. I don't know how far they've expanded since I was here last."

"Good thinking, Doby," Dave said, digging in the rucksack at his feet. "Here, do what I do." He handed the boy a small jar of green face paint. Next he removed a jar of brown and began painting the hollows of his face and neck. Doby followed suit, smearing it in wiggly lines up and down. They touched each other up doing ears and the backs of hands. Next Dave removed two camo bandannas and handed one to Doby, showing him how to tie it to cover his shiny hair. Finally they stood beside the quiet vehicle. Dave inspected Doby carefully, looking for any reflective surface. "Take your watch off and put it in your pocket," Dave indicated. A strip of dark webbing covered his own watch.

Into his pockets and around his waist Dave clipped on or strapped a two way radio with a thin microphone hooked over one ear, a pair of night vision binoculars and a small electronic drawing pad. On his right hip was a Smith and Wesson 9mm semi-automatic pistol with a four-inch silencer. The pistol was stuffed with especially loaded low velocity shells he and Vinny had made up to keep air speed down. When they'd tested it out on the water, it had hardly made a phffft sound. It wouldn't be very effective in the dense jungle but Dave fervently hoped he wouldn't have to use it.

"Where's my gun, Dave?" Doby asked innocently.

"What do you need a gun for?" Dave replied. "We're not going to shoot anybody today."

"What do you need a gun for," Doby countered, "if we're not going to shoot anybody?"

"Insurance."

"Well, I should have some insurance, too. Suppose something happens to you?" He looked so forlorn that Dave reluctantly reached back into the rucksack and brought out his featherweight Walther PPK 9mm semi-automatic pistol. It was in a black nylon shoulder holster. He thrust it at the youngster. "Here. You don't need it. But if you do, just point and shoot. There's no safety or anything to get in the way. And it's loud so only shoot in an emergency. If you can just run, do that. Remember, we're here only to gather intel."

"Right, gathering intel. What's intel?"

"Intelligence, data, information. Oh, yeah," Dave pulled out the monitoring device with the two nine volt batteries taped on. "I want to see if we can slip this into their camp." He smiled an evil grin. To Doby, Dave looked like the worst devil in the whole world at that moment and he shivered. Worse than Arnold Swartzenegger in Terminator. Even worse than Stallone in Rambo. They stood appraising each other. They wore identical camouflage trousers and long sleeve shirts and bandanas, on their feet were camouflage jungle boots. Dave's gear was in black pouches and Doby's gun was strapped over his shoulders. They were lean and mean. Dave nodded and the slipped into the bush, Doby in the lead.

They'd gone only a short distance when Dave brought Doby up short. "Listen, kid, if anything happens to me, don't try anything heroic. Just get your ass back to Tom. He'll know what to do, okay?"

"Right, Dave." Doby grinned and winked, then turned and resumed his march. The soft mold on the jungle floor quieted their footsteps and the dense canopy kept the undergrowth to a minimum. The jungle darkness enveloped them and Dave once again felt comfortable, his night vision returning, and his stealthiness reactivated like a well-remembered dance. They hardly noticed night deepening. Only when they emerged into the infrequent clearings and saw the stars overhead did they realize the hour.

By now they'd crested the ridge and headed for the lights below. Dave instructed Doby on how to speak quietly, breathing words into his ear, not hissing them, using a simple system of hand gestures and finger squeezes in the dark.

Silently they slipped from tree to tree, coming closer to the lights below. When they were no more than twenty yards from the outer circle of lights, they came upon the first sentry. Dave smelled his cigarette first and reached out to touch Doby. They halted silently, waiting, breathing through their mouths, squatting behind a clump of fragrant bushes. In a moment they could see his cigarette ember, then his outline against the lights behind.

He was squat and thick, a crumpled straw hat pulled down over his face. Stupid, Dave thought. Allowing the guards to smoke and the hat hid whatever came from above. Security was lax. Good. He gestured Doby to the right and they circled the camp.

They came to a tree that had a large crotch just over their heads and gave a full view of the encampment. Dave indicated to Doby to make a step for him with his hands. This Doby did and Dave vaulted lightly into the crotch. Reaching down, he pulled Doby up to him and silently slid out on a massive limb.

Dave made himself comfortable then pulled out the night vision binoculars and the electronic writing tablet. The binoculars slid over his head and were fixed in place with a set of plastic straps. Dave settled them comfortably and began his reconnaissance. To the south and backed up against a dark cliff was a building still under construction. It was approximately one hundred and fifty feet long by about fifty wide. Beside it was a prefab ten by forty and bordering the jungle on their side were several more prefabs, in different locations. There were two jeeps and a bulldozer parked next to a huge tank, which must be holding fuel. Beside it was another tank, plastic, which looked like it held water. One small building stood off to one side and had an antenna on its roof and a small satellite dish aimed heavenward. Leading out of the encampment was a short road and some more construction equipment parked by its side. Dave surmised that they were building an airstrip several hundred yards away. In the center of the clearing stood a Bell 206 Jet Ranger helicopter, painted a dark color with a logo Dave couldn't make out.

The cliff intrigued Dave. He reached up and pulled on Doby's shirtsleeve. "What's with the cliff? Why is the building right up against it?"

Doby leaned close to Dave and whispered, "It's a cave in there. It goes back into a bunch of passages and tunnels. Some are real small. We used to sneak in when we were kids," the teenager said.

"Any other way in?" Dave breathed.

Doby shrugged in the night, "Not that I know of."

Damn, Dave thought. *I'll have to go in one of these nights.* "Listen, I'm going to slip in and find a good place to plant this bug. You stay here and keep quiet. I'll be back in a few minutes. I want to get a look at the layout." Doby gave his hand a squeeze in reply.

Dave made a series of drawings on the faintly illuminated pad, labeling each one and storing it in

memory, before darkening the screen. He then
wedged the pad in the tree fork and slipped
noiselessly to the ground. This was their first
reconnaissance. Dave planned many more to totally
familiarize himself with the valley

A week later, he and Doby made their sixth
reconnaissance into the *Cholo* Valley, as they'd
come to call it. They were getting a pretty good feel
for the layout, the vehicles and personnel. They'd
begun building a model of the valley in the back
garage on a sheet of discarded plywood. Doby
supplied a quantity of toy trucks, planes, helicopters
and soldiers from a box of no longer used toys from
under his bed. He and Tom planned escape routes,
lines of fire, booby traps, and hiding places. On one
trip Dave had planted one of Tom's miniature TV
cameras with a transceiver pack high in a tree
overlooking the compound. One family member sat
at all times before the computer terminal to which it
was connected and monitored the progress of the
buildings and airstrip. The building against the cliff
was nearly completed and the bulldozer had hacked
out the basic outline of the airstrip, shoving trees
and stumps into the jungle beside the runway.
They'd watched while a group of the *Cholos*
unrolled a large roll of metal mesh onto the raw dirt.
Back in camp, an auxiliary generator had been air
lifted in by the Jet Ranger along with more building
materials.

Some of the buildings had started out as
sausage shaped balloons that were blown up by a
diesel-operated air compressor. When the balloons

were inflated they were approximately eight feet in diameter and twenty or thirty feet long. One group of men used a spray rig to coat the balloons with a chemical foam that expanded and hardened. The balloons were then deflated and extracted through a doorway-sized hole that had been cut with a portable saw. Some wet foam was sprayed on the outside, and branches, twigs, palm fronds, and banana leaves were adhered to the hut rendering them all but invisible.

Dave marveled at the high tech construction methods employed by the Colombians. But then he guessed they had to spend the cartel's money somehow.

This night Doby was comfortably ensconced in "their tree" while Dave ducked behind a jeep and then slipped against the wall of one of the half finished buildings, hidden in deep shadow. Quietly he crept toward the far end of the structure, the cliff looming over him. Once he lay perfectly still as a sentry paused in his round to light a cigarette.

As Dave passed the opened doorway of one of the prefabs, he could hear men inside laughing and joking in Spanish. He couldn't estimate their numbers, but there were a quite a few, judging by the collective noise.

He passed through the open end of the building, squeezing between it and the rock. The dark opening of the cave loomed, and he slipped the night vision goggles over his face once again. The eerie green light illuminated the inside of the black cavern. As he scanned from side to side, he could barely make out the walls and ceiling. Dave estimated its height to be over fifty feet and the depth even more. Dave moved inside. There was an enormous pile of crated equipment stored against one wall, and several workbenches pulled together. Back in one corner was a side passage. It was low and the walls were shiny as if made from porcelain. From a low pocket, Dave pulled out the small pouch he'd received from Alex. He shook several small, clear stones into his hand and carefully placed them against the wall of the passage about a foot in and several inches apart. He reached back and scraped some dust from the hard packed floor into his hand and lightly dusted the rough gems, concealing them from a casual look.

Quickly, Dave flitted to all corners of the cave, several times stopping to peer into side passages. It was now past midnight by his watch and he was well concealed. He thumbed the button on his transmitter. "Tom, Tom, come in."

Almost immediately, the reply came, "Five by five, Buddy-boy."

"Listen, this cave in the side of the cliff here is huge. It's loaded with crates and construction supplies. I'd have to guess they're for the airstrip. I've got it all in the computer. We'll be back in a couple of hours. Out." Dave didn't wait for a reply.

Back in the tree, Doby was getting restless waiting. And he had to pee. He squirmed around and pulled out the gun. "Pow, pow," he whispered, aiming for one of the buildings. Just then he heard a noise below him.

A voice called out in Spanish, "Hey *cabrone*, what you doin' up there? Get your ass down here." He poked Doby in the leg with a long barreled shotgun. Doby was paralyzed with fear. The man poked him again roughly. "If you don't come down, I'm gonna have to shoot you down."

As if by itself, the gun in Doby's hand turned and spat out a bullet at the surprised face. The loud boom echoed off the tree trunks, the buildings and the steel machinery. A muffled curse and a louder sound followed as the shotgun fired. The pellets hit the tree limb where Doby lay, and a few struck him in the leg, hurling him over the side and down onto the ground. Doby's shot had just scratched the surprised guard who now stood over him, one booted foot on his outstretched hand.

Dave had been finishing the activation of the homing device that he'd placed in one of the jeeps the week before and was on his way back to the tree when the shots rang out. *Shit*, he thought, *what kind of trouble has the kid gotten into now?*

He swiftly ran in the direction of the commotion. Behind him lights were flashing as men spilled out of the huts. Most were armed.

Just as Dave reached the tree, the guard was cocking his weapon, preparing to pull the trigger again. Dave bowled him over, attempting to get a grip on the long barrel. They fell over Doby, grappling for the gun.

"Run, kid. Run!" Dave yelled as he rolled on his back. Doby sat for a minute and then swiftly leaped to his feet and darted into the dark jungle. Behind him he heard the cocking of many weapons as a circle of mean looking men pointed pistols and automatic carbines at the two men on the moss covered ground.

That same morning on the Rio Dulce approaching Lake Peten Itza:

Rusty and Vinny were enjoying their second cup of coffee in the cockpit. Beside them stood a small, dark man in the military uniform of the Guatemalan Customs Service -- a colonel, he'd informed them. Rusty smiled, this guy was even shorter than Vinny.

When they'd checked in with Guatemalan Customs and Immigration, Colonel Rafaelo Perez had been summoned. He was overjoyed to see the two Americans. Many years ago he had lived in *Nuevo* York City and had helped build PT boats for the United States Navy. Now to have one he could actually ride upon was his life's delight. He stood on the bow like a small bronze statue, occasionally waving a slim swagger stick at passing boaters. They'd been on the water now for three days. Each evening they stopped at one of Senor Perez' far flung family's residences, been feted and worried over until their every comfort was assured. They topped off their fuel tanks and never worried about local police or government obstructions. Occasionally Colonel Perez took the wheel. As they sped along, Perez had a great grin on his face, contrasting to the look of consternation on Rusty's and outright terror on Vinny's.

They were entering a tributary of the river just off the northern shore of the large lake when the small colonel gestured at a row of sleek speedboats tied up at a narrow, well-maintained dock. Rusty eased back on the throttles and angled them across the stream. Several figures looked up at the approach of the large military craft. The colonel called to them, "You men, what are these boats doing here? I don't recall them from my last visit."

"*Si, mi Capitain*, we rent out these boats to *touristas* and the weekend city people," a tall man replied, a shotgun slung over his shoulder, barrel pointed down.

The colonel was puzzled, there were no weekend houses on this northern end of the lake and the tourists tended to stay near Santa Elena on the southern shore. Besides, only a mile to the north was the great nature preserve of the Peten with its impenetrable jungles all the way north to Tikal. And the great Mayan ruins accessible only by bumpy roads or aircraft. Something was not right.

He called again, "You men, we are coming alongside. Please have your identification cards ready." He motioned Rusty to nose into the dock so he could jump down. Slowly the men began fading away from the dock and drift back into the trees.

"Vinny, go below and get me a hammer and that blue wooden box from under my bed." Rusty paused for a minute. "Better get yourself some firepower, too." Vinny lowered himself through the companionway and began handing tools and supplies up to Rusty.

The big boat nosed into the dock, gently bumping the last boat in line. The boats looked like small cigarette boats, powerful engines and tiny cockpits -- not your usual fishing boats. Rusty eased the hammer onto the dashboard and moved the blue wooden box out of the way with his foot. Vinny popped up next to him trailing a stainless steel Ruger Mini-14 rifle and a handful of clips. These he slid next to the hammer.

The colonel jumped down to the dock, still calling to the men in the trees. Suddenly a shot rang out and the colonel ducked to his side, clutching his thigh. He rapidly crawled behind a low wooden shed on the dock, returning fire with the pistol he pulled from a snap flap holster.

A volley of shots rang out from the trees. Rusty ducked as Vinny flipped up the light rifle and slammed home a 30 shot clip. He rapidly squeezed off a number of shots, noting the muzzle flashes of the opposing weapons. Several shots peppered the lightly armored cockpit.

Rusty swore and picked up the hammer. With several rapid blows he splintered the lightweight wood around one of the guns. Tearing the shards away, he flipped open the heavy machinegun's receiver and slid into the pivoting chair. He fired one short burst into the row of boats and settled in to firing ten and twenty shot bursts from the .50 cal machine gun into the tree line. The trees were decimated; many falling and several cries were heard. The return fire lessened, then stopped. Rusty fired one more long burst and then quit. Vinny poked his head out of the cockpit and he, too, ceased firing. On the dock, the colonel crawled out from behind his hiding place and leaned back against the low wall.

His leg was bleeding and he was busy tying a flowery handkerchief to his thigh, pulling his shorts up to expose the wound. Vinny hopped down and ran the short distance to him.

"Colonel, Colonel, you okay? Lemme see that." He peered under the bloody makeshift bandage. "Ah, you'll be all right, it's just a flesh wound. He just grazed you." He leaned down and helped the older man to his feet. "Here, lean on me. Don't worry, me 'n Rusty'll get you patched up in no time."

They stumbled along the dock toward the gently bobbing bow. Rusty kept a keen lookout, swiveling back and forth in the gunner's seat.

"Thank you, *mi amigo*," the colonel panted. When they got to the boat, Rusty hurried to help, hauling up on the skinny arm while Vinny pushed from the dock. Soon they were all aboard, the colonel stretched out in Rusty's large bed, a bead of perspiration on his forehead. Vinny kept watch on the foredeck while Rusty expertly cleaned the long, ugly gash and bandaged it. He then gave the colonel a couple of morphine tablets and a shot of ampicillin for infection.

Just before the colonel fell asleep, he clutched Rusty's hand. "Destroy the boats. These people are *narcoticos.*" And with that, his hand dropped and his eyes closed.

Rusty crossed Colonel Perez' hands over his chest, checked his pulse and when he was satisfied that he was resting comfortably, clambered to his feet and ascended the ladder to the cockpit. Vinny was still peering over the coaming, his rifle at the ready, fresh clips lined up beside him.

"How's he doing, big guy?"

"He'll be okay. It's just a flesh wound. I gave him a couple of morphine tabs. He'll sleep it off and be fine in a few days." He hesitated. "He wants us to destroy the boats before we leave."

"I'm not going down there again," Vinny looked back over his shoulder indignantly. "You go, I'll cover you."

"Screw you, I ain't going either." He thought for a minute, then turned and, crouching over, lumbered down the deck to the forward torpedo tube. He reached inside and fiddled for a minute then withdrew his hand and ran back.

"What did you do?" asked Vinny, all jittery, eyes darting around, first at the tree line, then at Rusty, then back to the torpedo tube.

"I, ah, made an adjustment," the big man replied.

"To what, a dummy torpedo?"

"Well, not exactly. The forward torps are real. Me and Dave and Emile made em. The starboard one is high explosive and the port one is incendiary. I figure if we light off the port one when it gets in among the little boats, it should set 'em all off. Lemme take the wheel."

Rusty knocked the transmissions into reverse and slowly backed the big boat out into the lake. He handed a small key chain to Vinny. On it was a tiny keypad that looked like a car alarm. "When the torp gets near the boats, press the arm button. It's a remote and will go off on impact." He smiled. "Wish we had these remote control guys back in the Big One." He swung the boat in a long curving arc that took it back more than a mile. Coming out of the turn, he jammed the throttles forward. The boat leaped forward, the twin turbo-charged diesels gave a deep-throated roar that was deafening, pushing a bow wave higher than the gunwales. When they were within three hundred yards, Rusty flipped a red cover up and pressed a large button. The port torpedo leaped out of the open tube and dropped into the water in front of the boat, trailing a foamy wake as it sped toward its target. The smaller boats bobbed gently at their moorings, looking peaceful and innocent. As the torpedo's wake disappeared behind the boats in the center, Vinny pressed the small button. Rusty swung the PT boat in a powerful arc away from the target.

For a second nothing happened, and then the water erupted, boats climbing high in the air on a column of fire. As one, the fuel tanks on the boats exploded and added to the flames. The dock and the small shed disappeared in a fireball that rolled toward the tree line. What remained of the torpedo ran up on the beach carrying part of a boat with it.

Vinny stood in the cockpit swiveling around, a pair of binoculars glued to his eyes.

He jumped up and down thumping Rusty on his back. "Son-of-a-bitch, did you see that?"

By this time Rusty had slowed the boat and pointed it back around toward the remains of the dock and boats. On the shore pieces were smoldering, and one engine lay on its side half in the water. Of the dock and most of the boats, there was only debris scattered over the water and nearby shoreline. Although there was no fire, some of the trees on the edge of the jungle were scorched, leaves curled and blackened. More important, what had once been eight boats was no more.

Rusty motored on, looking for a small town or village where the Colonel could report to his superiors. As they quietly puttered, the radio on the console squealed. It was Tom.

"PT-108, this is airborne one. Come in."

"Airborne One, this is PT, over."

"Vinny, Rusty, give me your location and be prepared for pickup. Dave's been captured. Over."

CHAPTER 17

On board the Van De Groot *off the Yucatan Peninsula:*

It was night and black. The ship was silent, no lights showing. Overhead the stars gleamed like a handful of diamonds thrown onto a velvet rug. Jane Houllihan stood in the bow watching the phosphorescent wave curl back alongside the dark hull. The light breeze swirled her short hair around her head like a tiny zephyr. She liked the time alone and had been standing nearly immobile for more than an hour. Footsteps approached. She turned her head at their sound. It was her co-team leader, Julian LeDuc. She liked the quiet, unassuming man with his slim yet knotted muscles. Julian was from Paris and spoke with a peculiar, lilting inflection in

his voice. It was particularly noticeable when he
spoke English. In French, it could almost have been
called High French compared to Jane's guttural
Marseilles twang. Her's was full of swear words
and innuendo.

Jane liked Julian because he was kind and
polite and at the same time fierce, although the
fierceness only came out in battle. He kept a clear
head, and always noticed those around him. After a
battle or an operation, he was quick to hand out
compliments as well as criticism, and his criticism
was always tinged with instruction.

"Bonjour, Mademoiselle Houllihan," he smiled
in the darkness, his teeth flashing.

"Ah, Julian. How did I know it would be you?"
She smiled back and touched him on the arm. Jane
had a way of touching, lightly, feathery that bound
her team and the men in her life together. Though
she had no permanent man of her own, she
occasionally used or allowed herself to be used. She
wanted a man, especially before a battle, especially
before the popping of the guns and flash of the
mortars. And tonight, she decided, she wanted this
man, her equal.

"Perhaps you sent some," he hesitated,
searching for a word, "some telepathic thought to
seek me out. I was playing cards and suddenly I had
the strangest feeling I was supposed to come out
here." From under his arm he produced a bottle of
champagne and two glasses clinked in his pocket.
He withdrew them and handed them to her.

With a quick twist, he popped the cork and managed to fill the two glasses without spilling a drop. "To you, my angel. May the gods watch your back tomorrow, and if they are busy elsewhere, then may I."

They softly clinked glasses and sipped. They stood side by side staring out at the ocean. A gust of a breeze gave her a sudden chill and made her shiver. Julian put his arm around her and held her close, his head resting against hers.

"Ah, *Cherie*, would that we could leave this life and live somewhere in a small house overlooking the ocean, perhaps in Brittany or even Martinique." He sighed in a purely French manner, his breath a whisper against her ear.

She smiled at him. "But, Julian, you know you would miss the scrapping and the guns. Not to mention the other women. But thank you for the compliment." Jane smiled again and turned in his arm so that she was facing him. They stood for a moment nose to nose, looking deep into each other's eyes. Then she moved a hand up to his face and caressed it gently before kissing him on the eyelids, then the nose, and finally the mouth, just lightly brushing his lips with her own, back and forth. He licked her lips with the tip of his tongue.

She opened her mouth and took in his tongue, matching him. He lifted his hand and moved it beneath her light cotton sleeveless shirt, cupping the weight of her breast and lightly teasing the nipple with his thumb.

His touch warmed her, stirring old passions. Her kissing became more ardent, her hands tangled in his straight hair. She ground her hips against his. He pulled up her shirt exposing her breasts to his gaze and to the night breeze. Her creamy skin shone luminescent, the darker tips now fully erect. He bent to them and she held his head between her palms, guiding and moving him to her will. She was bent back now, partly over the rail, her hair swirling over her closed eyes. His lips found her flat stomach. He wrenched at her belt, then his own. In a moment he was inside her, her legs clasped around his waist, bent far out over the water, her breasts thrust up at the full moon. They ground and twisted, rather than thrust.

On the bridge, the captain and first mate watched in silence, passing a pair of binoculars back and forth. The ship was on automatic pilot and needed little attention. The mate stroked himself through his trousers, unconsciously, feeling a little guilty at what he was watching. The captain's eyes were bright, his breath coming in short gasps.

Below, the couple clenched each other tightly, then visibly relaxed. She brought her head back upright as he eased her back onto the deck. Always the gentleman, Julian handed her a fresh handkerchief. She wiped herself then reached and delicately fondled him before putting him away and zipping his fly. She then squatted and pulled up her shorts, her buttocks flashing for a moment. The captain let out a sigh and absently handed the mate the glasses.

He fumbled for a small flat bottle in a coat pocket, took a short pull and also handed it to the mate. "Almost, but not quite as good as having her yourself, wot?"

"Aye," the mate grunted. He was a thin man with gold-rimmed glasses and a receding hairline that made him look older than his twenty-nine years. He spoke out of one side of his mouth, an affectation that he practiced in a mirror, copying Humphry Bogart. He took a longer drink and had to visibly keep from gagging at the strong schnapps. This was his first trip with the teams.

Below, Jane and Julian kissed, and then separated. He strolled back along the starboard rail, hands in pockets and whistling to himself. Jane hurried back along the port side and down a companionway ladder. Two decks below she stepped over the high sill and pushed open a cabin door. In the dimly lit cabin she saw her roommate Marie book ended by the Broussard brothers, one on his knees behind her and the other holding her head to his groin. "Oops," she whispered and withdrew, silently closing the door. She guessed she wasn't the only horny one this night before battle. She went to the hanger deck to check her gear.

On the Unocal Oil platform in the Gulf of Mexico:

"Get that bird hung in the slings, Sergeant! Lieutenant Graham will be bringing in the number two bird any minute now. Chop-chop!" Colonel Sykes clapped his hands and the crew set about hauling the wide nylon straps around the squat fuselage of the Blackhawk helicopter. They'd already folded the four blades back and secured them. The flat whap-whap of the second chopper could be heard above them.

Sergeant Dodge waved the green-lighted wand around in a circle signaling the crane operator to lift and swing the bird up and off to the side. Then he switched the light off and pulled another light out of his pocket. This one was amber. He waved it around his head in a circle as the first bird swung clear. The second chopper, a twin engine AH-64D Apache attack helicopter dropped out of the sky as if a string had been cut. Dodge cursed and flung himself down and toward the edge of the heli-platform. The whup-whup grew deafeningly loud as the pilot pulled collective and flared the wide blades before settling on the wheels. The blades slowed and the whine of the engines came down in pitch, octave by octave until they were mute. Inside Lt. Graham flipped overhead switches and turned knobs. He dropped down to the deck. Behind him came Corporal Pagano, the skinny Italian kid. Lieutenant Graham had been giving him flying lessons, and Pagano was already a fairly good pilot. In fact, he'd taken off and flown most of the way from home base. But Graham knew that the colonel would be waiting for them on the platform and so he insisted on landing himself. He decided that Pagano's career as a pilot would have to wait for its public showing. The Army didn't like its pilots to be enlisted men, and Pagano would never be an officer.

"Okay, let's go, let's go. Into the mess hall. Let's get this show on the road!" Sykes led the men into the tower and double-timed it through the labyrinth of corridors and up and down ladders until they reached the small dining hall. A buffet style meal had been laid out, and the men hungrily filled their trays. After filling his own tray, Colonel Sykes took a seat at the head of the table.

They ate greedily and in a few minutes one of the men, a Corporal Mikkelsen, asked, "Colonel, have we got a fix on the Comanche?"

Sykes stopped eating, a forkful of potato salad halfway to his mouth. "What'd you say Mikkelsen?"

"A fix, sir, on the chopper. Do we have a fix?"

"What do you know about a fix, corporal?"

"Christ, colonel, do we have to keep reminding you that we know most things before they happen? There ain't no secrets in our crew." He shook his head disgustedly and began building himself a huge sandwich of sliced meat and cheese.

"All right, you know we've got a homing device on the Comanche and so we know where it is. It's in Guatemala, wise-ass." This last directed at Corporal Mikkelsen.

"Yeah, so what's the plan, colonel?" Lieutenant Graham spoke, his mouth full of food.

"Plan? We're armed to the teeth. We've got fourteen men. We know where they are, so we'll go in and get it. What the fuck can they do? There's only two of them."

"Colonel, with all due respect, that was your plan last time. How about something more specific this time? Please."

"Okay, Graham." He stood and pulled down a map of the western Caribbean showing the coast and the countries of Central America. "Listen up, girls." He picked up a pointer. "This is where we are." He indicated the platform in red in the Gulf of Mexico south of Texas. He consulted his watch and said, "At exactly 0450 we rendezvous with an Air Farce flying gas station at these co-ordinates." He again indicated the map, this time at a set of co-ordinates barely off the coast of Belize. "We're still in international waters so nobody can say anything. Then we fly inland over Belize. Those fucking greasers don't have shit for radar so we're in the clear. By the time they get finished wiping the taco grease off their hands, we'll be over Guatemala. The bird is being held in this valley, at the western end. He flipped the map out of the way and revealed a huge blowup of a satellite photo. The men were used to looking at satellite images and could discern patterns of vehicles, the gash of a primitive airstrip and buildings in the photo. The only helicopter indicated was a Jet Ranger.

"We land at the center of the airstrip after softening up the surrounding buildings. Lt. Graham, you will fly the Comanche. I'll hold at treetop height in the Apache and you, Pagano, will fly the Blackhawk out with the rest of the men." He smirked, "Yeah, lieutenant, I know all about you and Pagano."

Graham looked startled, then pleased that the colonel trusted a kid like Pagano with the Blackhawk.

Sykes tossed the pointer at Graham and said, "Now, does that look like a plan? I haven't been sitting on my ass like the rest of you girls waiting for something to happen." He sat down and propped his chair against the wall, feet up on the table. "Lieutenant, would you continue the briefing? You know armament, weapons, personal gear - that sort of thing." He lit up a crooked, black cheroot and watched the smoke drift toward the air conditioning vent.

Graham stood and continued, specifying jungle camouflage clothing and gear, light automatic weapons, night vision goggles, and flash-bang grenades. As he droned on the men grew restless. Finally he finished and the men filed out to retrieve their gear. Sykes put his hand on the younger man's shoulder. "Can this kid Pagano really fly the Blackhawk out, with men aboard, maybe under fire?"

Graham thought for a minute, then shrugged, "Only one way to find out, sir."

No shit, thought Sykes.

Early morning, Locarno hacienda:

The dusty truck came screeching to a halt outside the front door. The boy, Doby, was out before it was even stopped. A fat woman wearing camouflage trousers and holding a shotgun under her arm pulled open the door. The boy spoke to her rapidly in Spanish, and she indicated a spot in the nearby woods. He turned on his heel and ran as fast as his injured leg would carry him to the copse of trees.

"Senor Tom. Senor Tom! Where are you?"

Tom Novak stepped out from behind a tree. He wore the same camo trousers and shirt as the boy. His face was a mottled green and brown from the makeup and small twigs and sawgrass stuck out from his shoulders and hat. He just seemed to appear next to the nearly hysterical boy, as silent as a wraith. "*Que*?" asked Tom quietly.

"Oh, Senor Tom," the boy sobbed. "They have Senor Dave, the *Cholos*." He was speaking rapidly, and Tom strained to understand. "They were going to kill me and Senor Dave saved me but they took him." He gasped for breath.

Tom thought for a minute and put his hand over the boy's heaving shoulders. "Did they kill him?" he asked patiently. Inside his mind was racing but he knew it would be fruitless to rush the boy or appear excited.

"No, I don't think so. I heard no shots after I ran," he stopped and corrected himself. "…after I got away." He was getting his breathing and excitement under control in view of Tom's extraordinary calm.

"How long ago?" Tom asked.

"Maybe two hours ago. Maybe three. I don't know. They were chasing me and I ran a long distance, and then had to circle around to the truck. I came straight here." He paused, and then asked in a small voice, "Are you going after him?"

Tom looked at him thoughtfully, "Eventually." Just then he noticed the blood on the boy's leg. He squatted and ascertained that the wound wasn't too deep. "Best go in and get your Aunt Roberta or Alex to clean that up." He gently pushed the boy toward the hacienda, following at a leisurely pace.

Tom moved toward the helicopter now resting beside the garage. He activated a power switch and flipped on the radio. After finding the correct frequency, he thumbed a mike button,

"Vinny, Rusty, give me your location and be prepared for pickup. Dave's been captured. I need you. Over."

CHAPTER 18

Dave woke in the dark with a splitting headache. The right side of his face lay in the dirt.

He tried to lift his head but pain stabbed down his neck and across his shoulder blades. He lay still for another few minutes, breathing deeply, trying to clear his head. Suddenly he was jerked upright by a rope behind his back. The rope disappeared above him over a beam and encircled his upper arms. First to his knees, then to his unsteady feet, finally off the floor, his feet dangling, the rope cutting into his armpits. He grunted, clamping his lips tightly, the muscles at the side of his jaw aching. A light shone in his face, blinding him. He swung slowly, the light following his eyes. He used his other senses, hearing light footsteps following him. Smell of

something sweet. Sandalwood? Shaving lotion? He
waited, trying to isolate the pain, cup it, cradle it,
snare it, and put it into a smaller and smaller
compartment in his brain, expanding his thinking
part, taking in data, and processing it.

He waited, alternately tensing his muscles,
testing and feeling for broken bones, tears, and
bruises. He seemed to be complete, no parts missing
or inoperable. He waited, swinging gently.

Then, after an eternity came a voice out of the
surrounding blackness, "Good evening, Senor. I
hope you have had a restful sleep. I apologize for
my men who have been a little … discourteous."

Dave couldn't see who was speaking to him.
The light held steady in his eyes. He tried to see
around the edges of it. As he slowly twirled in the
air, the voice followed him. He estimated the man
speaking to him to be about six feet tall. He
couldn't quite follow the purring voice, the accent
was heavy and he wasn't thinking too clearly so he
just let his eyes slide closed. A moment later he felt
his shirt being roughly torn open, then two
pinpricks in his chest. He managed to open his eyes
again just as the grinning face came into focus.

A sudden jolt leapt through his body. He felt as
if his mind was on fire. His skin leapt and crackled
and his body jerked and pulled against the ropes. He
had absolutely no control. He tried to pull against it
but the fire was consuming him. Suddenly it
stopped and he slumped. The voice was close to his
ear.

"Now, once again, Senor; who are you and
what are you doing here?"

Dave barely managed to turn his head and look at the face. The man facing him was slim, dark hair narrowing to a widow's peak. The eyes disappeared into dark hollows beneath neatly groomed eyebrows. He was so close Dave could see the pinpricks of flesh where the brows had been tweezed. Odd, he thought.

Dave tried to remember his training in the Escape and Evasion classrooms in San Diego at the giant Naval base there, then in the Panamanian jungles where the Marines ran the Jungle Survival School for Navy personnel. Let's see, the instructions for when captured and interrogated were: name, rank, serial number, and date of birth. Then if tortured, lie, half lie, and finally the truth. It wasn't worth getting killed over. Dave felt that the name, rank and service number bit was a little late, since he wasn't on active duty, at the moment, and he couldn't remember his 20-year-old service number. Lies would work only he needed time to think of a good one. Maybe a half lie?

"My name is Sergeant Novak. I'm with the U.S. Army working with the Guatemalan Government forces here in the Peten rooting out the remnants of rebel guerrilla forces said to be operating here." He paused for a minute, his mind racing. Then he went on, "I'm part of a fifty man force in this area." He hoped the last would get him out of the pickle he seemed to be in.

The man facing him paused to reflect. "With all due respect, sergeant, or whatever you are, that story is so much bullshit. There are no insignia on your uniform. Miguel tells me you were with a boy. What do you take me for?" He held a small box up in front of Dave's nose so close it was almost blurry. A tiny light blinked and a thumb was held over the button. "You see this, *pendejo*?"

Dave did and nodded. It was a taser, a stun gun that operated with two wire leads, usually fired from the gun. The two tiny wires led down to Dave's chest. He could barely make them out stuck there like a heart monitor.

"Watch!" the voice whispered like a snake. He viscously jabbed the button. Dave jerked again, straining against the ropes, feet kicking. His guts knotted and he clenched his buttocks tightly, sweat boiling off his face in buckets.

1300 hours, Locarno hacienda:

Tom pulled the pickup truck away from the Comanche. A half-hour before, he'd fired it up and lifted it over the wall and onto the road in front of the sprawling house. He'd dropped it on its wheels and then ran for a truck. In a few minutes he had diesel fuel running into the chopper's tank.

Alex had ridden with him. "Thomas, I will come with you. We will get Senor Dave back."

Tom stepped back and wiped his hands dry on a small towel held by the silent Doby.
"Alex, baby, you have to stay here. There isn't room in the chopper for me, Rusty, and Vinny as it

is." Desperation was apparent in his voice. "I'll be back before dusk and we'll all go get him, but I need these guys." He looked at her beseechingly, gave her a quick squeeze, a kiss, and ran for the chopper.

They stood back as the big bird began to turn up, its fifty foot diameter rotor slowly started to move, then swiftly became a blur. They could see Tom in the pilot's seat putting on his helmet and speaking into a microphone. The noise was deafening. The woman and young boy put their hands over their ears and turned their heads away, as a swirling cloud of dust enveloping them. When they looked back, the chopper was just a speck on the horizon. Tom had the pedal to the metal, all right. He flew contour, frequently consulting his maps. As much as he tried to avoid civilization, there were times when he just couldn't help but fly over a house, a farm, or a small village, which hadn't made it to a three-year-old map. He was flying fast and loose, and was worried about the Guatemalan military tracking him, but he knew the Comanche was constructed using the latest radar hiding technology. The wheels were retracted and the smooth underbelly looked like some sort of sky creature to the people on the ground. Many crossed themselves and muttered a quick prayer.

He'd radioed Vinny and Rusty before leaving and received their co-ordinates. They had agreed to drop anchor in the middle of a bulge in the river. They'd also told him of the wounded customs colonel they had aboard. Tom cursed silently, then loudly, the cockpit filling with the sound of it. At last, worn out and thoroughly enraged, his outward appearance calmed, then grew icy. His lips thinned and his eyes slipped deep behind slitted lids. A cold fury took over. He'd get Dave if he had to slit the throat of every goddamn Colombian narcotic dealing asshole in Guatemala. The fury grew in him and enveloped him. He was one mean avenging angel and God help anyone who got in his way today.

1420 hours, Over the Gulf and closing with the Guatemalan coast:

Sykes was now flying the Apache with Graham following in the Blackhawk.

"Colonel Sykes," Lieutenant Graham called into his microphone. Ahead of him, in the twin engine Apache Colonel Sykes heard and reached for his switch.

"Yeah, Graham? What do you want?"

"Corporal. Mikkelsen reports that the signal is still in the same position at the eastern end of the valley. Our ETA will be," Mikkelsen held up five fingers, then two, "at approximately 1720 hours."

A thousand feet below them, a freighter silently sat in the water, smoke trickling out of her stack. No one paid it any attention.

"Lt. Graham, let's get low and come in through that notch at one o'clock." Sykes pointed though he knew Graham couldn't see him.

"Roger, sir."

Less than an hour before, they'd met an Air Force Tanker out over the Gulf, and both choppers refueled. In air refueling was something new to helicopter aviation. The refueling plane had to remain below and to one side of the helicopters so as not to interfere with the rotors. The chopper extended a telescoping tube out past the rotor path where the tanker coupled to the tube. The nozzle was guided up toward the tube and filled using the pumps inside the tanker plane. They'd arranged for another refueling the following day, and the pilot promised to return to station in twelve hours. The huge plane had lumbered off into the wispy gray clouds, climbing rapidly.

Sykes dropped the nose of his chopper and aimed for the u-shaped gap in the misty hills, Graham right on his tail.

1450 Hours, aboard the Jan de Groot:

Jane Houllihan and Julian LeDuc stood beside the captain and peered into the large radarscope. The captain pointed. "See those two blips there. They are headed for the coast." He paused a minute, rubbing his hand over the stubble on his chin. "I don't think they're commercial aircraft. They're flying too close to each other and too slow." He frowned.

"Private, perhaps?" Julian asked cautiously.

"Maybe, but they're also flying too slowly to be jets or even nice twin engine turbo-propeller aircraft. A small single engine plane would fly that slowly, but they were coming from the northeast. There is nothing up that way but water. Maybe from Belize but," here he frowned again and shook his head.

"Military?" asked Jane. She too frowned trying to put together the known facts and a logical sequence.

"Perhaps helicopters, captain?"

The captain shrugged his brawny shoulders again, "That would fit the profile but again, where did they come from? There is nothing up there." He turned and smiled. "Anyway, I thought I would call it to your attention." He indicated the doorway and gestured. "Happy hunting, soldiers. I will be waiting for your return."

Below on the wide deck, the three helicopters had been raised, assembled, and tested. A line of soldiers was loading each machine. By the time Julian and Jane reached the broad deck, everything was aboard.

Jane slipped on her web gear and took up her weapon, a Czech made AK-47. Julian checked her gear as she checked his. Then they boarded through the gaping doorway of the matte painted LodeRunner helicopter. The pilot and co-pilot awaited her signal. Jane slipped on the padded earphones and adjusted the thin microphone near her lips. Through the Plexiglas windows, she saw the rotors of the tiny Alouette II Scout chopper move, then a few minutes later, the larger rotor of the Falcon Gunship. Inside the LodeRunner, the team sat six abreast and back to back, ten in the team, two spares, a pilot, and co-pilot. Both the Falcon and the tiny Alouette each held two. Eighteen in all. She would have preferred to have another squad as back up. They had poor intelligence and unknowns in the area. *Ah, well* she sighed, *can't have everything. What was it the United States Marines say? Do you want to live forever?* She snorted and held up an upraised thumb where the pilot could see it.

The Alouette broke formation first and darted forward, a long curving arc, which took it to its assigned altitude of 500 feet. Behind it lumbered the LodeRunner, heavier and slower, its Allison engine screaming. To its right and slightly above was the Falcon, lean and shark-like. Since the Americans had developed the Cobra Gunship, just about every other helicopter manufacturer in the world had copied the design. The Brits had their own highly modified version of the Apache called the Longbow. The Russians had the Mi-28 Havoc, if they could ever keep it in production. The French had the SA-565 Panther, and the South Africans had the Rooivalk – Red Falcon, of course, and all the other nations had one or more variations. Jane and the others sat behind a Plexiglas contour covering almost hung out over the skids. The effect at five-hundred feet was dizzying and she closed her eyes.

Ahead of them, the pilot of the Alouette called back on the radio. "Captain Houllihan, I am going to take that pass just to our right and into the first of these valleys. What are we looking for?"

"Fly inland until you see a large river, then follow it north. Mr. Boettcher radioed that he will contact us as we get closer to our destination. That is all I know." She clicked off the microphone in disgust. Their lack of intelligence was distressing. She amended that to Boettcher's lack of intelligence. She and Julian would have liked at least two weeks with a mock-up to train their people. She wanted to know all the variables and a good idea about the unknowns. This operating blindly was bull, *merde*, as Julian would say. He sat next to her and she smiled at him.

Ahead and below them, the pilot of the Alouette thought he saw movement against the trees. It was a barely discernible object moving at great speed in a southerly direction. Before he could get a fix on radar, the object was gone. He shrugged, a small plane perhaps. Just as they were approaching a ridge, a pair of helicopters flew up ahead of them and disappeared over an adjoining ridge. They were quite low and actually flew between two very tall trees. The pilot radioed back once again. "Two helicopters ahead of us about five miles, captain. They're flying low and fast. I think they're military."

Jane was confused. She knew the government of Guatemala had nothing faster or more agile than Hueys or maybe a Jet Ranger, nothing capable of contour flying in the growing dusk. She triggered her mike, "Attention, all aircraft, maintain speed and direction. Keep a sharp eye out for enemy aircraft. At this point in our operation we must consider all aircraft to be enemy. Pilot, see if you can raise Mr. Boettcher on the assigned frequency."

"Aye, Ma'am." The pilot busied himself with a small notebook and pencil. Then he twisted some dials and called into the microphone, "Eagle One, Eagle One, this is the Crows Nest, over."

He tried several more times until a faint reply could be heard. "Crow's Nest, this is Eagle One. Crow's Nest this is Eagle One, do you copy? Over."

The day before, Michael Boettcher and his companion Dieter had entered the country at the run down airport in Guatemala City where a man known only as Karl met them. He passed them tickets for a ride in a light plane to the town of San Jose on the shore of Lake Peten Itza. The rickety plane landed on a dusty airstrip outside the town in the middle of the day. It was quite hot, but a steady breeze blew, coating them with a layer of fine-gritted dust. A man, who also identified himself as Karl, once again met them.

The first Karl had been a largish, sweaty man in a wilted suit that had once been white. He wore a battered Panama hat. This second one was also heavy, with a thick, corded neck, and a battered nose. He drove them north and into the Peten ostensibly to view the extensive Quiche Mayan ruins in Tikal. In the battered Toyota Land Cruiser, he had camouflage uniforms, weapons, stout boots and radio gear.

Boettcher, of course, had the list of assigned frequencies in the back of a money belt cinched around his waist. He didn't often take part in wet operations these days, preferring to leave such doings to the squads. However, since he was into this from the beginning, he felt it was his duty to see it to its conclusion.

Karl 2 had reported that the gems seemed to be coming from someplace in the vast Peten rain forest, but he thought he ought to report some unusual activity in a small valley near a town known only as El Zotz. They were proceeding there now. Karl reported that there seemed to be a cave or excavation, a landing strip for small aircraft, and helicopters could be seen moving in and out now and then. He thought it unusual for a small remote valley, and had heard nothing about a strike of gold or copper or some such mineral that would have required such activity.

Boettcher and Dieter quickly changed into the camo gear and checked their weapons. Boettcher slid a Walther PPK into a shoulder holster and gripped an American M-16 rifle. Behind him, Dieter slid a Glock .40-caliber pistol into a holster strapped to his waist. He, too, gripped a shabby, yet still useable M-16 rifle, its stock cracked and covered with several layers of duct tape. He grimaced and snorted. In front, the driver turned his head slightly. "I'm sorry, *Mien Herr,* this was all I could locate at such short notice. You will notice that the pistol is like new, eh?" He laughed heartily to himself.

They were now traveling through dense forest on a wide track that had been cleared years before. The road was quite good and the larger bumps had been filled recently. They occasionally passed a small clearing where some poor family was trying to hold back the encroaching jungle and scratch out a living. Once they passed a large logging operation, complete with diesel generator, sawmill, and mulching machines. The cleared land was smoking where the stumps were being burned out, and still farther, tractors were already beginning to plow the fallow earth.

"Where are we going, Karl?" Boettcher asked.

"The place has no name," Karl replied with a shrug. "It is just a valley like all these other valleys." He waved his hand in a dismissing fashion. Boettcher noticed that his middle finger was missing above the second joint. He saw Boettcher's look. "A small misunderstanding with the Indians many years ago. They liked me so much they wanted to keep a piece of me!" He said this in a loud voice and laughed uproariously at his own poor joke, slapping his hat down on his knee.

Boettcher looked at Dieter out of the corner of his eye. Dieter just raised his eyes to the sky and shook his head.

The sun slanted well into the west, shadows growing longer. He indicated to Karl to pull over. In a moment Karl found a wide spot in the road and wheeled the vehicle in, downshifting as he did so.

Boettcher and Dieter climbed out and Dieter opened the hood, leaning it back against the windscreen. Boettcher pulled a pair of battery cables out from under the rear seat and hooked up the radio. It was an ICOM M-700 marine grade single side band radio.

"It has been modified for the amateur radio bands, too, *Mien Herr*." Karl leaned in uncomfortably close to the white haired man. Up this close, he could see the caked white crystals in the lines of his face and the jaundiced tinge to his skin. Boettcher looked over his shoulder at the big man and gestured him away.

"Perhaps you should pay a call to nature, Karl. This is none of your business." He said quietly with no hint of rancor in his voice. Dieter was unfurling a long telescoping whip antenna and Boettcher motioned to him to come near once Karl was out of earshot. "Dieter, once we determine the location of this valley, we will dispose of this pig. We can return to the ship via one of our own aircraft."

"Yes sir," Dieter muttered almost under his breath.

At this point, Boettcher commenced waiting for the call from the aircraft aloft. He had Karl point out the location of the valley on a map and wrote in the co-ordinates as well as their own. They settled down to wait.

1650 hours, in the Rio Azul, just north of Lake Peten Itza:

"Colonel Perez," Rusty called desperately shaking the injured Guatemalan Customs officer gently by the shoulder. Vinny looked over his shoulder, twitching and nervously clasping and unclasping his hands. The man slept on, under the cover of morphine.

"Shit, Rusty, what did you have to give him so much for?" Vinny was agitatedly pacing the small cabin.

"Me? Look, little buddy, you were here, you coulda said no. How was I to know Tom would call us?" He pulled his captain's hat off and scratched the back of his head.

"Well, you better do something. Tommy will be here soon. Maybe we ought to leave him a note?" Vinny's voice was almost a cry of desperation.

"A note? A note? What the hell are we going to say? Sorry we shot up your country with all the illegal weapons we brought in with us - also illegally? Yeah he'll really like that," Rusty muttered, now getting to his feet. He turned to the small man, "Besides, we don't even know if he can read English. I sure as hell can't write in Spanish, can you?"

Vinny shook his head desperately. "No, but let's just leave him a note saying we'll be back in a while. He'll understand."

"Okay. Okay, you do it. I'll get our gear together and lash down the junk topside." He swiftly strode to the companionway ladder and hurried up. Vinny found a piece of paper and

quickly printed a note. Rummaging through a
drawer he found a safety pin and pinned it to the
colonel's tunic. With a last look, he patted the
colonel's hand and followed Rusty above.

"I left a pistol next to him. Let's set the deck
alarm and he should be okay"

"Good idea," said the big man. All their gear
was piled in the cockpit. Rusty had the radio turned
on and was waiting for a call from Tom. They heard
the chopper before the radio crackled to life. It came
in from the west and swooped down like an
avenging angel, black and swift. It came to a hover
about fifty feet off the water and fifty yards off the
port bow. The wave of air was terrific and they
crouched behind the cockpit coaming to get out of
its blast. The radio jarred Rusty into blindly
reaching for the dangling microphone.

"PT, this is Airborne One, over."

Rusty hastily pulled the mike closer and yelled
into it, "Airborne One, this is PT. Gotcha, Tommy!"

"You guys get ready. I'm going to come in on
your starboard side. The canopy in front opens on
the side near the deck. You first, Big Guy, then the
Vin man."

Rusty yelled, "Roger!" And cut off the power.

The black bird nosed toward them, the big rotor
now passing overhead. The men could barely
breathe under the rushing air. Rusty looked up to
see the nose of the craft appear over the rail. He
nudged Vinny, scooped up their gear and ran
forward. Vinny followed, holding onto the bigger
man's shirttail. Tom smiled and gestured with his
hand quickly recovering. The chopper wobbled and

weaved from side to side, though no more than a few inches at a time. Rusty saw the small handle and jerked it to the side. The canopy came loose and he lifted it skyward. It hinged on the opposite side and opened like a clamshell. Rusty lifted a massive leg in and squirmed to get his fat butt wedged into the too small seat. Vinny stood looking perplexed until Rusty waved him forward. Vinny yelled something but the words were torn from his lips and swept away. Rusty reached out a meaty paw and grabbed the front of his shirt and jerked him halfway into the cockpit. With his other hand he reached out and grabbed the back of his belt, sliding his thumb into the waistband of his trousers. As he jerked him fully in, Rusty reached up a meaty paw, and slammed and latched the canopy.

Tom saw what he was up to and quickly leapt the chopper high in the air before Vinny could see what was happening. Vinny squirmed into a position half in and half out of Rusty's lap. When he was able to see through the canopy on the opposite side, he gave a shriek and fainted dead away. Rusty kept his grip on the small man's pants and Tom laughed to himself.

The chopper streaked toward the northwest at full throttle, low and dark. It was like modern day death coming to take away the evil in the world. Tom thought about the movie "Ghost" where the bad guys were taken south by a group of goblin like creatures. Before the night was over, he'd make some of the *Cholos* wish there were only goblins hauling their skinny asses off to Hell.

In a short time, Tom lightly touched the chopper down in front of the Locarno hacienda. Tia Roberta and Senor Locarno came into the night, the light spilling out into the patio like liquid fire. They both held weapons at the ready. Tom told Rusty to stay where he was and quickly clambered down, ducking low to stay under the massive rotor.

"Where's Alex?" he demanded.

The old woman answered. "Gone to the next valley with the Mayans and Dominguez. When you didn't return right away, they went to rescue Senor Dave."

Tom cursed in Spanish then turned to Senor Locarno, "I thought I told you to keep the Mayans away from the valley for a few days?" His voice was harsh and accusatory.

The old man drew himself up, indignant. "I told them your wishes, Thomas, but it was the chief's son who was killed and this area," he swept his arm in a broad gesture. "is his home, not yours. His people, not yours."

"Yeah, yeah, I guess you're right, but why did Alex go? And why the hell did she take the kid?" Tom was fidgeting now, anxious to get away.

Again Tia Roberta answered, "She said that if you came, she had a radio. She would meet you there. Now go, Thomas, and may God be with you." She touched him gently on the side of his face.

Tom nodded and sprinted to the waiting helicopter squatting on its three wheels. The front canopy was almost closed, only Vinny's legs from the knees down sticking out. Rusty still had a firm grip on his belt. "Hang on guys, we're going to get

Dave. And Alex and Doby and a bunch of fucking
Mayans. Maybe some Colombians, a gang of
American Rangers, and a few South Africans while
we're at it. After that, I don't know what I'll do for
an encore," he muttered to himself.

The Americans:

Colonel Sykes flew in high over the trees,
watching his monitoring receiver out of one eye and
the night vision radar out of the other. "There it is!"
He called excitedly. "Hah, now we've got the
bastards." He dropped in lower, turning on the
infrared spotlight and camera and flipping a switch
on his console to change the screen to infrared
reception. The screen showed several hot spots
moving quickly and more coming from buildings.
"Shoot some of those fuckers, sergeant."

"Yes sir," Sergeant Rossiter had his tracking
helmet on and turned his head toward the nearest
group, the chin gun following his every movement.
His finger depressed the button on the front of the
stick between his legs. He quickly fired off several
short bursts, every tenth shell a tracer. The ropelike
stream flew out from under his feet and hosed some
of the white ghosts showing on his screen.

"Atta boy!" Sykes exulted. "Let's get that
building on the right at about three o'clock. Then
we'll call in the boys to get the chopper."

Sykes carefully lined up the crosshairs highlighted on his windscreen and thumbed the button for a Tow missile. It streaked away into the night and a sudden blossom of fire grew where a construction shed used to be. "Graham, get your ass down there. Find me that chopper. The readout says that it's at the southeast side about halfway to the cliff from the airstrip. I'll fly cover. You land on my flare."

"Roger that."

Sykes continued, "Rossiter, drop a green flare on my go." Without waiting for an answer, he flew low over the partially constructed airstrip. About 200 yards from the beginning, he hovered a minute. "Go!" he called and a green flare exploded from the belly of the craft.

"Got it." came the calm reply from Lieutenant Graham. Sykes slipped sideways just as the heavier Blackhawk fell past him. He saw it land lightly and half a dozen men slip into the jungle.

"You wait for them, Graham," Sykes ordered.

"But colonel, that's against regs. I'm supposed to be airborne. Shit, I'm a sitting duck here." Graham kept the big rotor turning, the helo just barely on the ground.

"That's an order, Graham. They'll be right back. I've got your cover." Sykes spat the words and thumbed his mike to internal. "Rossiter, I'm taking us back up. You've got the guns. Don't you let anybody back to my ship. You got that?"

"Roger that, sir!" Rossiter swiveled his head, constantly scanning the jungle and airstrip. Below, he could see their men fanned out and leapfrogging toward the buildings. One man leaping ahead of the other, slapping him on the shoulder. Sykes' men may be misfits, he thought, but they were professional soldiers and well trained.

But neither Sykes nor Graham was watching behind him as Tom slid in over the low ridge and found a pathway through the trees. It is doubtful they would have seen him anyway as the Comanche was made of radar absorbing Kevlar and carbon fibers. Most of its surfaces were angular and difficult to get a reflective pattern returned.

Tom whispered into his mike, "Alex? Alex, come in."

The hesitant, crackly reply came into his headphones, "Thomas, is that you?"

"Yeah, it's me. Where are you? What's happening?" Tom held the black bird in a hover, out of sight.

"I saw two helicopters come down. One landed and some men got out and ran toward the buildings. The other helicopter is up there." She pointed uselessly. "It's shooting at the *Cholos* and some of the buildings." She paused for breath and went on, "We don't know where David is yet, but the Mayans are searching for him. Please come down and help us." She paused again and just as Tom was about to ask her location, she interjected, "We are located just off the runway about twenty-five meters from the end. There is a large banyan tree just before me."

Tom scanned the terrain before him. He could see the Blackhawk sitting on the ground, its tail toward him. To his left he saw the banyan tree and beneath its branches a tiny light winked on and off. After lowering the wheels, Tom eased the chopper forward until it barely touched the ground. He gently tweaked the collective, slid it in under the tree and cut the power. Quickly, the struggling Vinny slid out of Rusty's grasp and dropped to the soft ground. He knelt there a minute rubbing his face into the mulch.

"Thank you, thank you, oh, thank you Lord!" He was still kissing the earth when Alex ran up with Doby in tow.

Tom and Rusty were busy handing gear out of the cockpits. Tom lowered the duffel bags to the ground. Alex ran up and threw her arms around his thick shoulders, nearly knocking him to the ground. "Thomas, I'm so glad you are here. I don't know what is happening. The Mayan's are searching for David now, but they have only primitive weapons and there are many armed men about." She paused, breathless.

Tom shouldered an M-16, slapping in a fifty shot banana clip. Behind him Rusty finally had Vinny up and was equipping them both with miniature radios and night vision goggles. They both carried M-16's and handguns. Tom checked their gear and Rusty checked his.

Tom turned to Alex, "Now there's going to be three more." He turned to his men, "Guys, shoot anything that moves. We'll stay together just on the left of the runway in the bush. Alex, you and the kid stay here and keep an eye on the chopper. You take the shotgun and Doby take a pistol."

Scratching his head, he was just turning to go when Rusty said, "We'll whistle when we come back. Don't shoot us, okay Alex?"

Alex smiled hesitatingly and just nodded. In an eye blink, Rusty and Vinny disappeared into the black jungle, footsteps muted. The jungle sounds returned to normal. Ahead, she heard the sound of firing. It was loud and staccato, but since it was directed in the opposite direction, it seemed somehow disconnected. Overhead, a helicopter buzzed, occasional bursts of gunfire splitting the night. Once a loud boom was heard and a bright flash of light made their eyes tear with after images. She and Doby settled down under the tree to wait.

Suddenly a new sound was heard. A muted popping close overhead flew by and was lost in the background. It was the Alouette helicopter searching, probing, radioing back to the LodeRunner and the Falcon hovering behind the ridge in back of the cliff. The pilot saw the strafing, the tracers, and finally, a truck explode. In the compound beside a large tank, a Jet Ranger was turning up.

"Herr Boettcher, a Jet Ranger helicopter is attempting to take off. The co-ordinates are…" Here, he read a series of time/distance numbers off his GPS receiver back to the pilot in the Falcon Gunship.

"Do not allow it to take off! *Hauptman* Streicher, are you in the gunship?"

"Yah, *Herr* Boettcher."

"Then please stop that Ranger."

The narrow Falcon helicopter lifted straight up and leaped over the top of the tall cliff. The pilot dove in on an angle searching for the now slowly lifting Jet Ranger. He caught it in his cross hairs and thumbed a button on his cyclic. A small ZT-35 laser guided anti-tank missile sped away and caught the Jet Ranger just about midpoint in the rotor blades. For an instant Streicher actually saw a blade fly off and slice a man in half before burying itself in the ground beside a Jeep. The helicopter weaved out of control, then plunged to the ground, the blades tearing themselves off and the fuselage coming to rest against the huge fuel tank.

At that minute, Boettcher ordered the LodeRunner up and over and into the fray. The team flipped their clear plastic covers back and prepared to descend. The team leaders, Jane and Julian LeDuc dropped knotted ropes to the ground and one by one, the team slid down into the center of the clearing. Boettcher and Dieter were the last. All around them was confusion, men running back and forth. There was a building on fire and several vehicles burning. The LodeRunner pulled back up and returned to its position behind the cliff. The Alouette went into a high hover and scanned the battleground with its night vision camera. The pilot kept up a running dialogue to the team leaders and Michael Boettcher. The team leaders were slowly advancing toward the cliff face, firing at anything that moved.

Tom jumped back behind a tree, bumping into Vinny, squashing him against Rusty's bulk. Rusty's big hand reached out and caught Vinny by the collar. "Steady, little buddy."

"Shh," whispered Tom. A burst of machine gun fire peppered the tree and the nearby bush causing them to drop to their knees. Tom flipped his night vision glasses down and peered at the buildings before him. Shit, he thought, he hoped Dave wasn't in one of the burning ones.

Vinny tugged at his back, "Tommy, how are we going to find out which building Dave's in?"

As Tom turned to answer him, a face loomed at him from the bushes. He reached for his gun and was swinging it around when Rusty's hand stopped him. Several more faces swam into view through the greenish light.

"These guys are Indians, Tommy. I don't think they're who we're after."

One of the Indians motioned him to follow. They crept through the night, bullets flying all around, helicopters flitting back and forth overhead. Several times they had to stop as men went running through the bush close to them, firing behind them as they ran. Once a swarthy fellow with long greasy hair ran right into Tom and tripped over him. They both fell to the ground, dazed. Before they could regain their senses, a tattooed hand reached out and raised the head, gripping it by the hair. With a grunt, the Indian slashed a large knife across the man's throat, nearly severing the head. Blood spurted across Tom, soaking his shirt. The Indian spit in the dead, staring eyes and then grinned at Tom. They jumped back to their feet and continued through the jungle, as quickly as they dared. In a minute, they were near the cliff face behind a small building.

Tom cautiously peered through a grimy window. In the glow from an oil lamp he saw a half-clothed man hanging by a rope, twitching in the night. Two thin wires dangled from his chest to a box lying on a rickety, wooden table beside him. It was his closest friend, Dave. His eyes were closed. Ahead of him three men crouched by a slightly open door. One raised a portable radio to his lips and snarled. Tom couldn't hear when he said for the noise. He slipped back down out of the light.

"Rusty, Vince. Dave's in there."

Before he could go on, Vinny started moving forward. Rusty's big paw reached out and gripped his collar. Tom grabbed the front of Rusty's shirt. "Listen, there are three guys in there with him." He paused. "They've been torturing him." He squatted with his back against the wall and wiped a hand over his sweaty face. Rusty and Vinny squatted next to him, faces close.

Tom made up his mind. "Okay, Vinny on my right, Rusty on my left. I'll knock out the window. I've got the guy in the middle. You two come in through the door." They nodded silently.

Tom made a fist, then shot up his index finger, then the middle. At the third, they leaped up, and Tom knocked out the glass. At the same moment, the door flew open and two strange men rushed into the building knocking the three *Cholos* off their feet. Three quick shots and the *Cholos* lay dead.

The two shooters stood with smoking guns pointed at the floor. The first man, a white haired man looked up at Dave, who hung twitching. The man's eyes went wide and Tom realized he was looking at the man who'd tried to kill him in New York. At that moment the man's gaze shifted past Dave to the window. Tom watched his arm come up almost as if in slow motion. Beside his face a gun boomed. Rusty fired while the arm was in motion. The white haired man spun, clutching his side. Vinny's gun boomed next, catching the other man in the stomach and dropping him to his knees. The white haired man moved quickly to the door, glanced back once and disappeared into the darkness.

Tom moved instantly to the corner where he crouched, gun held ready. Before him, a pair of men dressed in dirty white trousers and T-shirts crumpled, falling over their weapons. Tom noted that they were carrying what appeared to be Uzis. Suddenly, three figures dressed in black appeared, sprinting past them to the building guarding the cliff face.

Jesus, Tom thought, *You can't tell the players without a scorecard.*

The black-garbed men stopped at the door and
when it didn't yield at first touch, one stepped back
and fired a short burst at the lock. It exploded in a
shower of splinters. The others were vigilant, one
looking back and the other with his back against the
shooter. *Very professional*, Tom thought. They
disappeared inside.

At that moment, Tom whispered, "Let's go!"
and leapt for the door, Rusty and Vinny right behind
him. They entered, the oil lamp still shining, the
room bathed in a low golden hue. Tom took two
strides to Dave, ripped the probes from his chest
and flung them aside. Rusty yanked a black knife
out of a sheath strapped to his arm and with one
smooth motion sliced the cord holding Dave. Tom
was ready and dropped Dave across his shoulder.
Dave must have come awake for a moment because
he kicked and struggled, his hands still tied behind
his back. Rusty was about to slit the rope when
Vinny cautioned him with a headshake.

"Naw, he'll be easier to handle like this. We'll
cut him loose when we get out of here. You got him
okay, Tommy?"

Tom grunted under his burden. "Lead the way,
Vince." He couldn't hold Dave and his weapon. He
hated to do it but he laid the gun on the table. He
still had the PPK in a shoulder harness. The James
Bond gun, he smiled to himself. But a sobering
thought came to mind, the SS officer's gun, too.

Rusty crouched beside the door peering out. He
held up a thick hand and then waved them forward.
He slipped out, moving quickly for a man his size
and age. Vinny motioned with his gun barrel for

Tom to follow. As Tom stepped to the door, Vinny quickly shot out the light. The oil lamp dropped to the floor and spilled its oil in a puddle. Vinny flipped his night goggles down and waited until the puddle spread to a wooden crate then shot a short burst into it. The third shell was a tracer and the oil immediately flared. Vinny turned to leave, glanced once at the burgeoning fire and faded into the night, following Tom's bulk.

Inside the cave, Jane Houllihan turned on the flashlight strapped to her wrist. Julian and Jacques Broussard crouched behind two crates watching the door. They, too, wore night vision goggles. Jane methodically checked the crates noting their markings and speaking into a small radio. She moved back to the side passages, scratching at the walls and looking at the dusty floor. Occasionally she heard shots fired but they seemed distant and she was busy. Suddenly her flashlight glinted off something in the dust. She knelt and picked up what looked like a tiny bit of glass. Jane dug out a jeweler's loupe and screwed it into her right eye. It looked like a medium to high-grade diamond, a tiny occlusion in the upper right quadrant. She pulled what looked like a ballpoint pen out of her breast pocket and pushed the tip against the stone and pushed the clip. A tiny light blinked once, red. She smiled and pulled the thin boom microphone down to her mouth again.

"Mr. Boettcher. I have found the cave of gems. Your instructions?" She waited. The voice that replied was almost obscured by gunfire.

"Houllihan, we are pinned down near the northern end of the camp. Get what you can and blow the damn thing up. Meet back at the end of the runway. Out."

Jane flipped the mike up and flashed her light along the passage. Two more glints greeted her and she quickly stuffed them in a pocket and began her retreat. When she entered the main cavern, she tapped Jacques on the shoulder and relayed her order. He grinned and nodded.

Jane ran in a crouch to Julian's side. He glanced quickly at her and nodded at the doorway. Several black forms peered in, quickly retreating and appearing again.

Suddenly thin beams of red laser lights played about, darting this way and that. A voice boomed, "You in there. All we want is the helicopter. Let us have it and nobody else will get hurt."

Julian fired a couple of shots in the vicinity of the door and looked at Jane, shrugging eloquently. "*Cherie*, did you find a helicopter back there?"

She shook her head no, and mimicked his shrug. "There is no helicopter in here," she hollered and waited, muttering, "How in the name of Christ would they get a helicopter in here?"

A loud argument was going on outside. Finally a voice called out, "Can I send a man in to verify that information?"

Jane shook her head, stupid assholes, and yelled, "No weapons, hands in the air. He may bring a torch. One man only. Two minutes."

Reluctantly, Sergeant Dodge stepped in, one hand held high, a black, four-cell flashlight in his other. He quickly circled the cave, peering into corners, side passages and behind crates. Julian kept his bullpup trained on him at all times.

Jacques whispered urgently into his mike. "The charge is set. We must leave. We have only five minutes, Madame."

"Yes, Jacques," she snapped. Then, turning to the swiftly moving figure in black, "Your time is up. See? No helicopter. Get out and call your men off. We have set a charge to destroy this cave and we must evacuate." She motioned to Jacques to come forward.

Sergeant Dodge scuttled outside. As Jane and her two men moved toward the doorway, a raking burst of machine gun fire flattened them. They threw themselves down and crawled to one side of the doorway beside a pallet loaded with sacks of some powdery substance. "Now what, Jane?" Julian smiled a sardonic grin.

She smiled back and said, "You men! Do I have to do all the work?" She jerked a grenade loose from her tunic, pulled the pin and flipped it to Julian. He juggled it for a moment in panic and lobbed it out the door.

A voice screamed, "Down!" A loud boom followed and pieces of shrapnel peppered the walls of the cave, nearby boxes, and the bags beside them.

Julian raised his eyebrows and asked, "May I?"
He pulled a flash-bang grenade from his own tunic
and carefully tossed it in the same spot. Jane
grudgingly acquiesced and gestured toward the
door.

They heard another order, "Fall back!" and the
scuttling of feet.

"*Bon*," Julian breathed. "Jacques, have you got
smoke?" On the other side of the doorway Jacques
nodded. He pulled the pin from a canister with a
short handle and flung it through the door.

Jane silently counted, "Eight, nine, ten." The
pop of the smoke grenade was not as loud as the
previous two. As the smoke tendrils drifted into the
cave, Jane lunged for the doorway followed closely
by Julian and Jacques. As she ducked through the
doorway, a burst of gunfire caught her in the chest
climbing to her throat. Julian, close behind her was
shot in the arm and upper leg, the second spinning
him to the ground, Jane on top of him. Though both
wore Kevlar flack jackets, the burst was so close
and of sufficient power to penetrate Jane's vest
tearing holes on it and jamming pieces of the Kevlar
into her ribcage, breaking several ribs and spinning
the pieces into her lungs and heart. She died, face
down, looking into Julian's open eyes. A tear
trickled down her cheek and fell in his mouth. He
licked his lips and died a short while later, his blood
leaking out in a great puddle on the dirt floor.

Behind them Jacques dropped behind the
bodies and fired a burst over Jane's hip at the
unknown assailants. He slipped a last grenade from
his pocket and threw it out as far as he could and

leaped to his feet. Just as he took a step, the cavern behind him exploded in a huge, expanding fireball. He felt the heat and the pressure fling him forward and up, his arms and feet windmilling. In a split second he met the blast from his own grenade. It crushed him against the falling rock behind him. At this point he was more than twenty feet in the air, the shrapnel caught him and shredded his body, only the torso staying together in the Kevlar vest. He thought he remained surprisingly lucid as a bright light grew and grew, drawing him in. He thought he saw his mother's face just before the light blinded him. When it went out he was dead. What was left of his body hit the ground with a thud.

"Holy shit, did you see that?" Vinny was peering out from behind a huge steel tank. Beside him, Tom rested, Dave still on his shoulder, occasionally twitching uncontrollably. Rusty crouched behind Vinny, peering over his head.

"Lordy, Lordy." When the blast hit them, the huge tank rocked, creaking. A thin trickle of liquid dribbled past them and on the other side of the tank a heavy object fell to the ground. Rusty and Vinny had pulled their heads back behind the tank until the blast wave passed. Vinny peered out again.

Behind him Rusty muttered, "What the hell was that?"

Vinny was looking into the upside down fuselage of the wrecked Jet Ranger. It was still rocking on its rounded roof.

"Come on, you guys. Let's get the hell out of here," Tom called. Rusty scrambled to his feet and helped pull Tom up, the heavy burden making it difficult to stand unaided.

"Wait a minute," Vinny whispered, "I thought I saw somebody move in that chopper."

"Maybe, but this tank is full of gasoline so I'm hitting the road," Tom said, shifting his load a little.

"Me, too," Rusty replied, moving behind him, covering his back. Tom slipped into the jungle heading north.

"I'll be with you in a minute, guys." Vinny slipped out from behind the tank keeping the chopper cockpit between him and the now almost totally destroyed compound. He knelt down in the dirt and peered in through the cracked window. A bloody hand lay on the other side of the window, the fingers reflexively twitching. He grabbed the handle of the upside down door and jerked on it. It was jammed. He put a foot against the sidewall and jerked, once, twice. On the third pull, the door flew open and a white clad body tumbled out and fell at his feet landing on his side. Atop him fell a shiny aluminum suitcase. Vinny shoved the suitcase aside and knelt by the man and rolled him over. His shirt was bloody and the lower part of his torso was neatly sliced open. His intestines lay where he had fallen. Vinny jerked back as if slapped, falling over the case, kicking it. He scrabbled back on heels and palms, horror etched on his face.

A piece of paper crumpled under his hand. He jammed it into his shirt and glanced at the open case. His eyes widened and he quickly closed and latched it. "I'm sorry, fella, I don't think you're going to make it." He made the sign of the cross, touching his lips, belt and shoulders. He shook his head to clear the cobwebs, leapt to his feet and grabbed the heavy case. In the back of the chopper fuselage, he heard another scraping noise, but there was just no time to investigate. Just as he was making his way into the jungle following Tom and Rusty's passage, several shapes materialized before him. It was the Indians.

One nodded in the direction he was heading. A small, practically naked man with a machete clutched in his hand moved before Vinny, and he was roughly shoved in behind him.

They quickly caught up with Tom and Rusty who were following a faint trail paralleling the airstrip. To their right they heard the slowly turning rotors of the Blackhawk helicopter idling on the ground. Above, the two gunships were playing cat and mouse, ducking behind hills, diving into clearings. All the firing was slowly winding down. Of the dozen or so buildings and vehicles, most were either ablaze or smoldering ruins. Tom was near exhaustion. The figure on his back had nearly regained consciousness and was struggling. Tom finally slumped to the ground nearly at their destination, the big banyan tree. Dave was muttering to himself. Occasionally a few words

became lucid. Tom tried to shush him. Dave just
nodded.

Rusty fished his knife out of his sheath and slit
Dave's bonds inspecting his wounds with a
penlight. The skin inside Dave's upper arms was
worn through, as was a broad stripe on his back.
They both trickled blood. Rusty tried to wipe some
away with his shirtsleeve when one of the Mayans
touched his arm. He turned and a small, grizzled old
man with no teeth thrust a handful of large, broad
leaves into his hands.

"What the hell am I supposed to do with
these?" he asked suspiciously.

The old man gestured at Dave and wrapped a
leaf around his arm, securing it with a thin piece of
vine. Rusty shrugged and did the same with the
other arm. They were almost back to their chopper.

"Fall back! Fall back," Boettcher called into his
microphone when he saw the fireball explode from
the cave's mouth. He was shooting at shadows.
There were two men with him, Dieter and Giles
Broussard, both wounded. They crouched behind a
jeep and shot at shadows. He turned to Dieter, "The
objective has been accomplished. This is one mine
that won't open any time soon."

Dieter nodded and asked, "Who were the other
commandos?" He was puzzled. Was there such
security at a tiny emerald mine in the jungles of
Guatemala? And if their own gunship hadn't shot

the Jet Ranger out of the air, who had? He had noted that after they were on the ground, there seemed to be an awful lot of black clad figures running around. The ones in white and khaki, he understood as being the workers of the mine, but they seemed to be very well armed for miners.

Boettcher shrugged in the night. "Who cares, we did what we set out to do. Now let's get the hell out of here." He flipped down his microphone. "*Hauptman* Lomax, bring the troop carrier down on my signal." He paused, feeling in his pocket. "Broussard, hand me a flare."

Broussard did so and as Boettcher pulled the cap loose, he called on his mike, "*Hauptman* Streicher, if you would fly cover for us, we would be obliged. Watch for the flare." He threw the flare out into the end of the compound. Darkness closed in and in a few minutes a low flying helicopter dropped quickly to the ground on its skids, rotor flaring, blowing debris back and flattening the grass. Boettcher motioned Dieter and Broussard ahead. Across the compound a lone figure ran toward them one leg dragging.

A woman called in French, "Giles, *un moment, sil vous plait*!" As she got closer, Giles ran to aid her.

He called over his shoulder, "It is Marie. Hold your fire." He grabbed the girl under her armpit and practically threw her into the rear bay with Dieter and Boettcher. Were there only the two of them left?

"Wait," he called to the pilot, imperiously. "There may be others coming. Where is my brother?" He flipped his night vision goggles down and scanned the compound. There was nothing moving. The occasional hot spot flared in the eerie green light. He thumbed a button on the personnel band, "Jacques? Janie? Julian?"

Silence.

Boettcher raised a hand and swirled it in a circle. The pilot who was looking over his shoulder gave a curt nod and pulled up on the collective. The machine's tail lifted and the bird tilted, its motor whining as it climbed rapidly, barely skimming the trees. The pilots headed for the ship, which waited just past the twelve-mile limit.

As Sykes saw the blast from the cave mouth, he gave a yelp. "What the hell was that?" He waited impatiently. "Talk to me, people. Was that my chopper?"

A scratchy voice called back, "Colonel, some guys in black blew up the cave. Dodge went in. There was no chopper in there. I don't think anybody in there survived. It was a pretty big blast and half the fucking mountain came down. We got most of the guys in white and it's all quiet down here." He wiped his face. "What do you want us to do. Nobody's hit bad. You still got a signal?"

Sykes tried to look in all directions at once. A black shape flew between him and the fires below.

Sykes yelped, "There it is! I'm gonna go get it." He pushed the cyclic stick forward and glanced at his night radar screen. Nope, too big a pattern. But anything in the air was the enemy. "Get that fucker, Rossi!"

"Yes sir," Sergeant Rossiter acknowledged, swiveling his head and following the outline on his radar screen. The crosshairs wavered and fixed on the other chopper now maneuvering below and to his left.

"Nine o'clock, low, Rossi." The more nimble Apache dropped like someone had pulled the rug out from under them. A stream of tracers flew out of the chin gun and just missed the tail of the diving Falcon. "Shit, you missed. Try one of the Hellfires. I'll line up on him." Sykes hauled back on the collective and followed the other chopper up and into the starlit sky. The Apache climbed and slowed about a half-mile away. Sykes shot the Hellfire missile when the crosshairs were on its profile. Dead on. The Falcon waited a second then the tail boom swung behind it, narrowing the profile. The pilot slipped the aircraft sideways just a few feet and headed directly for Sykes. The missile just missed, flashing by within feet.

Let's go, Tommy, we've only got about a hunert yards t'go," Vinny said softly, leaning over Tom.

"I'm bushed. Gimmee a hand with him, will you?" Dave lay on the ground, head propped against a tree. One minute he was twitching and jerking uncontrollably, the next he seemed to be coming out of it. His voice was calm and he tried to help them. Rusty lifted Dave to his feet.

Tom hauled himself upright, gasping and sweating profusely. Rusty and Vinny leaned down and caught Dave under the arms. He helped as best he could, hanging onto the front of Rusty's shirt. They propped him against the bole of the tree, Rusty's big hand against his chest. Just then a group of figures ran past them down the runway toward a waiting chopper. In a few minutes the sound of the engines' whine was heard and then the rapid whup, whup, whup which faded quickly into the night.

"Let's go," Vinny urged. Rusty helped Tom with Dave. Unerringly, Vinny led them to the big banyan tree, where he stopped and whistled, the heavy briefcase slapping against his leg. As they came up to the hidden chopper, Alex stepped out with the shotgun raised. Doby stood next to her, the pistol gripped in both his hands.

Alex was the first to recognize them. She lowered her gun and ran to Tom. "What's wrong, Thomas? Is he dead?" Just then Dave jerked, an arm coiling tightly around Tom's back.

"Oof," Tom expelled a lungful of air and slid Dave to the ground. He was dripping with sweat. Around him were gathered Doby, Rusty and Vinny. "Keep an eye on Dave," he nudged him with his foot. "I'll get the bird turned up. Vin, you and Rusty get ready to go."

Vinny looked at Rusty, then at Tom. "What? In that eggbeater?" He snorted. "Not me."

"Yeah," Rusty chimed in. "One ride was enough."

"So, what are you guys going to do? Go back to the house with Alex?"

"Naw." Rusty scraped his foot in the dust. "We figure we'll swipe one of the leftover jeeps and head back to the boat." He paused, scratching his head. "I saw one off to the south kinda stuck into a clump of trees."

"Yeah," Vinny chimed in. "We just want to get the hell outta here." He looked down at Dave. "Can you handle him alone?"

"Yeah, sure. Don't worry about us." Tom paused. "I'll tell you what, we've got about half a belt of ammo. I'll fly cover for you until you're back aboard." He turned to Alex and Doby. "You two get back to the house. Keep close and be ready for anything, although," he gazed back at the ruined, still burning compound, "I don't think you'll have any more problems with our Colombian friends for a while." He smiled and pecked Alex on the cheek. "Be back in a couple of hours."

With that, Tom bent and hoisted the now conscious Dave to his feet. "Come on, Buddy-boy, we're going for a little ride." Dave was able to slide his arm over Tom's shoulder and half walk, half stumble with him toward the hidden helicopter.

Alex and Doby exchanged good-byes with Rusty and Vinny who then turned and faded into the trees. Vinny led the way back on the trail toward the

ruined buildings. In a few minutes they came to the
jeep that had been scorched but not destroyed. It
only took a minute for Vinny to slip under the dash
and hot-wire the 4-wheel drive vehicle. It started
instantly and Rusty slid his bulk into the passenger
side, gun trained out the side. "Let's amscray,
Vince."

"No kidding, Big guy." They threw their gear
in the back seat. The jeep crept forward and Vinny
looked once at the illuminated wrist compass he
wore, made a turn and slipped out of the compound
and along a jungle trail. They both wore their night
vision goggles and, though the path looked
otherworldly, were able to make reasonable
progress. They saw several bodies as they crept out
of the clearing but no one alive. They headed east
and a little south, hoping to hit one of the few roads
in the Peten.

Tom quickly dumped Dave into the front seat
of the black Comanche helicopter and strapped him
in. Dave kept muttering that he was all right, though
his arms spasmed occasionally. In a flash Tom was
in the rear seat and turning up the mighty engines,
the rotor blades crashing through the light brush. As
the torque came to full power, temperatures and
pressures leveled out, Tom got her light on her
wheels and eased forward until he was clear of the
trees. The stars were bright above him as he lifted
the big chopper up and slid it side to side, searching

for clearance through the canopy cover. Finally he was clear of the tallest branches and started searching with his infrared spotlight for moving heat spots. Way off to one side, he detected a faint blip. That must be the lads, he thought. At least they're going in the right direction.

Tom leveled off at five-hundred feet and slowly followed. The radar gave off a tinny bleep. "Shit," he muttered beneath his breath. "Who the fuck was that?" He couldn't get a reading from the radar, being too unfamiliar with the newest equipment. If he had, he would have noted that it was an Apache Gunship somewhat above and off to his right. And right now, the Apache had him in his radar.

"Rossi, Rossi, who's that?" Sykes was pointing a thin finger that the lighted screen.

"I dunno, boss, but it sure looks like our missing Comanche. See how it keeps fading in and out? It's that stealth shit." He turned the ship in a tight arc and followed. "Whooee, colonel! That must be it! Just about in the same place as the locator beacon."

Sykes looked at the small box taped to the control panel. The light was blinking rapidly, following the homing device in the jeep far below. "Got you, you bastard Novak!" He grinned at his reflection in the side window. "Go get 'em, Rossi. Force 'em down."

By now, Tom had detected the oncoming helicopter. He scanned around for a hill to hide behind but there was nothing but dense jungle below with only a few small clearings. Oh, well, try to out maneuver them was the best he could hope for. "Damn," he thought. "Here I am in the best fighting chopper in the world and I've only got a few shells left."

"Hang on, Buddy-boy," he yelled to Dave and dove down toward the blackness below. When he got as low as he dared, he pulled back on the stick and shot up in a tight ag turn, one practiced by agricultural sprayers to minimize time not directly over the crops. When he leveled off, he was face to face with the older, but no less deadly Apache. They were approaching each other at over one-hundred miles per hour. Tom thumbed the red button on the stick and a short burst exploded from under the nose. Then silence from the booming gun. He held the button down but the gun remained silent. The Apache deftly dodged the illuminated stream of shells, at the same time loosing off a short burst of its own.

Tom tried to crab sideways, but several of the bullets struck the clear Lexan canopy, which shattered, pieces blowing into his and Dave's lap and chest. One dagger shaped shard stuck in Dave's left shoulder while a smaller piece stuck into Tom's left ear.

Dave was fully awake now and mad as hell. "Go get those bastards," he bawled into his mike. "Gimmee a gun, dammit!" Tom pulled a Smith and Wesson 9mm automatic from a belt holster and slid it over the seat back and nudged Dave in the shoulder. Then he got back on the controls, hauled them up and swung around searching for their nemesis, the Apache.

Dave saw it before Tom did. "There he is! Get him! Get him!" Dave was pointing an arm to their left. Dave swore a blue streak and though Tom was concentrating on his flying, he marveled at Dave's inventiveness. He'd heard most of the words before, but Dave's combinations were truly inspirational.

The Apache was almost on them, coming at them on their left side. Dave was still yelling and waving the gun. Before he could stop him, Dave had undone his shoulder harness and was now standing on the cramped seat, left hand clutching the twisted framework of the canopy. Just as he started firing an uncontrollable spasm clutched at his tortured muscles. His right arm jerked and pulled back. The first shot hit their own nose, careening off into the black night, the next three slamming into the instrument panel shattering the instruments and starting a small fire. Dave emptied the gun at the other helicopter after steadying the gun with two hands. Sykes peeled off to his right in a screaming turn.

When Dave didn't make contact, he gave an exasperated scream and threw the gun at the retreating shape.

"Good job, Rossi, you got 'em. Well hang back and follow 'em down. Let's try not to do any more damage to the bird, but if you can get off a shot at the fuckers flying it, do it." Sykes smiled grimly. It was a shame shooting their own chopper down, but if it meant getting rid of that fuck Novak and his sidekick, he'd nuke them if he could.

Tom watched the instruments. Yep, the hydraulic pressure was steadily falling. "Hey, Wyatt Earp. You got us all right. I'm taking her down." He figured he had about three or four minutes at the most, then he'd have no controls. The night vision searchlight flickered and finally died, but not before Tom got a fix again on Vinny and Rusty. They were behind the speeding jeep by a couple of miles and coming their way rapidly. "Must have found a road," Tom mumbled absently.

Dave was slumped back in his seat gingerly touching the Lexan spear in his shoulder. It was just starting to throb a bit, the adrenaline slowly wearing off. He was dazed but coherent. "You okay?" he asked Tom.

"Yeah. Strap in. We're going down." He let the wheels down and saw moonlight glint off the occasional puddle on the road below. At least he hoped it was a road. The controls were getting spongy now and he figured a light but running landing would be just what the doctor ordered.

The bird came down with a thump at twenty miles an hour. The blades crashing through the small trees by the sides made an awful din, but Tom managed to keep them in the center of a straight stretch. He reached up and flipped an array of switches and twisted knobs until the rotor stopped and the lights went out.

In an instant he was out hauling his small bag with him and grabbing for the back of Dave's collar, "Come on. Come on. They'll be on us in a couple of minutes."

Dave stumbled out and they limped for the overhanging trees, Tom's arm around his waist. "Just like the old days, eh?" Tom had a wolfish grin on his thin lips.

Dave grinned back and said, "Lucy, you've got some 'splaining to do."

Behind them they could only hear the night crickets and the cooling and contracting of metal. Far above them, the whup, whup of helicopter blades could faintly be heard. They scrambled farther from their useless ship and ran alongside the road. In a minute they heard the harsh grinding of a straining gas engine.

The jeep with Rusty and Vinny came around a bend in the road and nearly collided with the downed aircraft. Vinny swerved at the last minute, bumping off the road and rapidly swerving back on it. Up ahead he saw two figures standing by the side of the dusty track, thumbs upraised in the universal signal. The jeep ground to a halt.

"Howdy sailors, going our way?" Tom tossed his duffel in the back. Dave was fumbling at the hood catches. "What's up, *Compadre*?"

Dave felt at the battery and found what he was looking for. The small box was still taped in place, alligator clips holding it to the battery. He yanked it free and held it up. "What we have here now is a failure to communicate!" He grinned and flipped it back toward the downed chopper, slammed the hood and jumped in the back.

"Let's boogie!" He shouted and Vinny yanked the gear lever into first and they were off in a cloud of dust.

"Where'd they go, Rossi? I lost the signal." Colonel Sykes frantically scanned his radarscope and looked out through the cockpit.

"I've got a fix on their last position, Colonel. We'll be there in about a minute." Rossiter brought the dragon-like helicopter down slowly, constantly scanning the gauges and scopes.

Colonel Sykes scratched at his throat, eyes glued to the screen before him. A small dot crawled toward the upper left-hand corner. It was moving too slowly for a low-level aircraft.

"What do you think that is, Rossi?" Sykes indicated the tiny blip.

"Ground traffic, sir. Probably some local farmer on his way to town." He frowned.

"Well, shoot him. It might be our boys." Sykes didn't care. He didn't want to take a chance on them getting away.

"Sir, I'm not going to shoot an unidentified, probably a local." *What are you, fucking nuts?* he muttered to himself.

"Yeah, I guess you're right. They're probably in the wreckage. Let's get on down there." By now they were hovering one-hundred feet above the downed Comanche. Sykes ignited the searchlight. It took some moments before his eyesight could adjust to the bright glare. The ship was surprisingly intact.

Rossiter landed the Apache just down the road from the silent craft. Sykes jumped down, gun drawn and ran in a crouch to the right side. He jumped up on a wheel and leveled the gun at the pilot's head - or where the pilot's head should be. The aircraft was empty, both helmets neatly sitting on the seats. He lifted the pilot's helmet. Beneath it Tom had neatly folded a glove palm up. All the fingers except one were folded in. The middle finger was extended in a universal sign. Sykes smiled and shook his head. "Always got to get the last word in, don't you?"

He walked back to the idling Apache Gunship and opened Rossiter's canopy. Cupping his hands to be heard, he yelled, "They're gone. Call the Blackhawk and get Dodge and Pagano down here. They can probably fix it well enough to fly. We're going home."

CHAPTER 19

The jeep slowed to a halt alongside a small crude dock. The sky was lightening in the east, and the tops of the trees swayed softly in the morning breeze. Dave hauled in lungs full of sweet air. They had stopped during the night and removed the plastic shard from Dave's shoulder and from Tom's ear. Vinny'd had a small first aid kit in his bag and they were well medicated and bandaged.

The PT boat floated serenely in the middle of the river. As they watched, a small figure appeared on deck and scanned them with a pair of binoculars. The figure waved an arm and Vinny returned the wave.

"Who the hell's that?" Tom asked. "Did you hire a boat boy to keep an eye on things?"

"Uh, no, Tommy. See, it's like this. That's the guy I told you about. He's a colonel in the Guatemalan Customs Service. His name's Perez and he got a little shot up and we kinda fixed him up an' left him when you came and got us." Vinny smiled weakly.

"Great. I suppose you left him aboard with the radio and all." Tom checked his shoulder holster, pulling out the small Walther PPK.

"What are you doing, Tom?" Dave asked edging closer to his friend.

"After all we've been through, I'll be damned if I'm going to do jail time for some bullshit customs violation." He pulled back the receiver inserting a shell in the chamber and cocking it. He flipped the safety on with his thumb and tucked the gun back into the small holster.

"Take it easy, everybody. Let's see what's up before we start anything." Rusty raised a big paw placatingly. "We've still got to figure out how to get out to the boat."

They stood on the bank in a silent row. The roar of a diesel engine being started suddenly broke the morning's silence. The tiny figure in the cockpit eased the throttle on one engine forward as he winched the anchor out of the river mud. The sky was light now, the sun peeping out from a low bank of clouds. The monkeys resumed their chatter and a macaw cried from a nearby tree.

The big boat nosed into the small dock and Rusty and Vinny scrambled aboard. Rusty took over the controls after clutching the small man to his chest. "You done good, little buddy."

The man smiled, white teeth seeming large in the small brown face.

Rusty held the boat alongside the dock until Tom and Dave could haul themselves up onto the wooden deck. They helped each other back to the cockpit where Rusty introduced them to Colonel Rafaelo Perez.

Colonel Perez shook each of their hands and made a small, stiff bow. Rusty took the boat out into the river's center again and headed them downstream. Colonel Perez made himself comfortable in a folding chair, a heavy porcelain mug of coffee in one hand, a thin, brown cigarette in the other, a contented look on his face.

"Your friends?" he asked casually.

"Yes," Rusty answered cautiously.

"Not hurt seriously, I hope?" he inquired just as casually, a trickle of smoke coming from his nostrils.

"No, no. A minor auto accident."

"Ah." A moment of silence. "One must be careful here in the back country."

"Yes." Rusty flicked his eyes from the river to the small man at his side.

"You are leaving soon?" asked Colonel Perez, taking a small sip of coffee.

"Yes, we thought that if we could get some fuel near the mouth of the river, we'd head back home." Rusty wasn't sure they were on safe ground yet.

"Yes, of course, of course. And, I assume that you will be donating that inoperative gun to our military museum?" he indicated with his cigarette the twin .50 caliber guns mounted above and to one side. The big boat drifted lazily with the current.

Rusty thought quickly, was he fishing for a handout or would the gun be enough? "Sure, colonel. It would be an honor if you would accept it. Perhaps a couple of belts of phony ammo, too?"

"Yes, of course, that goes without saying, my friend." He thought for a minute. "Do you have any other items of, shall we say, a military nature that you would like to donate to our museum?"

"How about that jeep we drove up in?" Rusty grinned at the little negotiator.

"Thank you. One of my men is already on his way to, ah, take possession of it." He smiled smugly. "You know, Mr. Rusty, I'd like to thank you and your friend for, ah, assisting me with those *narcoticos*. I have spoken with my headquarters and I am to receive a small promotion for my efforts." He sat silently for a time, watching the foliage drift by on either side.

"Colonel, I think I'll get myself something to eat and some coffee. Would you take the wheel, please?"

"Thank you, captain. I was hoping you'd allow me once more." A huge grin split his face as he eased himself into the captain's chair.

Rusty shook his head and went below. "Everything's okay guys."

CHAPTER 20

"Colonel Sykes is outside, General." The general's orderly, a buck sergeant, stuck his head in the door.

General Rutz, a grizzled 30-year veteran, looked up from his desk. The pink of his scalp showed through his close-cropped white hair. His desk was flanked by an American flag on one side and a regimental standard of the 82nd Airborne on the other. Between them were placed two crossed guns: a beautiful Kentucky long rifle, a .50 caliber, from the works of Hawken. The other was the most modern shoulder arm available. It was so new that it only had a numerical designation, the 866. It was matte black with titanium folding stock and a dual scope. The lower scope was a laser projector, smaller and narrower in diameter than the upper, which was a slim day or night scope, accurate to about fifteen-hundred yards. It was the general's habit to replace the later rifle periodically with the newest he could get his hands on. The general leaned forward on his elbows and ran a hand over his scalp. Finally he pushed himself to his feet. He stood no more that 5'6" and when fellow generals made sport of his height, he always replied that Audie Murphy, the most decorated soldier in World War II, stood only 5'5". The general stood twirling a pencil in his hand while he waited for the colonel to be shown in. He hated Sykes with a passion, but he also knew that the Army needed men like Sykes, and not only in wartime. So he reigned in his anger. Now he had to decide how to handle this arrogant asshole.

Colonel Sykes strode into the room, centered himself before the general's desk and snapped an exactly correct salute. His left hand fairly quivered as it lay against the seam of his trouser leg. The colonel's O.D. uniform was impeccably tailored and pressed. His rows of ribbons were perfectly aligned and his tie was even perfectly centered. His perfectness made the general nauseous.

"Colonel Sykes reporting as ordered, sir!" Sykes held his stiff at-attention pose, not making eye contact with the fireplug of a general. Sykes knew that the general had won his medals in the field just as he had, and was not a man to be fucked with.

"At ease, colonel." Rutz pursed his lips contemplating his next words. "I read your report, Sykes, and I must say that it was the most fascinating piece of fiction next to a Tom Clancy novel I have ever read. Yes sir, I had to stand on my fucking desk so the bullshit wouldn't cover my shoes." He shook his head ruefully and moved in front of Sykes so he was only inches from his face. "Yes sir. Do you really expect me to believe that crap about you staging a fake theft of an experimental chopper so you could go down and wipe out a nest of drug smugglers in fucking Guatemala?"

Sykes was about to speak but the general cut him off.

"Shut up, shut up. Don't say a fucking word. That last was what we generals call a rhetorical question, which means that you don't even attempt to answer it! Understand?"

Sykes gulped and nodded once, his Adam's apple bobbing.

General Rutz went on, "If it wasn't for this Dan Bagelman," he thrust a paper in the colonel's face, "from the D-fucking-EA, thanking you for the assistance you provided his whole department, I'd have you supervising road clearing at some flea ass base in the Aleutian Islands." The general walked away and resumed pacing, muttering to himself. "They want me to give you a fucking medal!" The general was near apoplexy, his face a bright red. He threw the letter down on his desk and glared at Sykes. He leaned across his desk and said in a low growl, "Well, it isn't going to happen. Nossir, it ain't going to ever happen! You were lucky to get back with your unit alive. It's a good thing one of those misfits of yours knows how to fix choppers or we'd have lost the Comanche, too!" He sat back in his chair, exhausted.

"Now get the fuck out of my sight. Go back to your unit and in the future you don't take a chopper off the base without my permission. You don't even take a nut or bolt from a chopper off this base without a goddamn chit from me. Is that clear?"

Sykes just nodded again, once. That's it? They weren't going to court-martial him or break up his unit? He was dismissed? He was about to ask if there was anything else when he thought better of it. So without a word, Colonel Sykes snapped to attention once again, whipped his arm up in a salute, about-faced and strode through the door, crisply shutting it behind him. He strode outside where his driver and Humvee waited. He looked around and breathed deeply, loving the smell, the crisp Texas air, the mile high clouds. His driver handed him a padded envelope.

"This came for you this morning, colonel." The driver, a PFC named Donninger started the Hummer and waited for the colonel.

Frowning, Sykes tore open the envelope. Inside was a glove similar to the one left on the seat of the downed Comanche. It was glued to a piece of cardboard in the classic insult. On it were written the words: You still owe me $50,000, asshole. And it was signed Dan Bagelman, DEA.

CHAPTER 21

The two old friends sat companionably across from each other in old, yet comfortable, wicker sofas. They drank homemade sangria, which was a deep red heady wine with pieces of fruit floating in it. A glistening pitcher sat on the low table between them. They spoke a guttural Spanish, one coarser than the other.

"So, Manuel, what do you think of the latest development in Guatemala?"

"*Jefe*, things happen that are sometimes beyond our control." He spoke calmly and carefully. He didn't want to anger the other man, for many men who had aroused *jefe* were now spending time with their ancestors.

The other man was fat but hard, his face dark and brutal. His thick arms rested on his thighs, the creamy white linen pulled tight. Manuel Nobriga, the *Jefe's* director of finance and friend since boyhood also wore white in the heat of the Cartagena summer. They were presently sitting in a sprawling living room on the 18th floor of one of many buildings the *jefe* owned in this and other cities.

"So how much did this thing that-is-beyond-our-control cost us?" he inquired pleasantly.

Manuel Nobriga pulled a small notebook out of his pocket and flipped a page or two. He took a deep breath and spoke clearly, "If we figure in the product we lost, the American dollars, the helicopter, the buildings, and jeeps, the figure was near $5.2 million. US dollars." He paused, then consulted his book again. "We also lost over fifty men including my sister's son Melu."

The Jefe stroked his full mustache. "Ah, yes, Melu. He was in charge of that particular operation, was he not?"

"Si. He will be missed by my sister and all of his family." Manuel bent his head respectfully.

"Yes, yes. He will be missed." El Jefe raised a finger at a large man stationed at the door at the end of the room. The room was brightly lit at that end, a suffused light coming in through the large glass doors, so when the figures emerged, it was as if they stepped out of the light.

The big man held a smaller, slimmer youth by his upper arm, the sausage-like fingers completely circling the youth's bicep. The youth staggered and leaned heavily against the big man.

As they came closer, Manuel could see that it was his nephew Melu. He leaped to his feet and started around the table. "How did you...?"

El Jefe held up a finely manicured hand. "*Alto*." Stop. He merely twitched a finger. The big man let Mel's arm go and Melu dropped to his knees.

Manuel made as if to move again and *jefe* merely looked at him. The look stopped Manuel cold. He slid back to a seat, this time on the edge of the sofa. The bodyguard retreated into the blaze of light until only his shoes could be seen on the highly polished hardwood floor.

"You mean, this Melu." It was a statement, not a question. The youth stayed on his knees, swaying slightly, his face aimed at the floor. Every so often he moaned low and guttural, like a dog hit by a car. His clothes were dirty and torn and there was dried blood in his hair and on his arm.

El Jefe pushed a leather-covered box across the table at Manuel. At first Manuel thought the Jefe was offering him a cigar and he was confused. *El Jefe* motioned him to open it, the barest flickering of a finger. Manuel pulled the box to him and slowly lifted the lid. Inside on a white satin covered cutout sat a small automatic pistol. It was finely made of satin finished stainless steel, or perhaps aluminum. The grips were rosewood and gleamed dully, their red hue offsetting the solidness and purposefulness of the shiny steel. It was almost as if the maker had tried to humanize the weapon with the beautiful, swirling wooden slabs. Manuel took up the gun, turning it in his hand. The balance was excellent. Manuel kept his trigger finger outside the guard as he'd been taught. Taught by *El Jefe* many years ago.

He looked up at his friend, his boss, and his enemy. Could he shoot his nephew? The thought rose in his throat with horror. He'd known Melu since babyhood, tried to keep him out of the business but he'd failed. The boy, now a young man, had fitted in to the rougher side first as a *corredor*, a runner, then later as an *asesino*, an assassin. The Guatemalan business had been Melu's, and his Uncle Manuel had backed him. It was a good plan and might have worked very much to their advantage if this thing that happened that-was-beyond-their-control had not happened. Manuel was still perplexed. What had drawn all the helicopter gunships? Why had their men in the Guatemalan government and police not forewarned them? No one seemed to know. How *El Jefe* had found his nephew and managed to bring him back alive was completely baffling to him, and he did not like to be baffled.

Now *El Jefe* was speaking, leaning across the low table and speaking low so only Manuel could hear. "My friend, it has been many years since you or I have had to commit an act of this nature." He shrugged. "Me," he pointed a thumb at his chest, "it makes no difference. But you," he pointed a thick finger at Manuel and shrugged, "maybe you need a reminder." He sat back, "Do it now."

EPILOGUE

Tom reached across the bar and snagged a French fry off Dave's plate. "It was trying to escape." Tom grinned. "I was just heading it off at the pass."

"Do you want some fries, Tom?" called Charlie from the kitchen.

"Nope," Tom replied filching another from Dave's lunch. "Can't. Not part of my diet."

Dave groaned. Not another of Tom's diets. Rusty slapped Tom and Dave on their backs. "Hi guys, what's up?" Dave looked over his shoulder at his large friend.

"Hey, Rus! When did you and Anna get back?" Rusty and Anna had been on a two-week vacation to Hawaii.

When the boys returned from Guatemala, they
doctored their wounds and rested. Tom stayed in the
small apartment above the bar while Dave and Chris
had retreated to their boat. It wasn't until several
days later that Vinny had come into the bar in the
late afternoon lugging a dirty aluminum briefcase.
Tom and Dave were nursing Bloody Marys. Chris
was in the kitchen with Charlie making up a
shopping list. Rusty and Anna were in the TV
corner watching a world cup soccer game with
Emile. Joan came in trailing Vinny, mouth going a
mile a minute.

"Wat'cha got, Vin? Something for me?
Something you brought back from wherever for all
of us?" She was looking over his shoulder, trying to
see what he had.

"Hey, guys, come here, I need a hand." He tried
hoisting the heavy case up onto one of the scarred
tables. Joan gave him a hand and they wrestled it to
the center. Tom and Dave dragged themselves off a
pair of bar stools and ambled over, drawing up
chairs around the old oak table. Chris came out of
the kitchen pushing a lock of hair behind her ear,
Charlie, the cook trailing behind. They all gathered
around the table in an assortment of chairs. Tom
hooked a leg around Dave's chair and pulled him
close.

"What's up?" Tom took a swig out of his glass.
Dave matched him and shrugged.

"Okay guys. Remember when we got back
from Guatemala, we were all pissing and moaning

about how much we'd spent and how we didn't make anything on the job?" He looked from one to the other, a silly grin splitting his face. He went on, "And you, Tom, were complaining about not being able to say good-bye to Alex. And, of course, none of us got any of the diamonds."

"White emeralds, *paisano*," interjected Joan.

"Whatever. Anyway, we figured we got screwed on everything, right?" Again he looked around the circle at the upturned faces and was answered with a couple of nods, a grunt or two and a scowl. He had the floor and the little man was enjoying his position immensely. He was determined to drag it out as long as he could.

"Well, we didn't!" He laughed and flipped back the lid with the flourish of a practiced magician. They all craned forward to see what was inside. The suitcase was filled with money. The top layer was loose and mixed with leaves and twigs. Beneath, the bills were neatly stacked and banded with thin rubber bands, two on each bundle. "Ha, ha!" He yelped and scooped up an armload of money and tossed it on the table. Then he upended the suitcase and spilled it over the plates and floral arrangement in its center.

A stunned silence greeted his display. Joan was the first to wake up. She whooped and hugged Vinny hard, "You wonderful little guinea!" She squealed again, "Where did you steal it?"

"It fell out of the Jet Ranger that crashed back there. I just grabbed it. I think it belonged to the dopers." He stuffed a bundle in each shirt pocket and danced around the table. "Now it's ours!"

In minutes they were all busy counting. The piles in the middle of the table grew to eye level. After more than fifteen minutes with all of them counting and making notes on napkins, Emile ran a total on his ever-present calculator. "It looks like two million, six-hundred and fifty-three thousand, eight hundred and twenty-four dollars." He snapped the flap closed and slipped it into his pocket. "Nice going, Vinny. Here's a tip." He slid a twenty out of the pile, folded it in half and tucked it into Vinny's mouth.

They worked out an equitable split after much argument, figuring, refiguring and making of lists. Vinny, Rusty, Tom, Dave, Chris, Anna, Joan and Charlie all got an equal share of $325,000 each, Charlie got an extra $10,000 for Ringo and Emile got $10,000 for new computer gear. The bar ate up the rest to repair the damage suffered in the gunfight, with a little added upgrading.

"Oh, guys, Hawaii was just wonderful! I ran into an old Navy buddy out at the Arizona monument. Anna and I spent almost the whole two weeks with them. They have a big house and a pool and, oh, Dave, he had the sweetest little Bertram cruiser you'd ever seen." Rusty paused and took a swig of the large, frosted brew Charlie slid across the bar. "Anna and Milly -- that's Mike's wife ... Oh, yeah, Mike's my old shipmate. Anyway, the girls went shopping in Waikiki while Mike and I cruised the island."

He reached into a colorful bag at his feet. "Look what I got you guys." With a flourish, he pulled out two large jars of macadamia nuts and set one down in front of each of them.

Tom grinned and rubbed his hands together, "Oh boy, oh boy! I just love macadamia nuts." He reached to unscrew the lid when Dave clapped a large hand down on top of the lid.

"Now, now, remember the old diet. Why, those nuts have more fat and calories than a couple of Big Macs." Dave smiled and flipped the jar over the counter to Charlie who deftly caught it in one outstretched hand. A few seconds went by and Charlie tossed a carrot onto the polished bar in front of Tom where it lay staring up at him. He pushed it with a forefinger. It rolled onto its back and lay still looking up at him.

Rusty clapped him again, hard on the meat of his back. "Aw, Tommy, don't worry. Look what else I got you." He pulled out a vividly printed Hawaiian shirt and Tom's eyes lit up.

"Hey, I'll wear this tonight!"

"Good, good. Dave, I got one for you, too. In fact, I got shirts for everybody!"

The party was in full swing that night when Tom came down the stairs. At the foot waited a pretty woman in Coast Guard khakis, a lieutenant. "Captain Roxy. I'm so glad you came." He strolled over to her and put his arm around her shoulders and steered her toward a large table in the center of the room where their whole entourage was already drinking and snacking.

The table was covered with bowls of tortilla chips, salsa, guacamole, sour cream, pretzels, mixed nuts, pate, crackers, and apple slices and, of course, macadamia nuts. Charlie and Chris had done it up right. Everyone was there wearing brightly colored Hawaiian shirts. The bar was jumping. It was Saturday night and all the locals packed the place. There were several boats anchored just outside the channel and a flock of inflatable dinghies were tied up at the dock wherever there was a gap between the boats.

On stage, Chris had hired a three-piece band. The leader was a longhaired youth named Jackie Montrose. He had a versatile style that could be warm and soothing during the ballads, and loud and booming during the more raucous numbers. His only problem was that he had a slight stutter and sometimes got stuck on a word. Most often, one of the other members of the group, Richie, the bassist, would give him a kick or whack him on the arm with the neck of the guitar. Until that time the guitar had a short and nearly electrocuted Jackie. Of course, Jackie hadn't noticed that, except for the extra loud yell in the middle of "Feelings," he hadn't stuttered again all that night.

Sometimes Bill Albert, the drummer would have to throw a drumstick at his gyrating back when Richie was wrapped up in a riff and couldn't respond in time. Ringo had taken to sweeping past the little stage and if he were in reach when a stutter started, would poke Jackie with the broom handle. Jackie would smile and wink at him as he finished the song. Ringo shyly nodded and moved on, occasionally scratching at the bandage on his buttock. Ringo's only change since the windfall was the new watch cap Charlie had bought him. It was black like his last one, but didn't itch. He didn't know it was cashmere.

At the table, everything was going swimmingly. Tom was snuggled in close to Captain Roxanne. They were sipping from a large frosted glass with a little umbrella and fruit in it. Dave had hired a couple of the vets from the VA home to help at the bar and Chris had asked a couple of her friends to help out waiting on tables. Charlie still presided in the kitchen but came out frequently to toss down a beer with the gang. Rusty was in the middle of a bawdy story and the ladies were laughing uproariously.

Victor, the mailman, cruised over with a large drink in his hand and slapped Dave on the back. "Hi, Davey. Hey, great party! Me an' Maureen are having a hell of a time." He wrapped his arm over Dave's shoulders and asked, "So what was in the package from Guatemala? Some dope? Ha, Ha!"

Dave looked puzzled, "What package?"

"The one I delivered this afternoon. Say, can I have the stamps for my kid? Mikey's into stamp collectin' now." He was slurring into Dave's ear and leaning on him, a dreamy smile on his face.

"Where'd you put it, Vic?"

"On the bar. I gave it to Charlie." Dave steered him back to his table and deposited him back with his wife. Then he walked over to the bar where Bull was busy handing drinks from his wheelchair up to Carter who was talking to a couple of the young Greek girls. The fact that he had only one arm and a prosthetic hand didn't seem to dampen his ardor. Bull laughed a deep rumbling laugh as he handed the drinks up to the skinny white guy.

Dave gave him a grin and a wink and looked over the busy bar looking for a package on the shelf. He finally located it under the cash register. Bull tossed it to him after Dave gestured toward the brightly stamped box. He brought it back to the table and handed it to Tom. "I think this was meant for you."

Tom unwrapped himself from Capt. Roxy and studied the address. "But it's addressed to you and Chris."

"Yeah, I know, buddy, but I still think it's for you. Go on, open it."

Tom did and revealed a colorfully painted tin box. He opened the lid and there lay a double row of hard candies in different colors." He looked baffled, shrugged, and popped one in his mouth. For a couple of moments he moved it around in his mouth with his tongue, and then noticed that it wasn't melting any longer. He took it out and held the sparkling center up to the light.

His eyes met Dave's and they smiled at each other.

"Good candy," Tom said.

"Very good candy," Dave agreed.

The following is a sample from Don
Kafrissen's new novel –

Gunfight on Clearwater Beach

The pistol was a long, heavy revolver,
obviously old and well used. Dave identified it as a
Colt Army model, single action six-shooter,
universally known as the Peacemaker. Dave hefted
it and looked down the barrel. It wasn't loaded. It
must have been a hundred years old, though. The
handle was wood, cherry, he guessed, well worn but
also well made. Stamped into the handle was an
inscription, two Rs entwined and beneath it a
scripted T.R. and 1889.

Captain barked a laugh. "Me carry a gun? Un,
uh, Nossir. It's been here all along."

Chely, a pretty waitress had been dipping a
napkin in a glass of water and swabbing the blood
off the bar. "Here? Where?" she demanded.

Artie chimed in, "Yeah, I don't keep a gun
here." He looked around and shrugged. "After those
two guys, maybe I should." He wrapped a handful
of ice cubes in a white cotton bar towel and handed
them to the black gentleman.

Captain picked up the gun in his free hand and
pointed the long barrel at an antique plaque hanging
on the wall beside the bar. The plaque was actually
an ornate frame containing an engraving depicting a
view of downtown Clearwater dated 1921.

Brooke looked puzzled. She walked over to it
and stood on tiptoes reading it. Tom casually leaned

over the bar to get a look at her rear encased in skintight brown wool slacks. Chris kicked him and glared, shaking her head minutely. Tom looked at her innocently.

Brooke tapped the plaque, running her slim fingers around the edge.

Captain shook his head and poked the barrel under the bottom edge. The plaque was hinged at the top and as he lifted it, revealed a box recessed into the wall. A string was attached to the bottom edge and disappeared behind the wall, attached to a weight to keep it closed. Artie smiled and held the trapdoor open, peering inside. There was nothing else in the box.

"How'd you know it was there, Mr. Toffelmeyer?" Dave asked?

The old man smiled, a faraway look on his face. He was silent a minute, thinking about the past. "Why, I put it there. In 1938. After the gunfight." He hoisted his skinny shanks back onto the stool. The bleeding was just about stopped now and he tilted his head forward and looked at the faces surrounding him. "You do know about the gunfight on the Beach, don't you?"

"Gunfight? What gunfight?" Artie asked. He looked around, "Any of you ever heard about a gunfight?" Artie and Brooke were originally from Detroit, the children of Albanian immigrants. They were self taught, and had purchased the restaurant and bar several years earlier. Their hard work and determination had pulled the old diner from a hangout for bums and down and outers to a classy hangout for lawyers and criminals -- in other words, a different breed of bums and down and outers. A step up or sideways?

No one had ever heard about the "gunfight.

"There was a gunfight in my bar?" asked Brooke. She leaned across the bar, the tan, silk top stretched tight. Chris kicked Tom before he could move his head.

"Oh, yess'm. Fact is, it is the only gunfight ever reported on Clearwater Beach." He shook his curly gray haired old head, grinning, his teeth gleaming in the early afternoon light. Then he was silent staring off into the distance again.

"Well, you can't just leave us there," complained Tom. "So who shot who?"

Just then a voice was heard from the door, "Shot? Was somebody shot? I'll get my bag?" A well turned out woman, medium height and weight dressed in a gray pleated skirt and a sleeveless yellow sweater strode over to the bar. She was definitely a stunner with a generous figure, billowy deep red hair, wide set blue eyes, and a no nonsense, take charge look on her face.

Tom hurriedly stood up and introduced her. "Bobbie, this is Chris and Dave, I told you about them." She shook hands with Chris and gave Dave a serious smile. When she smiled, her lips turned up at the corners. Dave noted that the smile didn't quite reach her eyes. "And this is Artie and Brooke. They own this joint." They how do you do'd.

"This chubby little twerp is Chely," Tom gestured with his beer at the dimpled waitress, short hair caught up fetchingly with a pair of clips. She waved a blood-spattered hand bringing an alarmed look to Bobbie's face. Chely noted the look and hurriedly said, "Oh, its O.K., it's not mine. It's his." She pointed to Captain Toffelmeyer.

"And this is Captain Octavious Toffelminer." Tom offered.

Captain shook his head and mumbled something about white folks. "Its Octavio Toffelmeyer, madam. Please call me Captain." He took her smooth hand and bowed gallantly over it, a small drop of blood dripping on it. "Oops, sorry."

"That's O.K." she replied. "I'm Barbara Young. Please call me Bobbie. What are you captain of?"

"Nothin', ma'am, just a nickname."

"Yep, that's right everybody, this is Bobbie, my friend and she's a nurse…"

"Nurse Practitioner," finished Bobbie. "So what's going on? Why do you two have blood on you?" She surveyed the two men with a practiced eye. "Thomas, have you been fighting with this nice man?"

"No, no, no, Miss Bobbie. Tom actually helped me out." He turned to Tom and said, "For which I'll be forever grateful." They shook hands again.

Hurriedly, Chris and Brooke encapsulated the events of the past half-hour for her, finishing with, "The Captain was just about to tell us about the gunfight on Clearwater Beach."

She snorted, "Yeah, right, a gunfight on the Beach? When was that, last week?" Her skepticism was readily apparent.

"No," piped in Brooke, "in 1938. Right, Captain?"

"Yep, that's right, Ma'am. Nineteen and thirty-eight." He mused for a long minute. "I'd a been 'bout thirteen back then and…"

"Wait a minute, Captain," interrupted Artie "Why don't we move into the big booth in the corner. That is, if you've got the time."

"Got nuthin' but time, son. I'm handing in my resignation tomorrow. You sure you all want to hear this story?"

"Oh, yes. Un-huh. Yep, Sure do." They all chorused.

Tom leaned over the bar and refilled his glass from the tap. "Put it on my tab," he grinned as Brooke glared at him.

"Chely, would you please get drinks for everybody," asked Brooke.

"O.K., but don't start 'til I get back." She took their orders and scampered away while the group settled themselves in the comfortable, semi-circular booth. It was just after lunch, the tables were clear. The only customers were courthouse regulars busy sipping their twentieth draft beer of the day. The dinner crowd wouldn't be in for another couple of hours.

"Let's see, where to start, where to start." Captain thought for a minute then looked around the table. "I guess I'd better start with the murder of Bob Brightwater by the Chief of Police of the City of Clearwater."

Also by
DON KAFRISSEN

Brothers Beyond Blood

Long Lost Brother

Missing Pieces

Mustang Charlie

Gunfight on Clearwater Beach

D'Amato's Place
(Short Story Collection)

On Top of Her Game

The Brooksville Terrorist

Stories in several anthologies including
Mosaic 2010 & Mosaic 2014

International Digital Book Publishing Industries

About the Author

Even though most authors may hope to write a best seller, it doesn't always work out that way. But Kafrissen was pleasantly surprised when his novel, BROTHERS BEYOND BLOOD began to make some serious sales, first the United States, then Europe and Japan. This was followed up by a sequel, LONG LOST BROTHER, another book that also attracted a lot of attention. A third book in this trilogy is in progress (aiming for 2016). Kafrissen has written a number of other popular novels and short story collections.

"Kafrissen is a multi-level writer," says one reviewer. *"His stories suck you in with action and characterization, but then they make you think and wonder ...."*

Kafrissen is a veteran of the U.S. Navy, and has visited 43 different countries. He's lived in a number places including Rhode Island, Canada, Texas, California, Vermont. He and his wife once lived on a 40' Endeavor sailboat, spending many happy years in the Caribbean. He is a graduate of Cranston High School East in R.I. and Queen's University's McArthur College in Ontario, Canada.

Today Don Kafrissen lives on five rural acres on Florida's West Coast with his wife Diane, 4 cats and 2 dogs. He and his wife built their own house, and are car people, taking part in many car shows and cruise-ins each year with their vintage autos. Don started the Brooksville Writers' Group several years ago, and now enjoys the friendship of many local authors.

For news, other books,
and to contact Don Kafrissen
Go to: http://idbpi.wordpress.com

IDBPI